EMILE

EMILE

Or, On Education

by

Jean-Jacques Rousseau

Translated by Barbara Foxley

First published 1782.
Republished 2015 by Cavalier Classics.

AUTHOR'S PREFACE

This collection of scattered thoughts and observations has little order or continuity; it was begun to give pleasure to a good mother who thinks for herself. My first idea was to write a tract a few pages long, but I was carried away by my subject, and before I knew what I was doing my tract had become a kind of book, too large indeed for the matter contained in it, but too small for the subject of which it treats. For a long time I hesitated whether to publish it or not, and I have often felt, when at work upon it, that it is one thing to publish a few pamphlets and another to write a book. After vain attempts to improve it, I have decided that it is my duty to publish it as it stands. I consider that public attention requires to be directed to this subject, and even if my own ideas are mistaken, my time will not have been wasted if I stir up others to form right ideas. A solitary who casts his writings before the public without any one to advertise them, without any party ready to defend them, one who does not even know what is thought and said about those writings, is at least free from one anxiety—if he is mistaken, no one will take his errors for gospel.

I shall say very little about the value of a good education, nor shall I stop to prove that the customary method of education is bad; this has been done again and again, and I do not wish to fill my book with things which everyone knows. I will merely state that, go as far back as you will, you will find a continual outcry against the established method, but no attempt to suggest a better. The literature and science of our day tend rather to destroy than to build up. We find fault after the manner of a master; to suggest, we must adopt another style, a style less in accordance with the pride of the philosopher. In spite of all those books, whose only aim, so they say, is public utility, the most useful of all arts, the art of training men, is still neglected. Even after Locke's book was written the subject remained almost untouched, and I fear that my book will leave it pretty much as it found it.

We know nothing of childhood; and with our mistaken notions the further we advance the further we go astray. The wisest writers devote themselves to what a man ought to know, without asking what a child is capable of learning. They are always looking for the man in the child, without considering what he is before he becomes a man. It is to this study that I have chiefly de-

1

voted myself, so that if my method is fanciful and unsound, my observations may still be of service. I may be greatly mistaken as to what ought to be done, but I think I have clearly perceived the material which is to be worked upon. Begin thus by making a more careful study of your scholars, for it is clear that you know nothing about them; yet if you read this book with that end in view, I think you will find that it is not entirely useless.

With regard to what will be called the systematic portion of the book, which is nothing more than the course of nature, it is here that the reader will probably go wrong, and no doubt I shall be attacked on this side, and perhaps my critics may be right. You will tell me, "This is not so much a treatise on education as the visions of a dreamer with regard to education." What can I do? I have not written about other people's ideas of education, but about my own. My thoughts are not those of others; this reproach has been brought against me again and again. But is it within my power to furnish myself with other eyes, or to adopt other ideas? It is within my power to refuse to be wedded to my own opinions and to refuse to think myself wiser than others. I cannot change my mind; I can distrust myself. This is all I can do, and this I have done. If I sometimes adopt a confident tone, it is not to impress the reader, it is to make my meaning plain to him. Why should I profess to suggest as doubtful that which is not a matter of doubt to myself? I say just what I think.

When I freely express my opinion, I have so little idea of claiming authority that I always give my reasons, so that you may weigh and judge them for yourselves; but though I would not obstinately defend my ideas, I think it my duty to put them forward; for the principles with regard to which I differ from other writers are not matters of indifference; we must know whether they are true or false, for on them depends the happiness or the misery of mankind. People are always telling me to make PRACTICABLE suggestions. You might as well tell me to suggest what people are doing already, or at least to suggest improvements which may be incorporated with the wrong methods at present in use. There are matters with regard to which such a suggestion is far more chimerical than my own, for in such a connection the good is corrupted and the bad is none the better for it. I would rather follow exactly the established method than adopt a better method by halves. There would be fewer contradictions in the man; he cannot aim at one and the same time at two different objects. Fathers and mothers, what you desire that you can do. May I count on your goodwill?

There are two things to be considered with regard to any scheme. In the first place, "Is it good in itself" In the second, "Can it be easily put into practice?"

With regard to the first of these it is enough that the scheme should be intelligible and feasible in itself, that what is good in it should be adapted to the nature of things, in this case, for example, that the proposed method of education should be suitable to man and adapted to the human heart.

The second consideration depends upon certain given conditions in particular cases; these conditions are accidental and therefore variable; they may vary indefinitely. Thus one kind of education would be possible in Switzerland and not in France; another would be adapted to the middle classes but not to the nobility. The scheme can be carried out, with more or less success, according to a multitude of circumstances, and its results can only be determined by its special application to one country or another, to this class or that. Now all these particular applications are not essential to my subject, and they form no part of my scheme. It is enough for me that, wherever men are born into the world, my suggestions with regard to them may be carried out, and when you have made them what I would have them be, you have done what is best for them and best for other people. If I fail to fulfil this promise, no doubt I am to blame; but if I fulfil my promise, it is your own fault if you ask anything more of me, for I have promised you nothing more.

BOOK I

God makes all things good; man meddles with them and they become evil. He forces one soil to yield the products of another, one tree to bear another's fruit. He confuses and confounds time, place, and natural conditions. He mutilates his dog, his horse, and his slave. He destroys and defaces all things; he loves all that is deformed and monstrous; he will have nothing as nature made it, not even man himself, who must learn his paces like a saddle-horse, and be shaped to his master's taste like the trees in his garden. Yet things would be worse without this education, and mankind cannot be made by halves. Under existing conditions a man left to himself from birth would be more of a monster than the rest. Prejudice, authority, necessity, example, all the social conditions into which we are plunged, would stifle nature in him and put nothing in her place. She would be like a sapling chance sown in the midst of the highway, bent hither and thither and soon crushed by the pass-ers-by.

Tender, anxious mother, [Footnote: The earliest education is most important and it undoubtedly is woman's work. If the author of nature had meant to assign it to men he would have given them milk to feed the child. Address your treatises on education to the women, for not only are they able to watch over it more closely than men, not only is their influence always predominant in education, its success concerns them more nearly, for most widows are at the mercy of their children, who show them very plainly whether their education was good or bad. The laws, always more concerned about property than about people, since their object is not virtue but peace, the laws give too little authority to the mother. Yet her position is more certain than that of the father, her duties are more trying; the right ordering of the family depends more upon her, and she is usually fonder of her children. There are occasions when a son may be excused for lack of respect for his father, but if a child could be so unnatural as to fail in respect for the mother who bore him and nursed him at her breast, who for so many years devoted herself to his care, such a monstrous wretch should be smothered at once as unworthy to live. You say mothers spoil their children, and no doubt that is wrong, but it is worse to deprave them as you do. The mother wants her child to be happy now. She is right, and if her method is wrong, she must be taught a better. Ambition, avarice, tyranny, the mistaken foresight of fathers, their neglect, their harshness, are a hundredfold more harmful to the child than the blind affection of the mother. Moreover, I must explain what I mean by a mother and that explanation follows.] I appeal to you. You can remove this young tree from the highway and shield it from the crushing force of social conventions. Tend and water it ere it dies. One day its fruit will reward your care. From the outset raise a wall round your child's soul; another may sketch the plan, you alone should carry it into execution.

Plants are fashioned by cultivation, man by education. If a man were born tall and strong, his size and strength would be of no good to him till he had learnt to use them; they would even harm him by preventing others from coming to his aid; [Footnote: Like them in externals, but without speech and without the ideas which are expressed by speech, he would be unable to make his wants known, while there would be nothing in his appearance to suggest that he needed their help.] left to himself he would die of want before he knew his needs. We lament the helplessness of infancy; we fail to perceive that the race would have perished had not man begun by being a child.

We are born weak, we need strength; helpless, we need aid; foolish, we need reason. All that we lack at birth, all that we need when we come to man's estate, is the gift of education.

This education comes to us from nature, from men, or from things. The inner growth of our organs and faculties is the education of nature, the use we learn to make of this growth is the education of men, what we gain by our experience of our surroundings is the education of things.

Thus we are each taught by three masters. If their teaching conflicts, the scholar is ill-educated and will never be at peace with himself; if their teaching agrees, he goes straight to his goal, he lives at peace with himself, he is well-educated.

Now of these three factors in education nature is wholly beyond our control, things are only partly in our power; the education of men is the only one controlled by us; and even here our power is largely illusory, for who can hope to direct every word and deed of all with whom the child has to do.

Viewed as an art, the success of education is almost impossible, since the essential conditions of success are beyond our control. Our efforts may bring us within sight of the goal, but fortune must favour us if we are to reach it.

What is this goal? As we have just shown, it is the goal of nature. Since all three modes of education must work together, the two that we can control must follow the lead of that which is beyond our control. Perhaps this word Nature has too vague a meaning. Let us try to define it.

Nature, we are told, is merely habit. What does that mean? Are there not habits formed under compulsion, habits which never stifle nature? Such, for example, are the habits of plants trained horizontally. The plant keeps its artificial shape, but the sap has not changed its course, and any new growth the plant may make will be vertical. It is the same with a man's disposition; while the conditions remain the same, habits, even the least natural of them, hold good; but change the conditions, habits vanish, nature reasserts herself. Education itself is but habit, for are there not people who forget or lose their education and others who keep it? Whence comes this difference? If the term nature is to be restricted to habits conformable to nature we need say no more.

We are born sensitive and from our birth onwards we are affected in various ways by our environment. As soon as we become conscious of our sensations we tend to seek or shun the things that cause them, at first because they are pleasant or unpleasant, then because they suit us or not, and at last because of judgments formed by means of the ideas of happiness and goodness which reason gives us. These tendencies gain strength and permanence with the growth of reason, but hindered by our habits they are more or less warped by our prejudices. Before this change they are what I call Nature within us.

Everything should therefore be brought into harmony with these natural tendencies, and that might well be if our three modes of education merely differed from one another; but what can be done when they conflict, when instead of training man for himself you try to train him for others? Harmony becomes impossible. Forced to combat either nature or society, you must make your choice between the man and the citizen, you cannot train both.

The smaller social group, firmly united in itself and dwelling apart from others, tends to withdraw itself from the larger society. Every patriot hates foreigners; they are only men, and nothing to him.[Footnote: Thus the wars of republics are more cruel than those of monarchies. But if the wars of kings are less cruel, their peace is terrible; better be their foe than their subject.] This defect is inevitable, but of little importance. The great thing is to be kind to our neighbours. Among strangers the Spartan was selfish, grasping, and unjust, but unselfishness, justice, and harmony ruled his home life. Distrust those cosmopolitans who search out remote duties in their books and neglect those that lie nearest. Such philosophers will love the Tartars to avoid loving their neighbour.

The natural man lives for himself; he is the unit, the whole, dependent only on himself and on his like. The citizen is but the numerator of a fraction, whose value depends on its denominator; his value depends upon the whole, that is, on the community. Good social institutions are those best fitted to make a man unnatural, to exchange his independence for dependence, to merge the unit in the group, so that he no longer regards himself as one, but as a part of the whole, and is only conscious of the common life. A citizen of Rome was neither Caius nor Lucius, he was a Roman; he ever loved his country better than his life. The captive Regulus professed himself a Carthaginian; as a foreigner he refused to take his seat in the Senate except at his master's bidding. He scorned the attempt to save his life. He had his will, and returned in triumph to a cruel death. There is no great likeness between Regulus and the men of our own day.

The Spartan Pedaretes presented himself for admission to the council of the Three Hundred and was rejected; he went away rejoicing that there were three hundred Spartans better than himself. I suppose he was in earnest; there is no reason to doubt it. That was a citizen.

A Spartan mother had five sons with the army. A Helot arrived; trembling she asked his news. "Your five sons are slain." "Vile slave, was that what I asked thee?" "We have won the victory." She hastened to the temple to render thanks to the gods. That was a citizen.

He who would preserve the supremacy of natural feelings in social life knows not what he asks. Ever at war with himself, hesitating between his wishes and his duties, he will be neither a man nor a citizen. He will be of no use to himself nor to others. He will be a man of our day, a Frenchman, an Englishman, one of the great middle class.

To be something, to be himself, and always at one with himself, a man must act as he speaks, must know what course he ought to take, and must follow that course with vigour and persistence. When I meet this miracle it will be time enough to decide whether he is a man or a citizen, or how he contrives to be both.

Two conflicting types of educational systems spring from these conflicting aims. One is public and common to many, the other private and domestic.

If you wish to know what is meant by public education, read Plato's Republic. Those who merely judge books by their titles take this for a treatise on politics, but it is the finest treatise on education ever written.

In popular estimation the Platonic Institute stands for all that is fanciful and unreal. For my own part I should have thought the system of Lycurgus far more impracticable had he merely committed it to writing. Plato only sought to purge man's heart; Lycurgus turned it from its natural course.

The public institute does not and cannot exist, for there is neither country nor patriot. The very words should be struck out of our language. The reason does not concern us at present, so that though I know it I refrain from stating it.

I do not consider our ridiculous colleges [Footnote: There are teachers dear to me in many schools and especially in the University of Paris, men for whom I have a great respect, men whom I believe to be quite capable of instructing young people, if they were not compelled to follow the established custom. I exhort one of them to publish the scheme of reform which he has thought out. Perhaps people would at length seek to cure the evil if they realised that there was a remedy.] as public institutes, nor do I include under this head a fashionable education, for this education facing two ways at once achieves nothing. It is only fit to turn out hypocrites, always professing to live for others, while thinking of themselves alone. These professions, however, deceive no one, for every one has his share in them; they are so much labour wasted.

Our inner conflicts are caused by these contradictions. Drawn this way by nature and that way by man, compelled to yield to both forces, we make a compromise and reach neither goal. We go through life, struggling and hesitating, and die before we have found peace, useless alike to ourselves and to others.

There remains the education of the home or of nature; but how will a man live with others if he is educated for himself alone? If the twofold aims could be resolved into one by removing the man's self-contradictions, one great obstacle to his happiness would be gone. To judge of this you must see the man full-grown; you must have noted his inclinations, watched his progress, followed his steps; in a word you must really know a natural man. When you have read this work, I think you will have made some progress in this inquiry.

What must be done to train this exceptional man! We can do much, but the chief thing is to prevent anything being done. To sail against the wind we merely follow one tack and another; to keep our position in a stormy sea we must cast anchor. Beware, young pilot, lest your boat slip its cable or drag its anchor before you know it.

In the social order where each has his own place a man must be educated for it. If such a one leave his own station he is fit for nothing else. His education is only useful when fate agrees with his parents' choice; if not, education harms the scholar, if only by the prejudices it has created. In Egypt, where the son was compelled to adopt his father's calling, education had at least a settled aim; where social grades remain fixed, but the men who form them are constantly changing, no one knows whether he is not harming his son by educating him for his own class.

In the natural order men are all equal and their common calling is that of manhood, so that a well-educated man cannot fail to do well in that calling and those related to it. It matters little to me whether my pupil is intended for the army, the church, or the law. Before his parents chose a calling for him nature called him to be a man. Life is the trade I would teach him. When he leaves me, I grant you, he will be neither a magistrate, a soldier, nor a priest; he will be a man. All that becomes a man he will learn as quickly as another. In vain will fate change his station, he will always be in his right place. "Occupavi te, fortuna, atque cepi; omnes-que aditus tuos interclusi, ut ad me aspirare non posses." The real object of our study is man and his environment. To my mind those of us who can best endure the good and evil of life are the best educated; hence it follows that true education consists less in precept than in practice. We begin to learn when we begin to live; our education begins with ourselves, our first teacher is our nurse. The ancients used the word "Education" in a different sense, it meant "Nurture." "Educit obstetrix," says Varro. "Educat nutrix, instituit paedagogus, docet magister." Thus, education, discipline, and instruction are three things as different in their purpose as the dame, the usher, and the teacher. But these distinctions are undesirable and the child should only follow one guide.

We must therefore look at the general rather than the particular, and consider our scholar as man in the abstract, man exposed to all the changes and chances of mortal life. If men were born attached to the soil of our country, if one season lasted all the year round, if every man's fortune were so firmly grasped that he could never lose it, then the established method of education would have certain advantages; the child brought up to his own calling would never leave it, he could never have to face the difficulties of any other condition. But when we consider the fleeting nature of human affairs, the restless and uneasy spirit of our times, when every generation overturns the work of its predecessor, can we conceive a more senseless plan than to educate a child as if he would never leave his room, as if he would always have his servants about him? If the wretched creature takes a single step up or down he is lost. This is not teaching him to bear pain; it is training him to feel it.

People think only of preserving their child's life; this is not enough, he must be taught to preserve his own life when he is a man, to bear the buffets of fortune, to brave wealth and poverty, to live at need among the snows of Iceland or on the scorching rocks of Malta. In vain you guard against death; he must needs die; and even if you do not kill him with your precautions, they are mistaken. Teach him to live rather than to avoid death: life is not breath, but action, the use of our senses, our mind, our faculties, every part of ourselves which makes us conscious of our being. Life consists less in length of days than in the keen sense of living. A man maybe buried at a hundred and may never have lived at all. He would have fared better had he died young.

Our wisdom is slavish prejudice, our customs consist in control, constraint, compulsion. Civilised man is born and dies a slave. The infant is bound up in swaddling clothes, the corpse is nailed down in his coffin. All his life long man is imprisoned by our institutions.

I am told that many midwives profess to improve the shape of the infant's head by rubbing, and they are allowed to do it. Our heads are not good enough as God made them, they must be moulded outside by the nurse and inside by the philosopher. The Caribs are better off than we are. The child has hardly left the mother's womb, it has hardly begun to move and stretch its limbs, when it is deprived of its freedom. It is wrapped in swaddling bands, laid down with its head fixed, its legs stretched out, and its arms by its sides; it is wound round with linen and bandages of all sorts so that it cannot move. It is fortunate if it has room to breathe, and it is laid on its side so that water which should flow from its mouth can escape, for it is not free to turn its head on one side for this purpose.

The new-born child requires to stir and stretch his limbs to free them from the stiffness resulting from being curled up so long. His limbs are stretched indeed, but he is not allowed to move them. Even the head is confined by a cap. One would think they were afraid the child should look as if it were alive.

Thus the internal impulses which should lead to growth find an insurmountable obstacle in the way of the necessary movements. The child exhausts his strength in vain struggles, or he gains strength very slowly. He was freer and less constrained in the womb; he has gained nothing by birth.

The inaction, the constraint to which the child's limbs are subjected can only check the circulation of the blood and humours; it can only hinder the child's growth in size and strength, and injure its constitution. Where these absurd precautions are absent, all the men are tall, strong, and well-made. Where children are swaddled, the country swarms with the hump-backed, the lame, the bow-legged, the rickety, and every kind of deformity. In our fear lest the body should become deformed by free movement, we hasten to deform it by putting it in a press. We make our children helpless lest they should hurt themselves.

Is not such a cruel bondage certain to affect both health and temper? Their first feeling is one of pain and suffering; they find every necessary movement hampered; more miserable than a galley slave, in vain they struggle, they become angry, they cry. Their first words you say are tears. That is so. From birth you are always checking them, your first gifts are fetters, your first treatment, torture. Their voice alone is free; why should they not raise it in complaint? They cry because you are hurting them; if you were swaddled you would cry louder still.

What is the origin of this senseless and unnatural custom? Since mothers have despised their first duty and refused to nurse their own children, they have had to be entrusted to hired nurses. Finding themselves the mothers of a stranger's children, without the ties of nature, they have merely tried to save themselves trouble. A child unswaddled would need constant watching; well swaddled it is cast into a corner and its cries are unheeded. So long as the nurse's negligence escapes notice, so long as the nursling does not break its arms or legs, what matter if it dies or becomes a weakling for life. Its limbs are kept safe at the expense of its body, and if anything goes wrong it is not the nurse's fault.

These gentle mothers, having got rid of their babies, devote themselves gaily to the pleasures of the town. Do they know how their children are being treated in the villages? If the nurse is at all busy, the child is hung up on a nail like a bundle of clothes and is left crucified while the nurse goes leisurely about her business. Children have been found in this position purple in the face, their tightly bandaged chest forbade the circulation of the blood, and it went to the head; so the sufferer was considered very quiet because he had not strength to cry. How long a child might survive under such conditions I do not know, but it could not be long. That, I fancy, is one of the chief advantages of swaddling clothes.

It is maintained that unswaddled infants would assume faulty positions and make movements which might injure the proper development of their limbs. That is one of the empty arguments of our false wisdom which has never been confirmed by experience. Out of all the crowds of children who grow up with the full use of their limbs among nations wiser than ourselves, you never find one who hurts himself or maims himself; their movements are too feeble to be dangerous, and when they assume an injurious position, pain warns them to change it.

We have not yet decided to swaddle our kittens and puppies; are they any the worse for this neglect? Children are heavier, I admit, but they are also weaker. They can scarcely move, how could they hurt themselves! If you lay them on their backs, they will lie there till they die, like the turtle, unable to turn itself over. Not content with having ceased to suckle their children, women no longer wish to do it; with the natural result motherhood becomes a burden; means are found to avoid it. They will destroy their work to begin it over again, and they thus turn to the injury of the race the charm which was given them for its increase. This practice, with other causes of depopulation, forbodes the coming fate of Europe. Her arts and sciences, her philosophy and morals, will shortly reduce her to a desert. She will be the home of wild beasts, and her inhabitants will hardly have changed for the worse.

I have sometimes watched the tricks of young wives who pretend that they wish to nurse their own children. They take care to be dissuaded from this whim. They contrive that husbands, doctors, and especially mothers should intervene. If a husband should let his wife nurse her own baby it would be the ruin of him; they would make him out a murderer who wanted to be rid of her. A prudent husband must sacrifice paternal affection to domestic peace. Fortunately for you there are women in the country districts more continent than your wives. You are still more fortunate if the time thus gained is not intended for another than yourself.

There can be no doubt about a wife's duty, but, considering the contempt in which it is held, it is doubtful whether it is not just as good for the child to be suckled by a stranger. This is a question for the doctors to settle, and in my opinion they have settled it according to the women's wishes, [Footnote: The league between the women and the doctors has always struck me as one of the oddest things in Paris. The doctors' reputation depends on the women, and by means of the doctors the women get their own way. It is easy to see what qualifications a doctor requires in Paris if he is to become celebrated.] and for my own part I think it is better that the child should suck the breast of a healthy nurse rather than of a petted mother, if he has any further evil to fear from her who has given him birth.

Ought the question, however, to be considered only from the physiological point of view? Does not the child need a mother's care as much as her milk? Other women, or even other animals, may give him the milk she denies him, but there is no substitute for a mother's love.

The woman who nurses another's child in place of her own is a bad mother; how can she be a good nurse? She may become one in time; use will overcome nature, but the child may perish a hundred times before his nurse has developed a mother's affection for him.

And this affection when developed has its drawbacks, which should make any feeling woman afraid to put her child out to nurse. Is she prepared to divide her mother's rights, or rather to abdicate them in favour of a stranger; to see her child loving another more than herself; to feel that the affection he

12

retains for his own mother is a favour, while his love for his foster-mother is a duty; for is not some affection due where there has been a mother's care?

To remove this difficulty, children are taught to look down on their nurses, to treat them as mere servants. When their task is completed the child is withdrawn or the nurse is dismissed. Her visits to her foster-child are discouraged by a cold reception. After a few years the child never sees her again. The mother expects to take her place, and to repair by her cruelty the results of her own neglect. But she is greatly mistaken; she is making an ungrateful foster-child, not an affectionate son; she is teaching him ingratitude, and she is preparing him to despise at a later day the mother who bore him, as he now despises his nurse.

How emphatically would I speak if it were not so hopeless to keep struggling in vain on behalf of a real reform. More depends on this than you realise. Would you restore all men to their primal duties, begin with the mothers; the results will surprise you. Every evil follows in the train of this first sin; the whole moral order is disturbed, nature is quenched in every breast, the home becomes gloomy, the spectacle of a young family no longer stirs the husband's love and the stranger's reverence. The mother whose children are out of sight wins scanty esteem; there is no home life, the ties of nature are not strengthened by those of habit; fathers, mothers, children, brothers, and sisters cease to exist. They are almost strangers; how should they love one another? Each thinks of himself first. When the home is a gloomy solitude pleasure will be sought elsewhere.

But when mothers deign to nurse their own children, then will be a reform in morals; natural feeling will revive in every heart; there will be no lack of citizens for the state; this first step by itself will restore mutual affection. The charms of home are the best antidote to vice. The noisy play of children, which we thought so trying, becomes a delight; mother and father rely more on each other and grow dearer to one another; the marriage tie is strengthened. In the cheerful home life the mother finds her sweetest duties and the father his pleasantest recreation. Thus the cure of this one evil would work a wide-spread reformation; nature would regain her rights. When women become good mothers, men will be good husbands and fathers.

My words are vain! When we are sick of worldly pleasures we do not return to the pleasures of the home. Women have ceased to be mothers, they do not and will not return to their duty. Could they do it if they would? The contrary custom is firmly established; each would have to overcome the opposition of her neighbours, leagued together against the example which some have never given and others do not desire to follow.

Yet there are still a few young women of good natural disposition who refuse to be the slaves of fashion and rebel against the clamour of other women, who fulfil the sweet task imposed on them by nature. Would that the reward in store for them might draw others to follow their example. My conclusion is based upon plain reason, and upon facts I have never seen disputed; and I venture to promise these worthy mothers the firm and steadfast affection of their husbands and the truly filial love of their children and the respect of all the world. Child-birth will be easy and will leave no ill-results, their health will be strong and vigorous, and they will see their daughters follow their example, and find that example quoted as a pattern to others.

No mother, no child; their duties are reciprocal, and when ill done by the one they will be neglected by the other. The child should love his mother before he knows what he owes her. If the voice of instinct is not strengthened by habit it soon dies, the heart is still-born. From the outset we have strayed from the path of nature.

There is another by-way which may tempt our feet from the path of nature. The mother may lavish excessive care on her child instead of neglecting him; she may make an idol of him; she may develop and increase his weakness to prevent him feeling it; she wards off every painful experience in the hope of withdrawing him from the power of nature, and fails to realise that for every trifling ill from which she preserves him the future holds in store many accidents and dangers, and that it is a cruel kindness to prolong the child's weakness when the grown man must bear fatigue.

Thetis, so the story goes, plunged her son in the waters of Styx to make him invulnerable. The truth of this allegory is apparent. The cruel mothers I speak of do otherwise; they plunge their children into softness, and they are preparing suffering for them, they open the way to every kind of ill, which their children will not fail to experience after they grow up.

Fix your eyes on nature, follow the path traced by her. She keeps children at work, she hardens them by all kinds of difficulties, she soon teaches them the meaning of pain and grief. They cut their teeth and are feverish, sharp colics bring on convulsions, they are choked by fits of coughing and tormented by worms, evil humours corrupt the blood, germs of various kinds ferment in it, causing dangerous eruptions. Sickness and danger play the chief part in infancy. One half of the children who are born die before their eighth year. The child who has overcome hardships has gained strength, and as soon as he can use his life he holds it more securely.

This is nature's law; why contradict it? Do you not see that in your efforts to improve upon her handiwork you are destroying it; her cares are wasted? To do from without what she does within is according to you to increase the danger twofold. On the contrary, it is the way to avert it; experience shows that children delicately nurtured are more likely to die. Provided we do not overdo it, there is less risk in using their strength than in sparing it. Accustom them therefore to the hardships they will have to face; train them to endure extremes of temperature, climate, and condition, hunger, thirst, and weariness. Dip them in the waters of Styx. Before bodily habits become fixed you may teach what habits you will without any risk, but once habits are established any change is fraught with peril. A child will bear changes which a man cannot bear, the muscles of the one are soft and flexible, they take whatever direction you give them without any effort; the muscles of the grown man are harder and they only change their accustomed mode of action when subjected to violence. So we can make a child strong without risking his life or health, and even if there were some risk, it should not be taken into consideration. Since human life is full of dangers, can we do better than face them at a time when they can do the least harm?

A child's worth increases with his years. To his personal value must be added the cost of the care bestowed upon him. For himself there is not only loss of life, but the consciousness of death. We must therefore think most of his future in our efforts for his preservation. He must be protected against the ills of youth before he reaches them: for if the value of life increases until the child reaches an age when he can be useful, what madness to spare some suffering in infancy only to multiply his pain when he reaches the age of reason. Is that what our master teaches us!

Man is born to suffer; pain is the means of his preservation. His childhood is happy, knowing only pain of body. These bodily sufferings are much less cruel, much less painful, than other forms of suffering, and they rarely lead to self-destruction. It is not the twinges of gout which make a man kill himself, it is mental suffering that leads to despair. We pity the sufferings of childhood; we should pity ourselves; our worst sorrows are of our own making.

The new-born infant cries, his early days are spent in crying. He is alternately petted and shaken by way of soothing him; sometimes he is threatened, sometimes beaten, to keep him quiet. We do what he wants or we make him do what we want, we submit to his whims or subject him to our own. There is no middle course; he must rule or obey. Thus his earliest ideas are those of the tyrant or the slave. He commands before he can speak, he obeys before he can act, and sometimes he is punished for faults before he is aware of them, or rather before they are committed. Thus early are the seeds of evil passions sown in his young heart. At a later day these are attributed to nature, and when we have taken pains to make him bad we lament his badness.

In this way the child passes six or seven years in the hands of women, the victim of his own caprices or theirs, and after they have taught him all sorts of things, when they have burdened his memory with words he cannot understand, or things which are of no use to him, when nature has been stifled by the passions they have implanted in him, this sham article is sent to a tutor. The tutor completes the development of the germs of artificiality which he finds already well grown, he teaches him everything except self-knowledge and self-control, the arts of life and happiness. When at length this infant slave and tyrant, crammed with knowledge but empty of sense, feeble alike in mind and body, is flung upon the world, and his helplessness, his pride, and his other vices are displayed, we begin to lament the wretchedness and perversity of mankind. We are wrong; this is the creature of our fantasy; the natural man is cast in another mould.

Would you keep him as nature made him? Watch over him from his birth. Take possession of him as soon as he comes into the world and keep him till he is a man; you will never succeed otherwise. The real nurse is the mother and the real teacher is the father. Let them agree in the ordering of their duties as well as in their method, let the child pass from one to the other. He will be better educated by a sensible though ignorant father than by the cleverest master in the world. For zeal will atone for lack of knowledge, rather than knowledge for lack of zeal. But the duties of public and private business! Duty indeed! Does a father's duty come last. [Footnote: When we read in Plutarch that Cato the Censor, who ruled Rome with such glory, brought up his own sons from the cradle, and so carefully that he left everything to be present when their nurse, that is to say their mother, bathed them; when we read in Suetonius that Augustus, the master of the world which he had conquered and which he himself governed, himself taught his grandsons to write, to swim, to understand the beginnings of science, and that he always had them with him, we cannot help smiling at the little people of those days who amused themselves with such follies, and who were too ignorant, no doubt, to attend to the great affairs of the great people of our own time.] It is not surprising that the man whose wife despises the duty of suckling her child should despise its education. There is no more charming picture than that of family life; but when one feature is wanting the whole is marred. If the mother is too delicate to nurse her child, the father will be too busy to teach him. Their children, scattered about in schools, convents, and colleges, will find the home of their affections elsewhere, or rather they will form the habit of caring for nothing. Brothers and sisters will scarcely know each other; when they are together in company they will behave as strangers. When there is no confidence between relations, when the family society ceases to give savour to life, its place is soon usurped by vice. Is there any man so stupid that he cannot see how all this hangs together?

A father has done but a third of his task when he begets children and provides a living for them. He owes men to humanity, citizens to the state. A man who can pay this threefold debt and neglect to do so is guilty, more guilty, perhaps, if he pays it in part than when he neglects it entirely. He has no right to be a father if he cannot fulfil a father's duties. Poverty, pressure of business, mistaken social prejudices, none of these can excuse a man from his duty, which is to support and educate his own children. If a man of any natural feeling neglects these sacred duties he will repent it with bitter tears and will never be comforted.

But what does this rich man do, this father of a family, compelled, so he says, to neglect his children? He pays another man to perform those duties which are his alone. Mercenary man! do you expect to purchase a second father for your child? Do not deceive yourself; it is not even a master you have hired for him, it is a flunkey, who will soon train such another as himself.

There is much discussion as to the characteristics of a good tutor. My first requirement, and it implies a good many more, is that he should not take up his task for reward. There are callings so great that they cannot be undertaken for money without showing our unfitness for them; such callings are those of the soldier and the teacher.

"But who must train my child?" "I have just told you, you should do it

16

yourself." "I cannot." "You cannot! Then find a friend. I see no other course."

A tutor! What a noble soul! Indeed for the training of a man one must either be a father or more than man. It is this duty you would calmly hand over to a hireling!

The more you think of it the harder you will find it. The tutor must have been trained for his pupil, his servants must have been trained for their master, so that all who come near him may have received the impression which is to be transmitted to him. We must pass from education to education, I know not how far. How can a child be well educated by one who has not been well educated himself!

Can such a one be found? I know not. In this age of degradation who knows the height of virtue to which man's soul may attain? But let us assume that this prodigy has been discovered. We shall learn what he should be from the consideration of his duties. I fancy the father who realises the value of a good tutor will contrive to do without one, for it will be harder to find one than to become such a tutor himself; he need search no further, nature herself having done half the work.

Some one whose rank alone is known to me suggested that I should educate his son. He did me a great honour, no doubt, but far from regretting my refusal, he ought to congratulate himself on my prudence. Had the offer been accepted, and had I been mistaken in my method, there would have been an education ruined; had I succeeded, things would have been worse—his son would have renounced his title and refused to be a prince.

I feel too deeply the importance of a tutor's duties and my own unfitness, ever to accept such a post, whoever offered it, and even the claims of friendship would be only an additional motive for my refusal. Few, I think, will be tempted to make me such an offer when they have read this book, and I beg any one who would do so to spare his pains. I have had enough experience of the task to convince myself of my own unfitness, and my circumstances would make it impossible, even if my talents were such as to fit me for it. I have thought it my duty to make this public declaration to those who apparently refuse to do me the honour of believing in the sincerity of my determination. If I am unable to undertake the more useful task, I will at least venture to attempt the easier one; I will follow the example of my predecessors and take up, not the task, but my pen; and instead of doing the right thing I will try to say it.

I know that in such an undertaking the author, who ranges at will among theoretical systems, utters many fine precepts impossible to practise, and even when he says what is practicable it remains undone for want of details and examples as to its application.

I have therefore decided to take an imaginary pupil, to assume on my own part the age, health, knowledge, and talents required for the work of his education, to guide him from birth to manhood, when he needs no guide but himself. This method seems to me useful for an author who fears lest he may stray from the practical to the visionary; for as soon as he departs from common practice he has only to try his method on his pupil; he will soon know, or the reader will know for him, whether he is following the development of the child and the natural growth of the human heart.

This is what I have tried to do. Lest my book should be unduly bulky, I have been content to state those principles the truth of which is self-evident. But as to the rules which call for proof, I have applied them to Emile or to others, and I have shown, in very great detail, how my theories may be put into practice. Such at least is my plan; the reader must decide whether I have succeeded. At first I have said little about Emile, for my earliest maxims of education, though very different from those generally accepted, are so plain that it is hard for a man of sense to refuse to accept them, but as I advance, my scholar, educated after another fashion than yours, is no longer an ordinary child, he needs a special system. Then he appears upon the scene more frequently, and towards the end I never lose sight of him for a moment, until, whatever he may say, he needs me no longer.

I pass over the qualities required in a good tutor; I take them for granted, and assume that I am endowed with them. As you read this book you will see how generous I have been to myself.

I will only remark that, contrary to the received opinion, a child's tutor should be young, as young indeed as a man may well be who is also wise. Were it possible, he should become a child himself, that he may be the companion of his pupil and win his confidence by sharing his games. Childhood and age have too little in common for the formation of a really firm affection. Children sometimes flatter old men; they never love them.

People seek a tutor who has already educated one pupil. This is too much; one man can only educate one pupil; if two were essential to success, what right would he have to undertake the first? With more experience you may know better what to do, but you are less capable of doing it; once this task has been well done, you will know too much of its difficulties to attempt it a second time—if ill done, the first attempt augurs badly for the second.

It is one thing to follow a young man about for four years, another to be his guide for five-and-twenty. You find a tutor for your son when he is already formed; I want one for him before he is born. Your man may change his pupil every five years; mine will never have but one pupil. You distinguish between the teacher and the tutor. Another piece of folly! Do you make any distinction between the pupil and the scholar? There is only one science for children to learn—the duties of man. This science is one, and, whatever Xenophon may say of the education of the Persians, it is indivisible. Besides, I prefer to call the man who has this knowledge master rather than teacher, since it is a question of guidance rather than instruction. He must not give precepts, he must let the scholar find them out for himself.

If the master is to be so carefully chosen, he may well choose his pupil, above all when he proposes to set a pattern for others. This choice cannot depend on the child's genius or character, as I adopt him before he is born, and they are only known when my task is finished. If I had my choice I would take a child of ordinary mind, such as I assume in my pupil. It is ordinary people who have to be educated, and their education alone can serve as a pattern for the education of their fellows. The others find their way alone.

The birthplace is not a matter of indifference in the education of man; it is only in temperate climes that he comes to his full growth. The disadvantages of extremes are easily seen. A man is not planted in one place like a tree, to stay there the rest of his life, and to pass from one extreme to another you must travel twice as far as he who starts half-way.

If the inhabitant of a temperate climate passes in turn through both extremes his advantage is plain, for although he may be changed as much as he who goes from one extreme to the other, he only removes half-way from his natural condition. A Frenchman can live in New Guinea or in Lapland, but a negro cannot live in Tornea nor a Samoyed in Benin. It seems also as if the brain were less perfectly organised in the two extremes. Neither the negroes nor the Laps are as wise as Europeans. So if I want my pupil to be a citizen of the world I will choose him in the temperate zone, in France for example, rather than elsewhere.

In the north with its barren soil men devour much food, in the fertile south they eat little. This produces another difference: the one is industrious, the other contemplative. Society shows us, in one and the same spot, a similar difference between rich and poor. The one dwells in a fertile land, the other in a barren land.

The poor man has no need of education. The education of his own station in life is forced upon him, he can have no other; the education received by the rich man from his own station is least fitted for himself and for society. Moreover, a natural education should fit a man for any position. Now it is more unreasonable to train a poor man for wealth than a rich man for poverty, for in proportion to their numbers more rich men are ruined and fewer poor men become rich. Let us choose our scholar among the rich; we shall at least have made another man; the poor may come to manhood without our help.

For the same reason I should not be sorry if Emile came of a good family. He will be another victim snatched from prejudice.

Emile is an orphan. No matter whether he has father or mother, having undertaken their duties I am invested with their rights. He must honour his parents, but he must obey me. That is my first and only condition.

I must add that there is just one other point arising out of this; we must never be separated except by mutual consent. This clause is essential, and I would have tutor and scholar so inseparable that they should regard their fate as one. If once they perceive the time of their separation drawing near, the time which must make them strangers to one another, they become strangers then and there; each makes his own little world, and both of them being busy in thought with the time when they will no longer be together, they remain together against their will. The disciple regards his master as the badge and scourge of childhood, the master regards his scholar as a heavy burden which he longs to be rid of. Both are looking forward to the time when they will part, and as there is never any real affection between them, there will be scant vigilance on the one hand, and on the other scant obedience.

But when they consider they must always live together, they must needs love one another, and in this way they really learn to love one another. The pupil is not ashamed to follow as a child the friend who will be with him in manhood; the tutor takes an interest in the efforts whose fruits he will enjoy, and the virtues he is cultivating in his pupil form a store laid up for his old age.

This agreement made beforehand assumes a normal birth, a strong, well-made, healthy child. A father has no choice, and should have no preference within the limits of the family God has given him; all his children are his alike, the same care and affection is due to all. Crippled or well-made, weak or strong, each of them is a trust for which he is responsible to the Giver, and nature is a party to the marriage contract along with husband and wife.

But if you undertake a duty not imposed upon you by nature, you must secure beforehand the means for its fulfilment, unless you would undertake duties you cannot fulfil. If you take the care of a sickly, unhealthy child, you are a sick nurse, not a tutor. To preserve a useless life you are wasting the time which should be spent in increasing its value, you risk the sight of a despairing mother reproaching you for the death of her child, who ought to have died long ago.

I would not undertake the care of a feeble, sickly child, should he live to four score years. I want no pupil who is useless alike to himself and others, one whose sole business is to keep himself alive, one whose body is always a hindrance to the training of his mind. If I vainly lavish my care upon him, what can I do but double the loss to society by robbing it of two men, instead of one? Let another tend this weakling for me; I am quite willing, I approve his charity, but I myself have no gift for such a task; I could never teach the art of living to one who needs all his strength to keep himself alive.

The body must be strong enough to obey the mind; a good servant must be strong. I know that intemperance stimulates the passions; in course of time it also destroys the body; fasting and penance often produce the same results in an opposite way. The weaker the body, the more imperious its demands; the stronger it is, the better it obeys. All sensual passions find their home in effeminate bodies; the less satisfaction they can get the keener their sting.

A feeble body makes a feeble mind. Hence the influence of physic, an art which does more harm to man than all the evils it professes to cure. I do not know what the doctors cure us of, but I know this: they infect us with very deadly diseases, cowardice, timidity, credulity, the fear of death. What matter if they make the dead walk, we have no need of corpses; they fail to give us men, and it is men we need.

Medicine is all the fashion in these days, and very naturally. It is the amusement of the idle and unemployed, who do not know what to do with their time, and so spend it in taking care of themselves. If by ill-luck they had happened to be born immortal, they would have been the most miserable of men; a life they could not lose would be of no value to them. Such men must have doctors to threaten and flatter them, to give them the only pleasure they can enjoy, the pleasure of not being dead.

I will say no more at present as to the uselessness of medicine. My aim is to consider its bearings on morals. Still I cannot refrain from saying that men employ the same sophism about medicine as they do about the search for truth. They assume that the patient is cured and that the seeker after truth finds it. They fail to see that against one life saved by the doctors you must set a hundred slain, and against the value of one truth discovered the errors which creep in with it. The science which instructs and the medicine which heals are no doubt excellent, but the science which misleads us and the medicine which kills us are evil. Teach us to know them apart. That is the real difficulty. If we were content to be ignorant of truth we should not be the dupes of falsehood; if we did not want to be cured in spite of nature, we should not be killed by the doctors. We should do well to steer clear of both, and we should evidently be the gainers. I do not deny that medicine is useful to some men; I assert that it is fatal to mankind.

You will tell me, as usual, that the doctors are to blame, that medicine herself is infallible. Well and good, then give us the medicine without the doctor, for when we have both, the blunders of the artist are a hundredfold greater than our hopes from the art. This lying art, invented rather for the ills of the mind than of the body, is useless to both alike; it does less to cure us of our diseases than to fill us with alarm. It does less to ward off death than to make us dread its approach. It exhausts life rather than prolongs it; should it even prolong life it would only be to the prejudice of the race, since it makes us set its precautions before society and our fears before our duties. It is the knowledge of danger that makes us afraid. If we thought ourselves invulnerable we should know no fear. The poet armed Achilles against danger and so robbed him of the merit of courage; on such terms any man would be an Achilles.

Would you find a really brave man? Seek him where there are no doctors, where the results of disease are unknown, and where death is little thought of. By nature a man bears pain bravely and dies in peace. It is the doctors with their rules, the philosophers with their precepts, the priests with their exhortations, who debase the heart and make us afraid to die.

Give me a pupil who has no need of these, or I will have nothing to do with him. No one else shall spoil my work, I will educate him myself or not at all. That wise man, Locke, who had devoted part of his life to the study of medicine, advises us to give no drugs to the child, whether as a precaution, or on account of slight ailments. I will go farther, and will declare that, as I never call in a doctor for myself, I will never send for one for Emile, unless his life is clearly in danger, when the doctor can but kill him.

I know the doctor will make capital out of my delay. If the child dies, he was called in too late; if he recovers, it is his doing. So be it; let the doctor boast, but do not call him in except in extremity.

As the child does not know how to be cured, he knows how to be ill. The one art takes the place of the other and is often more successful; it is the art of nature. When a beast is ill, it keeps quiet and suffers in silence; but we see fewer sickly animals than sick men. How many men have been slain by impatience, fear, anxiety, and above all by medicine, men whom disease would have spared, and time alone have cured. I shall be told that animals, who live according to nature, are less liable to disease than ourselves. Well, that way of living is just what I mean to teach my pupil; he should profit by it in the same way.

Hygiene is the only useful part of medicine, and hygiene is rather a virtue than a science. Temperance and industry are man's true remedies; work sharpens his appetite and temperance teaches him to control it.

To learn what system is most beneficial you have only to study those races remarkable for health, strength, and length of days. If common observation shows us that medicine neither increases health nor prolongs life, it follows that this useless art is worse than useless, since it wastes time, men, and things on what is pure loss. Not only must we deduct the time spent, not in using life, but preserving it, but if this time is spent in tormenting ourselves it is worse than wasted, it is so much to the bad, and to reckon fairly a corresponding share must be deducted from what remains to us. A man who lives ten years for himself and others without the help of doctors lives more for himself and others than one who spends thirty years as their victim. I have tried both, so I think I have a better right than most to draw my own conclusions.

For these reasons I decline to take any but a strong and healthy pupil, and these are my principles for keeping him in health. I will not stop to prove at length the value of manual labour and bodily exercise for strengthening the health and constitution; no one denies it. Nearly all the instances of long life are to be found among the men who have taken most exercise, who have endured fatigue and labour. [Footnote: I cannot help quoting the following passage from an English newspaper, as it throws much light on my opinions: "A certain Patrick O'Neil, born in 1647, has just married his seventh wife in 1760. In the seventeenth year of Charles II. he served in the dragoons and in other regiments up to 1740, when he took his discharge. He served in all the campaigns of William III. and Marlborough. This man has never drunk anything but small beer; he has always lived on vegetables, and has never eaten meat except on few occasions when he made a feast for his relations. He has always been accustomed to rise with the sun and go to bed at sunset unless prevented by his military duties. He is now in his 130th year; he is healthy, his hearing is good, and he walks with the help of a stick. In spite of his great age he is never idle, and every Sunday he goes to his parish church accompanied by his children, grandchildren, and great grandchildren."] Neither will I enter into details as to the care I shall take for this alone. It will be clear that it forms such an essential part of my practice that it is enough to get hold of the idea without further explanation.

When our life begins our needs begin too. The new-born infant must have a nurse. If his mother will do her duty, so much the better; her instructions will be given her in writing, but this advantage has its drawbacks, it removes the tutor from his charge. But it is to be hoped that the child's own interests, and her respect for the person to whom she is about to confide so precious a treasure, will induce the mother to follow the master's wishes, and whatever she does you may be sure she will do better than another. If we must have a strange nurse, make a good choice to begin with.

It is one of the misfortunes of the rich to be cheated on all sides; what wonder they think ill of mankind! It is riches that corrupt men, and the rich are rightly the first to feel the defects of the only tool they know. Everything is ill-done for them, except what they do themselves, and they do next to nothing. When a nurse must be selected the choice is left to the doctor. What happens? The best nurse is the one who offers the highest bribe. I shall not consult the doctor about Emile's nurse, I shall take care to choose her myself. I may not argue about it so elegantly as the surgeon, but I shall be more reliable, I shall be less deceived by my zeal than the doctor by his greed.

There is no mystery about this choice; its rules are well known, but I think we ought probably to pay more attention to the age of the milk as well as its quality. The first milk is watery, it must be almost an aperient, to purge the remains of the meconium curdled in the bowels of the new-born child. Little by little the milk thickens and supplies more solid food as the child is able to digest it. It is surely not without cause that nature changes the milk in the female of every species according to the age of the offspring.

Thus a new-born child requires a nurse who has recently become mother. There is, I know, a difficulty here, but as soon as we leave the path of nature there are difficulties in the way of all well-doing. The wrong course is the only right one under the circumstances, so we take it.

The nurse must be healthy alike in disposition and in body. The violence of the passions as well as the humours may spoil her milk. Moreover, to consider the body only is to keep only half our aim in view. The milk may be good and the nurse bad; a good character is as necessary as a good constitution. If you choose a vicious person, I do not say her foster-child will acquire her vices, but he will suffer for them. Ought she not to bestow on him day by day, along with her milk, a care which calls for zeal, patience, gentleness, and cleanliness. If she is intemperate and greedy her milk will soon be spoilt; if she is careless and hasty what will become of a poor little wretch left to her mercy, and unable either to protect himself or to complain. The wicked are never good for anything.

The choice is all the more important because her foster-child should have no other guardian, just as he should have no teacher but his tutor. This was the custom of the ancients, who talked less but acted more wisely than we. The nurse never left her foster-daughter; this is why the nurse is the confidante in most of their plays. A child who passes through many hands in turn, can never be well brought up.

At every change he makes a secret comparison, which continually tends to lessen his respect for those who control him, and with it their authority over him. If once he thinks there are grown-up people with no more sense than children the authority of age is destroyed and his education is ruined. A child should know no betters but its father and mother, or failing them its foster-mother and its tutor, and even this is one too many, but this division is inevitable, and the best that can be done in the way of remedy is that the man and woman who control him shall be so well agreed with regard to him that they seem like one.

The nurse must live rather more comfortably, she must have rather more substantial food, but her whole way of living must not be altered, for a sudden change, even a change for the better, is dangerous to health, and since her usual way of life has made her healthy and strong, why change it?

Country women eat less meat and more vegetables than towns-women, and this vegetarian diet seems favourable rather than otherwise to themselves and their children. When they take nurslings from the upper classes they eat meat and broth with the idea that they will form better chyle and supply more milk. I do not hold with this at all, and experience is on my side, for we do not find children fed in this way less liable to colic and worms.

That need not surprise us, for decaying animal matter swarms with worms, but this is not the case with vegetable matter. [Footnote: Women eat bread, vegetables, and dairy produce; female dogs and cats do the same; the she-wolves eat grass. This supplies vegetable juices to their milk. There are still those species which are unable to eat anything but flesh, if such there are, which I very much doubt.] Milk, although manufactured in the body of an animal, is a vegetable substance; this is shown by analysis; it readily turns acid, and far from showing traces of any volatile alkali like animal matter, it gives a neutral salt like plants.

The milk of herbivorous creatures is sweeter and more wholesome than the milk of the carnivorous; formed of a substance similar to its own, it keeps its goodness and becomes less liable to putrifaction. If quantity is considered, it is well known that farinaceous foods produce more blood than meat, so they ought to yield more milk. If a child were not weaned too soon, and if it were fed on vegetarian food, and its foster-mother were a vegetarian, I do not think it would be troubled with worms.

Milk derived from vegetable foods may perhaps be more liable to go sour, but I am far from considering sour milk an unwholesome food; whole nations have no other food and are none the worse, and all the array of absorbents seems to me mere humbug. There are constitutions which do not thrive on milk, others can take it without absorbents. People are afraid of the milk separating or curdling; that is absurd, for we know that milk always curdles in the stomach. This is how it becomes sufficiently solid to nourish children and young animals; if it did not curdle it would merely pass away without feeding them. [Footnote: Although the juices which nourish us are liquid, they must be extracted from solids. A hard-working man who ate nothing but soup would soon waste away. He would be far better fed on milk, just because it curdles.] In vain you dilute milk and use absorbents; whoever swallows milk digests cheese, this rule is without exception; rennet is made from a calf's stomach.

Instead of changing the nurse's usual diet, I think it would be enough to give food in larger quantities and better of its kind. It is not the nature of the food that makes a vegetable diet indigestible, but the flavouring that makes it unwholesome. Reform your cookery, use neither butter nor oil for frying. Butter, salt, and milk should never be cooked. Let your vegetables be cooked in water and only seasoned when they come to table. The vegetable diet, far from disturbing the nurse, will give her a plentiful supply of milk. [Footnote: Those who wish to study a full account of the advantages and disadvantages of the Pythagorean regime, may consult the works of Dr. Cocchi and his opponent Dr. Bianchi on this important subject.] If a vegetable diet is best for the child, how can meat food be best for his nurse? The things are contradictory.

Fresh air affects children's constitutions, particularly in early years. It enters every pore of a soft and tender skin, it has a powerful effect on their young bodies. Its effects can never be destroyed. So I should not agree with those who take a country woman from her village and shut her up in one room in a town and her nursling with her. I would rather send him to breathe the fresh air of the country than the foul air of the town. He will take his new mother's position, will live in her cottage, where his tutor will follow him. The reader will bear in mind that this tutor is not a paid servant, but the father's friend. But if this friend cannot be found, if this transfer is not easy, if none of my advice can be followed, you will say to me, "What shall I do instead?" I have told you already—"Do what you are doing;" no advice is needed there.

Men are not made to be crowded together in ant-hills, but scattered over the earth to till it. The more they are massed together, the more corrupt they become. Disease and vice are the sure results of over-crowded cities. Of all creatures man is least fitted to live in herds. Huddled together like sheep, men would very soon die. Man's breath is fatal to his fellows. This is literally as well as figuratively true.

Men are devoured by our towns. In a few generations the race dies out or becomes degenerate; it needs renewal, and it is always renewed from the country. Send your children to renew themselves, so to speak, send them to regain in the open fields the strength lost in the foul air of our crowded cities. Women hurry home that their children may be born in the town; they ought to do just the opposite, especially those who mean to nurse their own children. They would lose less than they think, and in more natural surroundings the pleasures associated by nature with maternal duties would soon destroy the taste for other delights.

The new-born infant is first bathed in warm water to which a little wine is usually added. I think the wine might be dispensed with. As nature does not produce fermented liquors, it is not likely that they are of much value to her creatures.

In the same way it is unnecessary to take the precaution of heating the water; in fact among many races the new-born infants are bathed with no more ado in rivers or in the sea. Our children, made tender before birth by the softness of their parents, come into the world with a constitution already enfeebled, which cannot be at once exposed to all the trials required to restore it to health. Little by little they must be restored to their natural vigour. Begin then by following this custom, and leave it off gradually. Wash your children often, their dirty ways show the need of this. If they are only wiped their skin is injured; but as they grow stronger gradually reduce the heat of the water, till at last you bathe them winter and summer in cold, even in ice-cold water. To avoid risk this change must be slow, gradual, and imperceptible, so you may use the thermometer for exact measurements.

This habit of the bath, once established, should never be broken off, it must be kept up all through life. I value it not only on grounds of cleanliness and present health, but also as a wholesome means of making the muscles supple, and accustoming them to bear without risk or effort extremes of heat and cold. As he gets older I would have the child trained to bathe occasionally in hot water of every bearable degree, and often in every degree of cold water. Now water being a denser fluid touches us at more points than air, so that, having learnt to bear all the variations of temperature in water, we shall scarcely feel this of the air. [Footnote: Children in towns are stifled by being kept indoors and too much wrapped up. Those who control them have still to learn that fresh air, far from doing them harm, will make them strong, while hot air will make them weak, will give rise to fevers, and will eventually kill them.]

When the child draws its first breath do not confine it in tight wrappings. No cap, no bandages, nor swaddling clothes. Loose and flowing flannel wrappers, which leave its limbs free and are not too heavy to check his movements, not too warm to prevent his feeling the air. [Footnote: I say "cradle" using the common word for want of a better, though I am convinced that it is never necessary and often harmful to rock children in the cradle.] Put him in a big cradle, well padded, where he can move easily and safely. As he begins to grow stronger, let him crawl about the room; let him develop and stretch his tiny limbs; you will see him gain strength from day to day. Compare him with a well swaddled child of the same age and you will be surprised at their different rates of progress. [Footnote: The ancient Peruvians wrapped their children in loose swaddling bands, leaving the arms quite free. Later they placed them unswaddled in a hole in the ground, lined with cloths, so that the lower part of the body was in the hole, and their arms were free and they could move the head and bend the body at will without falling or hurting themselves. When they began to walk they were enticed to come to the breast. The little negroes are often in a position much more difficult for sucking. They cling to the mother's hip, and cling so tightly that the mother's arm is often not needed to support them. They clasp the breast with their hand and continue sucking while their mother goes on with her ordinary work. These children begin to walk at two months, or rather to crawl. Later on they can run on all fours almost as well as on their feet. — Buffon. M. Buffon might also have quoted the example of England, where the senseless and barbarous swaddling clothes have become almost obsolete. Cf. La Longue Voyage de Siam, Le Beau Voyage de Canada, etc.]

You must expect great opposition from the nurses, who find a half strangled baby needs much less watching. Besides his dirtyness is more perceptible in an open garment; he must be attended to more frequently. Indeed, custom is an unanswerable argument in some lands and among all classes of people.

Do not argue with the nurses; give your orders, see them carried out, and spare no pains to make the attention you prescribe easy in practice. Why not take your share in it? With ordinary nurslings, where the body alone is thought of, nothing matters so long as the child lives and does not actually die, but with us, when education begins with life, the new-born child is already a disciple, not of his tutor, but of nature. The tutor merely studies under this master, and sees that his orders are not evaded. He watches over the infant, he observes it, he looks for the first feeble glimmering of intelligence, as the Moslem looks for the moment of the moon's rising in her first quarter.

We are born capable of learning, but knowing nothing, perceiving nothing. The mind, bound up within imperfect and half grown organs, is not even aware of its own existence. The movements and cries of the new-born child are purely reflex, without knowledge or will.

Suppose a child born with the size and strength of manhood, entering upon life full grown like Pallas from the brain of Jupiter; such a child-man would be a perfect idiot, an automaton, a statue without motion and almost without feeling; he would see and hear nothing, he would recognise no one, he could not turn his eyes towards what he wanted to see; not only would he perceive no external object, he would not even be aware of sensation through the several sense-organs. His eye would not perceive colour, his ear sounds, his body would be unaware of contact with neighbouring bodies, he would not even know he had a body, what his hands handled would be in his brain alone; all his sensations would be united in one place, they would exist only in the common "sensorium," he would have only one idea, that of self, to which he would refer all his sensations; and this idea, or rather this feeling, would be the only thing in which he excelled an ordinary child.

This man, full grown at birth, would also be unable to stand on his feet, he would need a long time to learn how to keep his balance; perhaps he would not even be able to try to do it, and you would see the big strong body left in one place like a stone, or creeping and crawling like a young puppy.

He would feel the discomfort of bodily needs without knowing what was the matter and without knowing how to provide for these needs. There is no immediate connection between the muscles of the stomach and those of the arms and legs to make him take a step towards food, or stretch a hand to seize it, even were he surrounded with it; and as his body would be full grown and his limbs well developed he would be without the perpetual restlessness and movement of childhood, so that he might die of hunger without stirring to seek food. However little you may have thought about the order and development of our knowledge, you cannot deny that such a one would be in the state of almost primitive ignorance and stupidity natural to man before he has learnt anything from experience or from his fellows.

We know then, or we may know, the point of departure from which we each start towards the usual level of understanding; but who knows the other extreme? Each progresses more or less according to his genius, his taste, his needs, his talents, his zeal, and his opportunities for using them. No philosopher, so far as I know, has dared to say to man, "Thus far shalt thou go and no further." We know not what nature allows us to be, none of us has measured the possible difference between man and man. Is there a mind so dead that this thought has never kindled it, that has never said in his pride, "How much have I already done, how much more may I achieve? Why should I lag behind my fellows?"

As I said before, man's education begins at birth; before he can speak or understand he is learning. Experience precedes instruction; when he recognises his nurse he has learnt much. The knowledge of the most ignorant man would surprise us if we had followed his course from birth to the present time. If all human knowledge were divided into two parts, one common to all, the other peculiar to the learned, the latter would seem very small compared with the former. But we scarcely heed this general experience, because it is acquired before the age of reason. Moreover, knowledge only attracts attention by its rarity, as in algebraic equations common factors count for nothing. Even animals learn much. They have senses and must learn to use them; they have needs, they must learn to satisfy them; they must learn to eat, walk, or fly. Quadrupeds which can stand on their feet from the first cannot walk for all that; from their first attempts it is clear that they lack confidence. Canaries who escape from their cage are unable to fly, having never used their wings. Living and feeling creatures are always learning. If plants could walk they would need senses and knowledge, else their species would die out. The child's first mental experiences are purely affective, he is only aware of pleasure and pain; it takes him a long time to acquire the definite sensations which show him things outside himself, but before these things present and withdraw themselves, so to speak, from his sight, taking size and shape for him, the recurrence of emotional experiences is beginning to subject the child to the rule of habit. You see his eyes constantly follow the light, and if the light comes from the side the eyes turn towards it, so that one must be careful to turn his head towards the light lest he should squint. He must also be accustomed from the first to the dark, or he will cry if he misses the light. Food and sleep, too, exactly measured, become necessary at regular intervals, and soon desire is no longer the effect of need, but of habit, or rather habit adds a fresh need to those of nature. You must be on your guard against this.

The only habit the child should be allowed to contract is that of having no habits; let him be carried on either arm, let him be accustomed to offer either hand, to use one or other indifferently; let him not want to eat, sleep, or do anything at fixed hours, nor be unable to be left alone by day or night. Prepare the way for his control of his liberty and the use of his strength by leaving his body its natural habit, by making him capable of lasting self-control, of doing all that he wills when his will is formed.

As soon as the child begins to take notice, what is shown him must be carefully chosen. The natural man is interested in all new things. He feels so feeble that he fears the unknown: the habit of seeing fresh things without ill effects destroys this fear. Children brought up in clean houses where there are no spiders are afraid of spiders, and this fear often lasts through life. I never saw peasants, man, woman, or child, afraid of spiders.

Since the mere choice of things shown him may make the child timid or brave, why should not his education begin before he can speak or understand? I would have him accustomed to see fresh things, ugly, repulsive, and strange beasts, but little by little, and far off till he is used to them, and till having seen others handle them he handles them himself. If in childhood he sees toads, snakes, and crayfish, he will not be afraid of any animal when he is grown up. Those who are continually seeing terrible things think nothing of them.

All children are afraid of masks. I begin by showing Emile a mask with a pleasant face, then some one puts this mask before his face; I begin to laugh, they all laugh too, and the child with them. By degrees I accustom him to less pleasing masks, and at last hideous ones. If I have arranged my stages skilfully, far from being afraid of the last mask, he will laugh at it as he did at the first. After that I am not afraid of people frightening him with masks.

When Hector bids farewell to Andromache, the young Astyanax, startled by the nodding plumes on the helmet, does not know his father; he flings himself weeping upon his nurse's bosom and wins from his mother a smile mingled with tears. What must be done to stay this terror? Just what Hector did; put the helmet on the ground and caress the child. In a calmer moment one would do more; one would go up to the helmet, play with the plumes, let the child feel them; at last the nurse would take the helmet and place it laughingly on her own head, if indeed a woman's hand dare touch the armour of Hector.

If Emile must get used to the sound of a gun, I first fire a pistol with a small charge. He is delighted with this sudden flash, this sort of lightning; I repeat the process with more powder; gradually I add a small charge without a wad, then a larger; in the end I accustom him to the sound of a gun, to fireworks, cannon, and the most terrible explosions.

I have observed that children are rarely afraid of thunder unless the peals are really terrible and actually hurt the ear, otherwise this fear only comes to them when they know that thunder sometimes hurts or kills. When reason begins to cause fear, let use reassure them. By slow and careful stages man and child learn to fear nothing.

In the dawn of life, when memory and imagination have not begun to function, the child only attends to what affects its senses. His sense experiences are the raw material of thought; they should, therefore, be presented to him in fitting order, so that memory may at a future time present them in the same order to his understanding; but as he only attends to his sensations it is enough, at first, to show him clearly the connection between these sensations and the things which cause them. He wants to touch and handle everything; do not check these movements which teach him invaluable lessons. Thus he learns to perceive the heat, cold, hardness, softness, weight, or lightness of bodies, to judge their size and shape and all their physical properties, by looking, feeling, [Footnote: Of all the senses that of smell is the latest to develop in children up to two or three years of age they appear to be insensible of pleasant or unpleasant odours; in this respect they are as indifferent or rather as insensible as many animals.] listening, and, above all, by comparing sight and touch, by judging with the eye what sensation they would cause to his hand.

It is only by movement that we learn the difference between self and not self; it is only by our own movements that we gain the idea of space. The child has not this idea, so he stretches out his hand to seize the object within his reach or that which is a hundred paces from him. You take this as a sign of tyranny, an attempt to bid the thing draw near, or to bid you bring it. Nothing of the kind, it is merely that the object first seen in his brain, then before his eyes, now seems close to his arms, and he has no idea of space beyond his reach. Be careful, therefore, to take him about, to move him from place to place, and to let him perceive the change in his surroundings, so as to teach him to judge of distances.

When he begins to perceive distances then you must change your plan, and only carry him when you please, not when he pleases; for as soon as he is no longer deceived by his senses, there is another motive for his effort. This change is remarkable and calls for explanation.

The discomfort caused by real needs is shown by signs, when the help of others is required. Hence the cries of children; they often cry; it must be so. Since they are only conscious of feelings, when those feelings are pleasant they enjoy them in silence; when they are painful they say so in their own way and demand relief. Now when they are awake they can scarcely be in a state of indifference, either they are asleep or else they are feeling something.

All our languages are the result of art. It has long been a subject of inquiry whether there ever was a natural language common to all; no doubt there is, and it is the language of children before they begin to speak. This language is inarticulate, but it has tone, stress, and meaning. The use of our own language has led us to neglect it so far as to forget it altogether. Let us study children and we shall soon learn it afresh from them. Nurses can teach us this language; they understand all their nurslings say to them, they answer them, and keep up long conversations with them; and though they use words, these words are quite useless. It is not the hearing of the word, but its accompanying intonation that is understood.

To the language of intonation is added the no less forcible language of gesture. The child uses, not its weak hands, but its face. The amount of expression in these undeveloped faces is extraordinary; their features change from one moment to another with incredible speed. You see smiles, desires, terror, come and go like lightning; every time the face seems different. The muscles of the face are undoubtedly more mobile than our own. On the other hand the eyes are almost expressionless. Such must be the sort of signs they use at an age when their only needs are those of the body. Grimaces are the sign of sensation, the glance expresses sentiment.

As man's first state is one of want and weakness, his first sounds are cries and tears. The child feels his needs and cannot satisfy them, he begs for help by his cries. Is he hungry or thirsty? there are tears; is he too cold or too hot? more tears; he needs movement and is kept quiet, more tears; he wants to sleep and is disturbed, he weeps. The less comfortable he is, the more he demands change. He has only one language because he has, so to say, only one kind of discomfort. In the imperfect state of his sense organs he does not distinguish their several impressions; all ills produce one feeling of sorrow.

These tears, which you think so little worthy of your attention, give rise to the first relation between man and his environment; here is forged the first link in the long chain of social order.

When the child cries he is uneasy, he feels some need which he cannot satisfy; you watch him, seek this need, find it, and satisfy it. If you can neither find it nor satisfy it, the tears continue and become tiresome. The child is petted to quiet him, he is rocked or sung to sleep; if he is obstinate, the nurse becomes impatient and threatens him; cruel nurses sometimes strike him. What strange lessons for him at his first entrance into life!

I shall never forget seeing one of these troublesome crying children thus beaten by his nurse. He was silent at once. I thought he was frightened, and said to myself, "This will be a servile being from whom nothing can be got but by harshness." I was wrong, the poor wretch was choking with rage, he could not breathe, he was black in the face. A moment later there were bitter cries, every sign of the anger, rage, and despair of this age was in his tones. I thought he would die. Had I doubted the innate sense of justice and injustice in man's heart, this one instance would have convinced me. I am sure that a drop of boiling liquid falling by chance on that child's hand would have hurt him less than that blow, slight in itself, but clearly given with the intention of hurting him.

This tendency to anger, vexation, and rage needs great care. Boerhaave thinks that most of the diseases of children are of the nature of convulsions, because the head being larger in proportion and the nervous system more extensive than in adults, they are more liable to nervous irritation. Take the greatest care to remove from them any servants who tease, annoy, or vex them. They are a hundredfold more dangerous and more fatal than fresh air and changing seasons. When children only experience resistance in things and never in the will of man, they do not become rebellious or passionate, and their health is better. This is one reason why the children of the poor, who are freer and more independent, are generally less frail and weakly, more vigorous than those who are supposed to be better brought up by being constantly thwarted; but you must always remember that it is one thing to refrain from thwarting them, but quite another to obey them. The child's first tears are prayers, beware lest they become commands; he begins by asking for aid, he ends by demanding service. Thus from his own weakness, the source of his first consciousness of dependence, springs the later idea of rule and tyranny; but as this idea is aroused rather by his needs than by our services, we begin to see moral results whose causes are not in nature; thus we see how important it is, even at the earliest age, to discern the secret meaning of the gesture or cry.

When the child tries to seize something without speaking, he thinks he can reach the object, for he does not rightly judge its distance; when he cries and stretches out his hands he no longer misjudges the distance, he bids the object approach, or orders you to bring it to him. In the first case bring it to him slowly; in the second do not even seem to hear his cries. The more he cries the less you should heed him. He must learn in good time not to give commands to men, for he is not their master, nor to things, for they cannot hear him. Thus when the child wants something you mean to give him, it is better to carry him to it rather than to bring the thing to him. From this he will draw a conclusion suited to his age, and there is no other way of suggesting it to him.

The Abbe Saint-Pierre calls men big children; one might also call children little men. These statements are true, but they require explanation. But when Hobbes calls the wicked a strong child, his statement is contradicted by facts. All wickedness comes from weakness. The child is only naughty because he is weak; make him strong and he will be good; if we could do everything we should never do wrong. Of all the attributes of the Almighty, goodness is that which it would be hardest to dissociate from our conception of Him. All nations who have acknowledged a good and an evil power, have always regarded the evil as inferior to the good; otherwise their opinion would have been absurd. Compare this with the creed of the Savoyard clergyman later on in this book.

Reason alone teaches us to know good and evil. Therefore conscience, which makes us love the one and hate the other, though it is independent of reason, cannot develop without it. Before the age of reason we do good or ill without knowing it, and there is no morality in our actions, although there is sometimes in our feeling with regard to other people's actions in relation to ourselves. A child wants to overturn everything he sees. He breaks and smashes everything he can reach; he seizes a bird as he seizes a stone, and strangles it without knowing what he is about.

Why so? In the first place philosophy will account for this by inbred sin, man's pride, love of power, selfishness, spite; perhaps it will say in addition to this that the child's consciousness of his own weakness makes him eager to use his strength, to convince himself of it. But watch that broken down old man reduced in the downward course of life to the weakness of a child; not only is he quiet and peaceful, he would have all about him quiet and peaceful too; the least change disturbs and troubles him, he would like to see universal calm. How is it possible that similar feebleness and similar passions should produce such different effects in age and in infancy, if the original cause were not different? And where can we find this difference in cause except in the bodily condition of the two. The active principle, common to both, is growing in one case and declining in the other; it is being formed in the one and destroyed in the other; one is moving towards life, the other towards death. The failing activity of the old man is centred in his heart, the child's overflowing activity spreads abroad. He feels, if we may say so, strong enough to give life to all about him. To make or to destroy, it is all one to him; change is what he seeks, and all change involves action. If he seems to enjoy destructive activity it is only that it takes time to make things and very little time to break them, so that the work of destruction accords better with his eagerness.

While the Author of nature has given children this activity, He takes care that it shall do little harm by giving them small power to use it. But as soon as they can think of people as tools to be used, they use them to carry out their wishes and to supplement their own weakness. This is how they become tiresome, masterful, imperious, naughty, and unmanageable; a development which does not spring from a natural love of power, but one which has been taught them, for it does not need much experience to realise how pleasant it is to set others to work and to move the world by a word.

As the child grows it gains strength and becomes less restless and unquiet and more independent. Soul and body become better balanced and nature no longer asks for more movement than is required for self-preservation. But the love of power does not die with the need that aroused it; power arouses and flatters self-love, and habit strengthens it; thus caprice follows upon need, and the first seeds of prejudice and obstinacy are sown.

FIRST MAXIM.—Far from being too strong, children are not strong enough for all the claims of nature. Give them full use of such strength as they have; they will not abuse it.

SECOND MAXIM.—Help them and supply the experience and strength they lack whenever the need is of the body.

THIRD MAXIM.—In the help you give them confine yourself to what is really needful, without granting anything to caprice or unreason; for they will not be tormented by caprice if you do not call it into existence, seeing it is no part of nature.

FOURTH MAXIM—Study carefully their speech and gestures, so that at an age when they are incapable of deceit you may discriminate between those desires which come from nature and those which spring from perversity.

The spirit of these rules is to give children more real liberty and less power, to let them do more for themselves and demand less of others; so that by teaching them from the first to confine their wishes within the limits of their powers they will scarcely feel the want of whatever is not in their power.

This is another very important reason for leaving children's limbs and bodies perfectly free, only taking care that they do not fall, and keeping anything that might hurt them out of their way.

The child whose body and arms are free will certainly cry much less than a child tied up in swaddling clothes. He who knows only bodily needs, only cries when in pain; and this is a great advantage, for then we know exactly when he needs help, and if possible we should not delay our help for an instant. But if you cannot relieve his pain, stay where you are and do not flatter him by way of soothing him; your caresses will not cure his colic, but he will remember what he must do to win them; and if he once finds out how to gain your attention at will, he is your master; the whole education is spoilt.

Their movements being less constrained, children will cry less; less wearied with their tears, people will not take so much trouble to check them. With fewer threats and promises, they will be less timid and less obstinate, and will remain more nearly in their natural state. Ruptures are produced less by letting children cry than by the means taken to stop them, and my evidence for this is the fact that the most neglected children are less liable to them than others. I am very far from wishing that they should be neglected; on the contrary, it is of the utmost importance that their wants should be anticipated, so that they need not proclaim their wants by crying. But neither would I have unwise care bestowed on them. Why should they think it wrong to cry when they find they can get so much by it? When they have learned the value of their silence they take good care not to waste it. In the end they will so exaggerate its importance that no one will be able to pay its price; then worn out with crying they become exhausted, and are at length silent.

Prolonged crying on the part of a child neither swaddled nor out of health, a child who lacks nothing, is merely the result of habit or obstinacy. Such tears are no longer the work of nature, but the work of the child's nurse, who could not resist its importunity and so has increased it, without considering that while she quiets the child to-day she is teaching him to cry louder to-morrow.

Moreover, when caprice or obstinacy is the cause of their tears, there is a sure way of stopping them by distracting their attention by some pleasant or conspicuous object which makes them forget that they want to cry. Most nurses excel in this art, and rightly used it is very useful; but it is of the utmost importance that the child should not perceive that you mean to distract his attention, and that he should be amused without suspecting you are thinking about him; now this is what most nurses cannot do.

Most children are weaned too soon. The time to wean them is when they cut their teeth. This generally causes pain and suffering. At this time the child instinctively carries everything he gets hold of to his mouth to chew it. To help forward this process he is given as a plaything some hard object such as ivory or a wolf's tooth. I think this is a mistake. Hard bodies applied to the gums do not soften them; far from it, they make the process of cutting the teeth more difficult and painful. Let us always take instinct as our guide; we never see puppies practising their budding teeth on pebbles, iron, or bones, but on wood, leather, rags, soft materials which yield to their jaws, and on which the tooth leaves its mark.

We can do nothing simply, not even for our children. Toys of silver, gold, coral, cut crystal, rattles of every price and kind; what vain and useless appliances. Away with them all! Let us have no corals or rattles; a small branch of a tree with its leaves and fruit, a stick of liquorice which he may suck and chew, will amuse him as well as these splendid trifles, and they will have this advantage at least, he will not be brought up to luxury from his birth.

It is admitted that pap is not a very wholesome food. Boiled milk and uncooked flour cause gravel and do not suit the stomach. In pap the flour is less thoroughly cooked than in bread and it has not fermented. I think bread and milk or rice-cream are better. If you will have pap, the flour should be lightly cooked beforehand. In my own country they make a very pleasant and wholesome soup from flour thus heated. Meat-broth or soup is not a very suitable food and should be used as little as possible. The child must first get used to chewing his food; this is the right way to bring the teeth through, and when the child begins to swallow, the saliva mixed with the food helps digestion.

I would have them first chew dried fruit or crusts. I should give them as playthings little bits of dry bread or biscuits, like the Piedmont bread, known in the country as "grisses." By dint of softening this bread in the mouth some of it is eventually swallowed the teeth come through of themselves, and the child is weaned almost imperceptibly. Peasants have usually very good digestions, and they are weaned with no more ado.

From the very first children hear spoken language; we speak to them before they can understand or even imitate spoken sounds. The vocal organs are still stiff, and only gradually lend themselves to the reproduction of the sounds heard; it is even doubtful whether these sounds are heard distinctly as we hear them. The nurse may amuse the child with songs and with very merry and varied intonation, but I object to her bewildering the child with a multitude of vain words of which it understands nothing but her tone of voice. I would have the first words he hears few in number, distinctly and often repeated, while the words themselves should be related to things which can first be shown to the child. That fatal facility in the use of words we do not understand begins earlier than we think. In the schoolroom the scholar listens to the verbiage of his master as he listened in the cradle to the babble of his nurse. I think it would be a very useful education to leave him in ignorance of both.

All sorts of ideas crowd in upon us when we try to consider the development of speech and the child's first words. Whatever we do they all learn to talk in the same way, and all philosophical speculations are utterly useless.

To begin with, they have, so to say, a grammar of their own, whose rules and syntax are more general than our own; if you attend carefully you will be surprised to find how exactly they follow certain analogies, very much mistaken if you like, but very regular; these forms are only objectionable because of their harshness or because they are not recognised by custom. I have just heard a child severely scolded by his father for saying, "Mon pere, irai-je-t-y?" Now we see that this child was following the analogy more closely than our grammarians, for as they say to him, "Vas-y," why should he not say, "Irai-je-t-y?" Notice too the skilful way in which he avoids the hiatus in irai-je-y or y-irai-je? Is it the poor child's fault that we have so unskilfully deprived the phrase of this determinative adverb "y," because we did not know what to do with it? It is an intolerable piece of pedantry and most superfluous attention to detail to make a point of correcting all children's little sins against the customary expression, for they always cure themselves with time. Always speak correctly before them, let them never be so happy with any one as with you, and be sure that their speech will be imperceptibly modelled upon yours without any correction on your part.

But a much greater evil, and one far less easy to guard against, is that they are urged to speak too much, as if people were afraid they would not learn to talk of themselves. This indiscreet zeal produces an effect directly opposite to what is meant. They speak later and more confusedly; the extreme attention paid to everything they say makes it unnecessary for them to speak distinctly, and as they will scarcely open their mouths, many of them contract a vicious pronunciation and a confused speech, which last all their life and make them almost unintelligible.

I have lived much among peasants, and I never knew one of them lisp, man or woman, boy or girl. Why is this? Are their speech organs differently made from our own? No, but they are differently used. There is a hillock facing my window on which the children of the place assemble for their games. Although they are far enough away, I can distinguish perfectly what they say, and often get good notes for this book. Every day my ear deceives me as to their age. I hear the voices of children of ten; I look and see the height and features of children of three or four. This experience is not confined to me; the townspeople who come to see me, and whom I consult on this point, all fall into the same mistake.

This results from the fact that, up to five or six, children in town, brought up in a room and under the care of a nursery governess, do not need to speak above a whisper to make themselves heard. As soon as their lips move people take pains to make out what they mean; they are taught words which they repeat inaccurately, and by paying great attention to them the people who are always with them rather guess what they meant to say than what they said.

It is quite a different matter in the country. A peasant woman is not always with her child; he is obliged to learn to say very clearly and loudly what he wants, if he is to make himself understood. Children scattered about the fields at a distance from their fathers, mothers and other children, gain practice in making themselves heard at a distance, and in adapting the loudness of the voice to the distance which separates them from those to whom they want to speak. This is the real way to learn pronunciation, not by stammering out a few vowels into the ear of an attentive governess. So when you question a peasant child, he may be too shy to answer, but what he says he says distinctly, while the nurse must serve as interpreter for the town child; without her one can understand nothing of what he is muttering between his teeth. [Footnote: There are exceptions to this; and often those children who at first are most difficult to hear, become the noisiest when they begin to raise their voices. But if I were to enter into all these details I should never make an end; every sensible reader ought to see that defect and excess, caused by the same abuse, are both corrected by my method. I regard the two maxims as inseparable—always enough—never too much. When the first is well established, the latter necessarily follows on it.]

As they grow older, the boys are supposed to be cured of this fault at college, the girls in the convent schools; and indeed both usually speak more clearly than children brought up entirely at home. But they are prevented from acquiring as clear a pronunciation as the peasants in this way—they are required to learn all sorts of things by heart, and to repeat aloud what they have learnt; for when they are studying they get into the way of gabbling and pronouncing carelessly and ill; it is still worse when they repeat their lessons; they cannot find the right words, they drag out their syllables. This is only possible when the memory hesitates, the tongue does not stammer of itself. Thus they acquire or continue habits of bad pronunciation. Later on you will see that Emile does not acquire such habits or at least not from this cause.

I grant you uneducated people and villagers often fall into the opposite extreme. They almost always speak too loud; their pronunciation is too exact, and leads to rough and coarse articulation; their accent is too pronounced, they choose their expressions badly, etc.

But, to begin with, this extreme strikes me as much less dangerous than the other, for the first law of speech is to make oneself understood, and the chief fault is to fail to be understood. To pride ourselves on having no accent is to pride ourselves on ridding our phrases of strength and elegance. Emphasis is the soul of speech, it gives it its feeling and truth. Emphasis deceives less than words; perhaps that is why well-educated people are so afraid of it. From the custom of saying everything in the same tone has arisen that of poking fun at people without their knowing it. When emphasis is proscribed, its place is taken by all sorts of ridiculous, affected, and ephemeral pronunciations, such as one observes especially among the young people about court. It is this affectation of speech and manner which makes Frenchmen disagreeable and repulsive to other nations on first acquaintance. Emphasis is found, not in their speech, but in their bearing. That is not the way to make themselves attractive.

All these little faults of speech, which you are so afraid the children will acquire, are mere trifles; they may be prevented or corrected with the greatest ease, but the faults which are taught them when you make them speak in a low, indistinct, and timid voice, when you are always criticising their tone and finding fault with their words, are never cured. A man who has only learnt to speak in society of fine ladies could not make himself heard at the head of his troops, and would make little impression on the rabble in a riot. First teach the child to speak to men; he will be able to speak to the women when required.

Brought up in all the rustic simplicity of the country, your children will gain a more sonorous voice; they will not acquire the hesitating stammer of town children, neither will they acquire the expressions nor the tone of the villagers, or if they do they will easily lose them; their master being with them from their earliest years, and more and more in their society the older they grow, will be able to prevent or efface by speaking correctly himself the impression of the peasants' talk. Emile will speak the purest French I know, but he will speak it more distinctly and with a better articulation than myself.

The child who is trying to speak should hear nothing but words he can understand, nor should he say words he cannot articulate; his efforts lead him to repeat the same syllable as if he were practising its clear pronunciation. When he begins to stammer, do not try to understand him. To expect to be always listened to is a form of tyranny which is not good for the child. See carefully to his real needs, and let him try to make you understand the rest. Still less should you hurry him into speech; he will learn to talk when he feels the want of it.

It has indeed been remarked that those who begin to speak very late never speak so distinctly as others; but it is not because they talked late that they are hesitating; on the contrary, they began to talk late because they hesitate; if not, why did they begin to talk so late? Have they less need of speech, have they been less urged to it? On the contrary, the anxiety aroused with the first suspicion of this backwardness leads people to tease them much more to begin to talk than those who articulated earlier; and this mistaken zeal may do much to make their speech confused, when with less haste they might have had time to bring it to greater perfection.

Children who are forced to speak too soon have no time to learn either to pronounce correctly or to understand what they are made to say; while left to themselves they first practise the easiest syllables, and then, adding to them little by little some meaning which their gestures explain, they teach you their own words before they learn yours. By this means they do not acquire your words till they have understood them. Being in no hurry to use them, they begin by carefully observing the sense in which you use them, and when they are sure of them they adopt them.

The worst evil resulting from the precocious use of speech by young children is that we not only fail to understand the first words they use, we misunderstand them without knowing it; so that while they seem to answer us correctly, they fail to understand us and we them. This is the most frequent cause of our surprise at children's sayings; we attribute to them ideas which they did not attach to their words. This lack of attention on our part to the real meaning which words have for children seems to me the cause of their earliest misconceptions; and these misconceptions, even when corrected, colour their whole course of thought for the rest of their life. I shall have several opportunities of illustrating these by examples later on.

Let the child's vocabulary, therefore, be limited; it is very undesirable that he should have more words than ideas, that he should be able to say more than he thinks. One of the reasons why peasants are generally shrewder than townsfolk is, I think, that their vocabulary is smaller. They have few ideas, but those few are thoroughly grasped.

The infant is progressing in several ways at once; he is learning to talk, eat, and walk about the same time. This is really the first phase of his life. Up till now, he was little more than he was before birth; he had neither feeling nor thought, he was barely capable of sensation; he was unconscious of his own existence.

"Vivit, et est vitae nescius ipse suae." —Ovid.

BOOK II

We have now reached the second phase of life; infancy, strictly so-called, is over; for the words infans and puer are not synonymous. The latter includes the former, which means literally "one who cannot speak;" thus Valerius speaks of puerum infantem. But I shall continue to use the word child (French enfant) according to the custom of our language till an age for which there is another term.

When children begin to talk they cry less. This progress is quite natural; one language supplants another. As soon as they can say "It hurts me," why should they cry, unless the pain is too sharp for words? If they still cry, those about them are to blame. When once Emile has said, "It hurts me," it will take a very sharp pain to make him cry.

If the child is delicate and sensitive, if by nature he begins to cry for nothing, I let him cry in vain and soon check his tears at their source. So long as he cries I will not go near him; I come at once when he leaves off crying. He will soon be quiet when he wants to call me, or rather he will utter a single cry. Children learn the meaning of signs by their effects; they have no other meaning for them. However much a child hurts himself when he is alone, he rarely cries, unless he expects to be heard.

Should he fall or bump his head, or make his nose bleed, or cut his fingers, I shall show no alarm, nor shall I make any fuss over him; I shall take no notice, at any rate at first. The harm is done; he must bear it; all my zeal could only frighten him more and make him more nervous. Indeed it is not the blow but the fear of it which distresses us when we are hurt. I shall spare him this suffering at least, for he will certainly regard the injury as he sees me regard it; if he finds that I hasten anxiously to him, if I pity him or comfort him, he will think he is badly hurt. If he finds I take no notice, he will soon recover himself, and will think the wound is healed when it ceases to hurt. This is the time for his first lesson in courage, and by bearing slight ills without fear we gradually learn to bear greater.

I shall not take pains to prevent Emile hurting himself; far from it, I should be vexed if he never hurt himself, if he grew up unacquainted with pain. To bear pain is his first and most useful lesson. It seems as if children were small and weak on purpose to teach them these valuable lessons without danger. The child has such a little way to fall he will not break his leg; if he knocks himself with a stick he will not break his arm; if he seizes a sharp knife he will not grasp it tight enough to make a deep wound. So far as I know, no child, left to himself, has ever been known to kill or maim itself, or even to do itself any serious harm, unless it has been foolishly left on a high place, or alone near the fire, or within reach of dangerous weapons. What is there to be said for all the paraphernalia with which the child is surrounded to shield him on every side so that he grows up at the mercy of pain, with neither courage nor experience, so that he thinks he is killed by a pin-prick and faints at the sight of blood?

With our foolish and pedantic methods we are always preventing children from learning what they could learn much better by themselves, while we neglect what we alone can teach them. Can anything be sillier than the pains taken to teach them to walk, as if there were any one who was unable to walk when he grows up through his nurse's neglect? How many we see walking badly all their life because they were ill taught?

Emile shall have no head-pads, no go-carts, no leading-strings; or at least as soon as he can put one foot before another he shall only be supported along pavements, and he shall be taken quickly across them. [Footnote: There is nothing so absurd and hesitating as the gait of those who have been kept too long in leading-strings when they were little. This is one of the observations which are considered trivial because they are true.] Instead of keeping him mewed up in a stuffy room, take him out into a meadow every day; let him run about, let him struggle and fall again and again, the oftener the better; he will learn all the sooner to pick himself up. The delights of liberty will make up for many bruises. My pupil will hurt himself oftener than yours, but he will always be merry; your pupils may receive fewer injuries, but they are always thwarted, constrained, and sad. I doubt whether they are any better off.

As their strength increases, children have also less need for tears. They can do more for themselves, they need the help of others less frequently. With strength comes the sense to use it. It is with this second phase that the real personal life has its beginning; it is then that the child becomes conscious of himself. During every moment of his life memory calls up the feeling of self; he becomes really one person, always the same, and therefore capable of joy or sorrow. Hence we must begin to consider him as a moral being.

Although we know approximately the limits of human life and our chances of attaining those limits, nothing is more uncertain than the length of the life of any one of us. Very few reach old age. The chief risks occur at the beginning of life; the shorter our past life, the less we must hope to live. Of all the children who are born scarcely one half reach adolescence, and it is very likely your pupil will not live to be a man.

What is to be thought, therefore, of that cruel education which sacrifices the present to an uncertain future, that burdens a child with all sorts of restrictions and begins by making him miserable, in order to prepare him for some far-off happiness which he may never enjoy? Even if I considered that education wise in its aims, how could I view without indignation those poor wretches subjected to an intolerable slavery and condemned like galley-slaves to endless toil, with no certainty that they will gain anything by it? The age of harmless mirth is spent in tears, punishments, threats, and slavery. You torment the poor thing for his good; you fail to see that you are calling Death to snatch him from these gloomy surroundings. Who can say how many children fall victims to the excessive care of their fathers and mothers? They are happy to escape from this cruelty; this is all that they gain from the ills they are forced to endure: they die without regretting, having known nothing of life but its sorrows.

Men, be kind to your fellow-men; this is your first duty, kind to every age and station, kind to all that is not foreign to humanity. What wisdom can you find that is greater than kindness? Love childhood, indulge its sports, its pleasures, its delightful instincts. Who has not sometimes regretted that age when laughter was ever on the lips, and when the heart was ever at peace? Why rob these innocents of the joys which pass so quickly, of that precious gift which they cannot abuse? Why fill with bitterness the fleeting days of early childhood, days which will no more return for them than for you? Fathers, can you tell when death will call your children to him? Do not lay up sorrow for yourselves by robbing them of the short span which nature has allotted to them. As soon as they are aware of the joy of life, let them rejoice in it, go that whenever God calls them they may not die without having tasted the joy of life.

How people will cry out against me! I hear from afar the shouts of that false wisdom which is ever dragging us onwards, counting the present as nothing, and pursuing without a pause a future which flies as we pursue, that false wisdom which removes us from our place and never brings us to any other.

Now is the time, you say, to correct his evil tendencies; we must increase suffering in childhood, when it is less keenly felt, to lessen it in manhood. But how do you know that you can carry out all these fine schemes; how do you know that all this fine teaching with which you overwhelm the feeble mind of the child will not do him more harm than good in the future? How do you know that you can spare him anything by the vexations you heap upon him now? Why inflict on him more ills than befit his present condition unless you are quite sure that these present ills will save him future ill? And what proof can you give me that those evil tendencies you profess to cure are not the result of your foolish precautions rather than of nature? What a poor sort of foresight, to make a child wretched in the present with the more or less doubtful hope of making him happy at some future day. If such blundering thinkers fail to distinguish between liberty and licence, between a merry child and a spoilt darling, let them learn to discriminate.

Let us not forget what befits our present state in the pursuit of vain fancies. Mankind has its place in the sequence of things; childhood has its place in the sequence of human life; the man must be treated as a man and the child as a child. Give each his place, and keep him there. Control human passions according to man's nature; that is all we can do for his welfare. The rest depends on external forces, which are beyond our control.

Absolute good and evil are unknown to us. In this life they are blended together; we never enjoy any perfectly pure feeling, nor do we remain for more than a moment in the same state. The feelings of our minds, like the changes in our bodies, are in a continual flux. Good and ill are common to all, but in varying proportions. The happiest is he who suffers least; the most miserable is he who enjoys least. Ever more sorrow than joy — this is the lot of all of us. Man's happiness in this world is but a negative state; it must be reckoned by the fewness of his ills.

Every feeling of hardship is inseparable from the desire to escape from it; every idea of pleasure from the desire to enjoy it. All desire implies a want, and all wants are painful; hence our wretchedness consists in the disproportion between our desires and our powers. A conscious being whose powers were equal to his desires would be perfectly happy.

What then is human wisdom? Where is the path of true happiness? The mere limitation of our desires is not enough, for if they were less than our powers, part of our faculties would be idle, and we should not enjoy our whole being; neither is the mere extension of our powers enough, for if our desires were also increased we should only be the more miserable. True happiness consists in decreasing the difference between our desires and our powers, in establishing a perfect equilibrium between the power and the will. Then only, when all its forces are employed, will the soul be at rest and man will find himself in his true position.

In this condition, nature, who does everything for the best, has placed him from the first. To begin with, she gives him only such desires as are necessary for self-preservation and such powers as are sufficient for their satisfaction. All the rest she has stored in his mind as a sort of reserve, to be drawn upon at need. It is only in this primitive condition that we find the equilibrium between desire and power, and then alone man is not unhappy. As soon as his potential powers of mind begin to function, imagination, more powerful than all the rest, awakes, and precedes all the rest. It is imagination which enlarges the bounds of possibility for us, whether for good or ill, and therefore stimulates and feeds desires by the hope of satisfying them. But the object which seemed within our grasp flies quicker than we can follow; when we think we have grasped it, it transforms itself and is again far ahead of us. We no longer perceive the country we have traversed, and we think nothing of it; that which lies before us becomes vaster and stretches still before us. Thus we exhaust our strength, yet never reach our goal, and the nearer we are to pleasure, the further we are from happiness.

On the other hand, the more nearly a man's condition approximates to this state of nature the less difference is there between his desires and his powers, and happiness is therefore less remote. Lacking everything, he is never less miserable; for misery consists, not in the lack of things, but in the needs which they inspire.

The world of reality has its bounds, the world of imagination is boundless; as we cannot enlarge the one, let us restrict the other; for all the sufferings which really make us miserable arise from the difference between the real and the imaginary. Health, strength, and a good conscience excepted, all the good things of life are a matter of opinion; except bodily suffering and remorse, all our woes are imaginary. You will tell me this is a commonplace; I admit it, but its practical application is no commonplace, and it is with practice only that we are now concerned.

What do you mean when you say, "Man is weak"? The term weak implies a relation, a relation of the creature to whom it is applied. An insect or a worm whose strength exceeds its needs is strong; an elephant, a lion, a conqueror, a hero, a god himself, whose needs exceed his strength is weak. The rebellious angel who fought against his own nature was weaker than the happy mortal who is living at peace according to nature. When man is content to be himself he is strong indeed; when he strives to be more than man he is weak indeed. But do not imagine that you can increase your strength by increasing your powers. Not so; if your pride increases more rapidly your strength is diminished. Let us measure the extent of our sphere and remain in its centre like the spider in its web; we shall have strength sufficient for our needs, we shall have no cause to lament our weakness, for we shall never be aware of it.

The other animals possess only such powers as are required for self-preservation; man alone has more. Is it not very strange that this superfluity should make him miserable? In every land a man's labour yields more than a bare living. If he were wise enough to disregard this surplus he would always have enough, for he would never have too much. "Great needs," said Favorin, "spring from great wealth; and often the best way of getting what we want is to get rid of what we have." By striving to increase our happiness we change it into wretchedness. If a man were content to live, he would live happy; and he would therefore be good, for what would he have to gain by vice?

If we were immortal we should all be miserable; no doubt it is hard to die, but it is sweet to think that we shall not live for ever, and that a better life will put an end to the sorrows of this world. If we had the offer of immortality here below, who would accept the sorrowful gift? [Footnote: You understand I am speaking of those who think, and not of the crowd.] What resources, what hopes, what consolation would be left against the cruelties of fate and man's injustice? The ignorant man never looks before; he knows little of the value of life and does not fear to lose it; the wise man sees things of greater worth and prefers them to it. Half knowledge and sham wisdom set us thinking about death and what lies beyond it; and they thus create the worst of our ills. The wise man bears life's ills all the better because he knows he must die. Life would be too dearly bought did we not know that sooner or later death will end it.

Our moral ills are the result of prejudice, crime alone excepted, and that depends on ourselves; our bodily ills either put an end to themselves or to us. Time or death will cure them, but the less we know how to bear it, the greater is our pain, and we suffer more in our efforts to cure our diseases than if we endured them. Live according to nature; be patient, get rid of the doctors; you will not escape death, but you will only die once, while the doctors make you die daily through your diseased imagination; their lying art, instead of prolonging your days, robs you of all delight in them. I am always asking what real good this art has done to mankind. True, the doctors cure some who would have died, but they kill millions who would have lived. If you are wise you will decline to take part in this lottery when the odds are so great against you. Suffer, die, or get better; but whatever you do, live while you are alive.

Human institutions are one mass of folly and contradiction. As our life loses its value we set a higher price upon it. The old regret life more than the young; they do not want to lose all they have spent in preparing for its enjoyment. At sixty it is cruel to die when one has not begun to live. Man is credited with a strong desire for self-preservation, and this desire exists; but we fail to perceive that this desire, as felt by us, is largely the work of man. In a natural state man is only eager to preserve his life while he has the means for its preservation; when self-preservation is no longer possible, he resigns himself to his fate and dies without vain torments. Nature teaches us the first law of resignation. Savages, like wild beasts, make very little struggle against death, and meet it almost without a murmur. When this natural law is overthrown reason establishes another, but few discern it, and man's resignation is never so complete as nature's.

Prudence! Prudence which is ever bidding us look forward into the future, a future which in many cases we shall never reach; here is the real source of all our troubles! How mad it is for so short-lived a creature as man to look forward into a future to which he rarely attains, while he neglects the present which is his? This madness is all the more fatal since it increases with years, and the old, always timid, prudent, and miserly, prefer to do without necessaries to-day that they may have luxuries at a hundred. Thus we grasp everything, we cling to everything; we are anxious about time, place, people, things, all that is and will be; we ourselves are but the least part of ourselves. We spread ourselves, so to speak, over the whole world, and all this vast expanse becomes sensitive. No wonder our woes increase when we may be wounded on every side. How many princes make themselves miserable for the loss of lands they never saw, and how many merchants lament in Paris over some misfortune in the Indies!

Is it nature that carries men so far from their real selves? Is it her will that each should learn his fate from others and even be the last to learn it; so that a man dies happy or miserable before he knows what he is about. There is a healthy, cheerful, strong, and vigorous man; it does me good to see him; his eyes tell of content and well-being; he is the picture of happiness. A letter comes by post; the happy man glances at it, it is addressed to him, he opens it and reads it. In a moment he is changed, he turns pale and falls into a swoon. When he comes to himself he weeps, laments, and groans, he tears his hair, and his shrieks re-echo through the air. You would say he was in convulsions. Fool, what harm has this bit of paper done you? What limb has it torn away? What crime has it made you commit? What change has it wrought in you to reduce you to this state of misery?

Had the letter miscarried, had some kindly hand thrown it into the fire, it strikes me that the fate of this mortal, at once happy and unhappy, would have offered us a strange problem. His misfortunes, you say, were real enough. Granted; but he did not feel them. What of that? His happiness was imaginary. I admit it; health, wealth, a contented spirit, are mere dreams. We no longer live in our own place, we live outside it. What does it profit us to live in such fear of death, when all that makes life worth living is our own?

Oh, man! live your own life and you will no longer be wretched. Keep to your appointed place in the order of nature and nothing can tear you from it. Do not kick against the stern law of necessity, nor waste in vain resistance the strength bestowed on you by heaven, not to prolong or extend your existence, but to preserve it so far and so long as heaven pleases. Your freedom and your power extend as far and no further than your natural strength; anything more is but slavery, deceit, and trickery. Power itself is servile when it depends upon public opinion; for you are dependent on the prejudices of others when you rule them by means of those prejudices. To lead them as you will, they must be led as they will. They have only to change their way of thinking and you are forced to change your course of action. Those who approach you need only contrive to sway the opinions of those you rule, or of the favourite by whom you are ruled, or those of your own family or theirs. Had you the genius of Themistocles, [Footnote: "You see that little boy," said Themistocles to his friends, "the fate of Greece is in his hands, for he rules his mother and his mother rules me, I rule the Athenians and the Athenians rule the Greeks." What petty creatures we should often find controlling great empires if we traced the course of power from the prince to those who secretly put that power in motion.] viziers, courtiers, priests, soldiers, servants, babblers, the very children themselves, would lead you like a child in the midst of your legions. Whatever you do, your actual authority can never extend beyond your own powers. As soon as you are obliged to see with another's eyes you must will what he wills. You say with pride, "My people are my subjects." Granted, but what are you? The subject of your ministers. And your ministers, what are they? The subjects of their clerks, their mistresses, the servants of their servants. Grasp all, usurp all, and then pour out your silver with both hands; set up your batteries, raise the gallows and the wheel; make laws, issue proclamations, multiply your spies, your soldiers, your hangmen, your prisons, and your chains. Poor little men, what good does it do you? You will be no better served, you will be none the less robbed and deceived, you will be no nearer absolute power. You will say continually, "It is our will," and you will continually do the will of others.

There is only one man who gets his own way—he who can get it single-handed; therefore freedom, not power, is the greatest good. That man is truly free who desires what he is able to perform, and does what he desires. This is my fundamental maxim. Apply it to childhood, and all the rules of education spring from it.

Society has enfeebled man, not merely by robbing him of the right to his own strength, but still more by making his strength insufficient for his needs. This is why his desires increase in proportion to his weakness; and this is why the child is weaker than the man. If a man is strong and a child is weak it is not because the strength of the one is absolutely greater than the strength of the other, but because the one can naturally provide for himself and the other cannot. Thus the man will have more desires and the child more caprices, a word which means, I take it, desires which are not true needs, desires which can only be satisfied with the help of others.

I have already given the reason for this state of weakness. Parental affection is nature's provision against it; but parental affection may be carried to excess, it may be wanting, or it may be ill applied. Parents who live under our ordinary social conditions bring their child into these conditions too soon. By increasing his needs they do not relieve his weakness; they rather increase it. They further increase it by demanding of him what nature does not demand, by subjecting to their will what little strength he has to further his own wishes, by making slaves of themselves or of him instead of recognising that mutual dependence which should result from his weakness or their affection.

The wise man can keep his own place; but the child who does not know what his place is, is unable to keep it. There are a thousand ways out of it, and it is the business of those who have charge of the child to keep him in his place, and this is no easy task. He should be neither beast nor man, but a child. He must feel his weakness, but not suffer through it; he must be dependent, but he must not obey; he must ask, not command. He is only subject to others because of his needs, and because they see better than he what he really needs, what may help or hinder his existence. No one, not even his father, has the right to bid the child do what is of no use to him.

When our natural tendencies have not been interfered with by human prejudice and human institutions, the happiness alike of children and of men consists in the enjoyment of their liberty. But the child's liberty is restricted by his lack of strength. He who does as he likes is happy provided he is self-sufficing; it is so with the man who is living in a state of nature. He who does what he likes is not happy if his desires exceed his strength; it is so with a child in like conditions. Even in a state of nature children only enjoy an imperfect liberty, like that enjoyed by men in social life. Each of us, unable to dispense with the help of others, becomes so far weak and wretched. We were meant to be men, laws and customs thrust us back into infancy. The rich and great, the very kings themselves are but children; they see that we are ready to relieve their misery; this makes them childishly vain, and they are quite proud of the care bestowed on them, a care which they would never get if they were grown men.

These are weighty considerations, and they provide a solution for all the conflicting problems of our social system. There are two kinds of dependence: dependence on things, which is the work of nature; and dependence on men, which is the work of society. Dependence on things, being non-moral, does no injury to liberty and begets no vices; dependence on men, being out of order, [Footnote: In my PRINCIPLES OF POLITICAL LAW it is proved that no private will can be ordered in the social system.] gives rise to every kind of vice, and through this master and slave become mutually depraved. If there is any cure for this social evil, it is to be found in the substitution of law for the individual; in arming the general will with a real strength beyond the power of any individual will. If the laws of nations, like the laws of nature, could never be broken by any human power, dependence on men would become dependence on things; all the advantages of a state of nature would be combined with all the advantages of social life in the commonwealth. The liberty which preserves a man from vice would be united with the morality which raises him to virtue.

Keep the child dependent on things only. By this course of education you will have followed the order of nature. Let his unreasonable wishes meet with physical obstacles only, or the punishment which results from his own actions, lessons which will be recalled when the same circumstances occur again. It is enough to prevent him from wrong doing without forbidding him to do wrong. Experience or lack of power should take the place of law. Give him, not what he wants, but what he needs. Let there be no question of obedience for him or tyranny for you. Supply the strength he lacks just so far as is required for freedom, not for power, so that he may receive your services with a sort of shame, and look forward to the time when he may dispense with them and may achieve the honour of self-help.

Nature provides for the child's growth in her own fashion, and this should never be thwarted. Do not make him sit still when he wants to run about, nor run when he wants to be quiet. If we did not spoil our children's wills by our blunders their desires would be free from caprice. Let them run, jump, and shout to their heart's content. All their own activities are instincts of the body for its growth in strength; but you should regard with suspicion those wishes which they cannot carry out for themselves, those which others must carry out for them. Then you must distinguish carefully between natural and artificial needs, between the needs of budding caprice and the needs which spring from the overflowing life just described.

I have already told you what you ought to do when a child cries for this thing or that. I will only add that as soon as he has words to ask for what he wants and accompanies his demands with tears, either to get his own way quicker or to over-ride a refusal, he should never have his way. If his words were prompted by a real need you should recognise it and satisfy it at once; but to yield to his tears is to encourage him to cry, to teach him to doubt your kindness, and to think that you are influenced more by his importunity than your own good-will. If he does not think you kind he will soon think you unkind; if he thinks you weak he will soon become obstinate; what you mean to give must be given at once. Be chary of refusing, but, having refused, do not change your mind.

Above all, beware of teaching the child empty phrases of politeness, which serve as spells to subdue those around him to his will, and to get him what he wants at once. The artificial education of the rich never fails to make them politely imperious, by teaching them the words to use so that no one will dare to resist them. Their children have neither the tone nor the manner of suppliants; they are as haughty or even more haughty in their entreaties than in their commands, as though they were more certain to be obeyed. You see at once that "If you please" means "It pleases me," and "I beg" means "I command." What a fine sort of politeness which only succeeds in changing the meaning of words so that every word is a command! For my own part, I would rather Emile were rude than haughty, that he should say "Do this" as a request, rather than "Please" as a command. What concerns me is his meaning, not his words.

There is such a thing as excessive severity as well as excessive indulgence, and both alike should be avoided. If you let children suffer you risk their health and life; you make them miserable now; if you take too much pains to spare them every kind of uneasiness you are laying up much misery for them in the future; you are making them delicate and over-sensitive; you are taking them out of their place among men, a place to which they must sooner or later return, in spite of all your pains. You will say I am falling into the same mistake as those bad fathers whom I blamed for sacrificing the present happiness of their children to a future which may never be theirs.

Not so; for the liberty I give my pupil makes up for the slight hardships to which he is exposed. I see little fellows playing in the snow, stiff and blue with cold, scarcely able to stir a finger. They could go and warm themselves if they chose, but they do not choose; if you forced them to come in they would feel the harshness of constraint a hundredfold more than the sharpness of the cold. Then what becomes of your grievance? Shall I make your child miserable by exposing him to hardships which he is perfectly ready to endure? I secure his present good by leaving him his freedom, and his future good by arming him against the evils he will have to bear. If he had his choice, would he hesitate for a moment between you and me?

Do you think any man can find true happiness elsewhere than in his natural state; and when you try to spare him all suffering, are you not taking him out of his natural state? Indeed I maintain that to enjoy great happiness he must experience slight ills; such is his nature. Too much bodily prosperity corrupts the morals. A man who knew nothing of suffering would be incapable of tenderness towards his fellow-creatures and ignorant of the joys of pity; he would be hard-hearted, unsocial, a very monster among men.

Do you know the surest way to make your child miserable? Let him have everything he wants; for as his wants increase in proportion to the ease with which they are satisfied, you will be compelled, sooner or later, to refuse his demands, and this unlooked-for refusal will hurt him more than the lack of what he wants. He will want your stick first, then your watch, the bird that flies, or the star that shines above him. He will want all he sets eyes on, and unless you were God himself, how could you satisfy him?

Man naturally considers all that he can get as his own. In this sense Hobbes' theory is true to a certain extent: Multiply both our wishes and the means of satisfying them, and each will be master of all. Thus the child, who has only to ask and have, thinks himself the master of the universe; he considers all men as his slaves; and when you are at last compelled to refuse, he takes your refusal as an act of rebellion, for he thinks he has only to command. All the reasons you give him, while he is still too young to reason, are so many pretences in his eyes; they seem to him only unkindness; the sense of injustice embitters his disposition; he hates every one. Though he has never felt grateful for kindness, he resents all opposition.

How should I suppose that such a child can ever be happy? He is the slave of anger, a prey to the fiercest passions. Happy! He is a tyrant, at once the basest of slaves and the most wretched of creatures. I have known children brought up like this who expected you to knock the house down, to give them the weather-cock on the steeple, to stop a regiment on the march so that they might listen to the band; when they could not get their way they screamed and cried and would pay no attention to any one. In vain everybody strove to please them; as their desires were stimulated by the ease with which they got their own way, they set their hearts on impossibilities, and found themselves face to face with opposition and difficulty, pain and grief. Scolding, sulking, or in a rage, they wept and cried all day. Were they really so greatly favoured? Weakness, combined with love of power, produces nothing but folly and suffering. One spoilt child beats the table; another whips the sea. They may beat and whip long enough before they find contentment.

If their childhood is made wretched by these notions of power and tyranny, what of their manhood, when their relations with their fellow-men begin to grow and multiply? They are used to find everything give way to them; what a painful surprise to enter society and meet with opposition on every side, to be crushed beneath the weight of a universe which they expected to move at will. Their insolent manners, their childish vanity, only draw down upon them mortification, scorn, and mockery; they swallow insults like water; sharp experience soon teaches them that they have realised neither their position nor their strength. As they cannot do everything, they think they can do nothing. They are daunted by unexpected obstacles, degraded by the scorn of men; they become base, cowardly, and deceitful, and fall as far below their true level as they formerly soared above it.

Let us come back to the primitive law. Nature has made children helpless and in need of affection; did she make them to be obeyed and feared? Has she given them an imposing manner, a stern eye, a loud and threatening voice with which to make themselves feared? I understand how the roaring of the lion strikes terror into the other beasts, so that they tremble when they behold his terrible mane, but of all unseemly, hateful, and ridiculous sights, was there ever anything like a body of statesmen in their robes of office with their chief at their head bowing down before a swaddled babe, addressing him in pompous phrases, while he cries and slavers in reply?

If we consider childhood itself, is there anything so weak and wretched as a child, anything so utterly at the mercy of those about it, so dependent on their pity, their care, and their affection? Does it not seem as if his gentle face and touching appearance were intended to interest every one on behalf of his weakness and to make them eager to help him? And what is there more offensive, more unsuitable, than the sight of a sulky or imperious child, who commands those about him, and impudently assumes the tones of a master towards those without whom he would perish?

On the other hand, do you not see how children are fettered by the weakness of infancy? Do you not see how cruel it is to increase this servitude by obedience to our caprices, by depriving them of such liberty as they have? a liberty which they can scarcely abuse, a liberty the loss of which will do so little good to them or us. If there is nothing more ridiculous than a haughty child, there is nothing that claims our pity like a timid child. With the age of reason the child becomes the slave of the community; then why forestall this by slavery in the home? Let this brief hour of life be free from a yoke which nature has not laid upon it; leave the child the use of his natural liberty, which, for a time at least, secures him from the vices of the slave. Bring me those harsh masters, and those fathers who are the slaves of their children, bring them both with their frivolous objections, and before they boast of their own methods let them for once learn the method of nature.

I return to practical matters. I have already said your child must not get what he asks, but what he needs; [Footnote: We must recognise that pain is often necessary, pleasure is sometimes needed. So there is only one of the child's desires which should never be complied with, the desire for power. Hence, whenever they ask for anything we must pay special attention to their motive in asking. As far as possible give them everything they ask for, provided it can really give them pleasure; refuse everything they demand from mere caprice or love of power.] he must never act from obedience, but from necessity.

The very words OBEY and COMMAND will be excluded from his vocabulary, still more those of DUTY and OBLIGATION; but the words strength, necessity, weakness, and constraint must have a large place in it. Before the age of reason it is impossible to form any idea of moral beings or social relations; so avoid, as far as may be, the use of words which express these ideas, lest the child at an early age should attach wrong ideas to them, ideas which you cannot or will not destroy when he is older. The first mistaken idea he gets into his head is the germ of error and vice; it is the first step that needs watching. Act in such a way that while he only notices external objects his ideas are confined to sensations; let him only see the physical world around him. If not, you may be sure that either he will pay no heed to you at all, or he will form fantastic ideas of the moral world of which you prate, ideas which you will never efface as long as he lives.

"Reason with children" was Locke's chief maxim; it is in the height of fashion at present, and I hardly think it is justified by its results; those children who have been constantly reasoned with strike me as exceedingly silly. Of all man's faculties, reason, which is, so to speak, compounded of all the rest, is the last and choicest growth, and it is this you would use for the child's early training. To make a man reasonable is the coping stone of a good education, and yet you profess to train a child through his reason! You begin at the wrong end, you make the end the means. If children understood reason they would not need education, but by talking to them from their earliest age in a language they do not understand you accustom them to be satisfied with words, to question all that is said to them, to think themselves as wise as their teachers; you train them to be argumentative and rebellious; and whatever you think you gain from motives of reason, you really gain from greediness, fear, or vanity with which you are obliged to reinforce your reasoning.

Most of the moral lessons which are and can be given to children may be reduced to this formula; Master. You must not do that.

Child. Why not?

Master. Because it is wrong.

Child. Wrong! What is wrong?

Master. What is forbidden you.

Child. Why is it wrong to do what is forbidden?

Master. You will be punished for disobedience.

Child. I will do it when no one is looking.

Master. We shall watch you.

Child. I will hide.

Master. We shall ask you what you were doing.

Child. I shall tell a lie.

Master. You must not tell lies.

Child. Why must not I tell lies?

Master. Because it is wrong, etc.

That is the inevitable circle. Go beyond it, and the child will not understand you. What sort of use is there in such teaching? I should greatly like to know what you would substitute for this dialogue. It would have puzzled Locke himself. It is no part of a child's business to know right and wrong, to perceive the reason for a man's duties.

Nature would have them children before they are men. If we try to invert this order we shall produce a forced fruit immature and flavourless, fruit which will be rotten before it is ripe; we shall have young doctors and old children. Childhood has its own ways of seeing, thinking, and feeling; nothing is more foolish than to try and substitute our ways; and I should no more expect judgment in a ten-year-old child than I should expect him to be five feet high. Indeed, what use would reason be to him at that age? It is the curb of strength, and the child does not need the curb.

When you try to persuade your scholars of the duty of obedience, you add to this so-called persuasion compulsion and threats, or still worse, flattery and bribes. Attracted by selfishness or constrained by force, they pretend to be convinced by reason. They see as soon as you do that obedience is to their advantage and disobedience to their disadvantage. But as you only demand disagreeable things of them, and as it is always disagreeable to do another's will, they hide themselves so that they may do as they please, persuaded that they are doing no wrong so long as they are not found out, but ready, if found out, to own themselves in the wrong for fear of worse evils. The reason for duty is beyond their age, and there is not a man in the world who could make them really aware of it; but the fear of punishment, the hope of forgiveness, importunity, the difficulty of answering, wrings from them as many confessions as you want; and you think you have convinced them when you have only wearied or frightened them.

What does it all come to? In the first place, by imposing on them a duty which they fail to recognise, you make them disinclined to submit to your tyranny, and you turn away their love; you teach them deceit, falsehood, and lying as a way to gain rewards or escape punishment; then by accustoming them to conceal a secret motive under the cloak of an apparent one, you yourself put into their hands the means of deceiving you, of depriving you of a knowledge of their real character, of answering you and others with empty words whenever they have the chance. Laws, you say, though binding on conscience, exercise the same constraint over grown-up men. That is so, but what are these men but children spoilt by education? This is just what you should avoid. Use force with children and reasoning with men; this is the natural order; the wise man needs no laws.

Treat your scholar according to his age. Put him in his place from the first, and keep him in it, so that he no longer tries to leave it. Then before he knows what goodness is, he will be practising its chief lesson. Give him no orders at all, absolutely none. Do not even let him think that you claim any authority over him. Let him only know that he is weak and you are strong, that his condition and yours puts him at your mercy; let this be perceived, learned, and felt. Let him early find upon his proud neck, the heavy yoke which nature has imposed upon us, the heavy yoke of necessity, under which every finite being must bow. Let him find this necessity in things, not in the caprices [Footnote: You may be sure the child will regard as caprice any will which opposes his own or any will which he does not understand. Now the child does not understand anything which interferes with his own fancies.] of man; let the curb be force, not authority. If there is something he should not do, do not forbid him, but prevent him without explanation or reasoning; what you give him, give it at his first word without prayers or entreaties, above all without conditions. Give willingly, refuse unwillingly, but let your refusal be irrevocable; let no entreaties move you; let your "No," once uttered, be a wall

53

of brass, against which the child may exhaust his strength some five or six times, but in the end he will try no more to overthrow it.

Thus you will make him patient, equable, calm, and resigned, even when he does not get all he wants; for it is in man's nature to bear patiently with the nature of things, but not with the ill-will of another. A child never rebels against, "There is none left," unless he thinks the reply is false. Moreover, there is no middle course; you must either make no demands on him at all, or else you must fashion him to perfect obedience. The worst education of all is to leave him hesitating between his own will and yours, constantly disputing whether you or he is master; I would rather a hundred times that he were master.

It is very strange that ever since people began to think about education they should have hit upon no other way of guiding children than emulation, jealousy, envy, vanity, greediness, base cowardice, all the most dangerous passions, passions ever ready to ferment, ever prepared to corrupt the soul even before the body is full-grown. With every piece of precocious instruction which you try to force into their minds you plant a vice in the depths of their hearts; foolish teachers think they are doing wonders when they are making their scholars wicked in order to teach them what goodness is, and then they tell us seriously, "Such is man." Yes, such is man, as you have made him. Every means has been tried except one, the very one which might succeed — well-regulated liberty. Do not undertake to bring up a child if you cannot guide him merely by the laws of what can or cannot be. The limits of the possible and the impossible are alike unknown to him, so they can be extended or contracted around him at your will. Without a murmur he is restrained, urged on, held back, by the hands of necessity alone; he is made adaptable and teachable by the mere force of things, without any chance for vice to spring up in him; for passions do not arise so long as they have accomplished nothing.

Give your scholar no verbal lessons; he should be taught by experience alone; never punish him, for he does not know what it is to do wrong; never make him say, "Forgive me," for he does not know how to do you wrong. Wholly unmoral in his actions, he can do nothing morally wrong, and he deserves neither punishment nor reproof.

Already I see the frightened reader comparing this child with those of our time; he is mistaken. The perpetual restraint imposed upon your scholars stimulates their activity; the more subdued they are in your presence, the more boisterous they are as soon as they are out of your sight. They must make amends to themselves in some way or other for the harsh constraint to which you subject them. Two schoolboys from the town will do more damage in the country than all the children of the village. Shut up a young gentleman and a young peasant in a room; the former will have upset and smashed everything before the latter has stirred from his place. Why is that, unless that the one hastens to misuse a moment's licence, while the other, always sure of freedom, does not use it rashly. And yet the village children, often flattered or constrained, are still very far from the state in which I would have them kept.

Let us lay it down as an incontrovertible rule that the first impulses of nature are always right; there is no original sin in the human heart, the how and why of the entrance of every vice can be traced. The only natural passion is self-love or selfishness taken in a wider sense. This selfishness is good in itself and in relation to ourselves; and as the child has no necessary relations to other people he is naturally indifferent to them; his self-love only becomes good or bad by the use made of it and the relations established by its means. Until the time is ripe for the appearance of reason, that guide of selfishness, the main thing is that the child shall do nothing because you are watching him or listening to him; in a word, nothing because of other people, but only what nature asks of him; then he will never do wrong.

I do not mean to say that he will never do any mischief, never hurt himself, never break a costly ornament if you leave it within his reach. He might do much damage without doing wrong, since wrong-doing depends on the harmful intention which will never be his. If once he meant to do harm, his whole education would be ruined; he would be almost hopelessly bad.

Greed considers some things wrong which are not wrong in the eyes of reason. When you leave free scope to a child's heedlessness, you must put anything he could spoil out of his way, and leave nothing fragile or costly within his reach. Let the room be furnished with plain and solid furniture; no mirrors, china, or useless ornaments. My pupil Emile, who is brought up in the country, shall have a room just like a peasant's. Why take such pains to adorn it when he will be so little in it? I am mistaken, however; he will ornament it for himself, and we shall soon see how.

But if, in spite of your precautions, the child contrives to do some damage, if he breaks some useful article, do not punish him for your carelessness, do not even scold him; let him hear no word of reproval, do not even let him see that he has vexed you; behave just as if the thing had come to pieces of itself; you may consider you have done great things if you have managed to hold your tongue.

May I venture at this point to state the greatest, the most important, the most useful rule of education? It is: Do not save time, but lose it. I hope that every-day readers will excuse my paradoxes; you cannot avoid paradox if you think for yourself, and whatever you may say I would rather fall into paradox than into prejudice. The most dangerous period in human life lies between birth and the age of twelve. It is the time when errors and vices spring up, while as yet there is no means to destroy them; when the means of destruction are ready, the roots have gone too deep to be pulled up. If the infant sprang at one bound from its mother's breast to the age of reason, the present type of education would be quite suitable, but its natural growth calls for quite a different training. The mind should be left undisturbed till its faculties have developed; for while it is blind it cannot see the torch you offer it, nor can it follow through the vast expanse of ideas a path so faintly traced by reason that the best eyes can scarcely follow it.

Therefore the education of the earliest years should be merely negative. It consists, not in teaching virtue or truth, but in preserving the heart from vice and from the spirit of error. If only you could let well alone, and get others to follow your example; if you could bring your scholar to the age of twelve strong and healthy, but unable to tell his right hand from his left, the eyes of his understanding would be open to reason as soon as you began to teach him. Free from prejudices and free from habits, there would be nothing in him to counteract the effects of your labours. In your hands he would soon become the wisest of men; by doing nothing to begin with, you would end with a prodigy of education.

Reverse the usual practice and you will almost always do right. Fathers and teachers who want to make the child, not a child but a man of learning, think it never too soon to scold, correct, reprove, threaten, bribe, teach, and reason. Do better than they; be reasonable, and do not reason with your pupil, more especially do not try to make him approve what he dislikes; for if reason is always connected with disagreeable matters, you make it distasteful to him, you discredit it at an early age in a mind not yet ready to understand it. Exercise his body, his limbs, his senses, his strength, but keep his mind idle as long as you can. Distrust all opinions which appear before the judgment to discriminate between them. Restrain and ward off strange impressions; and to prevent the birth of evil do not hasten to do well, for goodness is only possible when enlightened by reason. Regard all delays as so much time gained; you have achieved much, you approach the boundary without loss. Leave childhood to ripen in your children. In a word, beware of giving anything they need to-day if it can be deferred without danger to to-morrow.

There is another point to be considered which confirms the suitability of this method: it is the child's individual bent, which must be thoroughly known before we can choose the fittest moral training. Every mind has its own form, in accordance with which it must be controlled; and the success of the pains taken depends largely on the fact that he is controlled in this way and no other. Oh, wise man, take time to observe nature; watch your scholar well before you say a word to him; first leave the germ of his character free to show itself, do not constrain him in anything, the better to see him as he really is. Do you think this time of liberty is wasted? On the contrary, your scholar will be the better employed, for this is the way you yourself will learn not to lose a single moment when time is of more value. If, however, you begin to act before you know what to do, you act at random; you may make mistakes, and must retrace your steps; your haste to reach your goal will only take you further from it. Do not imitate the miser who loses much lest he should lose a little. Sacrifice a little time in early childhood, and it will be repaid you with usury when your scholar is older. The wise physician does not hastily give prescriptions at first sight, but he studies the constitution of the sick man before he prescribes anything; the treatment is begun later, but the patient is cured, while the hasty doctor kills him.

But where shall we find a place for our child so as to bring him up as a senseless being, an automaton? Shall we keep him in the moon, or on a desert island? Shall we remove him from human society? Will he not always have around him the sight and the pattern of the passions of other people? Will he never see children of his own age? Will he not see his parents, his neighbours, his nurse, his governess, his man-servant, his tutor himself, who after all will not be an angel? Here we have a real and serious objection. But did I tell you that an education according to nature would be an easy task? Oh, men! is it my fault that you have made all good things difficult? I admit that I am aware of these difficulties; perhaps they are insuperable; but nevertheless it is certain that we do to some extent avoid them by trying to do so. I am showing what we should try to attain, I do not say we can attain it, but I do say that whoever comes nearest to it is nearest to success.

Remember you must be a man yourself before you try to train a man; you yourself must set the pattern he shall copy. While the child is still unconscious there is time to prepare his surroundings, so that nothing shall strike his eye but what is fit for his sight. Gain the respect of every one, begin to win their hearts, so that they may try to please you. You will not be master of the child if you cannot control every one about him; and this authority will never suffice unless it rests upon respect for your goodness. There is no question of squandering one's means and giving money right and left; I never knew money win love. You must neither be harsh nor niggardly, nor must you merely pity misery when you can relieve it; but in vain will you open your purse if you do not open your heart along with it, the hearts of others will always be closed to you. You must give your own time, attention, affection, your very self; for whatever you do, people always perceive that your money is not you. There are proofs of kindly interest which produce more results and are really more useful than any gift; how many of the sick and wretched have more need of comfort than of charity; how many of the oppressed need protection rather than money? Reconcile those who are at strife, prevent lawsuits; incline children to duty, fathers to kindness; promote happy marriages; prevent annoyances; freely use the credit of your pupil's parents on behalf of the weak who cannot obtain justice, the weak who are oppressed by the strong. Be just, human, kindly. Do not give alms alone, give charity; works of mercy do more than money for the relief of suffering; love others and they will love you; serve them and they will serve you; be their brother and they will be your children.

This is one reason why I want to bring up Emile in the country, far from those miserable lacqueys, the most degraded of men except their masters; far from the vile morals of the town, whose gilded surface makes them seductive and contagious to children; while the vices of peasants, unadorned and in their naked grossness, are more fitted to repel than to seduce, when there is no motive for imitating them.

In the village a tutor will have much more control over the things he wishes to show the child; his reputation, his words, his example, will have a weight they would never have in the town; he is of use to every one, so every one is eager to oblige him, to win his esteem, to appeal before the disciple what the master would have him be; if vice is not corrected, public scandal is at least avoided, which is all that our present purpose requires.

Cease to blame others for your own faults; children are corrupted less by what they see than by your own teaching. With your endless preaching, moralising, and pedantry, for one idea you give your scholars, believing it to be good, you give them twenty more which are good for nothing; you are full of what is going on in your own minds, and you fail to see the effect you produce on theirs. In the continual flow of words with which you overwhelm them, do you think there is none which they get hold of in a wrong sense? Do you suppose they do not make their own comments on your long-winded explanations, that they do not find material for the construction of a system they can understand—one which they will use against you when they get the chance?

Listen to a little fellow who has just been under instruction; let him chatter freely, ask questions, and talk at his ease, and you will be surprised to find the strange forms your arguments have assumed in his mind; he confuses everything, and turns everything topsy-turvy; you are vexed and grieved by his unforeseen objections; he reduces you to be silent yourself or to silence him: and what can he think of silence in one who is so fond of talking? If ever he gains this advantage and is aware of it, farewell education; from that moment all is lost; he is no longer trying to learn, he is trying to refute you.

Zealous teachers, be simple, sensible, and reticent; be in no hurry to act unless to prevent the actions of others. Again and again I say, reject, if it may be, a good lesson for fear of giving a bad one. Beware of playing the tempter in this world, which nature intended as an earthly paradise for men, and do not attempt to give the innocent child the knowledge of good and evil; since you cannot prevent the child learning by what he sees outside himself, restrict your own efforts to impressing those examples on his mind in the form best suited for him.

The explosive passions produce a great effect upon the child when he sees them; their outward expression is very marked; he is struck by this and his attention is arrested. Anger especially is so noisy in its rage that it is impossible not to perceive it if you are within reach. You need not ask yourself whether this is an opportunity for a pedagogue to frame a fine disquisition. What! no fine disquisition, nothing, not a word! Let the child come to you; impressed by what he has seen, he will not fail to ask you questions. The answer is easy; it is drawn from the very things which have appealed to his senses. He sees a flushed face, flashing eyes, a threatening gesture, he hears cries; everything shows that the body is ill at ease. Tell him plainly, without affectation or mystery, "This poor man is ill, he is in a fever." You may take the opportunity of giving him in a few words some idea of disease and its effects; for that too belongs to nature, and is one of the bonds of necessity which he must recognise. By means of this idea, which is not false in itself, may he not early acquire a certain aversion to giving way to excessive passions, which he regards as diseases; and do you not think that such a notion, given at the right moment, will produce a more wholesome effect than the most tedious sermon? But consider the after effects of this idea; you have authority, if ever you find it necessary, to treat the rebellious child as a sick child; to keep him in his room, in bed if need be, to diet him, to make him afraid of his growing vices, to make him hate and dread them without ever regarding as a punishment the strict measures you will perhaps have to use for his recovery. If it happens that you yourself in a moment's heat depart from the calm and self-control which you should aim at, do not try to conceal your fault, but tell him frankly, with a gentle reproach, "My dear, you have hurt me."

Moreover, it is a matter of great importance that no notice should be taken in his presence of the quaint sayings which result from the simplicity of the ideas in which he is brought up, nor should they be quoted in a way he can understand. A foolish laugh may destroy six months' work and do irreparable damage for life. I cannot repeat too often that to control the child one must often control oneself.

I picture my little Emile at the height of a dispute between two neighbours going up to the fiercest of them and saying in a tone of pity, "You are ill, I am very sorry for you." This speech will no doubt have its effect on the spectators and perhaps on the disputants. Without laughter, scolding, or praise I should take him away, willing or no, before he could see this result, or at least before he could think about it; and I should make haste to turn his thoughts to other things, so that he would soon forget all about it.

I do not propose to enter into every detail, but only to explain general rules and to give illustrations in cases of difficulty. I think it is impossible to train a child up to the age of twelve in the midst of society, without giving him some idea of the relations between one man and another, and of the morality of human actions. It is enough to delay the development of these ideas as long as possible, and when they can no longer be avoided to limit them to present needs, so that he may neither think himself master of everything nor do harm to others without knowing or caring. There are calm and gentle characters which can be led a long way in their first innocence without any danger; but there are also stormy dispositions whose passions develop early; you must hasten to make men of them lest you should have to keep them in chains.

Our first duties are to ourselves; our first feelings are centred on self; all our instincts are at first directed to our own preservation and our own welfare. Thus the first notion of justice springs not from what we owe to others, but from what is due to us. Here is another error in popular methods of education. If you talk to children of their duties, and not of their rights, you are beginning at the wrong end, and telling them what they cannot understand, what cannot be of any interest to them.

If I had to train a child such as I have just described, I should say to myself, "A child never attacks people, [Footnote: A child should never be allowed to play with grown-up people as if they were his inferiors, nor even as if they were only his equals. If he ventured to strike any one in earnest, were it only the footman, were it the hangman himself, let the sufferer return his blows with interest, so that he will not want to do it again. I have seen silly women inciting children to rebellion, encouraging them to hit people, allowing themselves to be beaten, and laughing at the harmless blows, never thinking that those blows were in intention the blows of a murderer, and that the child who desires to beat people now will desire to kill them when he is grown up.] only things; and he soon learns by experience to respect those older and stronger than himself. Things, however, do not defend themselves. Therefore the first idea he needs is not that of liberty but of property, and that he may get this idea he must have something of his own." It is useless to enumerate his clothes, furniture, and playthings; although he uses these he knows not how or why he has come by them. To tell him they were given him is little better, for giving implies having; so here is property before his own, and it is the principle of property that you want to teach him; moreover, giving is a convention, and the child as yet has no idea of conventions. I hope my reader will note, in this and many other cases, how people think they have taught children thoroughly, when they have only thrust on them words which have no intelligible meaning to them. [Footnote: This is why most children want to take back what they have given, and cry if they cannot get it. They do not do this when once they know what a gift is; only they are more careful about giving things away.]

We must therefore go back to the origin of property, for that is where the first idea of it must begin. The child, living in the country, will have got some idea of field work; eyes and leisure suffice for that, and he will have both. In every age, and especially in childhood, we want to create, to copy, to produce, to give all the signs of power and activity. He will hardly have seen the gardener at work twice, sowing, planting, and growing vegetables, before he will want to garden himself.

According to the principles I have already laid down, I shall not thwart him; on the contrary, I shall approve of his plan, share his hobby, and work with him, not for his pleasure but my own; at least, so he thinks; I shall be his under-gardener, and dig the ground for him till his arms are strong enough to do it; he will take possession of it by planting a bean, and this is surely a more sacred possession, and one more worthy of respect, than that of Nunes Balboa, who took possession of South America in the name of the King of Spain, by planting his banner on the coast of the Southern Sea.

We water the beans every day, we watch them coming up with the greatest delight. Day by day I increase this delight by saying, "Those belong to you." To explain what that word "belong" means, I show him how he has given his time, his labour, and his trouble, his very self to it; that in this ground there is a part of himself which he can claim against all the world, as he could withdraw his arm from the hand of another man who wanted to keep it against his will.

One fine day he hurries up with his watering-can in his hand. What a scene of woe! Alas! all the beans are pulled up, the soil is dug over, you can scarcely find the place. Oh! what has become of my labour, my work, the beloved fruits of my care and effort? Who has stolen my property! Who has taken my beans? The young heart revolts; the first feeling of injustice brings its sorrow and bitterness; tears come in torrents, the unhappy child fills the air with cries and groans, I share his sorrow and anger; we look around us, we make inquiries. At last we discover that the gardener did it. We send for him.

But we are greatly mistaken. The gardener, hearing our complaint, begins to complain louder than we:

What, gentlemen, was it you who spoilt my work! I had sown some Maltese melons; the seed was given me as something quite out of the common, and I meant to give you a treat when they were ripe; but you have planted your miserable beans and destroyed my melons, which were coming up so nicely, and I can never get any more. You have behaved very badly to me and you have deprived yourselves of the pleasure of eating most delicious melons.

JEAN JACQUES. My poor Robert, you must forgive us. You had given your labour and your pains to it. I see we were wrong to spoil your work, but we will send to Malta for some more seed for you, and we will never dig the ground again without finding out if some one else has been beforehand with us.

ROBERT. Well, gentlemen, you need not trouble yourselves, for there is no more waste ground. I dig what my father tilled; every one does the same, and all the land you see has been occupied time out of mind.

EMILE. Mr. Robert, do people often lose the seed of Maltese melons?

ROBERT. No indeed, sir; we do not often find such silly little gentlemen as you. No one meddles with his neighbour's garden; every one respects other people's work so that his own may be safe.

EMILE. But I have not got a garden.

ROBERT. I don't care; if you spoil mine I won't let you walk in it, for you see I do not mean to lose my labour.

JEAN JACQUES. Could not we suggest an arrangement with this kind Robert? Let him give my young friend and myself a corner of his garden to cultivate, on condition that he has half the crop.

ROBERT. You may have it free. But remember I shall dig up your beans if you touch my melons.

In this attempt to show how a child may be taught certain primitive ideas we see how the notion of property goes back naturally to the right of the first occupier to the results of his work. That is plain and simple, and quite within the child's grasp. From that to the rights of property and exchange there is but a step, after which you must stop short.

You also see that an explanation which I can give in writing in a couple of pages may take a year in practice, for in the course of moral ideas we cannot advance too slowly, nor plant each step too firmly. Young teacher, pray consider this example, and remember that your lessons should always be in deeds rather than words, for children soon forget what they say or what is said to them, but not what they have done nor what has been done to them.

Such teaching should be given, as I have said, sooner or later, as the scholar's disposition, gentle or turbulent, requires it. The way of using it is unmistakable; but to omit no matter of importance in a difficult business let us take another example.

Your ill-tempered child destroys everything he touches. Do not vex yourself; put anything he can spoil out of his reach. He breaks the things he is using; do not be in a hurry to give him more; let him feel the want of them. He breaks the windows of his room; let the wind blow upon him night and day, and do not be afraid of his catching cold; it is better to catch cold than to be reckless. Never complain of the inconvenience he causes you, but let him feel it first. At last you will have the windows mended without saying anything. He breaks them again; then change your plan; tell him dryly and without anger, "The windows are mine, I took pains to have them put in, and I mean to keep them safe." Then you will shut him up in a dark place without a window. At this unexpected proceeding he cries and howls; no one heeds. Soon he gets tired and changes his tone; he laments and sighs; a servant appears, the rebel begs to be let out. Without seeking any excuse for refusing, the servant merely says, "I, too, have windows to keep," and goes away. At last, when the child has been there several hours, long enough to get very tired of it, long enough to make an impression on his memory, some one suggests to him that he should offer to make terms with you, so that you may set him free and he will never break windows again. That is just what he wants. He will send and ask you to come and see him; you will come, he will suggest his plan, and you will agree to it at once, saying, "That is a very good idea; it will suit us both; why didn't you think of it sooner?" Then without asking for any affirmation or confirmation of his promise, you will embrace him joyfully and take him back at once to his own room, considering this agreement as sacred as if he had confirmed it by a formal oath. What idea do you think he will form from these proceedings, as to the fulfilment of a promise and its usefulness? If I am not greatly mistaken, there is not a child upon earth, unless he is utterly spoilt already, who could resist this treatment, or one who would ever dream of breaking windows again on purpose. Follow out the whole train of thought. The naughty little fellow hardly thought when he was making a hole for his beans that he was hewing out a cell in which his own knowledge would soon imprison him. [Footnote: Moreover if the duty of keeping his word were not established in the child's mind by its own utility, the child's growing consciousness would soon impress it on him as a law of conscience, as an innate principle, only requiring suitable experiences for its development. This first outline is not sketched by man, it is engraved on the heart by the author of all justice. Take away the primitive law of contract and the obligation imposed by contract and there is nothing left of human society but vanity and empty show. He who only keeps his word because it is to his own profit is hardly more pledged than if he had given no promise at all. This principle is of the utmost importance, and deserves to be thoroughly studied, for man is now beginning to be at war with himself.]

We are now in the world of morals, the door to vice is open. Deceit and falsehood are born along with conventions and duties. As soon as we can do what we ought not to do, we try to hide what we ought not to have done. As soon as self-interest makes us give a promise, a greater interest may make us break it; it is merely a question of doing it with impunity; we naturally take refuge in concealment and falsehood. As we have not been able to prevent vice, we must punish it. The sorrows of life begin with its mistakes.

I have already said enough to show that children should never receive punishment merely as such; it should always come as the natural consequence of their fault. Thus you will not exclaim against their falsehood, you will not exactly punish them for lying, but you will arrange that all the ill effects of lying, such as not being believed when we speak the truth, or being accused of what we have not done in spite of our protests, shall fall on their heads when they have told a lie. But let us explain what lying means to the child.

There are two kinds of lies; one concerns an accomplished fact, the other concerns a future duty. The first occurs when we falsely deny or assert that we did or did not do something, or, to put it in general terms, when we knowingly say what is contrary to facts. The other occurs when we promise what we do not mean to perform, or, in general terms, when we profess an intention which we do not really mean to carry out. These two kinds of lie are sometimes found in combination, [Footnote: Thus the guilty person, accused of some evil deed, defends himself by asserting that he is a good man. His statement is false in itself and false in its application to the matter in hand.] but their differences are my present business.

He who feels the need of help from others, he who is constantly experiencing their kindness, has nothing to gain by deceiving them; it is plainly to his advantage that they should see things as they are, lest they should mistake his interests. It is therefore plain that lying with regard to actual facts is not natural to children, but lying is made necessary by the law of obedience; since obedience is disagreeable, children disobey as far as they can in secret, and the present good of avoiding punishment or reproof outweighs the remoter good of speaking the truth. Under a free and natural education why should your child lie? What has he to conceal from you? You do not thwart him, you do not punish him, you demand nothing from him. Why should he not tell everything to you as simply as to his little playmate? He cannot see anything more risky in the one course than in the other.

The lie concerning duty is even less natural, since promises to do or refrain from doing are conventional agreements which are outside the state of nature and detract from our liberty. Moreover, all promises made by children are in themselves void; when they pledge themselves they do not know what they are doing, for their narrow vision cannot look beyond the present. A child can hardly lie when he makes a promise; for he is only thinking how he can get out of the present difficulty, any means which has not an immediate result is the same to him; when he promises for the future he promises nothing, and his imagination is as yet incapable of projecting him into the future while he lives in the present. If he could escape a whipping or get a packet of sweets by promising to throw himself out of the window to-morrow, he would promise on the spot. This is why the law disregards all promises made by minors, and when fathers and teachers are stricter and demand that promises shall be kept, it is only when the promise refers to something the child ought to do even if he had made no promise.

The child cannot lie when he makes a promise, for he does not know what he is doing when he makes his promise. The case is different when he breaks his promise, which is a sort of retrospective falsehood; for he clearly remembers making the promise, but he fails to see the importance of keeping it. Unable to look into the future, he cannot foresee the results of things, and when he breaks his promises he does nothing contrary to his stage of reasoning.

Children's lies are therefore entirely the work of their teachers, and to teach them to speak the truth is nothing less than to teach them the art of lying. In your zeal to rule, control, and teach them, you never find sufficient means at your disposal. You wish to gain fresh influence over their minds by baseless maxims, by unreasonable precepts; and you would rather they knew their lessons and told lies, than leave them ignorant and truthful.

We, who only give our scholars lessons in practice, who prefer to have them good rather than clever, never demand the truth lest they should conceal it, and never claim any promise lest they should be tempted to break it. If some mischief has been done in my absence and I do not know who did it, I shall take care not to accuse Emile, nor to say, "Did you do it?" [Footnote: Nothing could be more indiscreet than such a question, especially if the child is guilty. Then if he thinks you know what he has done, he will think you are setting a trap for him, and this idea can only set him against you. If he thinks you do not know, he will say to himself, "Why should I make my fault known?" And here we have the first temptation to falsehood as the direct result of your foolish question.] For in so doing what should I do but teach him to deny it? If his difficult temperament compels me to make some agreement with him, I will take good care that the suggestion always comes from him, never from me; that when he undertakes anything he has always a present and effective interest in fulfilling his promise, and if he ever fails this lie will bring down on him all the unpleasant consequences which he sees arising from the natural order of things, and not from his tutor's vengeance. But far from having recourse to such cruel measures, I feel almost certain that Emile will not know for many years what it is to lie, and that when he does find out, he will be astonished and unable to understand what can be the use of it. It is quite clear that the less I make his welfare dependent on the will or the opinions of others, the less is it to his interest to lie.

When we are in no hurry to teach there is no hurry to demand, and we can take our time, so as to demand nothing except under fitting conditions. Then the child is training himself, in so far as he is not being spoilt. But when a fool of a tutor, who does not know how to set about his business, is always making his pupil promise first this and then that, without discrimination, choice, or proportion, the child is puzzled and overburdened with all these promises, and neglects, forgets or even scorns them, and considering them as so many empty phrases he makes a game of making and breaking promises. Would you have him keep his promise faithfully, be moderate in your claims upon him.

The detailed treatment I have just given to lying may be applied in many respects to all the other duties imposed upon children, whereby these duties are made not only hateful but impracticable. For the sake of a show of preaching virtue you make them love every vice; you instil these vices by forbidding them. Would you have them pious, you take them to church till they are sick of it; you teach them to gabble prayers until they long for the happy time when they will not have to pray to God. To teach them charity you make them give alms as if you scorned to give yourself. It is not the child, but the master, who should give; however much he loves his pupil he should vie with him for this honour; he should make him think that he is too young to deserve it. Alms-giving is the deed of a man who can measure the worth of his gift and the needs of his fellow-men. The child, who knows nothing of these, can have no merit in giving; he gives without charity, without kindness; he is almost ashamed to give, for, to judge by your practice and his own, he thinks it is only children who give, and that there is no need for charity when we are grown up.

Observe that the only things children are set to give are things of which they do not know the value, bits of metal carried in their pockets for which they have no further use. A child would rather give a hundred coins than one cake. But get this prodigal giver to distribute what is dear to him, his toys, his sweets, his own lunch, and we shall soon see if you have made him really generous.

People try yet another way; they soon restore what he gave to the child, so that he gets used to giving everything which he knows will come back to him. I have scarcely seen generosity in children except of these two types, giving what is of no use to them, or what they expect to get back again. "Arrange things," says Locke, "so that experience may convince them that the most generous giver gets the biggest share." That is to make the child superficially generous but really greedy. He adds that "children will thus form the habit of liberality." Yes, a usurer's liberality, which expects cent. per cent. But when it is a question of real giving, good-bye to the habit; when they do not get things back, they will not give. It is the habit of the mind, not of the hands, that needs watching. All the other virtues taught to children are like this, and to preach these baseless virtues you waste their youth in sorrow. What a sensible sort of education!

Teachers, have done with these shams; be good and kind; let your example sink into your scholars' memories till they are old enough to take it to heart. Rather than hasten to demand deeds of charity from my pupil I prefer to perform such deeds in his presence, even depriving him of the means of imitating me, as an honour beyond his years; for it is of the utmost importance that he should not regard a man's duties as merely those of a child. If when he sees me help the poor he asks me about it, and it is time to reply to his questions, [Footnote: It must be understood that I do not answer his questions when he wants; that would be to subject myself to his will and to place myself in the most dangerous state of dependence that ever a tutor was in.] I shall say, "My dear boy, the rich only exist, through the good-will of the poor, so they have promised to feed those who have not enough to live on, either in goods or labour." "Then you promised to do this?" "Certainly; I am only master of the wealth that passes through my hands on the condition attached to its ownership."

After this talk (and we have seen how a child may be brought to understand it) another than Emile would be tempted to imitate me and behave like a rich man; in such a case I should at least take care that it was done without ostentation; I would rather he robbed me of my privilege and hid himself to give. It is a fraud suitable to his age, and the only one I could forgive in him.

I know that all these imitative virtues are only the virtues of a monkey, and that a good action is only morally good when it is done as such and not because of others. But at an age when the heart does not yet feel anything, you must make children copy the deeds you wish to grow into habits, until they can do them with understanding and for the love of what is good. Man imitates, as do the beasts. The love of imitating is well regulated by nature; in society it becomes a vice. The monkey imitates man, whom he fears, and not the other beasts, which he scorns; he thinks what is done by his betters must be good. Among ourselves, our harlequins imitate all that is good to degrade it and bring it into ridicule; knowing their owners' baseness they try to equal what is better than they are, or they strive to imitate what they admire, and their bad taste appears in their choice of models, they would rather deceive others or win applause for their own talents than become wiser or better. Imitation has its roots in our desire to escape from ourselves. If I succeed in my undertaking, Emile will certainly have no such wish. So we must dispense with any seeming good that might arise from it.

Examine your rules of education; you will find them all topsy-turvy, especially in all that concerns virtue and morals. The only moral lesson which is suited for a child—the most important lesson for every time of life—is this: "Never hurt anybody." The very rule of well-doing, if not subordinated to this rule, is dangerous, false, and contradictory. Who is there who does no good? Every one does some good, the wicked as well as the righteous; he makes one happy at the cost of the misery of a hundred, and hence spring all our misfortunes. The noblest virtues are negative, they are also the most difficult, for they make little show, and do not even make room for that pleasure so dear to the heart of man, the thought that some one is pleased with us. If there be a man who does no harm to his neighbours, what good must he have accomplished! What a bold heart, what a strong character it needs! It is not in talking about this maxim, but in trying to practise it, that we discover both its greatness and its difficulty. [Footnote: The precept "Never hurt anybody," implies the greatest possible independence of human society; for in the social state one man's good is another man's evil. This relation is part of the nature of things; it is inevitable. You may apply this test to man in society and to the hermit to discover which is best. A distinguished author says, "None but the wicked can live alone." I say, "None but the good can live alone." This proposition, if less sententious, is truer and more logical than the other. If the wicked were alone, what evil would he do? It is among his fellows that he lays his snares for others. If they wish to apply this argument to the man of property, my answer is to be found in the passage to which this note is appended.]

This will give you some slight idea of the precautions I would have you take in giving children instruction which cannot always be refused without risk to themselves or others, or the far greater risk of the formation of bad habits, which would be difficult to correct later on; but be sure this necessity will not often arise with children who are properly brought up, for they cannot possibly become rebellious, spiteful, untruthful, or greedy, unless the seeds of these vices are sown in their hearts. What I have just said applies therefore rather to the exception than the rule. But the oftener children have the opportunity of quitting their proper condition, and contracting the vices of men, the oftener will these exceptions arise. Those who are brought up in the world must receive more precocious instruction than those who are brought up in retirement. So this solitary education would be preferable, even if it did nothing more than leave childhood time to ripen.

There is quite another class of exceptions: those so gifted by nature that they rise above the level of their age. As there are men who never get beyond infancy, so there are others who are never, so to speak, children, they are men almost from birth. The difficulty is that these cases are very rare, very difficult to distinguish; while every mother, who knows that a child may be a prodigy, is convinced that her child is that one. They go further; they mistake the common signs of growth for marks of exceptional talent. Liveliness, sharp sayings, romping, amusing simplicity, these are the characteristic marks of this age, and show that the child is a child indeed. Is it strange that a child who is encouraged to chatter and allowed to say anything, who is restrained neither by consideration nor convention, should chance to say something clever? Were he never to hit the mark, his case would be stranger than that of the astrologer who, among a thousand errors, occasionally predicts the truth. "They lie so often," said Henry IV., "that at last they say what is true." If you want to say something clever, you have only to talk long enough. May Providence watch over those fine folk who have no other claim to social distinction.

The finest thoughts may spring from a child's brain, or rather the best words may drop from his lips, just as diamonds of great worth may fall into his hands, while neither the thoughts nor the diamonds are his own; at that age neither can be really his. The child's sayings do not mean to him what they mean to us, the ideas he attaches to them are different. His ideas, if indeed he has any ideas at all, have neither order nor connection; there is nothing sure, nothing certain, in his thoughts. Examine your so-called prodigy. Now and again you will discover in him extreme activity of mind and extraordinary clearness of thought. More often this same mind will seem slack and spiritless, as if wrapped in mist. Sometimes he goes before you, sometimes he will not stir. One moment you would call him a genius, another a fool. You would be mistaken in both; he is a child, an eaglet who soars aloft for a moment, only to drop back into the nest.

Treat him, therefore, according to his age, in spite of appearances, and beware of exhausting his strength by over-much exercise. If the young brain grows warm and begins to bubble, let it work freely, but do not heat it any further, lest it lose its goodness, and when the first gases have been given off, collect and compress the rest so that in after years they may turn to life-giving heat and real energy. If not, your time and your pains will be wasted, you will destroy your own work, and after foolishly intoxicating yourself with these heady fumes, you will have nothing left but an insipid and worthless wine.

Silly children grow into ordinary men. I know no generalisation more certain than this. It is the most difficult thing in the world to distinguish between genuine stupidity, and that apparent and deceitful stupidity which is the sign of a strong character. At first sight it seems strange that the two extremes should have the same outward signs; and yet it may well be so, for at an age when man has as yet no true ideas, the whole difference between the genius and the rest consists in this: the latter only take in false ideas, while the former, finding nothing but false ideas, receives no ideas at all. In this he resembles the fool; the one is fit for nothing, the other finds nothing fit for him. The only way of distinguishing between them depends upon chance, which may offer the genius some idea which he can understand, while the fool is always the same. As a child, the young Cato was taken for an idiot by his parents; he was obstinate and silent, and that was all they perceived in him; it was only in Sulla's ante-chamber that his uncle discovered what was in him. Had he never found his way there, he might have passed for a fool till he reached the age of reason. Had Caesar never lived, perhaps this same Cato, who discerned his fatal genius, and foretold his great schemes, would have passed for a dreamer all his days. Those who judge children hastily are apt to be mistaken; they are often more childish than the child himself. I knew a middle-aged man, [Footnote: The Abbe de Condillac] whose friendship I esteemed an honour, who was reckoned a fool by his family. All at once he made his name as a philosopher, and I have no doubt posterity will give him a high place among the greatest thinkers and the profoundest metaphysicians of his day.

Hold childhood in reverence, and do not be in any hurry to judge it for good or ill. Leave exceptional cases to show themselves, let their qualities be tested and confirmed, before special methods are adopted. Give nature time to work before you take over her business, lest you interfere with her dealings. You assert that you know the value of time and are afraid to waste it. You fail to perceive that it is a greater waste of time to use it ill than to do nothing, and that a child ill taught is further from virtue than a child who has learnt nothing at all. You are afraid to see him spending his early years doing nothing. What! is it nothing to be happy, nothing to run and jump all day? He will never be so busy again all his life long. Plato, in his Republic, which is considered so stern, teaches the children only through festivals, games, songs, and amusements. It seems as if he had accomplished his purpose when he had taught them to be happy; and Seneca, speaking of the Roman lads in olden days, says, "They were always on their feet, they were never taught anything which kept them sitting." Were they any the worse for it in manhood? Do not be afraid, therefore, of this so-called idleness. What would you think of a man who refused to sleep lest he should waste part of his life? You would say, "He is mad; he is not enjoying his life, he is robbing himself of part of it; to avoid sleep he is hastening his death." Remember that these two cases are alike, and that childhood is the sleep of reason.

The apparent ease with which children learn is their ruin. You fail to see that this very facility proves that they are not learning. Their shining, polished brain reflects, as in a mirror, the things you show them, but nothing sinks in. The child remembers the words and the ideas are reflected back; his hearers understand them, but to him they are meaningless.

Although memory and reason are wholly different faculties, the one does not really develop apart from the other. Before the age of reason the child receives images, not ideas; and there is this difference between them: images are merely the pictures of external objects, while ideas are notions about those objects determined by their relations. An image when it is recalled may exist by itself in the mind, but every idea implies other ideas. When we image we merely perceive, when we reason we compare. Our sensations are merely passive, our notions or ideas spring from an active principle which judges. The proof of this will be given later.

I maintain, therefore, that as children are incapable of judging, they have no true memory. They retain sounds, form, sensation, but rarely ideas, and still more rarely relations. You tell me they acquire some rudiments of geometry, and you think you prove your case; not so, it is mine you prove; you show that far from being able to reason themselves, children are unable to retain the reasoning of others; for if you follow the method of these little geometricians you will see they only retain the exact impression of the figure and the terms of the demonstration. They cannot meet the slightest new objection; if the figure is reversed they can do nothing. All their knowledge is on the sensation-level, nothing has penetrated to their understanding. Their memory is little better than their other powers, for they always have to learn over again, when they are grown up, what they learnt as children.

I am far from thinking, however, that children have no sort of reason. [Footnote: I have noticed again and again that it is impossible in writing a lengthy work to use the same words always in the same sense. There is no language rich enough to supply terms and expressions sufficient for the modifications of our ideas. The method of defining every term and constantly substituting the definition for the term defined looks well, but it is impracticable. For how can we escape from our vicious circle? Definitions would be all very well if we did not use words in the making of them. In spite of this I am convinced that even in our poor language we can make our meaning clear, not by always using words in the same sense, but by taking care hat every time we use a word the sense in which we use it is sufficiently indicated by the sense of the context, so that each sentence in which the word occurs acts as a sort of definition. Sometimes I say children are incapable of reasoning. Sometimes I say they reason cleverly. I must admit that my words are often contradictory, but I do not think there is any contradiction in my ideas.] On the contrary, I think they reason very well with regard to things that affect their actual and sensible well-being. But people are mistaken as to the extent of their information, and they attribute to them knowledge they do not possess, and make them reason about things they cannot understand. Another mistake is to try to turn their attention to matters which do not concern them in the least, such as their future interest, their happiness when they are grown up, the opinion people will have of them when they are men — terms which are absolutely meaningless when addressed to creatures who are entirely without foresight. But all the forced studies of these poor little wretches are directed towards matters utterly remote from their minds. You may judge how much attention they can give to them.

The pedagogues, who make a great display of the teaching they give their pupils, are paid to say just the opposite; yet their actions show that they think just as I do. For what do they teach? Words! words! words! Among the various sciences they boast of teaching their scholars, they take good care never to choose those which might be really useful to them, for then they would be compelled to deal with things and would fail utterly; the sciences they choose are those we seem to know when we know their technical terms — heraldry, geography, chronology, languages, etc., studies so remote from man, and even more remote from the child, that it is a wonder if he can ever make any use of any part of them.

You will be surprised to find that I reckon the study of languages among the useless lumber of education; but you must remember that I am speaking of the studies of the earliest years, and whatever you may say, I do not believe any child under twelve or fifteen ever really acquired two languages.

If the study of languages were merely the study of words, that is, of the symbols by which language expresses itself, then this might be a suitable study for children; but languages, as they change the symbols, also modify the ideas which the symbols express. Minds are formed by language, thoughts take their colour from its ideas. Reason alone is common to all. Every language has its own form, a difference which may be partly cause and partly effect of differences in national character; this conjecture appears to be confirmed by the fact that in every nation under the sun speech follows the changes of manners, and is preserved or altered along with them.

By use the child acquires one of these different forms, and it is the only language he retains till the age of reason. To acquire two languages he must be able to compare their ideas, and how can he compare ideas he can barely understand? Everything may have a thousand meanings to him, but each idea can only have one form, so he can only learn one language. You assure me he learns several languages; I deny it. I have seen those little prodigies who are supposed to speak half a dozen languages. I have heard them speak first in German, then in Latin, French, or Italian; true, they used half a dozen different vocabularies, but they always spoke German. In a word, you may give children as many synonyms as you like; it is not their language but their words that you change; they will never have but one language.

To conceal their deficiencies teachers choose the dead languages, in which we have no longer any judges whose authority is beyond dispute. The familiar use of these tongues disappeared long ago, so they are content to imitate what they find in books, and they call that talking. If the master's Greek and Latin is such poor stuff, what about the children? They have scarcely learnt their primer by heart, without understanding a word of it, when they are set to translate a French speech into Latin words; then when they are more advanced they piece together a few phrases of Cicero for prose or a few lines of Vergil for verse. Then they think they can speak Latin, and who will contradict them?

In any study whatsoever the symbols are of no value without the idea of the things symbolised. Yet the education of the child in confined to those symbols, while no one ever succeeds in making him understand the thing signified. You think you are teaching him what the world is like; he is only learning the map; he is taught the names of towns, countries, rivers, which have no existence for him except on the paper before him. I remember seeing a geography somewhere which began with: "What is the world?" — "A sphere of cardboard." That is the child's geography. I maintain that after two years' work with the globe and cosmography, there is not a single ten-year-old child who could find his way from Paris to Saint Denis by the help of the rules he has learnt. I maintain that not one of these children could find his way by the map about the paths on his father's estate without getting lost. These are the young doctors who can tell us the position of Pekin, Ispahan, Mexico, and every country in the world.

You tell me the child must be employed on studies which only need eyes. That may be; but if there are any such studies, they are unknown to me.

It is a still more ridiculous error to set them to study history, which is considered within their grasp because it is merely a collection of facts. But what is meant by this word "fact"? Do you think the relations which determine the facts of history are so easy to grasp that the corresponding ideas are easily developed in the child's mind! Do you think that a real knowledge of events can exist apart from the knowledge of their causes and effects, and that history has so little relation to words that the one can be learnt without the other? If you perceive nothing in a man's actions beyond merely physical and external movements, what do you learn from history? Absolutely nothing; while this study, robbed of all that makes it interesting, gives you neither pleasure nor information. If you want to judge actions by their moral bearings, try to make these moral bearings intelligible to your scholars. You will soon find out if they are old enough to learn history.

Remember, reader, that he who speaks to you is neither a scholar nor a philosopher, but a plain man and a lover of truth; a man who is pledged to no one party or system, a hermit, who mixes little with other men, and has less opportunity of imbibing their prejudices, and more time to reflect on the things that strike him in his intercourse with them. My arguments are based less on theories than on facts, and I think I can find no better way to bring the facts home to you than by quoting continually some example from the observations which suggested my arguments.

I had gone to spend a few days in the country with a worthy mother of a family who took great pains with her children and their education. One morning I was present while the eldest boy had his lessons. His tutor, who had taken great pains to teach him ancient history, began upon the story of Alexander and lighted on the well-known anecdote of Philip the Doctor. There is a picture of it, and the story is well worth study. The tutor, worthy man, made several reflections which I did not like with regard to Alexander's courage, but I did not argue with him lest I should lower him in the eyes of his pupil. At dinner they did not fail to get the little fellow talking, French fashion. The eager spirit of a child of his age, and the confident expectation of applause, made him say a number of silly things, and among them from time to time there were things to the point, and these made people forget the rest. At last came the story of Philip the Doctor. He told it very distinctly and prettily. After the usual meed of praise, demanded by his mother and expected by the child himself, they discussed what he had said. Most of them blamed Alexander's rashness, some of them, following the tutor's example, praised his resolution, which showed me that none of those present really saw the beauty of the story. "For my own part," I said, "if there was any courage or any steadfastness at all in Alexander's conduct I think it was only a piece of bravado." Then every one agreed that it was a piece of bravado. I was getting angry, and would have replied, when a lady sitting beside me, who had not hitherto spoken, bent towards me and whispered in my ear. "Jean Jacques," said she, "say no more, they will never understand you." I looked at her, I recognised the wisdom of her advice, and I held my tongue.

Several things made me suspect that our young professor had not in the least understood the story he told so prettily. After dinner I took his hand in mine and we went for a walk in the park. When I had questioned him quietly, I discovered that he admired the vaunted courage of Alexander more than any one. But in what do you suppose he thought this courage consisted? Merely in swallowing a disagreeable drink at a single draught without hesitation and without any signs of dislike. Not a fortnight before the poor child had been made to take some medicine which he could hardly swallow, and the taste of it was still in his mouth. Death, and death by poisoning, were for him only disagreeable sensations, and senna was his only idea of poison. I must admit, however, that Alexander's resolution had made a great impression on his young mind, and he was determined that next time he had to take medicine he would be an Alexander. Without entering upon explanations which were clearly beyond his grasp, I confirmed him in his praiseworthy intention, and returned home smiling to myself over the great wisdom of parents and teachers who expect to teach history to children.

Such words as king, emperor, war, conquest, law, and revolution are easily put into their mouths; but when it is a question of attaching clear ideas to these words the explanations are very different from our talk with Robert the gardener.

I feel sure some readers dissatisfied with that "Say no more, Jean Jacques," will ask what I really saw to admire in the conduct of Alexander. Poor things! if you need telling, how can you comprehend it? Alexander believed in virtue, he staked his head, he staked his own life on that faith, his great soul was fitted to hold such a faith. To swallow that draught was to make a noble profession of the faith that was in him. Never did mortal man recite a finer creed. If there is an Alexander in our own days, show me such deeds.

If children have no knowledge of words, there is no study that is suitable for them. If they have no real ideas they have no real memory, for I do not call that a memory which only recalls sensations. What is the use of inscribing on their brains a list of symbols which mean nothing to them? They will learn the symbols when they learn the things signified; why give them the useless trouble of learning them twice over? And yet what dangerous prejudices are you implanting when you teach them to accept as knowledge words which have no meaning for them. The first meaningless phrase, the first thing taken for granted on the word of another person without seeing its use for himself, this is the beginning of the ruin of the child's judgment. He may dazzle the eyes of fools long enough before he recovers from such a loss. [Footnote: The learning of most philosophers is like the learning of children. Vast erudition results less in the multitude of ideas than in a multitude of images. Dates, names, places, all objects isolated or unconnected with ideas are merely retained in the memory for symbols, and we rarely recall any of these without seeing the right or left page of the book in which we read it, or the form in which we first saw it. Most science was of this kind till recently. The science of our times is another matter; study and observation are things of the past; we dream and the dreams of a bad night are given to us as philosophy. You will say I too am a dreamer; I admit it, but I do what the others fail to do, I give my dreams as dreams, and leave the reader to discover whether there is anything in them which may prove useful to those who are awake.]

No, if nature has given the child this plasticity of brain which fits him to receive every kind of impression, it was not that you should imprint on it the names and dates of kings, the jargon of heraldry, the globe and geography, all those words without present meaning or future use for the child, which flood of words overwhelms his sad and barren childhood. But by means of this plasticity all the ideas he can understand and use, all that concern his happiness and will some day throw light upon his duties, should be traced at an early age in indelible characters upon his brain, to guide him to live in such a way as befits his nature and his powers.

Without the study of books, such a memory as the child may possess is not left idle; everything he sees and hears makes an impression on him, he keeps a record of men's sayings and doings, and his whole environment is the book from which he unconsciously enriches his memory, till his judgment is able to profit by it.

To select these objects, to take care to present him constantly with those he may know, to conceal from him those he ought not to know, this is the real way of training his early memory; and in this way you must try to provide him with a storehouse of knowledge which will serve for his education in youth and his conduct throughout life. True, this method does not produce infant prodigies, nor will it reflect glory upon their tutors and governesses, but it produces men, strong, right-thinking men, vigorous both in mind and body, men who do not win admiration as children, but honour as men.

Emile will not learn anything by heart, not even fables, not even the fables of La Fontaine, simple and delightful as they are, for the words are no more the fable than the words of history are history. How can people be so blind as to call fables the child's system of morals, without considering that the child is not only amused by the apologue but misled by it? He is attracted by what is false and he misses the truth, and the means adopted to make the teaching pleasant prevent him profiting by it. Men may be taught by fables; children require the naked truth.

All children learn La Fontaine's fables, but not one of them understands them. It is just as well that they do not understand, for the morality of the fables is so mixed and so unsuitable for their age that it would be more likely to incline them to vice than to virtue. "More paradoxes!" you exclaim. Paradoxes they may be; but let us see if there is not some truth in them.

I maintain that the child does not understand the fables he is taught, for however you try to explain them, the teaching you wish to extract from them demands ideas which he cannot grasp, while the poetical form which makes it easier to remember makes it harder to understand, so that clearness is sacrificed to facility. Without quoting the host of wholly unintelligible and useless fables which are taught to children because they happen to be in the same book as the others, let us keep to those which the author seems to have written specially for children.

In the whole of La Fontaine's works I only know five or six fables conspicuous for child-like simplicity; I will take the first of these as an example, for it is one whose moral is most suitable for all ages, one which children get hold of with the least difficulty, which they have most pleasure in learning, one which for this very reason the author has placed at the beginning of his book. If his object were really to delight and instruct children, this fable is his masterpiece. Let us go through it and examine it briefly.

THE CROW AND THE FOX

"Maitre corbeau, sur un arbre perche" (Mr. Crow perched on a tree). — "Mr.!" what does that word really mean? What does it mean before a proper noun? What is its meaning here? What is a crow? What is "un arbre perche"? We do not say "on a tree perched," but perched on a tree. So we must speak of poetical inversions, we must distinguish between prose and verse.

"Tenait dans son bec un fromage" (Held a cheese in his beak) — What sort of a cheese? Swiss, Brie, or Dutch? If the child has never seen crows, what is the good of talking about them? If he has seen crows will he believe that they can hold a cheese in their beak? Your illustrations should always be taken from nature.

"Maitre renard, par l'odeur alleche" (Mr. Fox, attracted by the smell). — Another Master! But the title suits the fox, — who is master of all the tricks of his trade. You must explain what a fox is, and distinguish between the real fox and the conventional fox of the fables.

"Alleche." The word is obsolete; you will have to explain it. You will say it is only used in verse. Perhaps the child will ask why people talk differently in verse. How will you answer that question?

"Alleche, par l'odeur d'un fromage." The cheese was held in his beak by a crow perched on a tree; it must indeed have smelt strong if the fox, in his thicket or his earth, could smell it. This is the way you train your pupil in that spirit of right judgment, which rejects all but reasonable arguments, and is able to distinguish between truth and falsehood in other tales.

"Lui tient a peu pres ce langage" (Spoke to him after this fashion). — "Ce langage." So foxes talk, do they! They talk like crows! Mind what you are about, oh, wise tutor; weigh your answer before you give it, it is more important than you suspect.

"Eh! Bonjour, Monsieur le Corbeau!" ("Good-day, Mr. Crow!") — Mr.! The child sees this title laughed to scorn before he knows it is a title of honour. Those who say "Monsieur du Corbeau" will find their work cut out for them to explain that "du."

"Que vous etes joli! Que vous me semblez beau!" ("How handsome you are, how beautiful in my eyes!") — Mere padding. The child, finding the same thing repeated twice over in different words, is learning to speak carelessly. If you say this redundance is a device of the author, a part of the fox's scheme to make his praise seem all the greater by his flow of words, that is a valid excuse for me, but not for my pupil.

"Sans mentir, si votre ramage" ("Without lying, if your song"). — "Without

75

lying." So people do tell lies sometimes. What will the child think of you if you tell him the fox only says "Sans mentir" because he is lying?

"Se rapporte a votre plumage" ("Answered to your fine feathers").— "Answered!" What does that mean? Try to make the child compare qualities so different as those of song and plumage; you will see how much he understands.

"Vous seriez le phenix des hotes de ces bois!" ("You would be the phoenix of all the inhabitants of this wood!")—The phoenix! What is a phoenix? All of a sudden we are floundering in the lies of antiquity—we are on the edge of mythology.

"The inhabitants of this wood." What figurative language! The flatterer adopts the grand style to add dignity to his speech, to make it more attractive. Will the child understand this cunning? Does he know, how could he possibly know, what is meant by grand style and simple style?

"A ces mots le corbeau ne se sent pas de joie" (At these words, the crow is beside himself with delight).—To realise the full force of this proverbial expression we must have experienced very strong feeling.

"Et, pour montrer sa belle voix" (And, to show his fine voice).— Remember that the child, to understand this line and the whole fable, must know what is meant by the crow's fine voice.

"Il ouvre un large bec, laisse tomber sa proie" (He opens his wide beak and drops his prey).—This is a splendid line; its very sound suggests a picture. I see the great big ugly gaping beak, I hear the cheese crashing through the branches; but this kind of beauty is thrown away upon children.

"Le renard s'en saisit, et dit, 'Mon bon monsieur'" (The fox catches it, and says, "My dear sir").—So kindness is already folly. You certainly waste no time in teaching your children.

"Apprenez que tout flatteur" ("You must learn that every flatterer").—A general maxim. The child can make neither head nor tail of it.

"Vit au depens de celui qui l'ecoute" ("Lives at the expense of the person who listens to his flattery").—No child of ten ever understood that.

"Ce lecon vaut bien un fromage, sans doute" ("No doubt this lesson is well worth a cheese").—This is intelligible and its meaning is very good. Yet there are few children who could compare a cheese and a lesson, few who would not prefer the cheese. You will therefore have to make them understand that this is said in mockery. What subtlety for a child!

"Le corbeau, honteux et confus" (The crow, ashamed and confused).—A nothing pleonasm, and there is no excuse for it this time.

"Jura, mais un peu tard, qu'on ne l'y prendrait plus" (Swore, but rather too late, that he would not be caught in that way again).—"Swore." What master will be such a fool as to try to explain to a child the meaning of an oath?

What a host of details! but much more would be needed for the analysis of all the ideas in this fable and their reduction to the simple and elementary ideas of which each is composed. But who thinks this analysis necessary to make himself intelligible to children? Who of us is philosopher enough to be able to put himself in the child's place? Let us now proceed to the moral.

Should we teach a six-year-old child that there are people who flatter and lie for the sake of gain? One might perhaps teach them that there are people who make fools of little boys and laugh at their foolish vanity behind their backs. But the whole thing is spoilt by the cheese. You are teaching them how to make another drop his cheese rather than how to keep their own. This is my second paradox, and it is not less weighty than the former one.

Watch children learning their fables and you will see that when they have a chance of applying them they almost always use them exactly contrary to the author's meaning; instead of being on their guard against the fault which you would prevent or cure, they are disposed to like the vice by which one takes advantage of another's defects. In the above fable children laugh at the crow, but they all love the fox. In the next fable you expect them to follow the example of the grasshopper. Not so, they will choose the ant. They do not care to abase themselves, they will always choose the principal part—this is the choice of self-love, a very natural choice. But what a dreadful lesson for children! There could be no monster more detestable than a harsh and avaricious child, who realised what he was asked to give and what he refused. The ant does more; she teaches him not merely to refuse but to revile.

In all the fables where the lion plays a part, usually the chief part, the child pretends to be the lion, and when he has to preside over some distribution of good things, he takes care to keep everything for himself; but when the lion is overthrown by the gnat, the child is the gnat. He learns how to sting to death those whom he dare not attack openly.

From the fable of the sleek dog and the starving wolf he learns a lesson of licence rather than the lesson of moderation which you profess to teach him. I shall never forget seeing a little girl weeping bitterly over this tale, which had been told her as a lesson in obedience. The poor child hated to be chained up; she felt the chain chafing her neck; she was crying because she was not a wolf.

So from the first of these fables the child learns the basest flattery; from the second, cruelty; from the third, injustice; from the fourth, satire; from the fifth, insubordination. The last of these lessons is no more suitable for your pupils than for mine, though he has no use for it. What results do you expect to get from your teaching when it contradicts itself! But perhaps the same system of morals which furnishes me with objections against the fables supplies you with as many reasons for keeping to them. Society requires a rule of morality in our words; it also requires a rule of morality in our deeds; and these two rules are quite different. The former is contained in the Catechism and it is left there; the other is contained in La Fontaine's fables for children and his tales for mothers. The same author does for both.

Let us make a bargain, M. de la Fontaine. For my own part, I undertake to make your books my favourite study; I undertake to love you, and to learn from your fables, for I hope I shall not mistake their meaning. As to my pupil, permit me to prevent him studying any one of them till you have convinced me that it is good for him to learn things three-fourths of which are unintelligible to him, and until you can convince me that in those fables he can understand he will never reverse the order and imitate the villain instead of taking warning from his dupe.

When I thus get rid of children's lessons, I get rid of the chief cause of their sorrows, namely their books. Reading is the curse of childhood, yet it is almost the only occupation you can find for children. Emile, at twelve years old, will hardly know what a book is. "But," you say, "he must, at least, know how to read."

When reading is of use to him, I admit he must learn to read, but till then he will only find it a nuisance.

If children are not to be required to do anything as a matter of obedience, it follows that they will only learn what they perceive to be of real and present value, either for use or enjoyment; what other motive could they have for learning? The art of speaking to our absent friends, of hearing their words; the art of letting them know at first hand our feelings, our desires, and our longings, is an art whose usefulness can be made plain at any age. How is it that this art, so useful and pleasant in itself, has become a terror to children? Because the child is compelled to acquire it against his will, and to use it for purposes beyond his comprehension. A child has no great wish to perfect himself in the use of an instrument of torture, but make it a means to his pleasure, and soon you will not be able to keep him from it.

People make a great fuss about discovering the beat way to teach children to read. They invent "bureaux" [Footnote: Translator's note.—The "bureau" was a sort of case containing letters to be put together to form words. It was a favourite device for the teaching of reading and gave its name to a special method, called the bureau-method, of learning to read.] and cards, they turn the nursery into a printer's shop. Locke would have them taught to read by means of dice. What a fine idea! And the pity of it! There is a better way than any of those, and one which is generally overlooked—it consists in the desire to learn. Arouse this desire in your scholar and have done with your "bureaux" and your dice—any method will serve.

Present interest, that is the motive power, the only motive power that takes us far and safely. Sometimes Emile receives notes of invitation from his father or mother, his relations or friends; he is invited to a dinner, a walk, a boating expedition, to see some public entertainment. These notes are short, clear, plain, and well written. Some one must read them to him, and he cannot always find anybody when wanted; no more consideration is shown to him than he himself showed to you yesterday. Time passes, the chance is lost. The note is read to him at last, but it is too late. Oh! if only he had known how to read! He receives other notes, so short, so interesting, he would like to try to read them. Sometimes he gets help, sometimes none. He does his best, and at last he makes out half the note; it is something about going to-morrow to drink cream—Where? With whom? He cannot tell—how hard he tries to make out the rest! I do not think Emile will need a "bureau." Shall I proceed to the teaching of writing? No, I am ashamed to toy with these trifles in a treatise on education.

I will just add a few words which contain a principle of great importance. It is this—What we are in no hurry to get is usually obtained with speed and certainty. I am pretty sure Emile will learn to read and write before he is ten, just because I care very little whether he can do so before he is fifteen; but I would rather he never learnt to read at all, than that this art should be acquired at the price of all that makes reading useful. What is the use of reading to him if he always hates it? "Id imprimis cavere oportebit, ne studia, qui amare nondum potest, oderit, et amaritudinem semel perceptam etiam ultra rudes annos reformidet."—Quintil.

The more I urge my method of letting well alone, the more objections I perceive against it. If your pupil learns nothing from you, he will learn from others. If you do not instil truth he will learn falsehoods; the prejudices you fear to teach him he will acquire from those about him, they will find their way through every one of his senses; they will either corrupt his reason before it is fully developed or his mind will become torpid through inaction, and will become engrossed in material things. If we do not form the habit of thinking as children, we shall lose the power of thinking for the rest of our life.

I fancy I could easily answer that objection, but why should I answer every objection? If my method itself answers your objections, it is good; if not, it is good for nothing. I continue my explanation.

If, in accordance with the plan I have sketched, you follow rules which are just the opposite of the established practice, if instead of taking your scholar far afield, instead of wandering with him in distant places, in far-off lands, in remote centuries, in the ends of the earth, and in the very heavens themselves, you try to keep him to himself, to his own concerns, you will then find him able to perceive, to remember, and even to reason; this is nature's order. As the sentient being becomes active his discernment develops along with his strength. Not till his strength is in excess of what is needed for self-preservation, is the speculative faculty developed, the faculty adapted for using this superfluous strength for other purposes. Would you cultivate your pupil's intelligence, cultivate the strength it is meant to control. Give his body constant exercise, make it strong and healthy, in order to make him good and wise; let him work, let him do things, let him run and shout, let him be always on the go; make a man of him in strength, and he will soon be a man in reason.

Of course by this method you will make him stupid if you are always giving him directions, always saying come here, go there, stop, do this, don't do that. If your head always guides his hands, his own mind will become useless. But remember the conditions we laid down; if you are a mere pedant it is not worth your while to read my book.

It is a lamentable mistake to imagine that bodily activity hinders the working of the mind, as if these two kinds of activity ought not to advance hand in hand, and as if the one were not intended to act as guide to the other.

There are two classes of men who are constantly engaged in bodily activity, peasants and savages, and certainly neither of these pays the least attention to the cultivation of the mind. Peasants are rough, coarse, and clumsy; savages are noted, not only for their keen senses, but for great subtility of mind. Speaking generally, there is nothing duller than a peasant or sharper than a savage. What is the cause of this difference? The peasant has always done as he was told, what his father did before him, what he himself has always done; he is the creature of habit, he spends his life almost like an automaton on the same tasks; habit and obedience have taken the place of reason.

The case of the savage is very different; he is tied to no one place, he has no prescribed task, no superior to obey, he knows no law but his own will; he is therefore forced to reason at every step he takes. He can neither move nor walk without considering the consequences. Thus the more his body is exercised, the more alert is his mind; his strength and his reason increase together, and each helps to develop the other.

Oh, learned tutor, let us see which of our two scholars is most like the savage and which is most like the peasant. Your scholar is subject to a power which is continually giving him instruction; he acts only at the word of command; he dare not eat when he is hungry, nor laugh when he is merry, nor weep when he is sad, nor offer one hand rather than the other, nor stir a foot unless he is told to do it; before long he will not venture to breathe without orders. What would you have him think about, when you do all the thinking for him? He rests securely on your foresight, why should he think for himself? He knows you have undertaken to take care of him, to secure his welfare, and he feels himself freed from this responsibility. His judgment relies on yours; what you have not forbidden that he does, knowing that he runs no risk. Why should he learn the signs of rain? He knows you watch the clouds for him. Why should he time his walk? He knows there is no fear of your letting him miss his dinner hour. He eats till you tell him to stop, he stops when you tell him to do so; he does not attend to the teaching of his own stomach, but yours. In vain do you make his body soft by inaction; his understanding does not become subtle. Far from it, you complete your task of discrediting reason in his eyes, by making him use such reasoning power as he has on the things which seem of least importance to him. As he never finds his reason any use to him, he decides at last that it is useless. If he reasons badly he will be found fault with; nothing worse will happen to him; and he has been found fault with so often that he pays no attention to it, such a common danger no longer alarms him.

Yet you will find he has a mind. He is quick enough to chatter with the women in the way I spoke of further back; but if he is in danger, if he must come to a decision in difficult circumstances, you will find him a hundredfold more stupid and silly than the son of the roughest labourer.

As for my pupil, or rather Nature's pupil, he has been trained from the outset to be as self-reliant as possible, he has not formed the habit of constantly seeking help from others, still less of displaying his stores of learning. On the other hand, he exercises discrimination and forethought, he reasons about everything that concerns himself. He does not chatter, he acts. Not a word does he know of what is going on in the world at large, but he knows very thoroughly what affects himself. As he is always stirring he is compelled to notice many things, to recognise many effects; he soon acquires a good deal of experience. Nature, not man, is his schoolmaster, and he learns all the quicker because he is not aware that he has any lesson to learn. So mind and body work together. He is always carrying out his own ideas, not those of other people, and thus he unites thought and action; as he grows in health and strength he grows in wisdom and discernment. This is the way to attain later on to what is generally considered incompatible, though most great men have achieved it, strength of body and strength of mind, the reason of the philosopher and the vigour of the athlete.

Young teacher, I am setting before you a difficult task, the art of controlling without precepts, and doing everything without doing anything at all. This art is, I confess, beyond your years, it is not calculated to display your talents nor to make your value known to your scholar's parents; but it is the only road to success. You will never succeed in making wise men if you do not first make little imps of mischief. This was the education of the Spartans; they were not taught to stick to their books, they were set to steal their dinners. Were they any the worse for it in after life? Ever ready for victory, they crushed their foes in every kind of warfare, and the prating Athenians were as much afraid of their words as of their blows.

When education is most carefully attended to, the teacher issues his orders and thinks himself master, but it is the child who is really master. He uses the tasks you set him to obtain what he wants from you, and he can always make you pay for an hour's industry by a week's complaisance. You must always be making bargains with him. These bargains, suggested in your fashion, but carried out in his, always follow the direction of his own fancies, especially when you are foolish enough to make the condition some advantage he is almost sure to obtain, whether he fulfils his part of the bargain or not. The child is usually much quicker to read the master's thoughts than the master to read the child's feelings. And that is as it should be, for all the sagacity which the child would have devoted to self-preservation, had he been left to himself, is now devoted to the rescue of his native freedom from the chains of his tyrant; while the latter, who has no such pressing need to understand the child, sometimes finds that it pays him better to leave him in idleness or vanity.

Take the opposite course with your pupil; let him always think he is master while you are really master. There is no subjection so complete as that which preserves the forms of freedom; it is thus that the will itself is taken captive. Is not this poor child, without knowledge, strength, or wisdom, entirely at your mercy? Are you not master of his whole environment so far as it affects him? Cannot you make of him what you please? His work and play, his pleasure and pain, are they not, unknown to him, under your control? No doubt he ought only to do what he wants, but he ought to want to do nothing but what you want him to do. He should never take a step you have not foreseen, nor utter a word you could not foretell.

Then he can devote himself to the bodily exercises adapted to his age without brutalising his mind; instead of developing his cunning to evade an unwelcome control, you will then find him entirely occupied in getting the best he can out of his environment with a view to his present welfare, and you will be surprised by the subtlety of the means he devises to get for himself such things as he can obtain, and to really enjoy things without the aid of other people's ideas. You leave him master of his own wishes, but you do not multiply his caprices. When he only does what he wants, he will soon only do what he ought, and although his body is constantly in motion, so far as his sensible and present interests are concerned, you will find him developing all the reason of which he is capable, far better and in a manner much better fitted for him than in purely theoretical studies.

Thus when he does not find you continually thwarting him, when he no longer distrusts you, no longer has anything to conceal from you, he will neither tell you lies nor deceive you; he will show himself fearlessly as he really is, and you can study him at your ease, and surround him with all the lessons you would have him learn, without awaking his suspicions.

Neither will he keep a curious and jealous eye on your own conduct, nor take a secret delight in catching you at fault. It is a great thing to avoid this. One of the child's first objects is, as I have said, to find the weak spots in its rulers. Though this leads to spitefulness, it does not arise from it, but from the desire to evade a disagreeable control. Overburdened by the yoke laid upon him, he tries to shake it off, and the faults he finds in his master give him a good opportunity for this. Still the habit of spying out faults and delighting in them grows upon people. Clearly we have stopped another of the springs of vice in Emile's heart. Having nothing to gain from my faults, he will not be on the watch for them, nor will he be tempted to look out for the faults of others.

All these methods seem difficult because they are new to us, but they ought not to be really difficult. I have a right to assume that you have the knowledge required for the business you have chosen; that you know the usual course of development of the human thought, that you can study mankind and man, that you know beforehand the effect on your pupil's will of the various objects suited to his age which you put before him. You have the tools and the art to use them; are you not master of your trade?

You speak of childish caprice; you are mistaken. Children's caprices are never the work of nature, but of bad discipline; they have either obeyed or given orders, and I have said again and again, they must do neither. Your pupil will have the caprices you have taught him; it is fair you should bear the punishment of your own faults. "But how can I cure them?" do you say? That may still be done by better conduct on your own part and great patience. I once undertook the charge of a child for a few weeks; he was accustomed not only to have his own way, but to make every one else do as he pleased; he was therefore capricious. The very first day he wanted to get up at midnight, to try how far he could go with me. When I was sound asleep he jumped out of bed, got his dressing-gown, and waked me up. I got up and lighted the candle, which was all he wanted. After a quarter of an hour he became sleepy and went back to bed quite satisfied with his experiment. Two days later he repeated it, with the same success and with no sign of impatience on my part. When he kissed me as he lay down, I said to him very quietly, "My little dear, this is all very well, but do not try it again." His curiosity was aroused by this, and the very next day he did not fail to get up at the same time and woke me to see whether I should dare to disobey him. I asked what he wanted, and he told me he could not sleep. "So much the worse for you," I replied, and I lay quiet. He seemed perplexed by this way of speaking. He felt his way to the flint and steel and tried to strike a light. I could not help laughing when I heard him strike his fingers. Convinced at last that he could not manage it, he brought the steel to my bed; I told him I did not want it, and I turned my back to him. Then he began to rush wildly about the room, shouting, singing, making a great noise, knocking against chairs and tables, but taking, however, good care not to hurt himself seriously, but screaming loudly in the hope of alarming me. All this had no effect, but I perceived that though he was prepared for scolding or anger, he was quite unprepared for indifference.

However, he was determined to overcome my patience with his own obstinacy, and he continued his racket so successfully that at last I lost my temper. I foresaw that I should spoil the whole business by an unseemly outburst of passion. I determined on another course. I got up quietly, went to the tinder box, but could not find it; I asked him for it, and he gave it me, delighted to have won the victory over me. I struck a light, lighted the candle, took my young gentleman by the hand and led him quietly into an adjoining dressing-room with the shutters firmly fastened, and nothing he could break.

I left him there without a light; then locking him in I went back to my bed without a word. What a noise there was! That was what I expected, and took no notice. At last the noise ceased; I listened, heard him settling down, and I was quite easy about him. Next morning I entered the room at daybreak, and my little rebel was lying on a sofa enjoying a sound and much needed sleep after his exertions.

The matter did not end there. His mother heard that the child had spent a great part of the night out of bed. That spoilt the whole thing; her child was as good as dead. Finding a good chance for revenge, he pretended to be ill, not seeing that he would gain nothing by it. They sent for the doctor. Unluckily for the mother, the doctor was a practical joker, and to amuse himself with her terrors he did his best to increase them. However, he whispered to me, "Leave it to me, I promise to cure the child of wanting to be ill for some time to come." As a matter of fact he prescribed bed and dieting, and the child was handed over to the apothecary. I sighed to see the mother cheated on every hand except by me, whom she hated because I did not deceive her.

After pretty severe reproaches, she told me her son was delicate, that he was the sole heir of the family, his life must be preserved at all costs, and she would not have him contradicted. In that I thoroughly agreed with her, but what she meant by contradicting was not obeying him in everything. I saw I should have to treat the mother as I had treated the son. "Madam," I said coldly, "I do not know how to educate the heir to a fortune, and what is more, I do not mean to study that art. You can take that as settled." I was wanted for some days longer, and the father smoothed things over. The mother wrote to the tutor to hasten his return, and the child, finding he got nothing by disturbing my rest, nor yet by being ill, decided at last to get better and to go to sleep.

You can form no idea of the number of similar caprices to which the little tyrant had subjected his unlucky tutor; for his education was carried on under his mother's eye, and she would not allow her son and heir to be disobeyed in anything. Whenever he wanted to go out, you must be ready to take him, or rather to follow him, and he always took good care to choose the time when he knew his tutor was very busy. He wished to exercise the same power over me and to avenge himself by day for having to leave me in peace at night. I gladly agreed and began by showing plainly how pleased I was to give him pleasure; after that when it was a matter of curing him of his fancies I set about it differently.

In the first place, he must be shown that he was in the wrong. This was not difficult; knowing that children think only of the present, I took the easy advantage which foresight gives; I took care to provide him with some indoor amusement of which he was very fond. Just when he was most occupied with it, I went and suggested a short walk, and he sent me away. I insisted, but he paid no attention. I had to give in, and he took note of this sign of submission.

The next day it was my turn. As I expected, he got tired of his occupation; I, however, pretended to be very busy. That was enough to decide him. He came to drag me from my work, to take him at once for a walk. I refused; he persisted. "No," I said, "when I did what you wanted, you taught me how to get my own way; I shall not go out." "Very well," he replied eagerly, "I shall go out by myself." "As you please," and I returned to my work.

He put on his things rather uneasily when he saw I did not follow his example. When he was ready he came and made his bow; I bowed too; he tried to frighten me with stories of the expeditions he was going to make; to hear him talk you would think he was going to the world's end. Quite unmoved, I wished him a pleasant journey. He became more and more perplexed. However, he put a good face on it, and when he was ready to go out he told his foot man to follow him. The footman, who had his instructions, replied that he had no time, and that he was busy carrying out my orders, and he must obey me first. For the moment the child was taken aback. How could he think they would really let him go out alone, him, who, in his own eyes, was the most important person in the world, who thought that everything in heaven and earth was wrapped up in his welfare? However, he was beginning to feel his weakness, he perceived that he should find himself alone among people who knew nothing of him. He saw beforehand the risks he would run; obstinacy alone sustained him; very slowly and unwillingly he went downstairs. At last he went out into the street, consoling himself a little for the harm that might happen to himself, in the hope that I should be held responsible for it.

This was just what I expected. All was arranged beforehand, and as it meant some sort of public scene I had got his father's consent. He had scarcely gone a few steps, when he heard, first on this side then on that, all sorts of remarks about himself. "What a pretty little gentleman, neighbour? Where is he going all alone? He will get lost! I will ask him into our house." "Take care you don't. Don't you see he is a naughty little boy, who has been turned out of his own house because he is good for nothing? You must not stop naughty boys; let him go where he likes." "Well, well; the good God take care of him. I should be sorry if anything happened to him." A little further on he met some young urchins of about his own age who teased him and made fun of him. The further he got the more difficulties he found. Alone and unprotected he was at the mercy of everybody, and he found to his great surprise that his shoulder knot and his gold lace commanded no respect.

However, I had got a friend of mine, who was a stranger to him, to keep an eye on him. Unnoticed by him, this friend followed him step by step, and in due time he spoke to him. The role, like that of Sbrigani in Pourceaugnac, required an intelligent actor, and it was played to perfection. Without making the child fearful and timid by inspiring excessive terror, he made him realise so thoroughly the folly of his exploit that in half an hour's time he brought him home to me, ashamed and humble, and afraid to look me in the face.

To put the finishing touch to his discomfiture, just as he was coming in his father came down on his way out and met him on the stairs. He had to explain where he had been, and why I was not with him. [Footnote: In a case like this there is no danger in asking a child to tell the truth, for he knows very well that it cannot be hid, and that if he ventured to tell a lie he would be found out at once.] The poor child would gladly have sunk into the earth. His father did not take the trouble to scold him at length, but said with more severity than I should have expected, "When you want to go out by yourself, you can do so, but I will not have a rebel in my house, so when you go, take good care that you never come back."

As for me, I received him somewhat gravely, but without blame and without mockery, and for fear he should find out we had been playing with him, I declined to take him out walking that day. Next day I was well pleased to find that he passed in triumph with me through the very same people who had mocked him the previous day, when they met him out by himself. You may be sure he never threatened to go out without me again.

By these means and other like them I succeeded during the short time I was with him in getting him to do everything I wanted without bidding him or forbidding him to do anything, without preaching or exhortation, without wearying him with unnecessary lessons. So he was pleased when I spoke to him, but when I was silent he was frightened, for he knew there was something amiss, and he always got his lesson from the thing itself. But let us return to our subject.

The body is strengthened by this constant exercise under the guidance of nature herself, and far from brutalising the mind, this exercise develops in it the only kind of reason of which young children are capable, the kind of reason most necessary at every age. It teaches us how to use our strength, to perceive the relations between our own and neighbouring bodies, to use the natural tools, which are within our reach and adapted to our senses. Is there anything sillier than a child brought up indoors under his mother's eye, who, in his ignorance of weight and resistance, tries to uproot a tall tree or pick up a rock. The first time I found myself outside Geneva I tried to catch a galloping horse, and I threw stones at Mont Saleve, two leagues away; I was the laughing stock of the whole village, and was supposed to be a regular idiot. At eighteen we are taught in our natural philosophy the use of the lever; every village boy of twelve knows how to use a lever better than the cleverest mechanician in the academy. The lessons the scholars learn from one another in the playground are worth a hundredfold more than what they learn in the class-room.

Watch a cat when she comes into a room for the first time; she goes from place to place, she sniffs about and examines everything, she is never still for a moment; she is suspicious of everything till she has examined it and found out what it is. It is the same with the child when he begins to walk, and enters, so to speak, the room of the world around him. The only difference is that, while both use sight, the child uses his hands and the cat that subtle sense of smell which nature has bestowed upon it. It is this instinct, rightly or wrongly educated, which makes children skilful or clumsy, quick or slow, wise or foolish.

Man's primary natural goals are, therefore, to measure himself against his environment, to discover in every object he sees those sensible qualities which may concern himself, so his first study is a kind of experimental physics for his own preservation. He is turned away from this and sent to speculative studies before he has found his proper place in the world. While his delicate and flexible limbs can adjust themselves to the bodies upon which they are intended to act, while his senses are keen and as yet free from illusions, then is the time to exercise both limbs and senses in their proper business. It is the time to learn to perceive the physical relations between ourselves and things. Since everything that comes into the human mind enters through the gates of sense, man's first reason is a reason of sense-experience. It is this that serves as a foundation for the reason of the intelligence; our first teachers in natural philosophy are our feet, hands, and eyes. To substitute books for them does not teach us to reason, it teaches us to use the reason of others rather than our own; it teaches us to believe much and know little.

Before you can practise an art you must first get your tools; and if you are to make good use of those tools, they must be fashioned sufficiently strong to stand use. To learn to think we must therefore exercise our limbs, our senses, and our bodily organs, which are the tools of the intellect; and to get the best use out of these tools, the body which supplies us with them must be strong and healthy. Not only is it quite a mistake that true reason is developed apart from the body, but it is a good bodily constitution which makes the workings of the mind easy and correct.

While I am showing how the child's long period of leisure should be spent, I am entering into details which may seem absurd. You will say, "This is a strange sort of education, and it is subject to your own criticism, for it only teaches what no one needs to learn. Why spend your time in teaching what will come of itself without care or trouble? Is there any child of twelve who is ignorant of all you wish to teach your pupil, while he also knows what his master has taught him."

Gentlemen, you are mistaken. I am teaching my pupil an art, the acquirement of which demands much time and trouble, an art which your scholars certainly do not possess; it is the art of being ignorant; for the knowledge of any one who only thinks he knows, what he really does know is a very small matter. You teach science; well and good; I am busy fashioning the necessary tools for its acquisition. Once upon a time, they say the Venetians were displaying the treasures of the Cathedral of Saint Mark to the Spanish ambassador; the only comment he made was, "Qui non c'e la radice." When I see a tutor showing off his pupil's learning, I am always tempted to say the same to him.

Every one who has considered the manner of life among the ancients, attributes the strength of body and mind by which they are distinguished from the men of our own day to their gymnastic exercises. The stress laid by Montaigne upon this opinion, shows that it had made a great impression on him; he returns to it again and again. Speaking of a child's education he says, "To strengthen the mind you must harden the muscles; by training the child to labour you train him to suffering; he must be broken in to the hardships of gymnastic exercises to prepare him for the hardships of dislocations, colics, and other bodily ills." The philosopher Locke, the worthy Rollin, the learned Fleury, the pedant De Crouzas, differing as they do so widely from one another, are agreed in this one matter of sufficient bodily exercise for children. This is the wisest of their precepts, and the one which is certain to be neglected. I have already dwelt sufficiently on its importance, and as better reasons and more sensible rules cannot be found than those in Locke's book, I will content myself with referring to it, after taking the liberty of adding a few remarks of my own.

The limbs of a growing child should be free to move easily in his clothing; nothing should cramp their growth or movement; there should be nothing tight, nothing fitting closely to the body, no belts of any kind. The French style of dress, uncomfortable and unhealthy for a man, is especially bad for children. The stagnant humours, whose circulation is interrupted, putrify in a state of inaction, and this process proceeds more rapidly in an inactive and sedentary life; they become corrupt and give rise to scurvy; this disease, which is continually on the increase among us, was almost unknown to the ancients, whose way of dressing and living protected them from it. The hussar's dress, far from correcting this fault, increases it, and compresses the whole of the child's body, by way of dispensing with a few bands. The best plan is to keep children in frocks as long as possible and then to provide them with loose clothing, without trying to define the shape which is only another way of deforming it. Their defects of body and mind may all be traced to the same source, the desire to make men of them before their time.

There are bright colours and dull; children like the bright colours best, and they suit them better too. I see no reason why such natural suitability should not be taken into consideration; but as soon as they prefer a material because it is rich, their hearts are already given over to luxury, to every caprice of fashion, and this taste is certainly not their own. It is impossible to say how much education is influenced by this choice of clothes, and the motives for this choice. Not only do short-sighted mothers offer ornaments as rewards to their children, but there are foolish tutors who threaten to make their pupils wear the plainest and coarsest clothes as a punishment. "If you do not do your lessons better, if you do not take more care of your clothes, you shall be dressed like that little peasant boy." This is like saying to them, "Understand that clothes make the man." Is it to be wondered at that our young people profit by such wise teaching, that they care for nothing but dress, and that they only judge of merit by its outside.

If I had to bring such a spoilt child to his senses, I would take care that his smartest clothes were the most uncomfortable, that he was always cramped, constrained, and embarrassed in every way; freedom and mirth should flee before his splendour. If he wanted to take part in the games of children more simply dressed, they should cease their play and run away. Before long I should make him so tired and sick of his magnificence, such a slave to his gold-laced coat, that it would become the plague of his life, and he would be less afraid to behold the darkest dungeon than to see the preparations for his adornment. Before the child is enslaved by our prejudices his first wish is always to be free and comfortable. The plainest and most comfortable clothes, those which leave him most liberty, are what he always likes best.

There are habits of body suited for an active life and others for a sedentary life. The latter leaves the humours an equable and uniform course, and the body should be protected from changes in temperature; the former is constantly passing from action to rest, from heat to cold, and the body should be inured to these changes. Hence people, engaged in sedentary pursuits indoors, should always be warmly dressed, to keep their bodies as nearly as possible at the same temperature at all times and seasons. Those, however, who come and go in sun, wind, and rain, who take much exercise, and spend most of their time out of doors, should always be lightly clad, so as to get used to the changes in the air and to every degree of temperature without suffering inconvenience. I would advise both never to change their clothes with the changing seasons, and that would be the invariable habit of my pupil Emile. By this I do not mean that he should wear his winter clothes in summer like many people of sedentary habits, but that he should wear his summer clothes in winter like hard-working folk. Sir Isaac Newton always did this, and he lived to be eighty.

Emile should wear little or nothing on his head all the year round. The ancient Egyptians always went bareheaded; the Persians used to wear heavy tiaras and still wear large turbans, which according to Chardin are required by their climate. I have remarked elsewhere on the difference observed by Herodotus on a battle-field between the skulls of the Persians and those of the Egyptians. Since it is desirable that the bones of the skull should grow harder and more substantial, less fragile and porous, not only to protect the brain against injuries but against colds, fever, and every influence of the air, you should therefore accustom your children to go bare-headed winter and summer, day and night. If you make them wear a night-cap to keep their hair clean and tidy, let it be thin and transparent like the nets with which the Basques cover their hair. I am aware that most mothers will be more impressed by Chardin's observations than my arguments, and will think that all climates are the climate of Persia, but I did not choose a European pupil to turn him into an Asiatic.

Children are generally too much wrapped up, particularly in infancy. They should be accustomed to cold rather than heat; great cold never does them any harm, if they are exposed to it soon enough; but their skin is still too soft and tender and leaves too free a course for perspiration, so that they are inevitably exhausted by excessive heat. It has been observed that infant mortality is greatest in August. Moreover, it seems certain from a comparison of northern and southern races that we become stronger by bearing extreme cold rather than excessive heat. But as the child's body grows bigger and his muscles get stronger, train him gradually to bear the rays of the sun. Little by little you will harden him till he can face the burning heat of the tropics without danger.

Locke, in the midst of the manly and sensible advice he gives us, falls into inconsistencies one would hardly expect in such a careful thinker. The same man who would have children take an ice-cold bath summer and winter, will not let them drink cold water when they are hot, or lie on damp grass. But he would never have their shoes water-tight; and why should they let in more water when the child is hot than when he is cold, and may we not draw the same inference with regard to the feet and body that he draws with regard to the hands and feet and the body and face? If he would have a man all face, why blame me if I would have him all feet?

To prevent children drinking when they are hot, he says they should be trained to eat a piece of bread first. It is a strange thing to make a child eat because he is thirsty; I would as soon give him a drink when he is hungry. You will never convince me that our first instincts are so ill-regulated that we cannot satisfy them without endangering our lives. Were that so, the man would have perished over and over again before he had learned how to keep himself alive.

Whenever Emile is thirsty let him have a drink, and let him drink fresh water just as it is, not even taking the chill off it in the depths of winter and when he is bathed in perspiration. The only precaution I advise is to take care what sort of water you give him. If the water comes from a river, give it him just as it is; if it is spring-water let it stand a little exposed to the air before he drinks it. In warm weather rivers are warm; it is not so with springs, whose water has not been in contact with the air. You must wait till the temperature of the water is the same as that of the air. In winter, on the other hand, spring water is safer than river water. It is, however, unusual and unnatural to perspire greatly in winter, especially in the open air, for the cold air constantly strikes the skin and drives the perspiration inwards, and prevents the pores opening enough to give it passage. Now I do not intend Emile to take his exercise by the fireside in winter, but in the open air and among the ice. If he only gets warm with making and throwing snowballs, let him drink when he is thirsty, and go on with his game after drinking, and you need not be afraid of any ill effects. And if any other exercise makes him perspire let him drink cold water even in winter provided he is thirsty. Only take care to take him to get the water some little distance away. In such cold as I am supposing, he would have cooled down sufficiently when he got there to be able to drink without danger. Above all, take care to conceal these precautions from him. I would rather he were ill now and then, than always thinking about his health.

Since children take such violent exercise they need a great deal of sleep. The one makes up for the other, and this shows that both are necessary. Night is the time set apart by nature for rest. It is an established fact that sleep is quieter and calmer when the sun is below the horizon, and that our senses are less calm when the air is warmed by the rays of the sun. So it is certainly the healthiest plan to rise with the sun and go to bed with the sun. Hence in our country man and all the other animals with him want more sleep in winter than in summer. But town life is so complex, so unnatural, so subject to chances and changes, that it is not wise to accustom a man to such uniformity that he cannot do without it. No doubt he must submit to rules; but the chief rule is this—be able to break the rule if necessary. So do not be so foolish as to soften your pupil by letting him always sleep his sleep out. Leave him at first to the law of nature without any hindrance, but never forget that under our conditions he must rise above this law; he must be able to go to bed late and rise early, be awakened suddenly, or sit up all night without ill effects. Begin early and proceed gently, a step at a time, and the constitution adapts itself to the very conditions which would destroy it if they were imposed for the first time on the grown man.

In the next place he must be accustomed to sleep in an uncomfortable bed, which is the best way to find no bed uncomfortable. Speaking generally, a hard life, when once we have become used to it, increases our pleasant experiences; an easy life prepares the way for innumerable unpleasant experiences. Those who are too tenderly nurtured can only sleep on down; those who are used to sleep on bare boards can find them anywhere. There is no such thing as a hard bed for the man who falls asleep at once.

The body is, so to speak, melted and dissolved in a soft bed where one sinks into feathers and eider-down. The reins when too warmly covered become inflamed. Stone and other diseases are often due to this, and it invariably produces a delicate constitution, which is the seed-ground of every ailment.

The best bed is that in which we get the best sleep. Emile and I will prepare such a bed for ourselves during the daytime. We do not need Persian slaves to make our beds; when we are digging the soil we are turning our mattresses. I know that a healthy child may be made to sleep or wake almost at will. When the child is put to bed and his nurse grows weary of his chatter, she says to him, "Go to sleep." That is much like saying, "Get well," when he is ill. The right way is to let him get tired of himself. Talk so much that he is compelled to hold his tongue, and he will soon be asleep. Here is at least one use for sermons, and you may as well preach to him as rock his cradle; but if you use this narcotic at night, do not use it by day.

I shall sometimes rouse Emile, not so much to prevent his sleeping too much, as to accustom him to anything—even to waking with a start. Moreover, I should be unfit for my business if I could not make him wake himself, and get up, so to speak, at my will, without being called.

If he wakes too soon, I shall let him look forward to a tedious morning, so that he will count as gain any time he can give to sleep. If he sleeps too late I shall show him some favourite toy when he wakes. If I want him to wake at a given hour I shall say, "To-morrow at six I am going fishing," or "I shall take a walk to such and such a place. Would you like to come too?" He assents, and begs me to wake him. I promise, or do not promise, as the case requires. If he wakes too late, he finds me gone. There is something amiss if he does not soon learn to wake himself.

Moreover, should it happen, though it rarely does, that a sluggish child desires to stagnate in idleness, you must not give way to this tendency, which might stupefy him entirely, but you must apply some stimulus to wake him. You must understand that is no question of applying force, but of arousing some appetite which leads to action, and such an appetite, carefully selected on the lines laid down by nature, kills two birds with one stone.

If one has any sort of skill, I can think of nothing for which a taste, a very passion, cannot be aroused in children, and that without vanity, emulation, or jealousy. Their keenness, their spirit of imitation, is enough of itself; above all, there is their natural liveliness, of which no teacher so far has contrived to take advantage. In every game, when they are quite sure it is only play, they endure without complaint, or even with laughter, hardships which they would not submit to otherwise without floods of tears. The sports of the young savage involve long fasting, blows, burns, and fatigue of every kind, a proof that even pain has a charm of its own, which may remove its bitterness.

It is not every master, however, who knows how to season this dish, nor can every scholar eat it without making faces. However, I must take care or I shall be wandering off again after exceptions.

It is not to be endured that man should become the slave of pain, disease, accident, the perils of life, or even death itself; the more familiar he becomes with these ideas the sooner he will be cured of that over-sensitiveness which adds to the pain by impatience in bearing it; the sooner he becomes used to the sufferings which may overtake him, the sooner he shall, as Montaigne has put it, rob those pains of the sting of unfamiliarity, and so make his soul strong and invulnerable; his body will be the coat of mail which stops all the darts which might otherwise find a vital part. Even the approach of death, which is not death itself, will scarcely be felt as such; he will not die, he will be, so to speak, alive or dead and nothing more. Montaigne might say of him as he did of a certain king of Morocco, "No man ever prolonged his life so far into death." A child serves his apprenticeship in courage and endurance as well as in other virtues; but you cannot teach children these virtues by name alone; they must learn them unconsciously through experience.

But speaking of death, what steps shall I take with regard to my pupil and the smallpox? Shall he be inoculated in infancy, or shall I wait till he takes it in the natural course of things? The former plan is more in accordance with our practice, for it preserves his life at a time when it is of greater value, at the cost of some danger when his life is of less worth; if indeed we can use the word danger with regard to inoculation when properly performed.

But the other plan is more in accordance with our general principles — to leave nature to take the precautions she delights in, precautions she abandons whenever man interferes. The natural man is always ready; let nature inoculate him herself, she will choose the fitting occasion better than we.

Do not think I am finding fault with inoculation, for my reasons for exempting my pupil from it do not in the least apply to yours. Your training does not prepare them to escape catching smallpox as soon as they are exposed to infection. If you let them take it anyhow, they will probably die. I perceive that in different lands the resistance to inoculation is in proportion to the need for it; and the reason is plain. So I scarcely condescend to discuss this question with regard to Emile. He will be inoculated or not according to time, place, and circumstances; it is almost a matter of indifference, as far as he is concerned. If it gives him smallpox, there will be the advantage of knowing what to expect, knowing what the disease is; that is a good thing, but if he catches it naturally it will have kept him out of the doctor's hands, which is better.

An exclusive education, which merely tends to keep those who have received it apart from the mass of mankind, always selects such teaching as is costly rather than cheap, even when the latter is of more use. Thus all carefully educated young men learn to ride, because it is costly, but scarcely any of them learn to swim, as it costs nothing, and an artisan can swim as well as any one. Yet without passing through the riding school, the traveller learns to mount his horse, to stick on it, and to ride well enough for practical purposes; but in the water if you cannot swim you will drown, and we cannot swim unless we are taught. Again, you are not forced to ride on pain of death, while no one is sure of escaping such a common danger as drowning. Emile shall be as much at home in the water as on land. Why should he not be able to live in every element? If he could learn to fly, he should be an eagle; I would make him a salamander, if he could bear the heat.

People are afraid lest the child should be drowned while he is learning to swim; if he dies while he is learning, or if he dies because he has not learnt, it will be your own fault. Foolhardiness is the result of vanity; we are not rash when no one is looking. Emile will not be foolhardy, though all the world were watching him. As the exercise does not depend on its danger, he will learn to swim the Hellespont by swimming, without any danger, a stream in his father's park; but he must get used to danger too, so as not to be flustered by it. This is an essential part of the apprenticeship I spoke of just now. Moreover, I shall take care to proportion the danger to his strength, and I shall always share it myself, so that I need scarcely fear any imprudence if I take as much care for his life as for my own.

A child is smaller than a man; he has not the man's strength or reason, but he sees and hears as well or nearly as well; his sense of taste is very good, though he is less fastidious, and he distinguishes scents as clearly though less sensuously. The senses are the first of our faculties to mature; they are those most frequently overlooked or neglected.

To train the senses it is not enough merely to use them; we must learn to judge by their means, to learn to feel, so to speak; for we cannot touch, see, or hear, except as we have been taught.

There is a mere natural and mechanical use of the senses which strengthens the body without improving the judgment. It is all very well to swim, run, jump, whip a top, throw stones; but have we nothing but arms and legs? Have we not eyes and ears as well; and are not these organs necessary for the use of the rest? Do not merely exercise the strength, exercise all the senses by which it is guided; make the best use of every one of them, and check the results of one by the other. Measure, count, weigh, compare. Do not use force till you have estimated the resistance; let the estimation of the effect always precede the application of the means. Get the child interested in avoiding insufficient or superfluous efforts. If in this way you train him to calculate the effects of all his movements, and to correct his mistakes by experience, is it not clear that the more he does the wiser he will become?

Take the case of moving a heavy mass; if he takes too long a lever, he will waste his strength; if it is too short, he will not have strength enough; experience will teach him to use the very stick he needs. This knowledge is not beyond his years. Take, for example, a load to be carried; if he wants to carry as much as he can, and not to take up more than he can carry, must he not calculate the weight by the appearance? Does he know how to compare masses of like substance and different size, or to choose between masses of the same size and different substances? He must set to work to compare their specific weights. I have seen a young man, very highly educated, who could not be convinced, till he had tried it, that a bucket full of blocks of oak weighed less than the same bucket full of water.

All our senses are not equally under our control. One of them, touch, is always busy during our waking hours; it is spread over the whole surface of the body, like a sentinel ever on the watch to warn us of anything which may do us harm. Whether we will or not, we learn to use it first of all by experience, by constant practice, and therefore we have less need for special training for it. Yet we know that the blind have a surer and more delicate sense of touch than we, for not being guided by the one sense, they are forced to get from the touch what we get from sight. Why, then, are not we trained to walk as they do in the dark, to recognise what we touch, to distinguish things about us; in a word, to do at night and in the dark what they do in the daytime without sight? We are better off than they while the sun shines; in the dark it is their turn to be our guide. We are blind half our time, with this difference: the really blind always know what to do, while we are afraid to stir in the dark. We have lights, you say. What always artificial aids. Who can insure that they will always be at hand when required. I had rather Emil's eyes were in his finger tips, than in the chandler's shop.

If you are shut up in a building at night, clap your hands, you will know from the sound whether the space is large or small, if you are in the middle or in one corner. Half a foot from a wall the air, which is refracted and does not circulate freely, produces a different effect on your face. Stand still in one place and turn this way and that; a slight draught will tell you if there is a door open. If you are on a boat you will perceive from the way the air strikes your face not merely the direction in which you are going, but whether the current is bearing you slow or fast. These observations and many others like them can only be properly made at night; however much attention we give to them by daylight, we are always helped or hindered by sight, so that the results escape us. Yet here we use neither hand nor stick. How much may be learnt by touch, without ever touching anything!

I would have plenty of games in the dark! This suggestion is more valuable than it seems at first sight. Men are naturally afraid of the dark; so are some animals. [Footnote: This terror is very noticeable during great eclipses of the sun.] Only a few men are freed from this burden by knowledge, determination, and courage. I have seen thinkers, unbelievers, philosophers, exceedingly brave by daylight, tremble like women at the rustling of a leaf in the dark. This terror is put down to nurses' tales; this is a mistake; it has a natural cause. What is this cause? What makes the deaf suspicious and the lower classes superstitious? Ignorance of the things about us, and of what is taking place around us. [Footnote: Another cause has been well explained by a philosopher, often quoted in this work, a philosopher to whose wide views I am very greatly indebted.]

When under special conditions we cannot form a fair idea of distance, when we can only judge things by the size of the angle or rather of the image formed in our eyes, we cannot avoid being deceived as to the size of these objects. Every one knows by experience how when we are travelling at night we take a bush near at hand for a great tree at a distance, and vice versa. In the same way, if the objects were of a shape unknown to us, so that we could not tell their size in that way, we should be equally mistaken with regard to it. If a fly flew quickly past a few inches from our eyes, we should think it was a distant bird; a horse standing still at a distance from us in the midst of open country, in a position somewhat like that of a sheep, would be taken for a large sheep, so long as we did not perceive that it was a horse; but as soon as we recognise what it is, it seems as large as a horse, and we at once correct our former judgment.

Whenever one finds oneself in unknown places at night where we cannot judge of distance, and where we cannot recognise objects by their shape on account of the darkness, we are in constant danger of forming mistaken judgments as to the objects which present themselves to our notice. Hence that terror, that kind of inward fear experienced by most people on dark nights. This is foundation for the supposed appearances of spectres, or gigantic and terrible forms which so many people profess to have seen. They are generally told that they imagined these things, yet they may really have seen them, and it is quite possible they really saw what they say they did see; for it will always be the case that when we can only estimate the size of an object by the angle it forms in the eye, that object will swell and grow as we approach it; and if the spectator thought it several feet high when it was thirty or forty feet away, it will seem very large indeed when it is a few feet off; this must indeed astonish and alarm the spectator until he touches it and perceives what it is, for as soon as he perceives what it is, the object which seemed so gigantic will suddenly shrink and assume its real size, but if we run away or are afraid to approach, we shall certainly form no other idea of the thing than the image formed in the eye, and we shall have really seen a gigantic figure of alarming size and shape. There is, therefore, a natural ground for the tendency to see ghosts, and these appearances are not merely the creation of the imagination, as the men of science would have us think. — Buffon, Nat. Hist.

In the text I have tried to show that they are always partly the creation of the imagination, and with regard to the cause explained in this quotation, it is clear that the habit of walking by night should teach us to distinguish those appearances which similarity of form and diversity of distance lend to the objects seen in the dark. For if the air is light enough for us to see the outlines there must be more air between us and them when they are further off, so that we ought to see them less distinctly when further off, which should be enough, when we are used to it, to prevent the error described by M. Buffon. [Whichever explanation you prefer, my mode of procedure is still efficacious, and experience entirely confirms it.] Accustomed to perceive things from a distance and to calculate their effects, how can I help supposing, when I cannot see, that there are hosts of creatures and all sorts of movements all about me which may do me harm, and against which I cannot protect myself? In vain do I know I am safe where I am; I am never so sure of it as when I can actually see it, so that I have always a cause for fear which did not exist in broad daylight. I know, indeed, that a foreign body can scarcely act upon me without some slight sound, and how intently I listen! At the least sound which I cannot explain, the desire of self-preservation makes me picture everything that would put me on my guard, and therefore everything most calculated to alarm me.

I am just as uneasy if I hear no sound, for I might be taken unawares without a sound. I must picture things as they were before, as they ought to be; I must see what I do not see. Thus driven to exercise my imagination, it soon becomes my master, and what I did to reassure myself only alarms me more. I hear a noise, it is a robber; I hear nothing, it is a ghost. The watchfulness inspired by the instinct of self-preservation only makes me more afraid. Everything that ought to reassure me exists only for my reason, and the voice of instinct is louder than that of reason. What is the good of thinking there is nothing to be afraid of, since in that case there is nothing we can do?

The cause indicates the cure. In everything habit overpowers imagination; it is only aroused by what is new. It is no longer imagination, but memory which is concerned with what we see every day, and that is the reason of the maxim, "Ab assuetis non fit passio," for it is only at the flame of imagination that the passions are kindled. Therefore do not argue with any one whom you want to cure of the fear of darkness; take him often into dark places and be assured this practice will be of more avail than all the arguments of philosophy. The tiler on the roof does not know what it is to be dizzy, and those who are used to the dark will not be afraid.

There is another advantage to be gained from our games in the dark. But if these games are to be a success I cannot speak too strongly of the need for gaiety. Nothing is so gloomy as the dark: do not shut your child up in a dungeon, let him laugh when he goes, into a dark place, let him laugh when he comes out, so that the thought of the game he is leaving and the games he will play next may protect him from the fantastic imagination which might lay hold on him.

There comes a stage in life beyond which we progress backwards. I feel I have reached this stage. I am, so to speak, returning to a past career. The approach of age makes us recall the happy days of our childhood. As I grow old I become a child again, and I recall more readily what I did at ten than at thirty. Reader, forgive me if I sometimes draw my examples from my own experience. If this book is to be well written, I must enjoy writing it.

I was living in the country with a pastor called M. Lambercier. My companion was a cousin richer than myself, who was regarded as the heir to some property, while I, far from my father, was but a poor orphan. My big cousin Bernard was unusually timid, especially at night. I laughed at his fears, till M. Lambercier was tired of my boasting, and determined to put my courage to the proof. One autumn evening, when it was very dark, he gave me the church key, and told me to go and fetch a Bible he had left in the pulpit. To put me on my mettle he said something which made it impossible for me to refuse.

I set out without a light; if I had had one, it would perhaps have been even worse. I had to pass through the graveyard; I crossed it bravely, for as long as I was in the open air I was never afraid of the dark.

As I opened the door I heard a sort of echo in the roof; it sounded like voices and it began to shake my Roman courage. Having opened the door I tried to enter, but when I had gone a few steps I stopped. At the sight of the profound darkness in which the vast building lay I was seized with terror and my hair stood on end. I turned, I went out through the door, and took to my heels. In the yard I found a little dog, called Sultan, whose caresses reassured me. Ashamed of my fears, I retraced my steps, trying to take Sultan with me, but he refused to follow. Hurriedly I opened the door and entered the church. I was hardly inside when terror again got hold of me and so firmly that I lost my head, and though the pulpit was on the right, as I very well knew, I sought it on the left, and entangling myself among the benches I was completely lost. Unable to find either pulpit or door, I fell into an indescribable state of mind. At last I found the door and managed to get out of the church and run away as I had done before, quite determined never to enter the church again except in broad daylight.

I returned to the house; on the doorstep I heard M. Lambercier laughing, laughing, as I supposed, at me. Ashamed to face his laughter, I was hesitating to open the door, when I heard Miss Lambercier, who was anxious about me, tell the maid to get the lantern, and M. Lambercier got ready to come and look for me, escorted by my gallant cousin, who would have got all the credit for the expedition. All at once my fears departed, and left me merely surprised at my terror. I ran, I fairly flew, to the church; without losing my way, without groping about, I reached the pulpit, took the Bible, and ran down the steps. In three strides I was out of the church, leaving the door open. Breathless, I entered the room and threw the Bible on the table, frightened indeed, but throbbing with pride that I had done it without the proposed assistance.

You will ask if I am giving this anecdote as an example, and as an illustration, of the mirth which I say should accompany these games. Not so, but I give it as a proof that there is nothing so well calculated to reassure any one who is afraid in the dark as to hear sounds of laughter and talking in an adjoining room. Instead of playing alone with your pupil in the evening, I would have you get together a number of merry children; do not send them alone to begin with, but several together, and do not venture to send any one quite alone, until you are quite certain beforehand that he will not be too frightened.

I can picture nothing more amusing and more profitable than such games, considering how little skill is required to organise them. In a large room I should arrange a sort of labyrinth of tables, armchairs, chairs, and screens. In the inextricable windings of this labyrinth I should place some eight or ten sham boxes, and one real box almost exactly like them, but well filled with sweets. I should describe clearly and briefly the place where the right box would be found. I should give instructions sufficient to enable people more attentive and less excitable than children to find it. [Footnote: To practise them in attention, only tell them things which it is clearly to their present interest that they should understand thoroughly; above all be brief, never say a word more than necessary. But neither let your speech be obscure nor of doubtful meaning.] Then having made the little competitors draw lots, I should send first one and then another till the right box was found. I should increase the difficulty of the task in proportion to their skill.

Picture to yourself a youthful Hercules returning, box in hand, quite proud of his expedition. The box is placed on the table and opened with great ceremony. I can hear the bursts of laughter and the shouts of the merry party when, instead of the looked-for sweets, he finds, neatly arranged on moss or cotton-wool, a beetle, a snail, a bit of coal, a few acorns, a turnip, or some such thing. Another time in a newly whitewashed room, a toy or some small article of furniture would be hung on the wall and the children would have to fetch it without touching the wall. When the child who fetches it comes back, if he has failed ever so little to fulfil the conditions, a dab of white on the brim of his cap, the tip of his shoe, the flap of his coat or his sleeve, will betray his lack of skill.

This is enough, or more than enough, to show the spirit of these games. Do not read my book if you expect me to tell you everything.

What great advantages would be possessed by a man so educated, when compared with others. His feet are accustomed to tread firmly in the dark, and his hands to touch lightly; they will guide him safely in the thickest darkness. His imagination is busy with the evening games of his childhood, and will find it difficult to turn towards objects of alarm. If he thinks he hears laughter, it will be the laughter of his former playfellows, not of frenzied spirits; if he thinks there is a host of people, it will not be the witches' sabbath, but the party in his tutor's study. Night only recalls these cheerful memories, and it will never alarm him; it will inspire delight rather than fear. He will be ready for a military expedition at any hour, with or without his troop. He will enter the camp of Saul, he will find his way, he will reach the king's tent without waking any one, and he will return unobserved. Are the steeds of Rhesus to be stolen, you may trust him. You will scarcely find a Ulysses among men educated in any other fashion.

I have known people who tried to train the children not to fear the dark by startling them. This is a very bad plan; its effects are just the opposite of those desired, and it only makes children more timid. Neither reason nor habit can secure us from the fear of a present danger whose degree and kind are unknown, nor from the fear of surprises which we have often experienced. Yet how will you make sure that you can preserve your pupil from such accidents? I consider this the best advice to give him beforehand. I should say to Emile, "This is a matter of self-defence, for the aggressor does not let you know whether he means to hurt or frighten you, and as the advantage is on his side you cannot even take refuge in flight. Therefore seize boldly anything, whether man or beast, which takes you unawares in the dark. Grasp it, squeeze it with all your might; if it struggles, strike, and do not spare your blows; and whatever he may say or do, do not let him go till you know just who he is. The event will probably prove that you had little to be afraid of, but this way of treating practical jokers would naturally prevent their trying it again."

Although touch is the sense oftenest used, its discrimination remains, as I have already pointed out, coarser and more imperfect than that of any other sense, because we always use sight along with it; the eye perceives the thing first, and the mind almost always judges without the hand. On the other hand, discrimination by touch is the surest just because of its limitations; for extending only as far as our hands can reach, it corrects the hasty judgments of the other senses, which pounce upon objects scarcely perceived, while what we learn by touch is learnt thoroughly. Moreover, touch, when required, unites the force of our muscles to the action of the nerves; we associate by simultaneous sensations our ideas of temperature, size, and shape, to those of weight and density. Thus touch is the sense which best teaches us the action of foreign bodies upon ourselves, the sense which most directly supplies us with the knowledge required for self-preservation.

As the trained touch takes the place of sight, why should it not, to some extent, take the place of hearing, since sounds set up, in sonorous bodies, vibrations perceptible by touch? By placing the hand on the body of a 'cello one can distinguish without the use of eye or ear, merely by the way in which the wood vibrates and trembles, whether the sound given out is sharp or flat, whether it is drawn from the treble string or the bass. If our touch were trained to note these differences, no doubt we might in time become so sensitive as to hear a whole tune by means of our fingers. But if we admit this, it is clear that one could easily speak to the deaf by means of music; for tone and measure are no less capable of regular combination than voice and articulation, so that they might be used as the elements of speech.

There are exercises by which the sense of touch is blunted and deadened, and others which sharpen it and make it delicate and discriminating. The former, which employ much movement and force for the continued impression of hard bodies, make the skin hard and thick, and deprive it of its natural sensitiveness. The latter are those which give variety to this feeling, by slight and repeated contact, so that the mind is attentive to constantly recurring impressions, and readily learns to discern their variations. This difference is clear in the use of musical instruments. The harsh and painful touch of the 'cello, bass-viol, and even of the violin, hardens the finger-tips, although it gives flexibility to the fingers. The soft and smooth touch of the harpsichord makes the fingers both flexible and sensitive. In this respect the harpsichord is to be preferred.

The skin protects the rest of the body, so it is very important to harden it to the effects of the air that it may be able to bear its changes. With regard to this I may say I would not have the hand roughened by too servile application to the same kind of work, nor should the skin of the hand become hardened so as to lose its delicate sense of touch which keeps the body informed of what is going on, and by the kind of contact sometimes makes us shudder in different ways even in the dark.

Why should my pupil be always compelled to wear the skin of an ox under his foot? What harm would come of it if his own skin could serve him at need as a sole. It is clear that a delicate skin could never be of any use in this way, and may often do harm. The Genevese, aroused at midnight by their enemies in the depth of winter, seized their guns rather than their shoes. Who can tell whether the town would have escaped capture if its citizens had not been able to go barefoot?

Let a man be always fore-armed against the unforeseen. Let Emile run about barefoot all the year round, upstairs, downstairs, and in the garden. Far from scolding him, I shall follow his example; only I shall be careful to remove any broken glass. I shall soon proceed to speak of work and manual occupations. Meanwhile, let him learn to perform every exercise which encourages agility of body; let him learn to hold himself easily and steadily in any position, let him practise jumping and leaping, climbing trees and walls. Let him always find his balance, and let his every movement and gesture be regulated by the laws of weight, long before he learns to explain them by the science of statics. By the way his foot is planted on the ground, and his body supported on his leg, he ought to know if he is holding himself well or ill. An easy carriage is always graceful, and the steadiest positions are the most elegant. If I were a dancing master I would refuse to play the monkey tricks of Marcel, which are only fit for the stage where they are performed; but instead of keeping my pupil busy with fancy steps, I would take him to the foot of a cliff. There I would show him how to hold himself, how to carry his body and head, how to place first a foot then a hand, to follow lightly the steep, toilsome, and rugged paths, to leap from point to point, either up or down. He should emulate the mountain-goat, not the ballet dancer.

As touch confines its operations to the man's immediate surroundings, so sight extends its range beyond them; it is this which makes it misleading; man sees half his horizon at a glance. In the midst of this host of simultaneous impressions and the thoughts excited by them, how can he fail now and then to make mistakes? Thus sight is the least reliable of our senses, just because it has the widest range; it functions long before our other senses, and its work is too hasty and on too large a scale to be corrected by the rest. Moreover, the very illusions of perspective are necessary if we are to arrive at a knowledge of space and compare one part of space with another. Without false appearances we should never see anything at a distance; without the gradations of size and tone we could not judge of distance, or rather distance would have no existence for us. If two trees, one of which was a hundred paces from us and the other ten, looked equally large and distinct, we should think they were side by side. If we perceived the real dimensions of things, we should know nothing of space; everything would seem close to our eyes.

The angle formed between any objects and our eye is the only means by which our sight estimates their size and distance, and as this angle is the simple effect of complex causes, the judgment we form does not distinguish between the several causes; we are compelled to be inaccurate. For how can I tell, by sight alone, whether the angle at which an object appears to me smaller than another, indicates that it is really smaller or that it is further off.

Here we must just reverse our former plan. Instead of simplifying the sensation, always reinforce it and verify it by means of another sense. Subject the eye to the hand, and, so to speak, restrain the precipitation of the former sense by the slower and more reasoned pace of the latter. For want of this sort of practice our sight measurements are very imperfect. We cannot correctly, and at a glance, estimate height, length, breadth, and distance; and the fact that engineers, surveyors, architects, masons, and painters are generally quicker to see and better able to estimate distances correctly, proves that the fault is not in our eyes, but in our use of them. Their occupations give them the training we lack, and they check the equivocal results of the angle of vision by its accompanying experiences, which determine the relations of the two causes of this angle for their eyes.

Children will always do anything that keeps them moving freely. There are countless ways of rousing their interest in measuring, perceiving, and estimating distance. There is a very tall cherry tree; how shall we gather the cherries? Will the ladder in the barn be big enough? There is a wide stream; how shall we get to the other side? Would one of the wooden planks in the yard reach from bank to bank? From our windows we want to fish in the moat; how many yards of line are required? I want to make a swing between two trees; will two fathoms of cord be enough? They tell me our room in the new house will be twenty-five feet square; do you think it will be big enough for us? Will it be larger than this? We are very hungry; here are two villages, which can we get to first for our dinner?

An idle, lazy child was to be taught to run. He had no liking for this or any other exercise, though he was intended for the army. Somehow or other he had got it into his head that a man of his rank need know nothing and do nothing—that his birth would serve as a substitute for arms and legs, as well as for every kind of virtue. The skill of Chiron himself would have failed to make a fleet-footed Achilles of this young gentleman. The difficulty was increased by my determination to give him no kind of orders. I had renounced all right to direct him by preaching, promises, threats, emulation, or the desire to show off. How should I make him want to run without saying anything? I might run myself, but he might not follow my example, and this plan had other drawbacks. Moreover, I must find some means of teaching him through this exercise, so as to train mind and body to work together. This is how I, or rather how the teacher who supplied me with this illustration, set about it.

When I took him a walk of an afternoon I sometimes put in my pocket a couple of cakes, of a kind he was very fond of; we each ate one while we were out, and we came back well pleased with our outing. One day he noticed I had three cakes; he could have easily eaten six, so he ate his cake quickly and asked for the other. "No," said I, "I could eat it myself, or we might divide it, but I would rather see those two little boys run a race for it." I called them to us, showed them the cake, and suggested that they should race for it. They were delighted. The cake was placed on a large stone which was to be the goal; the course was marked out, we sat down, and at a given signal off flew the children! The victor seized the cake and ate it without pity in the sight of the spectators and of his defeated rival.

The sport was better than the cake; but the lesson did not take effect all at once, and produced no result. I was not discouraged, nor did I hurry; teaching is a trade at which one must be able to lose time and save it. Our walks were continued, sometimes we took three cakes, sometimes four, and from time to time there were one or two cakes for the racers. If the prize was not great, neither was the ambition of the competitors. The winner was praised and petted, and everything was done with much ceremony. To give room to run and to add interest to the race I marked out a longer course and admitted several fresh competitors. Scarcely had they entered the lists than all the passers-by stopped to watch. They were encouraged by shouting, cheering, and clapping. I sometimes saw my little man trembling with excitement, jumping up and shouting when one was about to reach or overtake another — to him these were the Olympian games.

However, the competitors did not always play fair, they got in each other's way, or knocked one another down, or put stones on the track. That led us to separate them and make them start from different places at equal distances from the goal. You will soon see the reason for this, for I must describe this important affair at length.

Tired of seeing his favourite cakes devoured before his eyes, the young lord began to suspect that there was some use in being a quick runner, and seeing that he had two legs of his own, he began to practise running on the quiet. I took care to see nothing, but I knew my stratagem had taken effect. When he thought he was good enough (and I thought so too), he pretended to tease me to give him the other cake. I refused; he persisted, and at last he said angrily, "Well, put it on the stone and mark out the course, and we shall see." "Very good," said I, laughing, "You will get a good appetite, but you will not get the cake." Stung by my mockery, he took heart, won the prize, all the more easily because I had marked out a very short course and taken care that the best runner was out of the way. It will be evident that, after the first step, I had no difficulty in keeping him in training. Soon he took such a fancy for this form of exercise that without any favour he was almost certain to beat the little peasant boys at running, however long the course.

The advantage thus obtained led unexpectedly to another. So long as he seldom won the prize, he ate it himself like his rivals, but as he got used to victory he grew generous, and often shared it with the defeated. That taught me a lesson in morals and I saw what was the real root of generosity.

While I continued to mark out a different starting place for each competitor, he did not notice that I had made the distances unequal, so that one of them, having farther to run to reach the goal, was clearly at a disadvantage. But though I left the choice to my pupil he did not know how to take advantage of it. Without thinking of the distance, he always chose the smoothest path, so that I could easily predict his choice, and could almost make him win or lose the cake at my pleasure. I had more than one end in view in this stratagem; but as my plan was to get him to notice the difference himself, I tried to make him aware of it. Though he was generally lazy and easy going, he was so eager in his sports and trusted me so completely that I had great difficulty in making him see that I was cheating him. When at last I managed to make him see it in spite of his excitement, he was angry with me. "What have you to complain of?" said I. "In a gift which I propose to give of my own free will am not I master of the conditions? Who makes you run? Did I promise to make the courses equal? Is not the choice yours? Do not you see that I am favouring you, and that the inequality you complain of is all to your advantage, if you knew how to use it?" That was plain to him; and to choose he must observe more carefully. At first he wanted to count the paces, but a child measures paces slowly and inaccurately; moreover, I decided to have several races on one day; and the game having become a sort of passion with the child, he was sorry to waste in measuring the portion of time intended for running. Such delays are not in accordance with a child's impatience; he tried therefore to see better and to reckon the distance more accurately at sight. It was now quite easy to extend and develop this power. At length, after some months' practice, and the correction of his errors, I so trained his power of judging at sight that I had only to place an imaginary cake on any distant object and his glance was nearly as accurate as the surveyor's chain.

Of all the senses, sight is that which we can least distinguish from the judgments of the mind; as it takes a long time to learn to see. It takes a long time to compare sight and touch, and to train the former sense to give a true report of shape and distance. Without touch, without progressive motion, the sharpest eyes in the world could give us no idea of space. To the oyster the whole world must seem a point, and it would seem nothing more to it even if it had a human mind. It is only by walking, feeling, counting, measuring the dimensions of things, that we learn to judge them rightly; but, on the other hand, if we were always measuring, our senses would trust to the instrument and would never gain confidence. Nor must the child pass abruptly from measurement to judgment; he must continue to compare the parts when he could not compare the whole; he must substitute his estimated aliquot parts for exact aliquot parts, and instead of always applying the measure by hand he must get used to applying it by eye alone. I would, however, have his first estimates tested by measurement, so that he may correct his errors, and if there is a false impression left upon the senses he may correct it by a better judgment. The same natural standards of measurement are in use almost everywhere, the man's foot, the extent of his outstretched arms, his height. When the child wants to measure the height of a room, his tutor may serve as a measuring rod; if he is estimating the height of a steeple let him measure it by the house; if he wants to know how many leagues of road there are, let him count the hours spent in walking along it. Above all, do not do this for him; let him do it himself.

One cannot learn to estimate the extent and size of bodies without at the same time learning to know and even to copy their shape; for at bottom this copying depends entirely on the laws of perspective, and one cannot estimate distance without some feeling for these laws. All children in the course of their endless imitation try to draw; and I would have Emile cultivate this art; not so much for art's sake, as to give him exactness of eye and flexibility of hand. Generally speaking, it matters little whether he is acquainted with this or that occupation, provided he gains clearness of sense—perception and the good bodily habits which belong to the exercise in question. So I shall take good care not to provide him with a drawing master, who would only set him to copy copies and draw from drawings. Nature should be his only teacher, and things his only models. He should have the real thing before his eyes, not its copy on paper. Let him draw a house from a house, a tree from a tree, a man from a man; so that he may train himself to observe objects and their appearance accurately and not to take false and conventional copies for truth. I would even train him to draw only from objects actually before him and not from memory, so that, by repeated observation, their exact form may be impressed on his imagination, for fear lest he should substitute absurd and fantastic forms for the real truth of things, and lose his sense of proportion and his taste for the beauties of nature.

Of course I know that in this way he will make any number of daubs before he produces anything recognisable, that it will be long before he attains to the graceful outline and light touch of the draughtsman; perhaps he will never have an eye for picturesque effect or a good taste in drawing. On the other hand, he will certainly get a truer eye, a surer hand, a knowledge of the real relations of form and size between animals, plants, and natural objects, together with a quicker sense of the effects of perspective. That is just what I wanted, and my purpose is rather that he should know things than copy them. I would rather he showed me a plant of acanthus even if he drew a capital with less accuracy.

Moreover, in this occupation as in others, I do not intend my pupil to play by himself; I mean to make it pleasanter for him by always sharing it with him. He shall have no other rival; but mine will be a continual rivalry, and there will be no risk attaching to it; it will give interest to his pursuits without awaking jealousy between us. I shall follow his example and take up a pencil; at first I shall use it as unskilfully as he. I should be an Apelles if I did not set myself daubing. To begin with, I shall draw a man such as lads draw on walls, a line for each arm, another for each leg, with the fingers longer than the arm. Long after, one or other of us will notice this lack of proportion; we shall observe that the leg is thick, that this thickness varies, that the length of the arm is proportionate to the body. In this improvement I shall either go side by side with my pupil, or so little in advance that he will always overtake me easily and sometimes get ahead of me. We shall get brushes and paints, we shall try to copy the colours of things and their whole appearance, not merely their shape. We shall colour prints, we shall paint, we shall daub; but in all our daubing we shall be searching out the secrets of nature, and whatever we do shall be done under the eye of that master.

We badly needed ornaments for our room, and now we have them ready to our hand. I will have our drawings framed and covered with good glass, so that no one will touch them, and thus seeing them where we put them, each of us has a motive for taking care of his own. I arrange them in order round the room, each drawing repeated some twenty or thirty times, thus showing the author's progress in each specimen, from the time when the house is merely a rude square, till its front view, its side view, its proportions, its light and shade are all exactly portrayed. These graduations will certainly furnish us with pictures, a source of interest to ourselves and of curiosity to others, which will spur us on to further emulation. The first and roughest drawings I put in very smart gilt frames to show them off; but as the copy becomes more accurate and the drawing really good, I only give it a very plain dark frame; it needs no other ornament than itself, and it would be a pity if the frame distracted the attention which the picture itself deserves. Thus we each aspire to a plain frame, and when we desire to pour scorn on each other's drawings, we condemn them to a gilded frame. Some day perhaps "the gilt frame" will become a proverb among us, and we shall be surprised to find how many people show what they are really made of by demanding a gilt frame.

I have said already that geometry is beyond the child's reach; but that is our own fault. We fail to perceive that their method is not ours, that what is for us the art of reasoning, should be for them the art of seeing. Instead of teaching them our way, we should do better to adopt theirs, for our way of learning geometry is quite as much a matter of imagination as of reasoning. When a proposition is enunciated you must imagine the proof; that is, you must discover on what proposition already learnt it depends, and of all the possible deductions from that proposition you must choose just the one required.

In this way the closest reasoner, if he is not inventive, may find himself at a loss. What is the result? Instead of making us discover proofs, they are dictated to us; instead of teaching us to reason, our memory only is employed.

Draw accurate figures, combine them together, put them one upon another, examine their relations, and you will discover the whole of elementary geometry in passing from one observation to another, without a word of definitions, problems, or any other form of demonstration but super-position. I do not profess to teach Emile geometry; he will teach me; I shall seek for relations, he will find them, for I shall seek in such a fashion as to make him find. For instance, instead of using a pair of compasses to draw a circle, I shall draw it with a pencil at the end of bit of string attached to a pivot. After that, when I want to compare the radii one with another, Emile will laugh at me and show me that the same thread at full stretch cannot have given distances of unequal length. If I wish to measure an angle of 60 degrees I describe from the apex of the angle, not an arc, but a complete circle, for with children nothing must be taken for granted. I find that the part of the circle contained between the two lines of the angle is the sixth part of a circle. Then I describe another and larger circle from the same centre, and I find the second arc is again the sixth part of its circle. I describe a third concentric circle with a similar result, and I continue with more and more circles till Emile, shocked at my stupidity, shows me that every arc, large or small, contained by the same angle will always be the sixth part of its circle. Now we are ready to use the protractor.

To prove that two adjacent angles are equal to two right angles people describe a circle. On the contrary I would have Emile observe the fact in a circle, and then I should say, "If we took away the circle and left the straight lines, would the angles have changed their size, etc.?"

Exactness in the construction of figures is neglected; it is taken for granted and stress is laid on the proof. With us, on the other hand, there will be no question of proof. Our chief business will be to draw very straight, accurate, and even lines, a perfect square, a really round circle. To verify the exactness of a figure we will test it by each of its sensible properties, and that will give us a chance to discover fresh properties day by day. We will fold the two semi-circles along the diameter, the two halves of the square by the diagonal; he will compare our two figures to see who has got the edges to fit moat exactly, i.e., who has done it best; we should argue whether this equal division would always be possible in parallelograms, trapezes, etc. We shall sometimes try to forecast the result of an experiment, to find reasons, etc.

Geometry means to my scholar the successful use of the rule and compass; he must not confuse it with drawing, in which these instruments are not used. The rule and compass will be locked up, so that he will not get into the way of messing about with them, but we may sometimes take our figures with us when we go for a walk, and talk over what we have done, or what we mean to do.

I shall never forget seeing a young man at Turin, who had learnt as a child the relations of contours and surfaces by having to choose every day isoperimetric cakes among cakes of every geometrical figure. The greedy little fellow had exhausted the art of Archimedes to find which were the biggest.

When the child flies a kite he is training eye and hand to accuracy; when he whips a top, he is increasing his strength by using it, but without learning anything. I have sometimes asked why children are not given the same games of skill as men; tennis, mall, billiards, archery, football, and musical instruments. I was told that some of these are beyond their strength, that the child's senses are not sufficiently developed for others. These do not strike me as valid reasons; a child is not as tall as a man, but he wears the same sort of coat; I do not want him to play with our cues at a billiard-table three feet high; I do not want him knocking about among our games, nor carrying one of our racquets in his little hand; but let him play in a room whose windows have been protected; at first let him only use soft balls, let his first racquets be of wood, then of parchment, and lastly of gut, according to his progress. You prefer the kite because it is less tiring and there is no danger. You are doubly wrong. Kite-flying is a sport for women, but every woman will run away from a swift ball. Their white skins were not meant to be hardened by blows and their faces were not made for bruises. But we men are made for strength; do you think we can attain it without hardship, and what defence shall we be able to make if we are attacked? People always play carelessly in games where there is no danger. A falling kite hurts nobody, but nothing makes the arm so supple as protecting the head, nothing makes the sight so accurate as having to guard the eye. To dash from one end of the room to another, to judge the rebound of a ball before it touches the ground, to return it with strength and accuracy, such games are not so much sports fit for a man, as sports fit to make a man of him.

The child's limbs, you say, are too tender. They are not so strong as those of a man, but they are more supple. His arm is weak, still it is an arm, and it should be used with due consideration as we use other tools. Children have no skill in the use of their hands. That is just why I want them to acquire skill; a man with as little practice would be just as clumsy. We can only learn the use of our limbs by using them. It is only by long experience that we learn to make the best of ourselves, and this experience is the real object of study to which we cannot apply ourselves too early.

What is done can be done. Now there is nothing commoner than to find nimble and skilful children whose limbs are as active as those of a man. They may be seen at any fair, swinging, walking on their hands, jumping, dancing on the tight rope. For many years past, troops of children have attracted spectators to the ballets at the Italian Comedy House. Who is there in Germany and Italy who has not heard of the famous pantomime company of Nicolini? Has it ever occurred to any one that the movements of these children were less finished, their postures less graceful, their ears less true, their dancing more clumsy than those of grown-up dancers? If at first the fingers are thick, short, and awkward, the dimpled hands unable to grasp anything, does this prevent many children from learning to read and write at an age when others cannot even hold a pen or pencil? All Paris still recalls the little English girl of ten who did wonders on the harpsichord. I once saw a little fellow of eight, the son of a magistrate, who was set like a statuette on the table among the dishes, to play on a fiddle almost as big as himself, and even artists were surprised at his execution.

To my mind, these and many more examples prove that the supposed incapacity of children for our games is imaginary, and that if they are unsuccessful in some of them, it is for want of practice.

You will tell me that with regard to the body I am falling into the same mistake of precocious development which I found fault with for the mind. The cases are very different: in the one, progress is apparent only; in the other it is real. I have shown that children have not the mental development they appear to have, while they really do what they seem to do. Besides, we must never forget that all this should be play, the easy and voluntary control of the movements which nature demands of them, the art of varying their games to make them pleasanter, without the least bit of constraint to transform them into work; for what games do they play in which I cannot find material for instruction for them? And even if I could not do so, so long as they are amusing themselves harmlessly and passing the time pleasantly, their progress in learning is not yet of such great importance. But if one must be teaching them this or that at every opportunity, it cannot be done without constraint, vexation, or tedium.

What I have said about the use of the two senses whose use is most constant and most important, may serve as an example of how to train the rest. Sight and touch are applied to bodies at rest and bodies in motion, but as hearing is only affected by vibrations of the air, only a body in motion can make a noise or sound; if everything were at rest we should never hear. At night, when we ourselves only move as we choose, we have nothing to fear but moving bodies; hence we need a quick ear, and power to judge from the sensations experienced whether the body which causes them is large or small, far off or near, whether its movements are gentle or violent. When once the air is set in motion, it is subject to repercussions which produce echoes, these renew the sensations and make us hear a loud or penetrating sound in another quarter. If you put your ear to the ground you may hear the sound of men's voices or horses' feet in a plain or valley much further off than when you stand upright.

As we have made a comparison between sight and touch, it will be as well to do the same for hearing, and to find out which of the two impressions starting simultaneously from a given body first reaches the sense-organ. When you see the flash of a cannon, you have still time to take cover; but when you hear the sound it is too late, the ball is close to you. One can reckon the distance of a thunderstorm by the interval between the lightning and the thunder. Let the child learn all these facts, let him learn those that are within his reach by experiment, and discover the rest by induction; but I would far rather he knew nothing at all about them, than that you should tell him.

In the voice we have an organ answering to hearing; we have no such organ answering to sight, and we do not repeat colours as we repeat sounds. This supplies an additional means of cultivating the ear by practising the active and passive organs one with the other.

Man has three kinds of voice, the speaking or articulate voice, the singing or melodious voice, and the pathetic or expressive voice, which serves as the language of the passions, and gives life to song and speech. The child has these three voices, just as the man has them, but he does not know how to use them in combination. Like us, he laughs, cries, laments, shrieks, and groans, but he does not know how to combine these inflexions with speech or song. These three voices find their best expression in perfect music. Children are incapable of such music, and their singing lacks feeling. In the same way their spoken language lacks expression; they shout, but they do not speak with emphasis, and there is as little power in their voice as there is emphasis in their speech. Our pupil's speech will be plainer and simpler still, for his passions are still asleep, and will not blend their tones with his. Do not, therefore, set him to recite tragedy or comedy, nor try to teach declamation so-called. He will have too much sense to give voice to things he cannot understand, or expression to feelings he has never known.

Teach him to speak plainly and distinctly, to articulate clearly, to pronounce correctly and without affectation, to perceive and imitate the right accent in prose and verse, and always to speak loud enough to be heard, but without speaking too loud—a common fault with school-children. Let there be no waste in anything.

The same method applies to singing; make his voice smooth and true, flexible and full, his ear alive to time and tune, but nothing more. Descriptive and theatrical music is not suitable at his age — —I would rather he sang no words; if he must have words, I would try to compose songs on purpose for him, songs interesting to a child, and as simple as his own thoughts.

You may perhaps suppose that as I am in no hurry to teach Emile to read and write, I shall not want to teach him to read music. Let us spare his brain the strain of excessive attention, and let us be in no hurry to turn his mind towards conventional signs. I grant you there seems to be a difficulty here, for if at first sight the knowledge of notes seems no more necessary for singing than the knowledge of letters for speaking, there is really this difference between them: When we speak, we are expressing our own thoughts; when we sing we are expressing the thoughts of others. Now in order to express them we must read them.

But at first we can listen to them instead of reading them, and a song is better learnt by ear than by eye. Moreover, to learn music thoroughly we must make songs as well as sing them, and the two processes must be studied together, or we shall never have any real knowledge of music. First give your young musician practice in very regular, well-cadenced phrases; then let him connect these phrases with the very simplest modulations; then show him their relation one to another by correct accent, which can be done by a fit choice of cadences and rests. On no account give him anything unusual, or anything that requires pathos or expression. A simple, tuneful air, always based on the common chords of the key, with its bass so clearly indicated that it is easily felt and accompanied, for to train his voice and ear he should always sing with the harpsichord.

We articulate the notes we sing the better to distinguish them; hence the custom of sol-faing with certain syllables. To tell the keys one from another they must have names and fixed intervals; hence the names of the intervals, and also the letters of the alphabet attached to the keys of the clavier and the notes of the scale. C and A indicate fixed sounds, invariable and always rendered by the same keys; Ut and La are different. Ut is always the dominant of a major scale, or the leading-note of a minor scale. La is always the dominant of a minor scale or the sixth of a major scale. Thus the letters indicate fixed terms in our system of music, and the syllables indicate terms homologous to the similar relations in different keys. The letters show the keys on the piano, and the syllables the degrees in the scale. French musicians have made a strange muddle of this. They have confused the meaning of the syllables with that of the letters, and while they have unnecessarily given us two sets of symbols for the keys of the piano, they have left none for the chords of the scales; so that Ut and C are always the same for them; this is not and ought not to be; if so, what is the use of C? Their method of sol-faing is, therefore, extremely and needlessly difficult, neither does it give any clear idea to the mind; since, by this method, Ut and Me, for example, may mean either a major third, a minor third, an augmented third, or a diminished third. What a strange thing that the country which produces the finest books about music should be the very country where it is hardest to learn music!

Let us adopt a simpler and clearer plan with our pupil; let him have only two scales whose relations remain unchanged, and indicated by the same symbols. Whether he sings or plays, let him learn to fix his scale on one of the twelve tones which may serve as a base, and whether he modulates in D, C, or G, let the close be always Ut or La, according to the scale. In this way he will understand what you mean, and the essential relations for correct singing and playing will always be present in his mind; his execution will be better and his progress quicker. There is nothing funnier than what the French call "natural sol-faing;" it consists in removing the real meaning of things and putting in their place other meanings which only distract us. There is nothing more natural than sol-faing by transposition, when the scale is transposed. But I have said enough, and more than enough, about music; teach it as you please, so long as it is nothing but play.

We are now thoroughly acquainted with the condition of foreign bodies in relation to our own, their weight, form, colour, density, size, distance, temperature, stability, or motion. We have learnt which of them to approach or avoid, how to set about overcoming their resistance or to resist them so as to prevent ourselves from injury; but this is not enough. Our own body is constantly wasting and as constantly requires to be renewed. Although we have the power of changing other substances into our own, our choice is not a matter of indifference. Everything is not food for man, and what may be food for him is not all equally suitable; it depends on his racial constitution, the country he lives in, his individual temperament, and the way of living which his condition demands.

If we had to wait till experience taught us to know and choose fit food for ourselves, we should die of hunger or poison; but a kindly providence which has made pleasure the means of self-preservation to sentient beings teaches us through our palate what is suitable for our stomach. In a state of nature there is no better doctor than a man's own appetite, and no doubt in a state of nature man could find the most palateable food the most wholesome.

Nor is this all. Our Maker provides, not only for those needs he has created, but for those we create for ourselves; and it is to keep the balance between our wants and our needs that he has caused our tastes to change and vary with our way of living. The further we are from a state of nature, the more we lose our natural tastes; or rather, habit becomes a second nature, and so completely replaces our real nature, that we have lost all knowledge of it.

From this it follows that the most natural tastes should be the simplest, for those are more easily changed; but when they are sharpened and stimulated by our fancies they assume a form which is incapable of modification. The man who so far has not adapted himself to one country can learn the ways of any country whatsoever; but the man who has adopted the habits of one particular country can never shake them off.

This seems to be true of all our senses, especially of taste. Our first food is milk; we only become accustomed by degrees to strong flavours; at first we dislike them. Fruit, vegetables, herbs, and then fried meat without salt or seasoning, formed the feasts of primitive man. When the savage tastes wine for the first time, he makes a grimace and spits it out; and even among ourselves a man who has not tasted fermented liquors before twenty cannot get used to them; we should all be sober if we did not have wine when we were children. Indeed, the simpler our tastes are, the more general they are; made dishes are those most frequently disliked. Did you ever meet with any one who disliked bread or water? Here is the finger of nature, this then is our rule. Preserve the child's primitive tastes as long as possible; let his food be plain and simple, let strong flavours be unknown to his palate, and do not let his diet be too uniform.

I am not asking, for the present, whether this way of living is healthier or no; that is not what I have in view. It is enough for me to know that my choice is more in accordance with nature, and that it can be more readily adapted to other conditions. In my opinion, those who say children should be accustomed to the food they will have when they are grown up are mistaken. Why should their food be the same when their way of living is so different? A man worn out by labour, anxiety, and pain needs tasty foods to give fresh vigour to his brain; a child fresh from his games, a child whose body is growing, needs plentiful food which will supply more chyle. Moreover the grown man has already a settled profession, occupation, and home, but who can tell what Fate holds in store for the child? Let us not give him so fixed a bent in any direction that he cannot change it if required without hardship. Do not bring him up so that he would die of hunger in a foreign land if he does not take a French cook about with him; do not let him say at some future time that France is the only country where the food is fit to eat. By the way, that is a strange way of praising one's country. On the other hand, I myself should say that the French are the only people who do not know what good food is, since they require such a special art to make their dishes eatable.

111

Of all our different senses, we are usually most affected by taste. Thus it concerns us more nearly to judge aright of what will actually become part of ourselves, than of that which will merely form part of our environment. Many things are matters of indifference to touch, hearing, and sight; but taste is affected by almost everything. Moreover the activity of this sense is wholly physical and material; of all the senses, it alone makes no appeal to the imagination, or at least, imagination plays a smaller part in its sensations; while imitation and imagination often bring morality into the impressions of the other senses. Thus, speaking generally, soft and pleasure-loving minds, passionate and truly sensitive dispositions, which are easily stirred by the other senses, are usually indifferent to this. From this very fact, which apparently places taste below our other senses and makes our inclination towards it the more despicable, I draw just the opposite conclusion—that the best way to lead children is by the mouth. Greediness is a better motive than vanity; for the former is a natural appetite directly dependent on the senses, while the latter is the outcome of convention, it is the slave of human caprice and liable to every kind of abuse. Believe me the child will cease to care about his food only too soon, and when his heart is too busy, his palate will be idle. When he is grown up greediness will be expelled by a host of stronger passions, while vanity will only be stimulated by them; for this latter passion feeds upon the rest till at length they are all swallowed up in it. I have sometimes studied those men who pay great attention to good eating, men whose first waking thought is—What shall we have to eat to-day? men who describe their dinner with as much detail as Polybius describes a combat. I have found these so-called men were only children of forty, without strength or vigour—fruges consumere nati. Gluttony is the vice of feeble minds. The gourmand has his brains in his palate, he can do nothing but eat; he is so stupid and incapable that the table is the only place for him, and dishes are the only things he knows anything about. Let us leave him to this business without regret; it is better for him and for us.

It is a small mind that fears lest greediness should take root in the child who is fit for something better. The child thinks of nothing but his food, the youth pays no heed to it at all; every kind of food is good, and we have other things to attend to. Yet I would not have you use the low motive unwisely. I would not have you trust to dainties rather than to the honour which is the reward of a good deed. But childhood is, or ought to be, a time of play and merry sports, and I do not see why the rewards of purely bodily exercises should not be material and sensible rewards. If a little lad in Majorca sees a basket on the tree-top and brings it down with his sling, is it not fair that he should get something by this, and a good breakfast should repair the strength spent in getting it. If a young Spartan, facing the risk of a hundred stripes, slips skilfully into the kitchen, and steals a live fox cub, carries it off in his garment, and is scratched, bitten till the blood comes, and for shame lest he should be caught the child allows his bowels to be torn out without a movement or a cry, is it not fair that he should keep his spoils, that he should eat his prey after it has eaten him? A good meal should never be a reward; but why should it not be sometimes the result of efforts made to get it. Emile does not consider the cake I put on the stone as a reward for good running; he knows that the only way to get the cake is to get there first.

This does not contradict my previous rules about simple food; for to tempt a child's appetite you need not stimulate it, you need only satisfy it; and the commonest things will do this if you do not attempt to refine children's taste. Their perpetual hunger, the result of their need for growth, will be the best sauce. Fruit, milk, a piece of cake just a little better than ordinary bread, and above all the art of dispensing these things prudently, by these means you may lead a host of children to the world's end, without on the one hand giving them a taste for strong flavours, nor on the other hand letting them get tired of their food.

The indifference of children towards meat is one proof that the taste for meat is unnatural; their preference is for vegetable foods, such as milk, pastry, fruit, etc. Beware of changing this natural taste and making children flesh-eaters, if not for their health's sake, for the sake of their character; for how can one explain away the fact that great meat-eaters are usually fiercer and more cruel than other men; this has been recognised at all times and in all places. The English are noted for their cruelty [Footnote: I am aware that the English make a boast of their humanity and of the kindly disposition of their race, which they call "good-natured people;" but in vain do they proclaim this fact; no one else says it of them.] while the Gaures are the gentlest of men. [Footnote: The Banians, who abstain from flesh even more completely than the Gaures, are almost as gentle as the Gaures themselves, but as their morality is less pure and their form of worship less reasonable they are not such good men.] All savages are cruel, and it is not their customs that tend in this direction; their cruelty is the result of their food. They go to war as to the chase, and treat men as they would treat bears. Indeed in England butchers are not allowed to give evidence in a court of law, no more can surgeons. [Footnote: One of the English translators of my book has pointed out my mistake, and both of them have corrected it. Butchers and surgeons are allowed to give evidence in the law courts, but butchers may not serve on juries in criminal cases, though surgeons are allowed to do so.] Great criminals prepare themselves for murder by drinking blood. Homer makes his flesh-eating Cyclops a terrible man, while his Lotus-eaters are so delightful that those who went to trade with them forgot even their own country to dwell among them.

"You ask me," said Plutarch, "why Pythagoras abstained from eating the flesh of beasts, but I ask you, what courage must have been needed by the first man who raised to his lips the flesh of the slain, who broke with his teeth the bones of a dying beast, who had dead bodies, corpses, placed before him and swallowed down limbs which a few moments ago were bleating, bellowing, walking, and seeing? How could his hand plunge the knife into the heart of a sentient creature, how could his eyes look on murder, how could he behold a poor helpless animal bled to death, scorched, and dismembered? how

113

can he bear the sight of this quivering flesh? does not the very smell of it turn his stomach? is he not repelled, disgusted, horror-struck, when he has to handle the blood from these wounds, and to cleanse his fingers from the dark and viscous bloodstains?

> *"The scorched skins wriggled upon the ground,*
> *The shrinking flesh bellowed upon the spit.*
> *Man cannot eat them without a shudder;*
> *He seems to hear their cries within his breast.*

"Thus must he have felt the first time he did despite to nature and made this horrible meal; the first time he hungered for the living creature, and desired to feed upon the beast which was still grazing; when he bade them slay, dismember, and cut up the sheep which licked his hands. It is those who began these cruel feasts, not those who abandon them, who should cause surprise, and there were excuses for those primitive men, excuses which we have not, and the absence of such excuses multiplies our barbarity a hundredfold.

"'Mortals, beloved of the gods,' says this primitive man, 'compare our times with yours; see how happy you are, and how wretched were we. The earth, newly formed, the air heavy with moisture, were not yet subjected to the rule of the seasons. Three-fourths of the surface of the globe was flooded by the ever-shifting channels of rivers uncertain of their course, and covered with pools, lakes, and bottomless morasses. The remaining quarter was covered with woods and barren forests. The earth yielded no good fruit, we had no instruments of tillage, we did not even know the use of them, and the time of harvest never came for those who had sown nothing. Thus hunger was always in our midst. In winter, mosses and the bark of trees were our common food. A few green roots of dogs-bit or heather were a feast, and when men found beech-mast, nuts, or acorns, they danced for joy round the beech or oak, to the sound of some rude song, while they called the earth their mother and their nurse. This was their only festival, their only sport; all the rest of man's life was spent in sorrow, pain, and hunger.

"'At length, when the bare and naked earth no longer offered us any food, we were compelled in self-defence to outrage nature, and to feed upon our companions in distress, rather than perish with them. But you, oh, cruel men! who forces you to shed blood? Behold the wealth of good things about you, the fruits yielded by the earth, the wealth of field and vineyard; the animals give their milk for your drink and their fleece for your clothing. What more do you ask? What madness compels you to commit such murders, when you have already more than you can eat or drink? Why do you slander our mother earth, and accuse her of denying you food? Why do you sin against Ceres, the inventor of the sacred laws, and against the gracious Bacchus, the comforter of man, as if their lavish gifts were not enough to preserve mankind? Have you the heart to mingle their sweet fruits with the bones upon your table, to eat with the milk the blood of the beasts which gave it? The lions and panthers, wild beasts as you call them, are driven to follow their natural instinct, and they kill other beasts that they may live. But, a hundredfold fiercer than they, you fight against your instincts without cause, and abandon yourselves to the most cruel pleasures. The animals you eat are not those who devour others; you do not eat the carnivorous beasts, you take them as your pattern. You only hunger for the sweet and gentle creatures which harm no one, which follow you, serve you, and are devoured by you as the reward of their service.

"'O unnatural murderer! if you persist in the assertion that nature has made you to devour your fellow-creatures, beings of flesh and blood, living and feeling like yourself, stifle if you can that horror with which nature makes you regard these horrible feasts; slay the animals yourself, slay them, I say, with your own hands, without knife or mallet; tear them with your nails like the lion and the bear, take this ox and rend him in pieces, plunge your claws into his hide; eat this lamb while it is yet alive, devour its warm flesh, drink its soul with its blood. You shudder! you dare not feel the living throbbing flesh between your teeth? Ruthless man; you begin by slaying the animal and then you devour it, as if to slay it twice. It is not enough. You turn against the dead flesh, it revolts you, it must be transformed by fire, boiled and roasted, seasoned and disguised with drugs; you must have butchers, cooks, turnspits, men who will rid the murder of its horrors, who will dress the dead bodies so that the taste deceived by these disguises will not reject what is strange to it, and will feast on corpses, the very sight of which would sicken you.'"

Although this quotation is irrelevant, I cannot resist the temptation to transcribe it, and I think few of my readers will resent it.

In conclusion, whatever food you give your children, provided you accustom them to nothing but plain and simple dishes, let them eat and run and play as much as they want; you may be sure they will never eat too much and will never have indigestion; but if you keep them hungry half their time, when they do contrive to evade your vigilance, they will take advantage of it as far as they can; they will eat till they are sick, they will gorge themselves till they can eat no more. Our appetite is only excessive because we try to impose on it rules other than those of nature, opposing, controlling, prescribing, adding, or substracting; the scales are always in our hands, but the scales are the measure of our caprices not of our stomachs. I return to my usual illustration; among peasants the cupboard and the apple-loft are always left open, and indigestion is unknown alike to children and grown-up people.

If, however, it happened that a child were too great an eater, though, under my system, I think it is impossible, he is so easily distracted by his favourite games that one might easily starve him without his knowing it. How is it that teachers have failed to use such a safe and easy weapon. Herodotus records that the Lydians, [Footnote: The ancient historians are full of opinions which may be useful, even if the facts which they present are false. But we do not know how to make any real use of history. Criticism and erudition are our only care; as if it mattered more that a statement were true or false than that we should be able to get a useful lesson from it. A wise man should consider history a tissue of fables whose morals are well adapted to the human heart.] under the pressure of great scarcity, decided to invent sports and other amusements with which to cheat their hunger, and they passed whole days without thought of food. Your learned teachers may have read this passage time after time without seeing how it might be applied to children. One of these teachers will probably tell me that a child does not like to leave his dinner for his lessons. You are right, sir—I was not thinking of that sort of sport.

The sense of smell is to taste what sight is to touch; it goes before it and gives it warning that it will be affected by this or that substance; and it inclines it to seek or shun this experience according to the impressions received beforehand. I have been told that savages receive impressions quite different from ours, and that they have quite different ideas with regard to pleasant or unpleasant odours. I can well believe it. Odours alone are slight sensations; they affect the imagination rather than the senses, and they work mainly through the anticipations they arouse. This being so, and the tastes of savages being so unlike the taste of civilised men, they should lead them to form very different ideas with regard to flavours and therefore with regard to the odours which announce them. A Tartar must enjoy the smell of a haunch of putrid horseflesh, much as a sportsman enjoys a very high partridge. Our idle sensations, such as the scents wafted from the flower beds, must pass unnoticed among men who walk too much to care for strolling in a garden, and do not work enough to find pleasure in repose. Hungry men would find little pleasure in scents which did not proclaim the approach of food.

Smell is the sense of the imagination; as it gives tone to the nerves it must have a great effect on the brain; that is why it revives us for the time, but eventually causes exhaustion. Its effects on love are pretty generally recognised. The sweet perfumes of a dressing-room are not so slight a snare as you may fancy them, and I hardly know whether to congratulate or condole with that wise and somewhat insensible person whose senses are never stirred by the scent of the flowers his mistress wears in her bosom.

Hence the sense of smell should not be over-active in early childhood; the imagination, as yet unstirred by changing passions, is scarcely susceptible of emotion, and we have not enough experience to discern beforehand from one sense the promise of another. This view is confirmed by observation, and it is certain that the sense of smell is dull and almost blunted in most children. Not that their sensations are less acute than those of grown-up people, but that there is no idea associated with them; they do not easily experience pleasure or pain, and are not flattered or hurt as we are. Without going beyond my system, and without recourse to comparative anatomy, I think we can easily see why women are generally fonder of perfumes than men.

It is said that from early childhood the Redskins of Canada, train their sense of smell to such a degree of subtlety that, although they have dogs, they do not condescend to use them in hunting—they are their own dogs. Indeed I believe that if children were trained to scent their dinner as a dog scents game, their sense of smell might be nearly as perfect; but I see no very real

116

advantage to be derived from this sense, except by teaching the child to observe the relation between smell and taste. Nature has taken care to compel us to learn these relations. She has made the exercise of the latter sense practically inseparable from that of the former, by placing their organs close together, and by providing, in the mouth, a direct pathway between them, so that we taste nothing without smelling it too. Only I would not have these natural relations disturbed in order to deceive the child, e.g.; to conceal the taste of medicine with an aromatic odour, for the discord between the senses is too great for deception, the more active sense overpowers the other, the medicine is just as distasteful, and this disagreeable association extends to every sensation experienced at the time; so the slightest of these sensations recalls the rest to his imagination and a very pleasant perfume is for him only a nasty smell; thus our foolish precautions increase the sum total of his unpleasant sensations at the cost of his pleasant sensations.

In the following books I have still to speak of the training of a sort of sixth sense, called common-sense, not so much because it is common to all men, but because it results from the well-regulated use of the other five, and teaches the nature of things by the sum-total of their external aspects. So this sixth sense has no special organ, it has its seat in the brain, and its sensations which are purely internal are called percepts or ideas. The number of these ideas is the measure of our knowledge; exactness of thought depends on their clearness and precision; the art of comparing them one with another is called human reason. Thus what I call the reasoning of the senses, or the reasoning of the child, consists in the formation of simple ideas through the associated experience of several sensations; what I call the reasoning of the intellect, consists in the formation, of complex ideas through the association of several simple ideas.

If my method is indeed that of nature, and if I am not mistaken in the application of that method, we have led our pupil through the region of sensation to the bounds of the child's reasoning; the first step we take beyond these bounds must be the step of a man. But before we make this fresh advance, let us glance back for a moment at the path we have hitherto followed. Every age, every station in life, has a perfection, a ripeness, of its own. We have often heard the phrase "a grown man;" but we will consider "a grown child." This will be a new experience and none the less pleasing.

The life of finite creatures is so poor and narrow that the mere sight of what is arouses no emotion. It is fancy which decks reality, and if imagination does not lend its charm to that which touches our senses, our barren pleasure is confined to the senses alone, while the heart remains cold. The earth adorned with the treasures of autumn displays a wealth of colour which the eye admires; but this admiration fails to move us, it springs rather from thought than from feeling. In spring the country is almost bare and leafless, the trees give no shade, the grass has hardly begun to grow, yet the heart is touched by the sight. In this new birth of nature, we feel the revival of our own life; the memories of past pleasures surround us; tears of delight, those companions of pleasure ever ready to accompany a pleasing sentiment, tremble on our eyelids. Animated, lively, and delightful though the vintage may be, we behold it without a tear.

And why is this? Because imagination adds to the sight of spring the image of the seasons which are yet to come; the eye sees the tender shoot, the mind's eye beholds its flowers, fruit, and foliage, and even the mysteries they may conceal. It blends successive stages into one moment's experience; we see things, not so much as they will be, but as we would have them be, for imagination has only to take her choice. In autumn, on the other hand, we only behold the present; if we wish to look forward to spring, winter bars the way, and our shivering imagination dies away among its frost and snow.

This is the source of the charm we find in beholding the beauties of childhood, rather than the perfection of manhood. When do we really delight in beholding a man? When the memory of his deeds leads us to look back over his life and his youth is renewed in our eyes. If we are reduced to viewing him as he is, or to picturing him as he will be in old age, the thought of declining years destroys all our pleasure. There is no pleasure in seeing a man hastening to his grave; the image of death makes all hideous.

But when I think of a child of ten or twelve, strong, healthy, well-grown for his age, only pleasant thoughts are called up, whether of the present or the future. I see him keen, eager, and full of life, free from gnawing cares and painful forebodings, absorbed in this present state, and delighting in a fullness of life which seems to extend beyond himself. I look forward to a time when he will use his daily increasing sense, intelligence and vigour, those growing powers of which he continually gives fresh proof. I watch the child with delight, I picture to myself the man with even greater pleasure. His eager life seems to stir my own pulses, I seem to live his life and in his vigour I renew my own.

The hour strikes, the scene is changed. All of a sudden his eye grows dim, his mirth has fled. Farewell mirth, farewell untrammelled sports in which he delighted. A stern, angry man takes him by the hand, saying gravely, "Come with me, sir," and he is led away. As they are entering the room, I catch a glimpse of books. Books, what dull food for a child of his age! The poor child allows himself to be dragged away; he casts a sorrowful look on all about him, and departs in silence, his eyes swollen with the tears he dare not shed, and his heart bursting with the sighs he dare not utter.

You who have no such cause for fear, you for whom no period of life is a time of weariness and tedium, you who welcome days without care and nights without impatience, you who only reckon time by your pleasures, come, my happy kindly pupil, and console us for the departure of that miserable creature. Come! Here he is and at his approach I feel a thrill of delight which I see he shares. It is his friend, his comrade, who meets him; when he sees me he knows very well that he will not be long without amusement; we are never dependent on each other, but we are always on good terms, and we are never so happy as when together.

His face, his bearing, his expression, speak of confidence and contentment; health shines in his countenance, his firm step speaks of strength; his colour, delicate but not sickly, has nothing of softness or effeminacy. Sun and wind have already set the honourable stamp of manhood on his countenance; his rounded muscles already begin to show some signs of growing individuality; his eyes, as yet unlighted by the flame of feeling, have at least all their native calm; They have not been darkened by prolonged sorrow, nor are his cheeks furrowed by ceaseless tears. Behold in his quick and certain movements the natural vigour of his age and the confidence of independence. His manner is free and open, but without a trace of insolence or vanity; his head which has not been bent over books does not fall upon his breast; there is no need to say, "Hold your head up," he will neither hang his head for shame or fear.

Make room for him, gentlemen, in your midst; question him boldly; have no fear of importunity, chatter, or impertinent questions. You need not be afraid that he will take possession of you and expect you to devote yourself entirely to him, so that you cannot get rid of him.

Neither need you look for compliments from him; nor will he tell you what I have taught him to say; expect nothing from him but the plain, simple truth, without addition or ornament and without vanity. He will tell you the wrong things he has done and thought as readily as the right, without troubling himself in the least as to the effect of his words upon you; he will use speech with all the simplicity of its first beginnings.

We love to augur well of our children, and we are continually regretting the flood of folly which overwhelms the hopes we would fain have rested on some chance phrase. If my scholar rarely gives me cause for such prophecies, neither will he give me cause for such regrets, for he never says a useless word, and does not exhaust himself by chattering when he knows there is no one to listen to him. His ideas are few but precise, he knows nothing by rote but much by experience. If he reads our books worse than other children, he reads far better in the book of nature; his thoughts are not in his tongue but in his brain; he has less memory and more judgment; he can only speak one language, but he understands what he is saying, and if his speech is not so good as that of other children his deeds are better.

He does not know the meaning of habit, routine, and custom; what he did yesterday has no control over what he is doing to-day; he follows no rule, submits to no authority, copies no pattern, and only acts or speaks as he pleases. So do not expect set speeches or studied manners from him, but just the faithful expression of his thoughts and the conduct that springs from his inclinations. [Footnote: Habit owes its charm to man's natural idleness, and this idleness grows upon us if indulged; it is easier to do what we have already done, there is a beaten path which is easily followed. Thus we may observe that habit is very strong in the aged and in the indolent, and very weak in the young and active. The rule of habit is only good for feeble hearts, and it makes them more and more feeble day by day. The only useful habit for children is to be accustomed to submit without difficulty to necessity, and the only useful habit for man is to submit without difficulty to the rule of reason. Every other habit is a vice.]

You will find he has a few moral ideas concerning his present state and none concerning manhood; what use could he make of them, for the child is not, as yet, an active member of society. Speak to him of freedom, of property, or even of what is usually done; he may understand you so far; he knows why his things are his own, and why other things are not his, and nothing more. Speak to him of duty or obedience; he will not know what you are talking about; bid him do something and he will pay no attention; but say to him, "If you will give me this pleasure, I will repay it when required," and he will hasten to give you satisfaction, for he asks nothing better than to extend his domain, to acquire rights over you, which will, he knows, be respected. Maybe he is not sorry to have a place of his own, to be reckoned of some account; but if he has formed this latter idea, he has already left the realms of nature, and you have failed to bar the gates of vanity.

For his own part, should he need help, he will ask it readily of the first person he meets. He will ask it of a king as readily as of his servant; all men are equals in his eyes. From his way of asking you will see he knows you owe him nothing, that he is asking a favour. He knows too that humanity moves you to grant this favour; his words are few and simple. His voice, his look, his gesture are those of a being equally familiar with compliance and refusal. It is neither the crawling, servile submission of the slave, nor the imperious tone of the master, it is a modest confidence in mankind; it is the noble and touching gentleness of a creature, free, yet sensitive and feeble, who asks aid of a being, free, but strong and kindly. If you grant his request he will not thank you, but he will feel he has incurred a debt. If you refuse he will neither complain nor insist; he knows it is useless; he will not say, "They refused to help me," but "It was impossible," and as I have already said, we do not rebel against necessity when once we have perceived it.

Leave him to himself and watch his actions without speaking, consider what he is doing and how he sets about it. He does not require to convince himself that he is free, so he never acts thoughtlessly and merely to show that he can do what he likes; does he not know that he is always his own master? He is quick, alert, and ready; his movements are eager as befits his age, but you will not find one which has no end in view. Whatever he wants, he will never attempt what is beyond his powers, for he has learnt by experience what those powers are; his means will always be adapted to the end in view, and he will rarely attempt anything without the certainty of success; his eye is keen and true; he will not be so stupid as to go and ask other people about what he sees; he will examine it on his own account, and before he asks he will try every means at his disposal to discover what he wants to know for himself. If he lights upon some unexpected difficulty, he will be less upset than others; if there is danger he will be less afraid. His imagination is still asleep and nothing has been done to arouse it; he only sees what is really there, and rates the danger at its true worth; so he never loses his head. He does not rebel against necessity, her hand is too heavy upon him; he has borne her yoke all his life long, he is well used to it; he is always ready for anything.

Work or play are all one to him, his games are his work; he knows no difference. He brings to everything the cheerfulness of interest, the charm of freedom, and he shows the bent of his own mind and the extent of his knowledge. Is there anything better worth seeing, anything more touching or more delightful, than a pretty child, with merry, cheerful glance, easy contented manner, open smiling countenance, playing at the most important things, or working at the lightest amusements?

Would you now judge him by comparison? Set him among other children and leave him to himself. You will soon see which has made most progress, which comes nearer to the perfection of childhood. Among all the children in the town there is none more skilful and none so strong. Among young peasants he is their equal in strength and their superior in skill. In everything within a child's grasp he judges, reasons, and shows a forethought beyond the rest. Is it a matter of action, running, jumping, or shifting things, raising weights or estimating distance, inventing games, carrying off prizes; you might say, "Nature obeys his word," so easily does he bend all things to his will. He is made to lead, to rule his fellows; talent and experience take the place of right and authority. In any garb, under any name, he will still be first; everywhere he will rule the rest, they will always feel his superiority, he will be master without knowing it, and they will serve him unawares.

He has reached the perfection of childhood; he has lived the life of a child; his progress has not been bought at the price of his happiness, he has gained both. While he has acquired all the wisdom of a child, he has been as free and happy as his health permits. If the Reaper Death should cut him off and rob us of our hopes, we need not bewail alike his life and death, we shall not have the added grief of knowing that we caused him pain; we will say, "His childhood, at least, was happy; we have robbed him of nothing that nature gave him."

The chief drawback to this early education is that it is only appreciated by the wise; to vulgar eyes the child so carefully educated is nothing but a rough little boy. A tutor thinks rather of the advantage to himself than to his pupil; he makes a point of showing that there has been no time wasted; he provides his pupil with goods which can be readily displayed in the shop window, accomplishments which can be shown off at will; no matter whether they are useful, provided they are easily seen. Without choice or discrimination he loads his memory with a pack of rubbish. If the child is to be examined he is set to display his wares; he spreads them out, satisfies those who behold them, packs up his bundle and goes his way. My pupil is poorer, he has no bundle to display, he has only himself to show. Now neither child nor man can be read at a glance. Where are the observers who can at once discern the characteristics of this child? There are such people, but they are few and far between; among a thousand fathers you will scarcely find one.

Too many questions are tedious and revolting to most of us and especially to children. After a few minutes their attention flags, they cease to listen to your everlasting questions and reply at random. This way of testing them is pedantic and useless; a chance word will often show their sense and intelligence better than much talking, but take care that the answer is neither a matter of chance nor yet learnt by heart. A man must needs have a good judgment if he is to estimate the judgment of a child.

I heard the late Lord Hyde tell the following story about one of his friends. He had returned from Italy after a three years' absence, and was anxious to test the progress of his son, a child of nine or ten. One evening he took a walk with the child and his tutor across a level space where the schoolboys were flying their kites. As they went, the father said to his son, "Where is the kite that casts this shadow?" Without hesitating and without glancing upwards the child replied, "Over the high road." "And indeed," said Lord Hyde, "the high road was between us and the sun." At these words, the father kissed his child, and having finished his examination he departed. The next day he sent the tutor the papers settling an annuity on him in addition to his salary.

What a father! and what a promising child! The question is exactly adapted to the child's age, the answer is perfectly simple; but see what precision it implies in the child's judgment. Thus did the pupil of Aristotle master the famous steed which no squire had ever been able to tame.

BOOK III

The whole course of man's life up to adolescence is a period of weakness; yet there comes a time during these early years when the child's strength overtakes the demands upon it, when the growing creature, though absolutely weak, is relatively strong. His needs are not fully developed and his present strength is more than enough for them. He would be a very feeble man, but he is a strong child.

What is the cause of man's weakness? It is to be found in the disproportion between his strength and his desires. It is our passions that make us weak, for our natural strength is not enough for their satisfaction. To limit our desires comes to the same thing, therefore, as to increase our strength. When we can do more than we want, we have strength enough and to spare, we are really strong. This is the third stage of childhood, the stage with which I am about to deal. I still speak of childhood for want of a better word; for our scholar is approaching adolescence, though he has not yet reached the age of puberty.

About twelve or thirteen the child's strength increases far more rapidly than his needs. The strongest and fiercest of the passions is still unknown, his physical development is still imperfect and seems to await the call of the will. He is scarcely aware of extremes of heat and cold and braves them with impunity. He needs no coat, his blood is warm; no spices, hunger is his sauce, no food comes amiss at this age; if he is sleepy he stretches himself on the ground and goes to sleep; he finds all he needs within his reach; he is not tormented by any imaginary wants; he cares nothing what others think; his desires are not beyond his grasp; not only is he self-sufficing, but for the first and last time in his life he has more strength than he needs.

I know beforehand what you will say. You will not assert that the child has more needs than I attribute to him, but you will deny his strength. You forget that I am speaking of my own pupil, not of those puppets who walk with difficulty from one room to another, who toil indoors and carry bundles of paper. Manly strength, you say, appears only with manhood; the vital spirits, distilled in their proper vessels and spreading through the whole body, can alone make the muscles firm, sensitive, tense, and springy, can alone cause real strength. This is the philosophy of the study; I appeal to that of experience. In the country districts, I see big lads hoeing, digging, guiding the plough, filling the wine-cask, driving the cart, like their fathers; you would take them for grown men if their voices did not betray them. Even in our towns, iron-workers', tool makers', and blacksmiths' lads are almost as strong as their masters and would be scarcely less skilful had their training begun earlier. If there is a difference, and I do not deny that there is, it is, I repeat, much less than the difference between the stormy passions of the man and the few wants of the child. Moreover, it is not merely a question of bodily strength, but more especially of strength of mind, which reinforces and directs the bodily strength.

This interval in which the strength of the individual is in excess of his wants is, as I have said, relatively though not absolutely the time of greatest strength. It is the most precious time in his life; it comes but once; it is very short, all too short, as you will see when you consider the importance of using it aright.

He has, therefore, a surplus of strength and capacity which he will never have again. What use shall he make of it? He will strive to use it in tasks which will help at need. He will, so to speak, cast his present surplus into the storehouse of the future; the vigorous child will make provision for the feeble man; but he will not store his goods where thieves may break in, nor in barns which are not his own. To store them aright, they must be in the hands and the head, they must be stored within himself. This is the time for work, instruction, and inquiry. And note that this is no arbitrary choice of mine, it is the way of nature herself.

Human intelligence is finite, and not only can no man know everything, he cannot even acquire all the scanty knowledge of others. Since the contrary of every false proposition is a truth, there are as many truths as falsehoods. We must, therefore, choose what to teach as well as when to teach it. Some of the information within our reach is false, some is useless, some merely serves to puff up its possessor. The small store which really contributes to our welfare alone deserves the study of a wise man, and therefore of a child whom one would have wise. He must know not merely what is, but what is useful.

From this small stock we must also deduct those truths which require a full grown mind for their understanding, those which suppose a knowledge of man's relations to his fellow-men—a knowledge which no child can acquire; these things, although in themselves true, lead an inexperienced mind into mistakes with regard to other matters.

We are now confined to a circle, small indeed compared with the whole of human thought, but this circle is still a vast sphere when measured by the child's mind. Dark places of the human understanding, what rash hand shall dare to raise your veil? What pitfalls does our so-called science prepare for the miserable child. Would you guide him along this dangerous path and draw the veil from the face of nature? Stay your hand. First make sure that neither he nor you will become dizzy. Beware of the specious charms of error and the intoxicating fumes of pride. Keep this truth ever before you— Ignorance never did any one any harm, error alone is fatal, and we do not lose our way through ignorance but through self-confidence.

His progress in geometry may serve as a test and a true measure of the growth of his intelligence, but as soon as he can distinguish between what is useful and what is useless, much skill and discretion are required to lead him towards theoretical studies. For example, would you have him find a mean proportional between two lines, contrive that he should require to find a square equal to a given rectangle; if two mean proportionals are required, you must first contrive to interest him in the doubling of the cube. See how we are gradually approaching the moral ideas which distinguish between good and evil. Hitherto we have known no law but necessity, now we are considering what is useful; we shall soon come to what is fitting and right.

Man's diverse powers are stirred by the same instinct. The bodily activity, which seeks an outlet for its energies, is succeeded by the mental activity which seeks for knowledge. Children are first restless, then curious; and this curiosity, rightly directed, is the means of development for the age with which we are dealing. Always distinguish between natural and acquired tendencies. There is a zeal for learning which has no other foundation than a wish to appear learned, and there is another which springs from man's natural curiosity about all things far or near which may affect himself. The innate desire for comfort and the impossibility of its complete satisfaction impel him to the endless search for fresh means of contributing to its satisfaction. This is the first principle of curiosity; a principle natural to the human heart, though its growth is proportional to the development of our feeling and knowledge. If a man of science were left on a desert island with his books and instruments and knowing that he must spend the rest of his life there, he would scarcely trouble himself about the solar system, the laws of attraction, or the differential calculus. He might never even open a book again; but he would never rest till he had explored the furthest corner of his island, however large it might be. Let us therefore omit from our early studies such knowledge as has no natural attraction for us, and confine ourselves to such things as instinct impels us to study.

Our island is this earth; and the most striking object we behold is the sun. As soon as we pass beyond our immediate surroundings, one or both of these must meet our eye. Thus the philosophy of most savage races is mainly directed to imaginary divisions of the earth or to the divinity of the sun.

What a sudden change you will say. Just now we were concerned with what touches ourselves, with our immediate environment, and all at once we are exploring the round world and leaping to the bounds of the universe. This change is the result of our growing strength and of the natural bent of the mind. While we were weak and feeble, self-preservation concentrated our attention on ourselves; now that we are strong and powerful, the desire for a wider sphere carries us beyond ourselves as far as our eyes can reach. But as the intellectual world is still unknown to us, our thoughts are bounded by the visible horizon, and our understanding only develops within the limits of our vision.

Let us transform our sensations into ideas, but do not let us jump all at once from the objects of sense to objects of thought. The latter are attained by means of the former. Let the senses be the only guide for the first workings of reason. No book but the world, no teaching but that of fact. The child who reads ceases to think, he only reads. He is acquiring words not knowledge.

Teach your scholar to observe the phenomena of nature; you will soon rouse his curiosity, but if you would have it grow, do not be in too great a hurry to satisfy this curiosity. Put the problems before him and let him solve them himself. Let him know nothing because you have told him, but because he has learnt it for himself. Let him not be taught science, let him discover it. If ever you substitute authority for reason he will cease to reason; he will be a mere plaything of other people's thoughts.

You wish to teach this child geography and you provide him with globes, spheres, and maps. What elaborate preparations! What is the use of all these symbols; why not begin by showing him the real thing so that he may at least know what you are talking about?

One fine evening we are walking in a suitable place where the wide horizon gives us a full view of the setting sun, and we note the objects which mark the place where it sets. Next morning we return to the same place for a breath of fresh air before sun-rise. We see the rays of light which announce the sun's approach; the glow increases, the east seems afire, and long before the sun appears the light leads us to expect its return. Every moment you expect to see it. There it is at last! A shining point appears like a flash of lightning and soon fills the whole space; the veil of darkness rolls away, man perceives his dwelling place in fresh beauty. During the night the grass has assumed a fresher green; in the light of early dawn, and gilded by the first rays of the sun, it seems covered with a shining network of dew reflecting the light and colour. The birds raise their chorus of praise to greet the Father of life, not one of them is mute; their gentle warbling is softer than by day, it expresses the langour of a peaceful waking. All these produce an impression of freshness which seems to reach the very soul. It is a brief hour of enchantment which no man can resist; a sight so grand, so fair, so delicious, that none can behold it unmoved.

Fired with this enthusiasm, the master wishes to impart it to the child. He expects to rouse his emotion by drawing attention to his own. Mere folly! The splendour of nature lives in man's heart; to be seen, it must be felt. The child sees the objects themselves, but does not perceive their relations, and cannot hear their harmony. It needs knowledge he has not yet acquired, feelings he has not yet experienced, to receive the complex impression which results from all these separate sensations. If he has not wandered over arid plains, if his feet have not been scorched by the burning sands of the desert, if he has not breathed the hot and oppressive air reflected from the glowing rocks, how shall he delight in the fresh air of a fine morning. The scent of flowers, the beauty of foliage, the moistness of the dew, the soft turf beneath his feet, how shall all these delight his senses. How shall the song of the birds arouse voluptuous emotion if love and pleasure are still unknown to him? How shall he behold with rapture the birth of this fair day, if his imagination cannot paint the joys it may bring in its track? How can he feel the beauty of nature, while the hand that formed it is unknown?

Never tell the child what he cannot understand: no descriptions, no eloquence, no figures of speech, no poetry. The time has not come for feeling or taste. Continue to be clear and cold; the time will come only too soon when you must adopt another tone.

Brought up in the spirit of our maxims, accustomed to make his own tools and not to appeal to others until he has tried and failed, he will examine everything he sees carefully and in silence. He thinks rather than questions. Be content, therefore, to show him things at a fit season; then, when you see that his curiosity is thoroughly aroused, put some brief question which will set him trying to discover the answer.

On the present occasion when you and he have carefully observed the rising sun, when you have called his attention to the mountains and other objects visible from the same spot, after he has chattered freely about them, keep quiet for a few minutes as if lost in thought and then say, "I think the sun set over there last night; it rose here this morning. How can that be?" Say no more; if he asks questions, do not answer them; talk of something else. Let him alone, and be sure he will think about it.

To train a child to be really attentive so that he may be really impressed by any truth of experience, he must spend anxious days before he discovers that truth. If he does not learn enough in this way, there is another way of drawing his attention to the matter. Turn the question about. If he does not know how the sun gets from the place where it sets to where it rises, he knows at least how it travels from sunrise to sunset, his eyes teach him that. Use the second question to throw light on the first; either your pupil is a regular dunce or the analogy is too clear to be missed. This is his first lesson in cosmography.

As we always advance slowly from one sensible idea to another, and as we give time enough to each for him to become really familiar with it before we go on to another, and lastly as we never force our scholar's attention, we are still a long way from a knowledge of the course of the sun or the shape of the earth; but as all the apparent movements of the celestial bodies depend on the same principle, and the first observation leads on to all the rest, less effort is needed, though more time, to proceed from the diurnal revolution to the calculation of eclipses, than to get a thorough understanding of day and night.

Since the sun revolves round the earth it describes a circle, and every circle must have a centre; that we know already. This centre is invisible, it is in the middle of the earth, but we can mark out two opposite points on the earth's surface which correspond to it. A skewer passed through the three points and prolonged to the sky at either end would represent the earth's axis and the sun's daily course. A round teetotum revolving on its point represents the sky turning on its axis, the two points of the teetotum are the two poles; the child will be delighted to find one of them, and I show him the tail of the Little bear. Here is another game for the dark. Little by little we get to know the stars, and from this comes a wish to know the planets and observe the constellations.

We saw the sun rise at midsummer, we shall see it rise at Christmas or some other fine winter's day; for you know we are no lie-a-beds and we enjoy the cold. I take care to make this second observation in the same place as the first, and if skilfully lead up to, one or other will certainly exclaim, "What a funny thing! The sun is not rising in the same place; here are our landmarks, but it is rising over there. So there is the summer east and the winter east, etc." Young teacher, you are on the right track. These examples should show you how to teach the sphere without any difficulty, taking the earth for the earth and the sun for the sun.

As a general rule—never substitute the symbol for the thing signified, unless it is impossible to show the thing itself; for the child's attention is so taken up with the symbol that he will forget what it signifies.

I consider the armillary sphere a clumsy disproportioned bit of apparatus. The confused circles and the strange figures described on it suggest witchcraft and frighten the child. The earth is too small, the circles too large and too numerous, some of them, the colures, for instance, are quite useless, and the thickness of the pasteboard gives them an appearance of solidity so that they are taken for circular masses having a real existence, and when you tell the child that these are imaginary circles, he does not know what he is looking at and is none the wiser.

We are unable to put ourselves in the child's place, we fail to enter into his thoughts, we invest him with our own ideas, and while we are following our own chain of reasoning, we merely fill his head with errors and absurdities.

Should the method of studying science be analytic or synthetic? People dispute over this question, but it is not always necessary to choose between them. Sometimes the same experiments allow one to use both analysis and synthesis, and thus to guide the child by the method of instruction when he fancies he is only analysing. Then, by using both at once, each method confirms the results of the other. Starting from opposite ends, without thinking of following the same road, he will unexpectedly reach their meeting place and this will be a delightful surprise. For example, I would begin geography at both ends and add to the study of the earth's revolution the measurement of its divisions, beginning at home. While the child is studying the sphere and is thus transported to the heavens, bring him back to the divisions of the globe and show him his own home.

His geography will begin with the town he lives in and his father's country house, then the places between them, the rivers near them, and then the sun's aspect and how to find one's way by its aid. This is the meeting place.

Let him make his own map, a very simple map, at first containing only two places; others may be added from time to time, as he is able to estimate their distance and position. You see at once what a good start we have given him by making his eye his compass.

No doubt he will require some guidance in spite of this, but very little, and that little without his knowing it. If he goes wrong let him alone, do not correct his mistakes; hold your tongue till he finds them out for himself and corrects them, or at most arrange something, as opportunity offers, which may show him his mistakes. If he never makes mistakes he will never learn anything thoroughly. Moreover, what he needs is not an exact knowledge of local topography, but how to find out for himself. No matter whether he carries maps in his head provided he understands what they mean, and has a clear idea of the art of making them. See what a difference there is already between the knowledge of your scholars and the ignorance of mine. They learn maps, he makes them. Here are fresh ornaments for his room.

Remember that this is the essential point in my method — Do not teach the child many things, but never to let him form inaccurate or confused ideas. I care not if he knows nothing provided he is not mistaken, and I only acquaint him with truths to guard him against the errors he might put in their place. Reason and judgment come slowly, prejudices flock to us in crowds, and from these he must be protected. But if you make science itself your object, you embark on an unfathomable and shoreless ocean, an ocean strewn with reefs from which you will never return. When I see a man in love with knowledge, yielding to its charms and flitting from one branch to another unable to stay his steps, he seems to me like a child gathering shells on the sea-shore, now picking them up, then throwing them aside for others which he sees beyond them, then taking them again, till overwhelmed by their number and unable to choose between them, he flings them all away and returns empty handed.

Time was long during early childhood; we only tried to pass our time for fear of using it ill; now it is the other way; we have not time enough for all that would be of use. The passions, remember, are drawing near, and when they knock at the door your scholar will have no ear for anything else. The peaceful age of intelligence is so short, it flies so swiftly, there is so much to be done, that it is madness to try to make your child learned. It is not your business to teach him the various sciences, but to give him a taste for them and methods of learning them when this taste is more mature. That is assuredly a fundamental principle of all good education.

This is also the time to train him gradually to prolonged attention to a given object; but this attention should never be the result of constraint, but of interest or desire; you must be very careful that it is not too much for his strength, and that it is not carried to the point of tedium. Watch him, therefore, and whatever happens, stop before he is tired, for it matters little what he learns; it does matter that he should do nothing against his will.

If he asks questions let your answers be enough to whet his curiosity but not enough to satisfy it; above all, when you find him talking at random and overwhelming you with silly questions instead of asking for information, at once refuse to answer; for it is clear that he no longer cares about the matter in hand, but wants to make you a slave to his questions. Consider his motives rather than his words. This warning, which was scarcely needed before, becomes of supreme importance when the child begins to reason.

There is a series of abstract truths by means of which all the sciences are related to common principles and are developed each in its turn. This relationship is the method of the philosophers. We are not concerned with it at present. There is quite another method by which every concrete example suggests another and always points to the next in the series. This succession, which stimulates the curiosity and so arouses the attention required by every object in turn, is the order followed by most men, and it is the right order for all children. To take our bearings so as to make our maps we must find meridians. Two points of intersection between the equal shadows morning and evening supply an excellent meridian for a thirteen-year-old astronomer. But these meridians disappear, it takes time to trace them, and you are obliged to work in one place. So much trouble and attention will at last become irksome. We foresaw this and are ready for it.

Again I must enter into minute and detailed explanations. I hear my readers murmur, but I am prepared to meet their disapproval; I will not sacrifice the most important part of this book to your impatience. You may think me as long-winded as you please; I have my own opinion as to your complaints.

Long ago my pupil and I remarked that some substances such as amber, glass, and wax, when well rubbed, attracted straws, while others did not. We accidentally discover a substance which has a more unusual property, that of attracting filings or other small particles of iron from a distance and without rubbing. How much time do we devote to this game to the exclusion of everything else! At last we discover that this property is communicated to the iron itself, which is, so to speak, endowed with life. We go to the fair one day [Footnote: I could not help laughing when I read an elaborate criticism of this little tale by M. de Formy. "This conjuror," says he, "who is afraid of a child's competition and preaches to his tutor is the sort of person we meet with in the world in which Emile and such as he are living." This witty M. de Formy could not guess that this little scene was arranged beforehand, and that the juggler was taught his part in it; indeed I did not state this fact. But I have said again and again that I was not writing for people who expected to be told everything.] and a conjuror has a wax duck floating in a basin of water, and he makes it follow a bit of bread. We are greatly surprised, but we do not call him a wizard, never having heard of such persons. As we are continually observing effects whose causes are unknown to us, we are in no hurry to make up our minds, and we remain in ignorance till we find an opportunity of learning.

When we get home we discuss the duck till we try to imitate it. We take a needle thoroughly magnetised, we imbed it in white wax, shaped as far as possible like a duck, with the needle running through the body, so that its eye forms the beak. We put the duck in water and put the end of a key near its beak, and you will readily understand our delight when we find that our duck follows the key just as the duck at the fair followed the bit of bread. Another time we may note the direction assumed by the duck when left in the basin; for the present we are wholly occupied with our work and we want nothing more.

The same evening we return to the fair with some bread specially prepared in our pockets, and as soon as the conjuror has performed his trick, my little doctor, who can scarcely sit still, exclaims, "The trick is quite easy; I can do it myself." "Do it then." He at once takes the bread with a bit of iron hidden in it from his pocket; his heart throbs as he approaches the table and holds out the bread, his hand trembles with excitement. The duck approaches and follows his hand. The child cries out and jumps for joy. The applause, the shouts of the crowd, are too much for him, he is beside himself. The conjuror, though disappointed, embraces him, congratulates him, begs the honour of his company on the following day, and promises to collect a still greater crowd to applaud his skill. My young scientist is very proud of himself and is beginning to chatter, but I check him at once and take him home overwhelmed with praise.

The child counts the minutes till to-morrow with absurd anxiety. He invites every one he meets, he wants all mankind to behold his glory; he can scarcely wait till the appointed hour. He hurries to the place; the hall is full already; as he enters his young heart swells with pride. Other tricks are to come first. The conjuror surpasses himself and does the most surprising things. The child sees none of these; he wriggles, perspires, and hardly breathes; the time is spent in fingering with a trembling hand the bit of bread in his pocket. His turn comes at last; the master announces it to the audience with all ceremony; he goes up looking somewhat shamefaced and takes out his bit of bread. Oh fleeting joys of human life! the duck, so tame yesterday, is quite wild to-day; instead of offering its beak it turns tail and swims away; it avoids the bread and the hand that holds it as carefully as it followed them yesterday. After many vain attempts accompanied by derisive shouts from the audience the child complains that he is being cheated, that is not the same duck, and he defies the conjuror to attract it.

The conjuror, without further words, takes a bit of bread and offers it to the duck, which at once follows it and comes to the hand which holds it. The child takes the same bit of bread with no better success; the duck mocks his efforts and swims round the basin. Overwhelmed with confusion he abandons the attempt, ashamed to face the crowd any longer. Then the conjuror takes the bit of bread the child brought with him and uses it as successfully as his own. He takes out the bit of iron before the audience — another laugh at our expense — then with this same bread he attracts the duck as before. He repeats the experiment with a piece of bread cut by a third person in full view of the audience. He does it with his glove, with his finger-tip. Finally he goes into the middle of the room and in the emphatic tones used by such persons he declares that his duck will obey his voice as readily as his hand; he speaks and the duck obeys; he bids him go to the right and he goes, to come back again and he comes. The movement is as ready as the command. The growing applause completes our discomfiture. We slip away unnoticed and shut ourselves up in our room, without relating our successes to everybody as we had expected.

Next day there is a knock at the door. When I open it there is the conjuror, who makes a modest complaint with regard to our conduct. What had he done that we should try to discredit his tricks and deprive him of his livelihood? What is there so wonderful in attracting a duck that we should purchase this honour at the price of an honest man's living? "My word, gentlemen! had I any other trade by which I could earn a living I would not pride myself on this. You may well believe that a man who has spent his life at this miserable trade knows more about it than you who only give your spare time to it. If I did not show you my best tricks at first, it was because one must not be so foolish as to display all one knows at once. I always take care to keep my best tricks for emergencies; and I have plenty more to prevent young folks from meddling. However, I have come, gentlemen, in all kindness, to show you the trick that gave you so much trouble; I only beg you not to use it to my hurt, and to be more discreet in future." He then shows us his apparatus, and to our great surprise we find it is merely a strong magnet in the hand of a boy concealed under the table. The man puts up his things, and after we have offered our thanks and apologies, we try to give him something. He refuses it. "No, gentlemen," says he, "I owe you no gratitude and I will not accept your gift. I leave you in my debt in spite of all, and that is my only revenge. Generosity may be found among all sorts of people, and I earn my pay by doing my tricks not by teaching them."

As he is going he blames me out-right. "I can make excuses for the child," he says, "he sinned in ignorance. But you, sir, should know better. Why did you let him do it? As you are living together and you are older than he, you should look after him and give him good advice. Your experience should be his guide. When he is grown up he will reproach, not only himself, but you, for the faults of his youth."

When he is gone we are greatly downcast. I blame myself for my easygoing ways. I promise the child that another time I will put his interests first and warn him against faults before he falls into them, for the time is coming when our relations will be changed, when the severity of the master must give way to the friendliness of the comrade; this change must come gradually, you must look ahead, and very far ahead.

We go to the fair again the next day to see the trick whose secret we know. We approach our Socrates, the conjuror, with profound respect, we scarcely dare to look him in the face. He overwhelms us with politeness, gives us the best places, and heaps coals of fire on our heads. He goes through his performance as usual, but he lingers affectionately over the duck, and often glances proudly in our direction. We are in the secret, but we do not tell. If my pupil did but open his mouth he would be worthy of death.

There is more meaning than you suspect in this detailed illustration. How many lessons in one! How mortifying are the results of a first impulse towards vanity! Young tutor, watch this first impulse carefully. If you can use it to bring about shame and disgrace, you may be sure it will not recur for many a day. What a fuss you will say. Just so; and all to provide a compass which will enable us to dispense with a meridian!

Having learnt that a magnet acts through other bodies, our next business is to construct a bit of apparatus similar to that shown us. A bare table, a shallow bowl placed on it and filled with water, a duck rather better finished than the first, and so on. We often watch the thing and at last we notice that the duck, when at rest, always turns the same way. We follow up this observation; we examine the direction, we find that it is from south to north. Enough! we have found our compass or its equivalent; the study of physics is begun.

There are various regions of the earth, and these regions differ in temperature. The variation is more evident as we approach the poles; all bodies expand with heat and contract with cold; this is best measured in liquids and best of all in spirits; hence the thermometer. The wind strikes the face, then the air is a body, a fluid; we feel it though we cannot see it. I invert a glass in water; the water will not fill it unless you leave a passage for the escape of the air; so air is capable of resistance. Plunge the glass further in the water; the water will encroach on the air-space without filling it entirely; so air yields somewhat to pressure. A ball filled with compressed air bounces better than one filled with anything else; so air is elastic. Raise your arm horizontally from the water when you are lying in your bath; you will feel a terrible weight on it; so air is a heavy body. By establishing an equilibrium between air and other fluids its weight can be measured, hence the barometer, the siphon, the air-gun, and the air-pump. All the laws of statics and hydrostatics are discovered by such rough experiments. For none of these would I take the child into a physical cabinet; I dislike that array of instruments and apparatus. The scientific atmosphere destroys science. Either the child is frightened by these instruments or his attention, which should be fixed on their effects, is distracted by their appearance.

We shall make all our apparatus ourselves, and I would not make it beforehand, but having caught a glimpse of the experiment by chance we mean to invent step by step an instrument for its verification. I would rather our apparatus was somewhat clumsy and imperfect, but our ideas clear as to what the apparatus ought to be, and the results to be obtained by means of it. For my first lesson in statics, instead of fetching a balance, I lay a stick across the back of a chair, I measure the two parts when it is balanced; add equal or unequal weights to either end; by pulling or pushing it as required, I find at last that equilibrium is the result of a reciprocal proportion between the amount of the weights and the length of the levers. Thus my little physicist is ready to rectify a balance before ever he sees one.

Undoubtedly the notions of things thus acquired for oneself are clearer and much more convincing than those acquired from the teaching of others; and not only is our reason not accustomed to a slavish submission to authority, but we develop greater ingenuity in discovering relations, connecting ideas and inventing apparatus, than when we merely accept what is given us and allow our minds to be enfeebled by indifference, like the body of a man whose servants always wait on him, dress him and put on his shoes, whose horse carries him, till he loses the use of his limbs. Boileau used to boast that he had taught Racine the art of rhyming with difficulty. Among the many short cuts to science, we badly need some one to teach us the art of learning with difficulty.

The most obvious advantage of these slow and laborious inquiries is this: the scholar, while engaged in speculative studies, is actively using his body, gaining suppleness of limb, and training his hands to labour so that he will be able to make them useful when he is a man. Too much apparatus, designed to guide us in our experiments and to supplement the exactness of our senses, makes us neglect to use those senses. The theodolite makes it unnecessary to estimate the size of angles; the eye which used to judge distances with much precision, trusts to the chain for its measurements; the steel yard dispenses with the need of judging weight by the hand as I used to do. The more ingenious our apparatus, the coarser and more unskilful are our senses. We surround ourselves with tools and fail to use those with which nature has provided every one of us.

But when we devote to the making of these instruments the skill which did instead of them, when for their construction we use the intelligence which enabled us to dispense with them, this is gain not loss, we add art to nature, we gain ingenuity without loss of skill. If instead of making a child stick to his books I employ him in a workshop, his hands work for the development of his mind. While he fancies himself a workman he is becoming a philosopher. Moreover, this exercise has other advantages of which I shall speak later; and you will see how, through philosophy in sport, one may rise to the real duties of man.

I have said already that purely theoretical science is hardly suitable for children, even for children approaching adolescence; but without going far into theoretical physics, take care that all their experiments are connected together by some chain of reasoning, so that they may follow an orderly sequence in the mind, and may be recalled at need; for it is very difficult to remember isolated facts or arguments, when there is no cue for their recall.

In your inquiry into the laws of nature always begin with the commonest and most conspicuous phenomena, and train your scholar not to accept these phenomena as causes but as facts. I take a stone and pretend to place it in the air; I open my hand, the stone falls. I see Emile watching my action and I say, "Why does this stone fall?"

What child will hesitate over this question? None, not even Emile, unless I have taken great pains to teach him not to answer. Every one will say, "The stone falls because it is heavy." "And what do you mean by heavy?" "That which falls." "So the stone falls because it falls?" Here is a poser for my little philosopher. This is his first lesson in systematic physics, and whether he learns physics or no it is a good lesson in common-sense.

As the child develops in intelligence other important considerations require us to be still more careful in our choice of his occupations. As soon as he has sufficient self-knowledge to understand what constitutes his well-being, as soon as he can grasp such far-reaching relations as to judge what is good for him and what is not, then he is able to discern the difference between work and play, and to consider the latter merely as relaxation. The objects of real utility may be introduced into his studies and may lead him to more prolonged attention than he gave to his games. The ever-recurring law of necessity soon teaches a man to do what he does not like, so as to avert evils which he would dislike still more. Such is the use of foresight, and this foresight, well or ill used, is the source of all the wisdom or the wretchedness of mankind.

Every one desires happiness, but to secure it he must know what happiness is. For the natural man happiness is as simple as his life; it consists in the absence of pain; health, freedom, the necessaries of life are its elements. The happiness of the moral man is another matter, but it does not concern us at present. I cannot repeat too often that it is only objects which can be perceived by the senses which can have any interest for children, especially children whose vanity has not been stimulated nor their minds corrupted by social conventions.

As soon as they foresee their needs before they feel them, their intelligence has made a great step forward, they are beginning to know the value of time. They must then be trained to devote this time to useful purposes, but this usefulness should be such as they can readily perceive and should be within the reach of their age and experience. What concerns the moral order and the customs of society should not yet be given them, for they are not in a condition to understand it. It is folly to expect them to attend to things vaguely described as good for them, when they do not know what this good is, things which they are assured will be to their advantage when they are grown up, though for the present they take no interest in this so-called advantage, which they are unable to understand.

Let the child do nothing because he is told; nothing is good for him but what he recognises as good. When you are always urging him beyond his present understanding, you think you are exercising a foresight which you really lack. To provide him with useless tools which he may never require, you deprive him of man's most useful tool—common-sense. You would have him docile as a child; he will be a credulous dupe when he grows up. You are always saying, "What I ask is for your good, though you cannot understand it. What does it matter to me whether you do it or not; my efforts are entirely on your account." All these fine speeches with which you hope to make him good, are preparing the way, so that the visionary, the tempter, the charlatan, the rascal, and every kind of fool may catch him in his snare or draw him into his folly.

A man must know many things which seem useless to a child, but need the child learn, or can he indeed learn, all that the man must know? Try to teach the child what is of use to a child and you will find that it takes all his time. Why urge him to the studies of an age he may never reach, to the neglect of those studies which meet his present needs? "But," you ask, "will it not be too late to learn what he ought to know when the time comes to use it?" I cannot tell; but this I do know, it is impossible to teach it sooner, for our real teachers are experience and emotion, and man will never learn what befits a man except under its own conditions. A child knows he must become a man; all the ideas he may have as to man's estate are so many opportunities for his instruction, but he should remain in complete ignorance of those ideas which are beyond his grasp. My whole book is one continued argument in support of this fundamental principle of education.

As soon as we have contrived to give our pupil an idea of the word "Useful," we have got an additional means of controlling him, for this word makes a great impression on him, provided that its meaning for him is a meaning relative to his own age, and provided he clearly sees its relation to his own well-being. This word makes no impression on your scholars because you have taken no pains to give it a meaning they can understand, and because other people always undertake to supply their needs so that they never require to think for themselves, and do not know what utility is.

"What is the use of that?" In future this is the sacred formula, the formula by which he and I test every action of our lives. This is the question with which I invariably answer all his questions; it serves to check the stream of foolish and tiresome questions with which children weary those about them. These incessant questions produce no result, and their object is rather to get a hold over you than to gain any real advantage. A pupil, who has been really taught only to want to know what is useful, questions like Socrates; he never asks a question without a reason for it, for he knows he will be required to give his reason before he gets an answer.

See what a powerful instrument I have put into your hands for use with your pupil. As he does not know the reason for anything you can reduce him to silence almost at will; and what advantages do your knowledge and experience give you to show him the usefulness of what you suggest. For, make no mistake about it, when you put this question to him, you are teaching him to put it to you, and you must expect that whatever you suggest to him in the future he will follow your own example and ask, "What is the use of this?"

Perhaps this is the greatest of the tutor's difficulties. If you merely try to put the child off when he asks a question, and if you give him a single reason he is not able to understand, if he finds that you reason according to your own ideas, not his, he will think what you tell him is good for you but not for him; you will lose his confidence and all your labour is thrown away. But what master will stop short and confess his faults to his pupil? We all make it a rule never to own to the faults we really have. Now I would make it a rule to admit even the faults I have not, if I could not make my reasons clear to him; as my conduct will always be intelligible to him, he will never doubt me and I shall gain more credit by confessing my imaginary faults than those who conceal their real defects.

In the first place do not forget that it is rarely your business to suggest what he ought to learn; it is for him to want to learn, to seek and to find it. You should put it within his reach, you should skilfully awaken the desire and supply him with means for its satisfaction. So your questions should be few and well-chosen, and as he will always have more questions to put to you than you to him, you will always have the advantage and will be able to ask all the oftener, "What is the use of that question?" Moreover, as it matters little what he learns provided he understands it and knows how to use it, as soon as you cannot give him a suitable explanation give him none at all. Do not hesitate to say, "I have no good answer to give you; I was wrong, let us drop the subject." If your teaching was really ill-chosen there is no harm in dropping it altogether; if it was not, with a little care you will soon find an opportunity of making its use apparent to him.

I do not like verbal explanations. Young people pay little heed to them, nor do they remember them. Things! Things! I cannot repeat it too often. We lay too much stress upon words; we teachers babble, and our scholars follow our example.

Suppose we are studying the course of the sun and the way to find our bearings, when all at once Emile interrupts me with the question, "What is the use of that?" what a fine lecture I might give, how many things I might take occasion to teach him in reply to his question, especially if there is any one there. I might speak of the advantages of travel, the value of commerce, the special products of different lands and the peculiar customs of different nations, the use of the calendar, the way to reckon the seasons for agriculture, the art of navigation, how to steer our course at sea, how to find our way without knowing exactly where we are. Politics, natural history, astronomy, even morals and international law are involved in my explanation, so as to give my pupil some idea of all these sciences and a great wish to learn them. When I have finished I shall have shown myself a regular pedant, I shall have made a great display of learning, and not one single idea has he understood. He is longing to ask me again, "What is the use of taking one's bearings?" but he dare not for fear of vexing me. He finds it pays best to pretend to listen to what he is forced to hear. This is the practical result of our fine systems of education.

But Emile is educated in a simpler fashion. We take so much pains to teach him a difficult idea that he will have heard nothing of all this. At the first word he does not understand, he will run away, he will prance about the room, and leave me to speechify by myself. Let us seek a more commonplace explanation; my scientific learning is of no use to him.

We were observing the position of the forest to the north of Montmorency when he interrupted me with the usual question, "What is the use of that?" "You are right," I said. "Let us take time to think it over, and if we find it is no use we will drop it, for we only want useful games." We find something else to do and geography is put aside for the day.

Next morning I suggest a walk before breakfast; there is nothing he would like better; children are always ready to run about, and he is a good walker. We climb up to the forest, we wander through its clearings and lose ourselves; we have no idea where we are, and when we want to retrace our steps we cannot find the way. Time passes, we are hot and hungry; hurrying vainly this way and that we find nothing but woods, quarries, plains, not a landmark to guide us. Very hot, very tired, very hungry, we only get further astray. At last we sit down to rest and to consider our position. I assume that Emile has been educated like an ordinary child. He does not think, he begins to cry; he has no idea we are close to Montmorency, which is hidden from our view by a mere thicket; but this thicket is a forest to him, a man of his size is buried among bushes. After a few minutes' silence I begin anxiously — —

JEAN JACQUES. My dear Emile, what shall we do get out?

EMILE. I am sure I do not know. I am tired, I am hungry, I am thirsty. I cannot go any further.

JEAN JACQUES. Do you suppose I am any better off? I would cry too if I could make my breakfast off tears. Crying is no use, we must look about us. Let us see your watch; what time is it?

EMILE. It is noon and I am so hungry!

JEAN JACQUES. Just so; it is noon and I am so hungry too.

EMILE. You must be very hungry indeed.

JEAN JACQUES. Unluckily my dinner won't come to find me. It is twelve o'clock. This time yesterday we were observing the position of the forest from Montmorency. If only we could see the position of Montmorency from the forest.

EMILE. But yesterday we could see the forest, and here we cannot see the town.

JEAN JACQUES. That is just it. If we could only find it without seeing it.

EMILE. Oh! my dear friend!

JEAN JACQUES. Did not we say the forest was...

EMILE. North of Montmorency.

JEAN JACQUES. Then Montmorency must lie...

EMILE. South of the forest.

JEAN JACQUES. We know how to find the north at midday.

EMILE. Yes, by the direction of the shadows.

JEAN JACQUES. But the south?

EMILE. What shall we do?

JEAN JACQUES. The south is opposite the north.

EMILE. That is true; we need only find the opposite of the shadows. That is the south! That is the south! Montmorency must be over there! Let us look for it there!

JEAN JACQUES. Perhaps you are right; let us follow this path through the wood.

EMILE. (Clapping his hands.) Oh, I can see Montmorency! there it is, quite plain, just in front of us! Come to luncheon, come to dinner, make haste! Astronomy is some use after all.

Be sure that he thinks this if he does not say it; no matter which, provided I do not say it myself. He will certainly never forget this day's lesson as long as he lives, while if I had only led him to think of all this at home, my lecture would have been forgotten the next day. Teach by doing whenever you can, and only fall back upon words when doing is out of the question.

The reader will not expect me to have such a poor opinion of him as to supply him with an example of every kind of study; but, whatever is taught, I cannot too strongly urge the tutor to adapt his instances to the capacity of his scholar; for once more I repeat the risk is not in what he does not know, but in what he thinks he knows.

I remember how I once tried to give a child a taste for chemistry. After showing him several metallic precipitates, I explained how ink was made. I told him how its blackness was merely the result of fine particles of iron separated from the vitriol and precipitated by an alkaline solution. In the midst of my learned explanation the little rascal pulled me up short with the question I myself had taught him. I was greatly puzzled. After a few moments' thought I decided what to do. I sent for some wine from the cellar of our landlord, and some very cheap wine from a wine-merchant. I took a small [Footnote: Before giving any explanation to a child a little bit of apparatus serves to fix his attention.] flask of an alkaline solution, and placing two glasses before me filled with the two sorts of wine, I said.

Food and drink are adulterated to make them seem better than they really are. These adulterations deceive both the eye and the palate, but they are unwholesome and make the adulterated article even worse than before in spite of its fine appearance.

All sorts of drinks are adulterated, and wine more than others; for the fraud is more difficult to detect, and more profitable to the fraudulent person.

Sour wine is adulterated with litharge; litharge is a preparation of lead. Lead in combination with acids forms a sweet salt which corrects the harsh taste of the sour wine, but it is poisonous. So before we drink wine of doubtful quality we should be able to tell if there is lead in it. This is how I should do it.

Wine contains not merely an inflammable spirit as you have seen from the brandy made from it; it also contains an acid as you know from the vinegar made from it.

This acid has an affinity for metals, it combines with them and forms salts, such as iron-rust, which is only iron dissolved by the acid in air or water, or such as verdegris, which is only copper dissolved in vinegar.

But this acid has a still greater affinity for alkalis than for metals, so that when we add alkalis to the above-mentioned salts, the acid sets free the metal with which it had combined, and combines with the alkali.

Then the metal, set free by the acid which held it in solution, is precipitated and the liquid becomes opaque.

If then there is litharge in either of these glasses of wine, the acid holds the litharge in solution. When I pour into it an alkaline solution, the acid will be forced to set the lead free in order to combine with the alkali. The lead, no longer held in solution, will reappear, the liquor will become thick, and after a time the lead will be deposited at the bottom of the glass.

If there is no lead [Footnote: The wine sold by retail dealers in Paris is rarely free from lead, though some of it does not contain litharge, for the counters are covered with lead and when the wine is poured into the measures and some of it spilt upon the counter and the measures left standing on the counter, some of the lead is always dissolved. It is strange that so obvious and dangerous an abuse should be tolerated by the police. But indeed well-to-do people, who rarely drink these wines, are not likely to be poisoned by them.] nor other metal in the wine the alkali will slowly [Footnote: The vegetable acid is very gentle in its action. If it were a mineral acid and less diluted, the combination would not take place without effervescence.] combine with the acid, all will remain clear and there will be no precipitate.

Then I poured my alkaline solution first into one glass and then into the other. The wine from our own house remained clear and unclouded, the other at once became turbid, and an hour later the lead might be plainly seen, precipitated at the bottom of the glass.

"This," said I, "is a pure natural wine and fit to drink; the other is adulterated and poisonous. You wanted to know the use of knowing how to make ink. If you can make ink you can find out what wines are adulterated."

I was very well pleased with my illustration, but I found it made little impression on my pupil. When I had time to think about it I saw I had been a fool, for not only was it impossible for a child of twelve to follow my explanations, but the usefulness of the experiment did not appeal to him; he had tasted both glasses of wine and found them both good, so he attached no meaning to the word "adulterated" which I thought I had explained so nicely. Indeed, the other words, "unwholesome" and "poison," had no meaning whatever for him; he was in the same condition as the boy who told the story of Philip and his doctor. It is the condition of all children.

The relation of causes and effects whose connection is unknown to us, good and ill of which we have no idea, the needs we have never felt, have no existence for us. It is impossible to interest ourselves in them sufficiently to make us do anything connected with them. At fifteen we become aware of the happiness of a good man, as at thirty we become aware of the glory of Paradise. If we had no clear idea of either we should make no effort for their attainment; and even if we had a clear idea of them, we should make little or no effort unless we desired them and unless we felt we were made for them. It is easy to convince a child that what you wish to teach him is useful, but it is useless to convince if you cannot also persuade. Pure reason may lead us to approve or censure, but it is feeling which leads to action, and how shall we care about that which does not concern us?

Never show a child what he cannot see. Since mankind is almost unknown to him, and since you cannot make a man of him, bring the man down to the level of the child. While you are thinking what will be useful to him when he is older, talk to him of what he knows he can use now. Moreover, as soon as he begins to reason let there be no comparison with other children, no rivalry, no competition, not even in running races. I would far rather he did not learn anything than have him learn it through jealousy or self-conceit. Year by year I shall just note the progress he had made, I shall compare the results with those of the following year, I shall say, "You have grown so much; that is the ditch you jumped, the weight you carried, the distance you flung a pebble, the race you ran without stopping to take breath, etc.; let us see what you can do now."

In this way he is stimulated to further effort without jealousy. He wants to excel himself as he ought to do; I see no reason why he should not emulate his own performances.

I hate books; they only teach us to talk about things we know nothing about. Hermes, they say, engraved the elements of science on pillars lest a deluge should destroy them. Had he imprinted them on men's hearts they would have been preserved by tradition. Well-trained minds are the pillars on which human knowledge is most deeply engraved.

Is there no way of correlating so many lessons scattered through so many books, no way of focussing them on some common object, easy to see, interesting to follow, and stimulating even to a child? Could we but discover a state in which all man's needs appear in such a way as to appeal to the child's mind, a state in which the ways of providing for these needs are as easily developed, the simple and stirring portrayal of this state should form the earliest training of the child's imagination.

Eager philosopher, I see your own imagination at work. Spare yourself the trouble; this state is already known, it is described, with due respect to you, far better than you could describe it, at least with greater truth and simplicity. Since we must have books, there is one book which, to my thinking, supplies the best treatise on an education according to nature. This is the first book Emile will read; for a long time it will form his whole library, and it will always retain an honoured place. It will be the text to which all our talks about natural science are but the commentary. It will serve to test our progress towards a right judgment, and it will always be read with delight, so long as our taste is unspoilt. What is this wonderful book? Is it Aristotle? Pliny? Buffon? No; it is Robinson Crusoe.

Robinson Crusoe on his island, deprived of the help of his fellow-men, without the means of carrying on the various arts, yet finding food, preserving his life, and procuring a certain amount of comfort; this is the thing to interest people of all ages, and it can be made attractive to children in all sorts of ways. We shall thus make a reality of that desert island which formerly served as an illustration. The condition, I confess, is not that of a social being, nor is it in all probability Emile's own condition, but he should use it as a standard of comparison for all other conditions. The surest way to raise him above prejudice and to base his judgments on the true relations of things, is to put him in the place of a solitary man, and to judge all things as they would be judged by such a man in relation to their own utility.

This novel, stripped of irrelevant matter, begins with Robinson's shipwreck on his island, and ends with the coming of the ship which bears him from it, and it will furnish Emile with material, both for work and play, during the whole period we are considering. His head should be full of it, he should always be busy with his castle, his goats, his plantations. Let him learn in detail, not from books but from things, all that is necessary in such a case. Let him think he is Robinson himself; let him see himself clad in skins, wearing a tall cap, a great cutlass, all the grotesque get-up of Robinson Crusoe, even to the umbrella which he will scarcely need. He should anxiously consider what steps to take; will this or that be wanting. He should examine his hero's conduct; has he omitted nothing; is there nothing he could have done better? He should carefully note his mistakes, so as not to fall into them himself in similar circumstances, for you may be sure he will plan out just such a settlement for himself. This is the genuine castle in the air of this happy age, when the child knows no other happiness but food and freedom.

What a motive will this infatuation supply in the hands of a skilful teacher who has aroused it for the purpose of using it. The child who wants to build a storehouse on his desert island will be more eager to learn than the master to teach. He will want to know all sorts of useful things and nothing else; you will need the curb as well as the spur. Make haste, therefore, to establish him on his island while this is all he needs to make him happy; for the day is at hand, when, if he must still live on his island, he will not be content to live alone, when even the companionship of Man Friday, who is almost disregarded now, will not long suffice.

The exercise of the natural arts, which may be carried on by one man alone, leads on to the industrial arts which call for the cooperation of many hands. The former may be carried on by hermits, by savages, but the others can only arise in a society, and they make society necessary. So long as only bodily needs are recognised man is self-sufficing; with superfluity comes the need for division and distribution of labour, for though one man working alone can earn a man's living, one hundred men working together can earn the living of two hundred. As soon as some men are idle, others must work to make up for their idleness.

Your main object should be to keep out of your scholar's way all idea of such social relations as he cannot understand, but when the development of knowledge compels you to show him the mutual dependence of mankind, instead of showing him its moral side, turn all his attention at first towards industry and the mechanical arts which make men useful to one another. While you take him from one workshop to another, let him try his hand at every trade you show him, and do not let him leave it till he has thoroughly learnt why everything is done, or at least everything that has attracted his attention. With this aim you should take a share in his work and set him an example. Be yourself the apprentice that he may become a master; you may expect him to learn more in one hour's work than he would retain after a whole day's explanation.

The value set by the general public on the various arts is in inverse ratio to their real utility. They are even valued directly according to their uselessness. This might be expected. The most useful arts are the worst paid, for the number of workmen is regulated by the demand, and the work which everybody requires must necessarily be paid at a rate which puts it within the reach of the poor. On the other hand, those great people who are called artists, not artisans, who labour only for the rich and idle, put a fancy price on their trifles; and as the real value of this vain labour is purely imaginary, the price itself adds to their market value, and they are valued according to their costliness. The rich think so much of these things, not because they are useful, but because they are beyond the reach of the poor. Nolo habere bona, nisi quibus populus inviderit.

What will become of your pupils if you let them acquire this foolish prejudice, if you share it yourself? If, for instance, they see you show more politeness in a jeweller's shop than in a locksmith's. What idea will they form of the true worth of the arts and the real value of things when they see, on the one hand, a fancy price and, on the other, the price of real utility, and that the more a thing costs the less it is worth? As soon as you let them get hold of these ideas, you may give up all attempt at further education; in spite of you they will be like all the other scholars—you have wasted fourteen years.

Emile, bent on furnishing his island, will look at things from another point of view. Robinson would have thought more of a toolmaker's shop than all Saide's trifles put together. He would have reckoned the toolmaker a very worthy man, and Saide little more than a charlatan.

"My son will have to take the world as he finds it, he will not live among the wise but among fools; he must therefore be acquainted with their follies, since they must be led by this means. A real knowledge of things may be a good thing in itself, but the knowledge of men and their opinions is better, for in human society man is the chief tool of man, and the wisest man is he who best knows the use of this tool. What is the good of teaching children an imaginary system, just the opposite of the established order of things, among which they will have to live? First teach them wisdom, then show them the follies of mankind."

These are the specious maxims by which fathers, who mistake them for prudence, strive to make their children the slaves of the prejudices in which they are educated, and the puppets of the senseless crowd, which they hope to make subservient to their passions. How much must be known before we attain to a knowledge of man. This is the final study of the philosopher, and you expect to make it the first lesson of the child! Before teaching him our sentiments, first teach him to judge of their worth. Do you perceive folly when you mistake it for wisdom? To be wise we must discern between good and evil. How can your child know men, when he can neither judge of their judgments nor unravel their mistakes? It is a misfortune to know what they think, without knowing whether their thoughts are true or false. First teach him things as they really are, afterwards you will teach him how they appear to us. He will then be able to make a comparison between popular ideas and truth, and be able to rise above the vulgar crowd; for you are unaware of the prejudices you adopt, and you do not lead a nation when you are like it. But if you begin to teach the opinions of other people before you teach how to judge of their worth, of one thing you may be sure, your pupil will adopt those opinions whatever you may do, and you will not succeed in uprooting them. I am therefore convinced that to make a young man judge rightly, you must form his judgment rather than teach him your own.

So far you see I have not spoken to my pupil about men; he would have too much sense to listen to me. His relations to other people are as yet not sufficiently apparent to him to enable him to judge others by himself. The only person he knows is himself, and his knowledge of himself is very imperfect. But if he forms few opinions about others, those opinions are correct. He knows nothing of another's place, but he knows his own and keeps to it. I have bound him with the strong cord of necessity, instead of social laws, which are beyond his knowledge. He is still little more than a body; let us treat him as such.

Every substance in nature and every work of man must be judged in relation to his own use, his own safety, his own preservation, his own comfort. Thus he should value iron far more than gold, and glass than diamonds; in the same way he has far more respect for a shoemaker or a mason than for a Lempereur, a Le Blanc, or all the jewellers in Europe. In his eyes a confectioner is a really great man, and he would give the whole academy of sciences for the smallest pastrycook in Lombard Street. Goldsmiths, engravers, gilders, and embroiderers, he considers lazy people, who play at quite useless games. He does not even think much of a clockmaker. The happy child enjoys Time without being a slave to it; he uses it, but he does not know its value. The freedom from passion which makes every day alike to him, makes any means of measuring time unnecessary. When I assumed that Emile had a watch, [Footnote: When our hearts are abandoned to the sway of passion, then it is that we need a measure of time. The wise man's watch is his equable temper and his peaceful heart. He is always punctual, and he always knows the time.] just as I assumed that he cried, it was a commonplace Emile that I chose to serve my purpose and make myself understood. The real Emile, a child so different from the rest, would not serve as an illustration for anything.

There is an order no less natural and even more accurate, by which the arts are valued according to bonds of necessity which connect them; the highest class consists of the most independent, the lowest of those most dependent on others. This classification, which suggests important considerations on the order of society in general, is like the preceding one in that it is subject to the same inversion in popular estimation, so that the use of raw material is the work of the lowest and worst paid trades, while the oftener the material changes hands, the more the work rises in price and in honour. I do not ask whether industry is really greater and more deserving of reward when engaged in the delicate arts which give the final shape to these materials, than in the labour which first gave them to man's use; but this I say, that in everything the art which is most generally useful and necessary, is undoubtedly that which most deserves esteem, and that art which requires the least help from others, is more worthy of honour than those which are dependent on other arts, since it is freer and more nearly independent. These are the true laws of value in the arts; all others are arbitrary and dependent on popular prejudice.

Agriculture is the earliest and most honourable of arts; metal work I put next, then carpentry, and so on. This is the order in which the child will put them, if he has not been spoilt by vulgar prejudices. What valuable considerations Emile will derive from his Robinson in such matters. What will he think when he sees the arts only brought to perfection by sub-division, by the infinite multiplication of tools. He will say, "All those people are as silly as they are ingenious; one would think they were afraid to use their eyes and their hands, they invent so many tools instead. To carry on one trade they become the slaves of many others; every single workman needs a whole town. My friend and I try to gain skill; we only make tools we can take about with us; these people, who are so proud of their talents in Paris, would be no use at all on our island; they would have to become apprentices."

Reader, do not stay to watch the bodily exercises and manual skill of our pupil, but consider the bent we are giving to his childish curiosity; consider his common-sense, his inventive spirit, his foresight; consider what a head he will have on his shoulders. He will want to know all about everything he sees or does, to learn the why and the wherefore of it; from tool to tool he will go back to the first beginning, taking nothing for granted; he will decline to learn anything that requires previous knowledge which he has not acquired. If he sees a spring made he will want to know how they got the steel from the mine; if he sees the pieces of a chest put together, he will want to know how the tree was cut down; when at work he will say of each tool, "If I had not got this, how could I make one like it, or how could I get along without it?"

It is, however, difficult to avoid another error. When the master is very fond of certain occupations, he is apt to assume that the child shares his tastes; beware lest you are carried away by the interest of your work, while the child is bored by it, but is afraid to show it. The child must come first, and you must devote yourself entirely to him. Watch him, study him constantly, without his knowing it; consider his feelings beforehand, and provide against those which are undesirable, keep him occupied in such a way that he not only feels the usefulness of the thing, but takes a pleasure in understanding the purpose which his work will serve.

The solidarity of the arts consists in the exchange of industry, that of commerce in the exchange of commodities, that of banks in the exchange of money or securities. All these ideas hang together, and their foundation has already been laid in early childhood with the help of Robert the gardener. All we have now to do is to substitute general ideas for particular, and to enlarge these ideas by means of numerous examples, so as to make the child understand the game of business itself, brought home to him by means of particular instances of natural history with regard to the special products of each country, by particular instances of the arts and sciences which concern navigation and the difficulties of transport, greater or less in proportion to the distance between places, the position of land, seas, rivers, etc.

There can be no society without exchange, no exchange without a common standard of measurement, no common standard of measurement without equality. Hence the first law of every society is some conventional equality either in men or things.

Conventional equality between men, a very different thing from natural equality, leads to the necessity for positive law, i.e., government and kings. A child's political knowledge should be clear and restricted; he should know nothing of government in general, beyond what concerns the rights of property, of which he has already some idea.

Conventional equality between things has led to the invention of money, for money is only one term in a comparison between the values of different sorts of things; and in this sense money is the real bond of society; but anything may be money; in former days it was cattle; shells are used among many tribes at the present day; Sparta used iron; Sweden, leather; while we use gold and silver.

Metals, being easier to carry, have generally been chosen as the middle term of every exchange, and these metals have been made into coin to save the trouble of continual weighing and measuring, for the stamp on the coin is merely evidence that the coin is of given weight; and the sole right of coining money is vested in the ruler because he alone has the right to demand the recognition of his authority by the whole nation.

The stupidest person can perceive the use of money when it is explained in this way. It is difficult to make a direct comparison between various things, for instance, between cloth and corn; but when we find a common measure, in money, it is easy for the manufacturer and the farmer to estimate the value of the goods they wish to exchange in terms of this common measure. If a given quantity of cloth is worth a given some of money, and a given quantity of corn is worth the same sum of money, then the seller, receiving the corn in exchange for his cloth, makes a fair bargain. Thus by means of money it becomes possible to compare the values of goods of various kinds.

Be content with this, and do not touch upon the moral effects of this institution. In everything you must show clearly the use before the abuse. If you attempt to teach children how the sign has led to the neglect of the thing signified, how money is the source of all the false ideas of society, how countries rich in silver must be poor in everything else, you will be treating these children as philosophers, and not only as philosophers but as wise men, for you are professing to teach them what very few philosophers have grasped.

What a wealth of interesting objects, towards which the curiosity of our pupil may be directed without ever quitting the real and material relations he can understand, and without permitting the formation of a single idea beyond his grasp! The teacher's art consists in this: To turn the child's attention from trivial details and to guide his thoughts continually towards relations of importance which he will one day need to know, that he may judge rightly of good and evil in human society. The teacher must be able to adapt the conversation with which he amuses his pupil to the turn already given to his mind. A problem which another child would never heed will torment Emile half a year.

We are going to dine with wealthy people; when we get there everything is ready for a feast, many guests, many servants, many dishes, dainty and elegant china. There is something intoxicating in all these preparations for pleasure and festivity when you are not used to them. I see how they will affect my young pupil. While dinner is going on, while course follows course, and conversation is loud around us, I whisper in his ear, "How many hands do you suppose the things on this table passed through before they got here?" What a crowd of ideas is called up by these few words. In a moment the mists of excitement have rolled away. He is thinking, considering, calculating, and anxious. The child is philosophising, while philosophers, excited by wine or perhaps by female society, are babbling like children. If he asks questions I decline to answer and put him off to another day. He becomes impatient, he forgets to eat and drink, he longs to get away from table and talk as he pleases. What an object of curiosity, what a text for instruction. Nothing has so far succeeded in corrupting his healthy reason; what will he think of luxury when he finds that every quarter of the globe has been ransacked, that some 2,000,000 men have laboured for years, that many lives have perhaps been sacrificed, and all to furnish him with fine clothes to be worn at midday and laid by in the wardrobe at night.

Be sure you observe what private conclusions he draws from all his observations. If you have watched him less carefully than I suppose, his thoughts may be tempted in another direction; he may consider himself a person of great importance in the world, when he sees so much labour concentrated on the preparation of his dinner. If you suspect his thoughts will take this direction you can easily prevent it, or at any rate promptly efface the false impression. As yet he can only appropriate things by personal enjoyment, he can only judge of their fitness or unfitness by their outward effects. Compare a plain rustic meal, preceded by exercise, seasoned by hunger, freedom, and delight, with this magnificent but tedious repast. This will suffice to make him realise that he has got no real advantage from the splendour of the feast, that his stomach was as well satisfied when he left the table of the peasant, as when he left the table of the banker; from neither had he gained anything he could really call his own.

Just fancy what a tutor might say to him on such an occasion. Consider the two dinners and decide for yourself which gave you most pleasure, which seemed the merriest, at which did you eat and drink most heartily, which was the least tedious and required least change of courses? Yet note the difference—this black bread you so enjoy is made from the peasant's own harvest; his wine is dark in colour and of a common kind, but wholesome and refreshing; it was made in his own vineyard; the cloth is made of his own hemp, spun and woven in the winter by his wife and daughters and the maid; no hands but theirs have touched the food. His world is bounded by the nearest mill and the next market. How far did you enjoy all that the produce of distant lands and the service of many people had prepared for you at the other dinner? If you did not get a better meal, what good did this wealth do you? how much of it was made for you? Had you been the master of the house, the tutor might say, it would have been of still less use to you; for the anxiety of displaying your enjoyment before the eyes of others would have robbed you of it; the pains would be yours, the pleasure theirs.

This may be a very fine speech, but it would be thrown away upon Emile, as he cannot understand it, and he does not accept second-hand opinions. Speak more simply to him. After these two experiences, say to him some day, "Where shall we have our dinner to-day? Where that mountain of silver covered three quarters of the table and those beds of artificial flowers on looking glass were served with the dessert, where those smart ladies treated you as a toy and pretended you said what you did not mean; or in that village two leagues away, with those good people who were so pleased to see us and gave us such delicious cream?" Emile will not hesitate; he is not vain and he is no chatterbox; he cannot endure constraint, and he does not care for fine dishes; but he is always ready for a run in the country and is very fond of good fruit and vegetables, sweet cream and kindly people. [Footnote: This taste, which I assume my pupil to have acquired, is a natural result of his education. Moreover, he has nothing foppish or affected about him, so that the ladies take little notice of him and he is less petted than other children; therefore he does not care for them, and is less spoilt by their company; he is not yet of an age to feel its charm. I have taken care not to teach him to kiss their hands, to pay them compliments, or even to be more polite to them than to men. It is my constant rule to ask nothing from him but what he can understand, and there is no good reason why a child should treat one sex differently from the other.] On our way, the thought will occur to him, "All those people who laboured to prepare that grand feast were either wasting their time or they have no idea how to enjoy themselves."

My example may be right for one child and wrong for the rest. If you enter into their way of looking at things you will know how to vary your instances as required; the choice depends on the study of the individual temperament, and this study in turn depends on the opportunities which occur to show this temperament. You will not suppose that, in the three or four years at our disposal, even the most gifted child can get an idea of all the arts and sciences, sufficient to enable him to study them for himself when he is older; but by bringing before him what he needs to know, we enable him to develop his own tastes, his own talents, to take the first step towards the object which appeals to his individuality and to show us the road we must open up to aid the work of nature.

There is another advantage of these trains of limited but exact bits of knowledge; he learns by their connection and interdependence how to rank them in his own estimation and to be on his guard against those prejudices, common to most men, which draw them towards the gifts they themselves cultivate and away from those they have neglected. The man who clearly sees the whole, sees where each part should be; the man who sees one part clearly and knows it thoroughly may be a learned man, but the former is a wise man, and you remember it is wisdom rather than knowledge that we hope to acquire.

However that may be, my method does not depend on my examples; it depends on the amount of a man's powers at different ages, and the choice of occupations adapted to those powers. I think it would be easy to find a method which appeared to give better results, but if it were less suited to the type, sex, and age of the scholar, I doubt whether the results would really be as good.

At the beginning of this second period we took advantage of the fact that our strength was more than enough for our needs, to enable us to get outside ourselves. We have ranged the heavens and measured the earth; we have sought out the laws of nature; we have explored the whole of our island. Now let us return to ourselves, let us unconsciously approach our own dwelling. We are happy indeed if we do not find it already occupied by the dreaded foe, who is preparing to seize it.

What remains to be done when we have observed all that lies around us? We must turn to our own use all that we can get, we must increase our comfort by means of our curiosity. Hitherto we have provided ourselves with tools of all kinds, not knowing which we require. Perhaps those we do not want will be useful to others, and perhaps we may need theirs. Thus we discover the use of exchange; but for this we must know each other's needs, what tools other people use, what they can offer in exchange. Given ten men, each of them has ten different requirements. To get what he needs for himself each must work at ten different trades; but considering our different talents, one will do better at this trade, another at that. Each of them, fitted for one thing, will work at all, and will be badly served. Let us form these ten men into a society, and let each devote himself to the trade for which he is best adapted, and let him work at it for himself and for the rest. Each will reap the advantage of the others' talents, just as if they were his own; by practice each will perfect his own talent, and thus all the ten, well provided for, will still have something to spare for others. This is the plain foundation of all our institutions. It is not my aim to examine its results here; I have done so in another book (Discours sur l'inegalite).

According to this principle, any one who wanted to consider himself as an isolated individual, self-sufficing and independent of others, could only be utterly wretched. He could not even continue to exist, for finding the whole earth appropriated by others while he had only himself, how could he get the means of subsistence? When we leave the state of nature we compel others to do the same; no one can remain in a state of nature in spite of his fellow-creatures, and to try to remain in it when it is no longer practicable, would really be to leave it, for self-preservation is nature's first law.

Thus the idea of social relations is gradually developed in the child's mind, before he can really be an active member of human society. Emile sees that to get tools for his own use, other people must have theirs, and that he can get in exchange what he needs and they possess. I easily bring him to feel the need of such exchange and to take advantage of it.

"Sir, I must live," said a miserable writer of lampoons to the minister who reproved him for his infamous trade. "I do not see the necessity," replied the great man coldly. This answer, excellent from the minister, would have been barbarous and untrue in any other mouth. Every man must live; this argument, which appeals to every one with more or less force in proportion to his humanity, strikes me as unanswerable when applied to oneself. Since our dislike of death is the strongest of those aversions nature has implanted in us, it follows that everything is permissible to the man who has no other means of living. The principles, which teach the good man to count his life a little thing and to sacrifice it at duty's call, are far removed from this primitive simplicity. Happy are those nations where one can be good without effort, and just without conscious virtue. If in this world there is any condition so miserable that one cannot live without wrong-doing, where the citizen is driven into evil, you should hang, not the criminal, but those who drove him into crime.

As soon as Emile knows what life is, my first care will be to teach him to preserve his life. Hitherto I have made no distinction of condition, rank, station, or fortune; nor shall I distinguish between them in the future, since man is the same in every station; the rich man's stomach is no bigger than the poor man's, nor is his digestion any better; the master's arm is neither longer nor stronger than the slave's; a great man is no taller than one of the people, and indeed the natural needs are the same to all, and the means of satisfying them should be equally within the reach of all. Fit a man's education to his real self, not to what is no part of him. Do you not see that in striving to fit him merely for one station, you are unfitting him for anything else, so that some caprice of Fortune may make your work really harmful to him? What could be more absurd than a nobleman in rags, who carries with him into his poverty the prejudices of his birth? What is more despicable than a rich man fallen into poverty, who recalls the scorn with which he himself regarded the poor, and feels that he has sunk to the lowest depth of degradation? The one may become a professional thief, the other a cringing servant, with this fine saying, "I must live."

You reckon on the present order of society, without considering that this order is itself subject to inscrutable changes, and that you can neither foresee nor provide against the revolution which may affect your children. The great become small, the rich poor, the king a commoner. Does fate strike so seldom that you can count on immunity from her blows? The crisis is approaching, and we are on the edge of a revolution. [Footnote: In my opinion it is impossible that the great kingdoms of Europe should last much longer. Each of them has had its period of splendour, after which it must inevitably decline. I have my own opinions as to the special applications of this general statement, but this is not the place to enter into details, and they are only too evident to everybody.] Who can answer for your fate? What man has made, man may destroy. Nature's characters alone are ineffaceable, and nature makes neither the prince, the rich man, nor the nobleman. This satrap whom you have educated for greatness, what will become of him in his degradation? This farmer of the taxes who can only live on gold, what will he do in poverty? This haughty fool who cannot use his own hands, who prides himself on what is not really his, what will he do when he is stripped of all? In that day, happy will he be who can give up the rank which is no longer his, and be still a man in Fate's despite. Let men praise as they will that conquered monarch who like a madman would be buried beneath the fragments of his throne; I behold him with scorn; to me he is merely a crown, and when that is gone he is nothing. But he who loses his crown and lives without it, is more than a king; from the rank of a king, which may be held by a coward, a villain, or madman, he rises to the rank of a man, a position few can fill. Thus he triumphs over Fortune, he dares to look her in the face; he depends on himself alone, and when he has nothing left to show but himself he is not a nonentity, he is somebody. Better a thousandfold the king of Corinth a schoolmaster at Syracuse, than a wretched Tarquin, unable to be anything but a king, or the heir of the ruler of three kingdoms, the sport of all who would scorn his poverty, wandering from court to court in search of help, and finding nothing but insults, for want of knowing any trade but one which he can no longer practise.

The man and the citizen, whoever he may be, has no property to invest in society but himself, all his other goods belong to society in spite of himself, and when a man is rich, either he does not enjoy his wealth, or the public enjoys it too; in the first case he robs others as well as himself; in the second he gives them nothing. Thus his debt to society is still unpaid, while he only pays with his property. "But my father was serving society while he was acquiring his wealth." Just so; he paid his own debt, not yours. You owe more to others than if you had been born with nothing, since you were born under favourable conditions. It is not fair that what one man has done for society should pay another's debt, for since every man owes all that he is, he can only pay his own debt, and no father can transmit to his son any right to be of no use to mankind. "But," you say, "this is just what he does when he leaves me his wealth, the reward of his labour." The man who eats in idleness what he has not himself earned, is a thief, and in my eyes, the man who lives on an income paid him by the state for doing nothing, differs little from a high-wayman who lives on those who travel his way. Outside the pale of society, the solitary, owing nothing to any man, may live as he pleases, but in society either he lives at the cost of others, or he owes them in labour the cost of his keep; there is no exception to this rule. Man in society is bound to work; rich or poor, weak or strong, every idler is a thief.

Now of all the pursuits by which a man may earn his living, the nearest to a state of nature is manual labour; of all stations that of the artisan is least dependent on Fortune. The artisan depends on his labour alone, he is a free man while the ploughman is a slave; for the latter depends on his field where the crops may be destroyed by others. An enemy, a prince, a powerful neigh-bour, or a law-suit may deprive him of his field; through this field he may be harassed in all sorts of ways. But if the artisan is ill-treated his goods are soon packed and he takes himself off. Yet agriculture is the earliest, the most hon-est of trades, and more useful than all the rest, and therefore more honourable for those who practise it. I do not say to Emile, "Study agriculture," he is al-ready familiar with it. He is acquainted with every kind of rural labour, it was his first occupation, and he returns to it continually. So I say to him, "Culti-vate your father's lands, but if you lose this inheritance, or if you have none to lose, what will you do? Learn a trade."

"A trade for my son! My son a working man! What are you thinking of, sir?" Madam, my thoughts are wiser than yours; you want to make him fit for nothing but a lord, a marquis, or a prince; and some day he may be less than nothing. I want to give him a rank which he cannot lose, a rank which will always do him honour; I want to raise him to the status of a man, and, what-ever you may say, he will have fewer equals in that rank than in your own.

The letter killeth, the spirit giveth life. Learning a trade matters less than overcoming the prejudices he despises. You will never be reduced to earning your livelihood; so much the worse for you. No matter; work for honour, not for need: stoop to the position of a working man, to rise above your own. To conquer Fortune and everything else, begin by independence. To rule through public opinion, begin by ruling over it.

Remember I demand no talent, only a trade, a genuine trade, a mere me-chanical art, in which the hands work harder than the head, a trade which does not lead to fortune but makes you independent of her. In households far removed from all danger of want I have known fathers carry prudence to such a point as to provide their children not only with ordinary teaching but with knowledge by means of which they could get a living if anything hap-pened. These far-sighted parents thought they were doing a great thing. It is nothing, for the resources they fancy they have secured depend on that very fortune of which they would make their children independent; so that unless they found themselves in circumstances fitted for the display of their talents, they would die of hunger as if they had none.

As soon as it is a question of influence and intrigue you may as well use these means to keep yourself in plenty, as to acquire, in the depths of poverty, the means of returning to your former position. If you cultivate the arts which depend on the artist's reputation, if you fit yourself for posts which are only obtained by favour, how will that help you when, rightly disgusted with the world, you scorn the steps by which you must climb. You have studied politics and state-craft, so far so good; but how will you use this knowledge, if you cannot gain the ear of the ministers, the favourites, or the officials? if you have not the secret of winning their favour, if they fail to find you a rogue to their taste? You are an architect or a painter; well and good; but your talents must be displayed. Do you suppose you can exhibit in the salon without further ado? That is not the way to set about it. Lay aside the rule and the pencil, take a cab and drive from door to door; there is the road to fame. Now you must know that the doors of the great are guarded by porters and flunkeys, who only understand one language, and their ears are in their palms. If you wish to teach what you have learned, geography, mathematics, languages, music, drawing, even to find pupils, you must have friends who will sing your praises. Learning, remember, gains more credit than skill, and with no trade but your own none will believe in your skill. See how little you can depend on these fine "Resources," and how many other resources are required before you can use what you have got. And what will become of you in your degradation? Misfortune will make you worse rather than better. More than ever the sport of public opinion, how will you rise above the prejudices on which your fate depends? How will you despise the vices and the baseness from which you get your living? You were dependent on wealth, now you are dependent on the wealthy; you are still a slave and a poor man into the bargain. Poverty without freedom, can a man sink lower than this!

But if instead of this recondite learning adapted to feed the mind, not the body, you have recourse, at need, to your hands and your handiwork, there is no call for deceit, your trade is ready when required. Honour and honesty will not stand in the way of your living. You need no longer cringe and lie to the great, nor creep and crawl before rogues, a despicable flatterer of both, a borrower or a thief, for there is little to choose between them when you are penniless. Other people's opinions are no concern of yours, you need not pay court to any one, there is no fool to flatter, no flunkey to bribe, no woman to win over. Let rogues conduct the affairs of state; in your lowly rank you can still be an honest man and yet get a living. You walk into the first workshop of your trade. "Master, I want work." "Comrade, take your place and work." Before dinner-time you have earned your dinner. If you are sober and industrious, before the week is out you will have earned your keep for another week; you will have lived in freedom, health, truth, industry, and righteousness. Time is not wasted when it brings these returns.

Emile shall learn a trade. "An honest trade, at least," you say. What do you mean by honest? Is not every useful trade honest? I would not make an embroiderer, a gilder, a polisher of him, like Locke's young gentleman. Neither would I make him a musician, an actor, or an author.[Footnote: You are an author yourself, you will reply. Yes, for my sins; and my ill deeds, which I think I have fully expiated, are no reason why others should be like me. I do not write to excuse my faults, but to prevent my readers from copying them.] With the exception of these and others like them, let him choose his own trade, I do not mean to interfere with his choice. I would rather have him a shoemaker than a poet, I would rather he paved streets than painted flowers on china. "But," you will say, "policemen, spies, and hangmen are useful people." There would be no use for them if it were not for the government. But let that pass. I was wrong. It is not enough to choose an honest trade, it must be a trade which does not develop detestable qualities in the mind, qualities incompatible with humanity. To return to our original expression, "Let us choose an honest trade," but let us remember there can be no honesty without usefulness.

A famous writer of this century, whose books are full of great schemes and narrow views, was under a vow, like the other priests of his communion, not to take a wife. Finding himself more scrupulous than others with regard to his neighbour's wife, he decided, so they say, to employ pretty servants, and so did his best to repair the wrong done to the race by his rash promise. He thought it the duty of a citizen to breed children for the state, and he made his children artisans. As soon as they were old enough they were taught whatever trade they chose; only idle or useless trades were excluded, such as that of the wigmaker who is never necessary, and may any day cease to be required, so long as nature does not get tired of providing us with hair.

This spirit shall guide our choice of trade for Emile, or rather, not our choice but his; for the maxims he has imbibed make him despise useless things, and he will never be content to waste his time on vain labours; his trade must be of use to Robinson on his island.

When we review with the child the productions of art and nature, when we stimulate his curiosity and follow its lead, we have great opportunities of studying his tastes and inclinations, and perceiving the first spark of genius, if he has any decided talent in any direction. You must, however, be on your guard against the common error which mistakes the effects of environment for the ardour of genius, or imagines there is a decided bent towards any one of the arts, when there is nothing more than that spirit of emulation, common to men and monkeys, which impels them instinctively to do what they see others doing, without knowing why. The world is full of artisans, and still fuller of artists, who have no native gift for their calling, into which they were driven in early childhood, either through the conventional ideas of other people, or because those about them were deceived by an appearance of zeal, which would have led them to take to any other art they saw practised. One hears a drum and fancies he is a general; another sees a building and wants to be an architect. Every one is drawn towards the trade he sees before him if he thinks it is held in honour.

I once knew a footman who watched his master drawing and painting and took it into his head to become a designer and artist. He seized a pencil which he only abandoned for a paint-brush, to which he stuck for the rest of his days. Without teaching or rules of art he began to draw everything he saw. Three whole years were devoted to these daubs, from which nothing but his duties could stir him, nor was he discouraged by the small progress resulting from his very mediocre talents. I have seen him spend the whole of a broiling summer in a little ante-room towards the south, a room where one was suffocated merely passing through it; there he was, seated or rather nailed all day to his chair, before a globe, drawing it again and again and yet again, with invincible obstinacy till he had reproduced the rounded surface to his own satisfaction. At last with his master's help and under the guidance of an artist he got so far as to abandon his livery and live by his brush. Perseverance does instead of talent up to a certain point; he got so far, but no further. This honest lad's perseverance and ambition are praiseworthy; he will always be respected for his industry and steadfastness of purpose, but his paintings will always be third-rate. Who would not have been deceived by his zeal and taken it for real talent! There is all the difference in the world between a liking and an aptitude. To make sure of real genius or real taste in a child calls for more accurate observations than is generally suspected, for the child displays his wishes not his capacity, and we judge by the former instead of considering the latter. I wish some trustworthy person would give us a treatise on the art of child-study. This art is well worth studying, but neither parents nor teachers have mastered its elements.

Perhaps we are laying too much stress on the choice of a trade; as it is a manual occupation, Emile's choice is no great matter, and his apprenticeship is more than half accomplished already, through the exercises which have hitherto occupied him. What would you have him do? He is ready for anything. He can handle the spade and hoe, he can use the lathe, hammer, plane, or file; he is already familiar with these tools which are common to many trades. He only needs to acquire sufficient skill in the use of any one of them to rival the speed, the familiarity, and the diligence of good workmen, and he will have a great advantage over them in suppleness of body and limb, so that he can easily take any position and can continue any kind of movements without effort. Moreover his senses are acute and well-practised, he knows the principles of the various trades; to work like a master of his craft he only needs experience, and experience comes with practice. To which of these trades which are open to us will he give sufficient time to make himself master of it? That is the whole question.

Give a man a trade befitting his sex, to a young man a trade befitting his age. Sedentary indoor employments, which make the body tender and effeminate, are neither pleasing nor suitable. No lad ever wanted to be a tailor. It takes some art to attract a man to this woman's work.[Footnote: There were no tailors among the ancients; men's clothes were made at home by the women.] The same hand cannot hold the needle and the sword. If I were king I would only allow needlework and dressmaking to be done by women and cripples who are obliged to work at such trades. If eunuchs were required I think the Easterns were very foolish to make them on purpose. Why not take those provided by nature, that crowd of base persons without natural feeling? There would be enough and to spare. The weak, feeble, timid man is condemned by nature to a sedentary life, he is fit to live among women or in their fashion. Let him adopt one of their trades if he likes; and if there must be eunuchs let them take those men who dishonour their sex by adopting trades unworthy of it. Their choice proclaims a blunder on the part of nature; correct it one way or other, you will do no harm.

An unhealthy trade I forbid to my pupil, but not a difficult or dangerous one. He will exercise himself in strength and courage; such trades are for men not women, who claim no share in them. Are not men ashamed to poach upon the women's trades?

> "Luctantur paucae, comedunt coliphia paucae.
> Vos lanam trahitis, calathisque peracta refertis
> Vellera." – Juven. Sat. II. V. 55.

Women are not seen in shops in Italy, and to persons accustomed to the streets of England and France nothing could look gloomier. When I saw drapers selling ladies ribbons, pompons, net, and chenille, I thought these delicate ornaments very absurd in the coarse hands fit to blow the bellows and strike the anvil. I said to myself, "In this country women should set up as steel-polishers and armourers." Let each make and sell the weapons of his or her own sex; knowledge is acquired through use.

I know I have said too much for my agreeable contemporaries, but I sometimes let myself be carried away by my argument. If any one is ashamed to be seen wearing a leathern apron or handling a plane, I think him a mere slave of public opinion, ready to blush for what is right when people poke fun at it. But let us yield to parents' prejudices so long as they do not hurt the children. To honour trades we are not obliged to practise every one of them, so long as we do not think them beneath us. When the choice is ours and we are under no compulsion, why not choose the pleasanter, more attractive and more suitable trade. Metal work is useful, more useful, perhaps, than the rest, but unless for some special reason Emile shall not be a blacksmith, a locksmith nor an iron-worker. I do not want to see him a Cyclops at the forge. Neither would I have him a mason, still less a shoemaker. All trades must be carried on, but when the choice is ours, cleanliness should be taken into account; this is not a matter of class prejudice, our senses are our guides. In conclusion, I do not like those stupid trades in which the workmen mechanically perform the same action without pause and almost without mental effort. Weaving, stocking-knitting, stone-cutting; why employ intelligent men on such work? it is merely one machine employed on another.

All things considered, the trade I should choose for my pupil, among the trades he likes, is that of a carpenter. It is clean and useful; it may be carried on at home; it gives enough exercise; it calls for skill and industry, and while fashioning articles for everyday use, there is scope for elegance and taste. If your pupil's talents happened to take a scientific turn, I should not blame you if you gave him a trade in accordance with his tastes, for instance, he might learn to make mathematical instruments, glasses, telescopes, etc.

When Emile learns his trade I shall learn it too. I am convinced he will never learn anything thoroughly unless we learn it together. So we shall both serve our apprenticeship, and we do not mean to be treated as gentlemen, but as real apprentices who are not there for fun; why should not we actually be apprenticed? Peter the Great was a ship's carpenter and drummer to his own troops; was not that prince at least your equal in birth and merit? You understand this is addressed not to Emile but to you — to you, whoever you may be.

Unluckily we cannot spend the whole of our time at the workshop. We are not only 'prentice-carpenters but 'prentice-men—a trade whose apprenticeship is longer and more exacting than the rest. What shall we do? Shall we take a master to teach us the use of the plane and engage him by the hour like the dancing-master? In that case we should be not apprentices but students, and our ambition is not merely to learn carpentry but to be carpenters. Once or twice a week I think we should spend the whole day at our master's; we should get up when he does, we should be at our work before him, we should take our meals with him, work under his orders, and after having had the honour of supping at his table we may if we please return to sleep upon our own hard beds. This is the way to learn several trades at once, to learn to do manual work without neglecting our apprenticeship to life.

Let us do what is right without ostentation; let us not fall into vanity through our efforts to resist it. To pride ourselves on our victory over prejudice is to succumb to prejudice. It is said that in accordance with an old custom of the Ottomans, the sultan is obliged to work with his hands, and, as every one knows, the handiwork of a king is a masterpiece. So he royally distributes his masterpieces among the great lords of the Porte and the price paid is in accordance with the rank of the workman. It is not this so-called abuse to which I object; on the contrary, it is an advantage, and by compelling the lords to share with him the spoils of the people it is so much the less necessary for the prince to plunder the people himself. Despotism needs some such relaxation, and without it that hateful rule could not last.

The real evil in such a custom is the idea it gives that poor man of his own worth. Like King Midas he sees all things turn to gold at his touch, but he does not see the ass' ears growing. Let us keep Emile's hands from money lest he should become an ass, let him take the work but not the wages. Never let his work be judged by any standard but that of the work of a master. Let it be judged as work, not because it is his. If anything is well done, I say, "That is a good piece of work," but do not ask who did it. If he is pleased and proud and says, "I did it," answer indifferently, "No matter who did it, it is well done."

Good mother, be on your guard against the deceptions prepared for you. If your son knows many things, distrust his knowledge; if he is unlucky enough to be rich and educated in Paris he is ruined. As long as there are clever artists he will have every talent, but apart from his masters he will have none. In Paris a rich man knows everything, it is the poor who are ignorant. Our capital is full of amateurs, especially women, who do their work as M. Gillaume invents his colours. Among the men I know three striking exceptions, among the women I know no exceptions, and I doubt if there are any. In a general way a man becomes an artist and a judge of art as he becomes a Doctor of Laws and a magistrate.

If then it is once admitted that it is a fine thing to have a trade, your children would soon have one without learning it. They would become postmasters like the councillors of Zurich. Let us have no such ceremonies for Emile; let it be the real thing not the sham. Do not say what he knows, let him learn in silence. Let him make his masterpiece, but not be hailed as master; let him be a workman not in name but in deed.

If I have made my meaning clear you ought to realise how bodily exercise and manual work unconsciously arouse thought and reflexion in my pupil, and counteract the idleness which might result from his indifference to men's judgments, and his freedom from passion. He must work like a peasant and think like a philosopher, if he is not to be as idle as a savage. The great secret of education is to use exercise of mind and body as relaxation one to the other.

But beware of anticipating teaching which demands more maturity of mind. Emile will not long be a workman before he discovers those social inequalities he had not previously observed. He will want to question me in turn on the maxims I have given him, maxims he is able to understand. When he derives everything from me, when he is so nearly in the position of the poor, he will want to know why I am so far removed from it. All of a sudden he may put scathing questions to me. "You are rich, you tell me, and I see you are. A rich man owes his work to the community like the rest because he is a man. What are you doing for the community?" What would a fine tutor say to that? I do not know. He would perhaps be foolish enough to talk to the child of the care he bestows upon him. The workshop will get me out of the difficulty. "My dear Emile that is a very good question; I will undertake to answer for myself, when you can answer for yourself to your own satisfaction. Meanwhile I will take care to give what I can spare to you and to the poor, and to make a table or a bench every week, so as not to be quite useless."

We have come back to ourselves. Having entered into possession of himself, our child is now ready to cease to be a child. He is more than ever conscious of the necessity which makes him dependent on things. After exercising his body and his senses you have exercised his mind and his judgment. Finally we have joined together the use of his limbs and his faculties. We have made him a worker and a thinker; we have now to make him loving and tender-hearted, to perfect reason through feeling. But before we enter on this new order of things, let us cast an eye over the stage we are leaving behind us, and perceive as clearly as we can how far we have got.

At first our pupil had merely sensations, now he has ideas; he could only feel, now he reasons. For from the comparison of many successive or simultaneous sensations and the judgment arrived at with regard to them, there springs a sort of mixed or complex sensation which I call an idea.

The way in which ideas are formed gives a character to the human mind. The mind which derives its ideas from real relations is thorough; the mind which relies on apparent relations is superficial. He who sees relations as they are has an exact mind; he who fails to estimate them aright has an inaccurate mind; he who concocts imaginary relations, which have no real existence, is a madman; he who does not perceive any relation at all is an imbecile. Clever men are distinguished from others by their greater or less aptitude for the comparison of ideas and the discovery of relations between them.

Simple ideas consist merely of sensations compared one with another. Simple sensations involve judgments, as do the complex sensations which I call simple ideas. In the sensation the judgment is purely passive; it affirms that I feel what I feel. In the percept or idea the judgment is active; it connects, compares, it discriminates between relations not perceived by the senses. That is the whole difference; but it is a great difference. Nature never deceives us; we deceive ourselves.

I see some one giving an ice-cream to an eight-year-old child; he does not know what it is and puts the spoon in his mouth. Struck by the cold he cries out, "Oh, it burns!" He feels a very keen sensation, and the heat of the fire is the keenest sensation he knows, so he thinks that is what he feels. Yet he is mistaken; cold hurts, but it does not burn; and these two sensations are different, for persons with more experience do not confuse them. So it is not the sensation that is wrong, but the judgment formed with regard to it.

It is just the same with those who see a mirror or some optical instrument for the first time, or enter a deep cellar in the depths of winter or at midsummer, or dip a very hot or cold hand into tepid water, or roll a little ball between two crossed fingers. If they are content to say what they really feel, their judgment, being purely passive, cannot go wrong; but when they judge according to appearances, their judgment is active; it compares and establishes by induction relations which are not really perceived. Then these inductions may or may not be mistaken. Experience is required to correct or prevent error.

Show your pupil the clouds at night passing between himself and the moon; he will think the moon is moving in the opposite direction and that the clouds are stationary. He will think this through a hasty induction, because he generally sees small objects moving and larger ones at rest, and the clouds seems larger than the moon, whose distance is beyond his reckoning. When he watches the shore from a moving boat he falls into the opposite mistake and thinks the earth is moving because he does not feel the motion of the boat and considers it along with the sea or river as one motionless whole, of which the shore, which appears to move, forms no part.

The first time a child sees a stick half immersed in water he thinks he sees a broken stick; the sensation is true and would not cease to be true even if he knew the reason of this appearance. So if you ask him what he sees, he replies, "A broken stick," for he is quite sure he is experiencing this sensation. But when deceived by his judgment he goes further and, after saying he sees a broken stick, he affirms that it really is broken he says what is not true. Why? Because he becomes active and judges no longer by observation but by induction, he affirms what he does not perceive, i.e., that the judgment he receives through one of his senses would be confirmed by another.

Since all our errors arise in our judgment, it is clear, that had we no need for judgment, we should not need to learn; we should never be liable to mistakes, we should be happier in our ignorance than we can be in our knowledge. Who can deny that a vast number of things are known to the learned, which the unlearned will never know? Are the learned any nearer truth? Not so, the further they go the further they get from truth, for their pride in their judgment increases faster than their progress in knowledge, so that for every truth they acquire they draw a hundred mistaken conclusions. Every one knows that the learned societies of Europe are mere schools of falsehood, and there are assuredly more mistaken notions in the Academy of Sciences than in a whole tribe of American Indians.

The more we know, the more mistakes we make; therefore ignorance is the only way to escape error. Form no judgments and you will never be mistaken. This is the teaching both of nature and reason. We come into direct contact with very few things, and these are very readily perceived; the rest we regard with profound indifference. A savage will not turn his head to watch the working of the finest machinery or all the wonders of electricity. "What does that matter to me?" is the common saying of the ignorant; it is the fittest phrase for the wise.

Unluckily this phrase will no longer serve our turn. Everything matters to us, as we are dependent on everything, and our curiosity naturally increases with our needs. This is why I attribute much curiosity to the man of science and none to the savage. The latter needs no help from anybody; the former requires every one, and admirers most of all.

You will tell me I am going beyond nature. I think not. She chooses her instruments and orders them, not according to fancy, but necessity. Now a man's needs vary with his circumstances. There is all the difference in the world between a natural man living in a state of nature, and a natural man living in society. Emile is no savage to be banished to the desert, he is a savage who has to live in the town. He must know how to get his living in a town, how to use its inhabitants, and how to live among them, if not of them.

In the midst of so many new relations and dependent on them, he must reason whether he wants to or no. Let us therefore teach him to reason correctly.

The best way of learning to reason aright is that which tends to simplify our experiences, or to enable us to dispense with them altogether without falling into error. Hence it follows that we must learn to confirm the experiences of each sense by itself, without recourse to any other, though we have been in the habit of verifying the experience of one sense by that of another. Then each of our sensations will become an idea, and this idea will always correspond to the truth. This is the sort of knowledge I have tried to accumulate during this third phase of man's life.

This method of procedure demands a patience and circumspection which few teachers possess; without them the scholar will never learn to reason. For example, if you hasten to take the stick out of the water when the child is deceived by its appearance, you may perhaps undeceive him, but what have you taught him? Nothing more than he would soon have learnt for himself. That is not the right thing to do. You have not got to teach him truths so much as to show him how to set about discovering them for himself. To teach him better you must not be in such a hurry to correct his mistakes. Let us take Emile and myself as an illustration.

To begin with, any child educated in the usual way could not fail to answer the second of my imaginary questions in the affirmative. He will say, "That is certainly a broken stick." I very much doubt whether Emile will give the same reply. He sees no reason for knowing everything or pretending to know it; he is never in a hurry to draw conclusions. He only reasons from evidence and on this occasion he has not got the evidence. He knows how appearances deceive us, if only through perspective.

Moreover, he knows by experience that there is always a reason for my slightest questions, though he may not see it at once; so he has not got into the habit of giving silly answers; on the contrary, he is on his guard, he considers things carefully and attentively before answering. He never gives me an answer unless he is satisfied with it himself, and he is hard to please. Lastly we neither of us take any pride in merely knowing a thing, but only in avoiding mistakes. We should be more ashamed to deceive ourselves with bad reasoning, than to find no explanation at all. There is no phrase so appropriate to us, or so often on our lips, as, "I do not know;" neither of us are ashamed to use it. But whether he gives the silly answer or whether he avoids it by our convenient phrase "I do not know," my answer is the same. "Let us examine it."

This stick immersed half way in the water is fixed in an upright position. To know if it is broken, how many things must be done before we take it out of the water or even touch it.

1. First we walk round it, and we see that the broken part follows us. So it is only our eye that changes it; looks do not make things move.

2. We look straight down on that end of the stick which is above the water, the stick is no longer bent, [Footnote: I have since found by more exact experiment that this is not the case. Refraction acts in a circle, and the stick appears larger at the end which is in the water, but this makes no difference to the strength of the argument, and the conclusion is correct.] the end near our eye exactly hides the other end. Has our eye set the stick straight?

3. We stir the surface of the water; we see the stick break into several pieces, it moves in zigzags and follows the ripples of the water. Can the motion we gave the water suffice to break, soften, or melt the stick like this?

4. We draw the water off, and little by little we see the stick straightening itself as the water sinks. Is not this more than enough to clear up the business and to discover refraction? So it is not true that our eyes deceive us, for nothing more has been required to correct the mistakes attributed to it.

Suppose the child were stupid enough not to perceive the result of these experiments, then you must call touch to the help of sight. Instead of taking the stick out of the water, leave it where it is and let the child pass his hand along it from end to end; he will feel no angle, therefore the stick is not broken.

You will tell me this is not mere judgment but formal reasoning. Just so; but do not you see that as soon as the mind has got any ideas at all, every judgment is a process of reasoning? So that as soon as we compare one sensation with another, we are beginning to reason. The art of judging and the art of reasoning are one and the same.

Emile will never learn dioptrics unless he learns with this stick. He will not have dissected insects nor counted the spots on the sun; he will not know what you mean by a microscope or a telescope. Your learned pupils will laugh at his ignorance and rightly, I intend him to invent these instruments before he uses them, and you will expect that to take some time.

This is the spirit of my whole method at this stage. If the child rolls a little ball between two crossed fingers and thinks he feels two balls, I shall not let him look until he is convinced there is only one.

This explanation will suffice, I hope, to show plainly the progress made by my pupil hitherto and the route followed by him. But perhaps the number of things I have brought to his notice alarms you. I shall crush his mind beneath this weight of knowledge. Not so, I am rather teaching him to be ignorant of things than to know them. I am showing him the path of science, easy indeed, but long, far-reaching and slow to follow. I am taking him a few steps along this path, but I do not allow him to go far.

Compelled to learn for himself, he uses his own reason not that of others, for there must be no submission to authority if you would have no submission to convention. Most of our errors are due to others more than ourselves. This continual exercise should develop a vigour of mind like that acquired by the body through labour and weariness. Another advantage is that his progress is in proportion to his strength, neither mind nor body carries more than it can bear. When the understanding lays hold of things before they are stored in the memory, what is drawn from that store is his own; while we are in danger of never finding anything of our own in a memory over-burdened with undigested knowledge.

Emile knows little, but what he knows is really his own; he has no half-knowledge. Among the few things he knows and knows thoroughly this is the most valuable, that there are many things he does not know now but may know some day, many more that other men know but he will never know, and an infinite number which nobody will ever know. He is large-minded, not through knowledge, but through the power of acquiring it; he is open-minded, intelligent, ready for anything, and, as Montaigne says, capable of learning if not learned. I am content if he knows the "Wherefore" of his actions and the "Why" of his beliefs. For once more my object is not to supply him with exact knowledge, but the means of getting it when required, to teach him to value it at its true worth, and to love truth above all things. By this method progress is slow but sure, and we never need to retrace our steps.

Emile's knowledge is confined to nature and things. The very name of history is unknown to him, along with metaphysics and morals. He knows the essential relations between men and things, but nothing of the moral relations between man and man. He has little power of generalisation, he has no skill in abstraction. He perceives that certain qualities are common to certain things, without reasoning about these qualities themselves. He is acquainted with the abstract idea of space by the help of his geometrical figures; he is acquainted with the abstract idea of quantity by the help of his algebraical symbols. These figures and signs are the supports on which these ideas may be said to rest, the supports on which his senses repose. He does not attempt to know the nature of things, but only to know things in so far as they affect himself. He only judges what is outside himself in relation to himself, and his judgment is exact and certain. Caprice and prejudice have no part in it. He values most the things which are of use to himself, and as he never departs from this standard of values, he owes nothing to prejudice.

Emile is industrious, temperate, patient, stedfast, and full of courage. His imagination is still asleep, so he has no exaggerated ideas of danger; the few ills he feels he knows how to endure in patience, because he has not learnt to rebel against fate. As to death, he knows not what it means; but accustomed as he is to submit without resistance to the law of necessity, he will die, if die he must, without a groan and without a struggle; that is as much as we can demand of nature, in that hour which we all abhor. To live in freedom, and to be independent of human affairs, is the best way to learn how to die.

In a word Emile is possessed of all that portion of virtue which concerns himself. To acquire the social virtues he only needs a knowledge of the relations which make those virtues necessary; he only lacks knowledge which he is quite ready to receive.

He thinks not of others but of himself, and prefers that others should do the same. He makes no claim upon them, and acknowledges no debt to them. He is alone in the midst of human society, he depends on himself alone, for he is all that a boy can be at his age. He has no errors, or at least only such as are inevitable; he has no vices, or only those from which no man can escape. His body is healthy, his limbs are supple, his mind is accurate and unprejudiced, his heart is free and untroubled by passion. Pride, the earliest and the most natural of passions, has scarcely shown itself. Without disturbing the peace of others, he has passed his life contented, happy, and free, so far as nature allows. Do you think that the earlier years of a child, who has reached his fifteenth year in this condition, have been wasted?

BOOK I?

How swiftly life passes here below! The first quarter of it is gone before we know how to use it; the last quarter finds us incapable of enjoying life. At first we do not know how to live; and when we know how to live it is too late. In the interval between these two useless extremes we waste three-fourths of our time sleeping, working, sorrowing, enduring restraint and every kind of suffering. Life is short, not so much because of the short time it lasts, but because we are allowed scarcely any time to enjoy it. In vain is there a long interval between the hour of death and that of birth; life is still too short, if this interval is not well spent.

We are born, so to speak, twice over; born into existence, and born into life; born a human being, and born a man. Those who regard woman as an imperfect man are no doubt mistaken, but they have external resemblance on their side. Up to the age of puberty children of both sexes have little to distinguish them to the eye, the same face and form, the same complexion and voice, everything is the same; girls are children and boys are children; one name is enough for creatures so closely resembling one another. Males whose development is arrested preserve this resemblance all their lives; they are always big children; and women who never lose this resemblance seem in many respects never to be more than children.

But, speaking generally, man is not meant to remain a child. He leaves childhood behind him at the time ordained by nature; and this critical moment, short enough in itself, has far-reaching consequences.

As the roaring of the waves precedes the tempest, so the murmur of rising passions announces this tumultuous change; a suppressed excitement warns us of the approaching danger. A change of temper, frequent outbreaks of anger, a perpetual stirring of the mind, make the child almost ungovernable. He becomes deaf to the voice he used to obey; he is a lion in a fever; he distrusts his keeper and refuses to be controlled.

With the moral symptoms of a changing temper there are perceptible changes in appearance. His countenance develops and takes the stamp of his character; the soft and sparse down upon his cheeks becomes darker and stiffer. His voice grows hoarse or rather he loses it altogether. He is neither a child nor a man and cannot speak like either of them. His eyes, those organs of the soul which till now were dumb, find speech and meaning; a kindling fire illumines them, there is still a sacred innocence in their ever brightening glance, but they have lost their first meaningless expression; he is already aware that they can say too much; he is beginning to learn to lower his eyes and blush, he is becoming sensitive, though he does not know what it is that he feels; he is uneasy without knowing why. All this may happen gradually and give you time enough; but if his keenness becomes impatience, his eagerness madness, if he is angry and sorry all in a moment, if he weeps without cause, if in the presence of objects which are beginning to be a source of danger his pulse quickens and his eyes sparkle, if he trembles when a woman's hand touches his, if he is troubled or timid in her presence, O Ulysses, wise Ulysses! have a care! The passages you closed with so much pains are open; the winds are unloosed; keep your hand upon the helm or all is lost.

This is the second birth I spoke of; then it is that man really enters upon life; henceforth no human passion is a stranger to him. Our efforts so far have been child's play, now they are of the greatest importance. This period when education is usually finished is just the time to begin; but to explain this new plan properly, let us take up our story where we left it.

Our passions are the chief means of self-preservation; to try to destroy them is therefore as absurd as it is useless; this would be to overcome nature, to reshape God's handiwork. If God bade man annihilate the passions he has given him, God would bid him be and not be; He would contradict himself. He has never given such a foolish commandment, there is nothing like it written on the heart of man, and what God will have a man do, He does not leave to the words of another man. He speaks Himself; His words are written in the secret heart.

Now I consider those who would prevent the birth of the passions almost as foolish as those who would destroy them, and those who think this has been my object hitherto are greatly mistaken.

But should we reason rightly, if from the fact that passions are natural to man, we inferred that all the passions we feel in ourselves and behold in others are natural? Their source, indeed, is natural; but they have been swollen by a thousand other streams; they are a great river which is constantly growing, one in which we can scarcely find a single drop of the original stream. Our natural passions are few in number; they are the means to freedom, they tend to self-preservation. All those which enslave and destroy us have another source; nature does not bestow them on us; we seize on them in her despite.

The origin of our passions, the root and spring of all the rest, the only one which is born with man, which never leaves him as long as he lives, is self-love; this passion is primitive, instinctive, it precedes all the rest, which are in a sense only modifications of it. In this sense, if you like, they are all natural. But most of these modifications are the result of external influences, without which they would never occur, and such modifications, far from being advantageous to us, are harmful. They change the original purpose and work against its end; then it is that man finds himself outside nature and at strife with himself.

Self-love is always good, always in accordance with the order of nature. The preservation of our own life is specially entrusted to each one of us, and our first care is, and must be, to watch over our own life; and how can we continually watch over it, if we do not take the greatest interest in it?

Self-preservation requires, therefore, that we shall love ourselves; we must love ourselves above everything, and it follows directly from this that we love what contributes to our preservation. Every child becomes fond of its nurse; Romulus must have loved the she-wolf who suckled him. At first this attachment is quite unconscious; the individual is attracted to that which contributes to his welfare and repelled by that which is harmful; this is merely blind instinct. What transforms this instinct into feeling, the liking into love, the aversion into hatred, is the evident intention of helping or hurting us. We do not become passionately attached to objects without feeling, which only follow the direction given them; but those from which we expect benefit or injury from their internal disposition, from their will, those we see acting freely for or against us, inspire us with like feelings to those they exhibit towards us. Something does us good, we seek after it; but we love the person who does us good; something harms us and we shrink from it, but we hate the person who tries to hurt us.

The child's first sentiment is self-love, his second, which is derived from it, is love of those about him; for in his present state of weakness he is only aware of people through the help and attention received from them. At first his affection for his nurse and his governess is mere habit. He seeks them because he needs them and because he is happy when they are there; it is rather perception than kindly feeling. It takes a long time to discover not merely that they are useful to him, but that they desire to be useful to him, and then it is that he begins to love them.

So a child is naturally disposed to kindly feeling because he sees that every one about him is inclined to help him, and from this experience he gets the habit of a kindly feeling towards his species; but with the expansion of his relations, his needs, his dependence, active or passive, the consciousness of his relations to others is awakened, and leads to the sense of duties and preferences. Then the child becomes masterful, jealous, deceitful, and vindictive. If he is not compelled to obedience, when he does not see the usefulness of what he is told to do, he attributes it to caprice, to an intention of tormenting him, and he rebels. If people give in to him, as soon as anything opposes him he regards it as rebellion, as a determination to resist him; he beats the chair or table for disobeying him. Self-love, which concerns itself only with ourselves, is content to satisfy our own needs; but selfishness, which is always comparing self with others, is never satisfied and never can be; for this feeling, which prefers ourselves to others, requires that they should prefer us to themselves, which is impossible. Thus the tender and gentle passions spring from self-love, while the hateful and angry passions spring from selfishness. So it is the fewness of his needs, the narrow limits within which he can compare himself with others, that makes a man really good; what makes him really bad is a multiplicity of needs and dependence on the opinions of others. It is easy to see how we can apply this principle and guide every passion of children and men towards good or evil. True, man cannot always live alone, and it will be hard therefore to remain good; and this difficulty will increase of necessity as his relations with others are extended. For this reason, above all, the dangers of social life demand that the necessary skill and care shall be devoted to guarding the human heart against the depravity which springs from fresh needs.

Man's proper study is that of his relation to his environment. So long as he only knows that environment through his physical nature, he should study himself in relation to things; this is the business of his childhood; when he begins to be aware of his moral nature, he should study himself in relation to his fellow-men; this is the business of his whole life, and we have now reached the time when that study should be begun.

As soon as a man needs a companion he is no longer an isolated creature, his heart is no longer alone. All his relations with his species, all the affections of his heart, come into being along with this. His first passion soon arouses the rest.

The direction of the instinct is uncertain. One sex is attracted by the other; that is the impulse of nature. Choice, preferences, individual likings, are the work of reason, prejudice, and habit; time and knowledge are required to make us capable of love; we do not love without reasoning or prefer without comparison. These judgments are none the less real, although they are formed unconsciously. True love, whatever you may say, will always be held in honour by mankind; for although its impulses lead us astray, although it does not bar the door of the heart to certain detestable qualities, although it even gives rise to these, yet it always presupposes certain worthy characteristics, without which we should be incapable of love. This choice, which is supposed to be contrary to reason, really springs from reason. We say Love is blind because his eyes are better than ours, and he perceives relations which we cannot discern. All women would be alike to a man who had no idea of virtue or beauty, and the first comer would always be the most charming. Love does not spring from nature, far from it; it is the curb and law of her desires; it is love that makes one sex indifferent to the other, the loved one alone excepted.

We wish to inspire the preference we feel; love must be mutual. To be loved we must be worthy of love; to be preferred we must be more worthy than the rest, at least in the eyes of our beloved. Hence we begin to look around among our fellows; we begin to compare ourselves with them, there is emulation, rivalry, and jealousy. A heart full to overflowing loves to make itself known; from the need of a mistress there soon springs the need of a friend He who feels how sweet it is to be loved, desires to be loved by everybody; and there could be no preferences if there were not many that fail to find satisfaction. With love and friendship there begin dissensions, enmity, and hatred. I behold deference to other people's opinions enthroned among all these divers passions, and foolish mortals, enslaved by her power, base their very existence merely on what other people think.

Expand these ideas and you will see where we get that form of selfishness which we call natural selfishness, and how selfishness ceases to be a simple feeling and becomes pride in great minds, vanity in little ones, and in both feeds continually at our neighbour's cost. Passions of this kind, not having any germ in the child's heart, cannot spring up in it of themselves; it is we who sow the seeds, and they never take root unless by our fault. Not so with the young man; they will find an entrance in spite of us. It is therefore time to change our methods.

Let us begin with some considerations of importance with regard to the critical stage under discussion. The change from childhood to puberty is not so clearly determined by nature but that it varies according to individual temperament and racial conditions. Everybody knows the differences which have been observed with regard to this between hot and cold countries, and every one sees that ardent temperaments mature earlier than others; but we may be mistaken as to the causes, and we may often attribute to physical causes what is really due to moral: this is one of the commonest errors in the philosophy of our times. The teaching of nature comes slowly; man's lessons are mostly premature. In the former case, the senses kindle the imagination, in the latter the imagination kindles the senses; it gives them a precocious activity which cannot fail to enervate the individual and, in the long run, the race. It is a more general and more trustworthy fact than that of climatic influences, that puberty and sexual power is always more precocious among educated and civilised races, than among the ignorant and barbarous. [Footnote: "In towns," says M. Buffon, "and among the well-to-do classes, children accustomed to plentiful and nourishing food sooner reach this state; in the country and among the poor, children are more backward, because of their poor and scanty food." I admit the fact but not the explanation, for in the districts where the food of the villagers is plentiful and good, as in the Valais and even in some of the mountain districts of Italy, such as Friuli, the age of puberty for both sexes is quite as much later than in the heart of the towns, where, in order to gratify their vanity, people are often extremely parsimonious in the matter of food, and where most people, in the words of the proverb, have a velvet coat and an empty belly. It is astonishing to find in these mountainous regions big lads as strong as a man with shrill voices and smooth chins, and tall girls, well developed in other respects, without any trace of the periodic functions of their sex. This difference is, in my opinion, solely due to the fact that in the simplicity of their manners the imagination remains calm and peaceful, and does not stir the blood till much later, and thus their temperament is much less precocious.] Children are preternaturally quick to discern immoral habits under the cloak of decency with which they are concealed. The prim speech imposed upon them, the lessons in good behaviour, the veil of mystery you profess to hang before their eyes, serve but to stimulate their curiosity. It is plain, from the way you set about it, that they are meant to learn what you profess to conceal; and of all you teach them this is most quickly assimilated.

Consult experience and you will find how far this foolish method hastens the work of nature and ruins the character. This is one of the chief causes of physical degeneration in our towns. The young people, prematurely exhausted, remain small, puny, and misshapen, they grow old instead of growing up, like a vine forced to bear fruit in spring, which fades and dies before autumn.

To know how far a happy ignorance may prolong the innocence of children, you must live among rude and simple people. It is a sight both touching and amusing to see both sexes, left to the protection of their own hearts, continuing the sports of childhood in the flower of youth and beauty, showing by their very familiarity the purity of their pleasures. When at length those delightful young people marry, they bestow on each other the first fruits of their person, and are all the dearer therefore. Swarms of strong and healthy children are the pledges of a union which nothing can change, and the fruit of the virtue of their early years.

If the age at which a man becomes conscious of his sex is deferred as much by the effects of education as by the action of nature, it follows that this age may be hastened or retarded according to the way in which the child is brought up; and if the body gains or loses strength in proportion as its development is accelerated or retarded, it also follows that the more we try to retard it the stronger and more vigorous will the young man be. I am still speaking of purely physical consequences; you will soon see that this is not all.

From these considerations I arrive at the solution of the question so often discussed—Should we enlighten children at an early period as to the objects of their curiosity, or is it better to put them off with decent shams? I think we need do neither. In the first place, this curiosity will not arise unless we give it a chance. We must therefore take care not to give it an opportunity. In the next place, questions one is not obliged to answer do not compel us to deceive those who ask them; it is better to bid the child hold his tongue than to tell him a lie. He will not be greatly surprised at this treatment if you have already accustomed him to it in matters of no importance. Lastly, if you decide to answer his questions, let it be with the greatest plainness, without mystery or confusion, without a smile. It is much less dangerous to satisfy a child's curiosity than to stimulate it.

Let your answers be always grave, brief, decided, and without trace of hesitation. I need not add that they should be true. We cannot teach children the danger of telling lies to men without realising, on the man's part, the danger of telling lies to children. A single untruth on the part of the master will destroy the results of his education.

Complete ignorance with regard to certain matters is perhaps the best thing for children; but let them learn very early what it is impossible to conceal from them permanently. Either their curiosity must never be aroused, or it must be satisfied before the age when it becomes a source of danger. Your conduct towards your pupil in this respect depends greatly on his individual circumstances, the society in which he moves, the position in which he may find himself, etc. Nothing must be left to chance; and if you are not sure of keeping him in ignorance of the difference between the sexes till he is sixteen, take care you teach him before he is ten.

I do not like people to be too fastidious in speaking with children, nor should they go out of their way to avoid calling a spade a spade; they are always found out if they do. Good manners in this respect are always perfectly simple; but an imagination soiled by vice makes the ear over-sensitive and compels us to be constantly refining our expressions. Plain words do not matter; it is lascivious ideas which must be avoided.

Although modesty is natural to man, it is not natural to children. Modesty only begins with the knowledge of evil; and how should children without this knowledge of evil have the feeling which results from it? To give them lessons in modesty and good conduct is to teach them that there are things shameful and wicked, and to give them a secret wish to know what these things are. Sooner or later they will find out, and the first spark which touches the imagination will certainly hasten the awakening of the senses. Blushes are the sign of guilt; true innocence is ashamed of nothing.

Children have not the same desires as men; but they are subject like them to the same disagreeable needs which offend the senses, and by this means they may receive the same lessons in propriety. Follow the mind of nature which has located in the same place the organs of secret pleasures and those of disgusting needs; she teaches us the same precautions at different ages, sometimes by means of one idea and sometimes by another; to the man through modesty, to the child through cleanliness.

I can only find one satisfactory way of preserving the child's innocence, to surround him by those who respect and love him. Without this all our efforts to keep him in ignorance fail sooner or later; a smile, a wink, a careless gesture tells him all we sought to hide; it is enough to teach him to perceive that there is something we want to hide from him. The delicate phrases and expressions employed by persons of politeness assume a knowledge which children ought not to possess, and they are quite out of place with them, but when we truly respect the child's innocence we easily find in talking to him the simple phrases which befit him. There is a certain directness of speech which is suitable and pleasing to innocence; this is the right tone to adopt in order to turn the child from dangerous curiosity. By speaking simply to him about everything you do not let him suspect there is anything left unsaid. By connecting coarse words with the unpleasant ideas which belong to them, you quench the first spark of imagination; you do not forbid the child to say these words or to form these ideas; but without his knowing it you make him unwilling to recall them. And how much confusion is spared to those who speaking from the heart always say the right thing, and say it as they themselves have felt it!

"Where do little children come from?" This is an embarrassing question, which occurs very naturally to children, one which foolishly or wisely answered may decide their health and their morals for life. The quickest way for a mother to escape from it without deceiving her son is to tell him to hold his tongue. That will serve its turn if he has always been accustomed to it in matters of no importance, and if he does not suspect some mystery from this new way of speaking. But the mother rarely stops there. "It is the married people's secret," she will say, "little boys should not be so curious." That is all very well so far as the mother is concerned, but she may be sure that the little boy, piqued by her scornful manner, will not rest till he has found out the married people's secret, which will very soon be the case.

Let me tell you a very different answer which I heard given to the same question, one which made all the more impression on me, coming, as it did, from a woman, modest in speech and behaviour, but one who was able on occasion, for the welfare of her child and for the cause of virtue, to cast aside the false fear of blame and the silly jests of the foolish. Not long before the child had passed a small stone which had torn the passage, but the trouble was over and forgotten. "Mamma," said the eager child, "where do little children come from?" "My child," replied his mother without hesitation, "women pass them with pains that sometimes cost their life." Let fools laugh and silly people be shocked; but let the wise inquire if it is possible to find a wiser answer and one which would better serve its purpose.

In the first place the thought of a need of nature with which the child is well acquainted turns his thoughts from the idea of a mysterious process. The accompanying ideas of pain and death cover it with a veil of sadness which deadens the imagination and suppresses curiosity; everything leads the mind to the results, not the causes, of child-birth. This is the information to which this answer leads. If the repugnance inspired by this answer should permit the child to inquire further, his thoughts are turned to the infirmities of human nature, disgusting things, images of pain. What chance is there for any stimulation of desire in such a conversation? And yet you see there is no departure from truth, no need to deceive the scholar in order to teach him.

Your children read; in the course of their reading they meet with things they would never have known without reading. Are they students, their imagination is stimulated and quickened in the silence of the study. Do they move in the world of society, they hear a strange jargon, they see conduct which makes a great impression on them; they have been told so continually that they are men that in everything men do in their presence they at once try to find how that will suit themselves; the conduct of others must indeed serve as their pattern when the opinions of others are their law. Servants, dependent on them, and therefore anxious to please them, flatter them at the expense of their morals; giggling governesses say things to the four-year-old child which the most shameless woman would not dare to say to them at fifteen. They soon forget what they said, but the child has not forgotten what he heard. Loose conversation prepares the way for licentious conduct; the child is debauched by the cunning lacquey, and the secret of the one guarantees the secret of the other.

The child brought up in accordance with his age is alone. He knows no attachment but that of habit, he loves his sister like his watch, and his friend like his dog. He is unconscious of his sex and his species; men and women are alike unknown; he does not connect their sayings and doings with himself, he neither sees nor hears, or he pays no heed to them; he is no more concerned with their talk than their actions; he has nothing to do with it. This is no artificial error induced by our method, it is the ignorance of nature. The time is at hand when that same nature will take care to enlighten her pupil, and then only does she make him capable of profiting by the lessons without danger. This is our principle; the details of its rules are outside my subject; and the means I suggest with regard to other matters will still serve to illustrate this.

Do you wish to establish law and order among the rising passions, prolong the period of their development, so that they may have time to find their proper place as they arise. Then they are controlled by nature herself, not by man; your task is merely to leave it in her hands. If your pupil were alone, you would have nothing to do; but everything about him enflames his imagination. He is swept along on the torrent of conventional ideas; to rescue him you must urge him in the opposite direction. Imagination must be curbed by feeling and reason must silence the voice of conventionality. Sensibility is the source of all the passions, imagination determines their course. Every creature who is aware of his relations must be disturbed by changes in these relations and when he imagines or fancies he imagines others better adapted to his nature. It is the errors of the imagination which transmute into vices the passions of finite beings, of angels even, if indeed they have passions; for they must needs know the nature of every creature to realise what relations are best adapted to themselves.

This is the sum of human wisdom with regard to the use of the passions. First, to be conscious of the true relations of man both in the species and the individual; second, to control all the affections in accordance with these relations.

But is man in a position to control his affections according to such and such relations? No doubt he is, if he is able to fix his imagination on this or that object, or to form this or that habit. Moreover, we are not so much concerned with what a man can do for himself, as with what we can do for our pupil through our choice of the circumstances in which he shall be placed. To show the means by which he may be kept in the path of nature is to show plainly enough how he might stray from that path.

So long as his consciousness is confined to himself there is no morality in his actions; it is only when it begins to extend beyond himself that he forms first the sentiments and then the ideas of good and ill, which make him indeed a man, and an integral part of his species. To begin with we must therefore confine our observations to this point.

These observations are difficult to make, for we must reject the examples before our eyes, and seek out those in which the successive developments follow the order of nature.

A child sophisticated, polished, and civilised, who is only awaiting the power to put into practice the precocious instruction he has received, is never mistaken with regard to the time when this power is acquired. Far from awaiting it, he accelerates it; he stirs his blood to a premature ferment; he knows what should be the object of his desires long before those desires are experienced. It is not nature which stimulates him; it is he who forces the hand of nature; she has nothing to teach him when he becomes a man; he was a man in thought long before he was a man in reality.

The true course of nature is slower and more gradual. Little by little the blood grows warmer, the faculties expand, the character is formed. The wise workman who directs the process is careful to perfect every tool before he puts it to use; the first desires are preceded by a long period of unrest, they are deceived by a prolonged ignorance, they know not what they want. The blood ferments and bubbles; overflowing vitality seeks to extend its sphere. The eye grows brighter and surveys others, we begin to be interested in those about us, we begin to feel that we are not meant to live alone; thus the heart is thrown open to human affection, and becomes capable of attachment.

The first sentiment of which the well-trained youth is capable is not love but friendship. The first work of his rising imagination is to make known to him his fellows; the species affects him before the sex. Here is another advantage to be gained from prolonged innocence; you may take advantage of his dawning sensibility to sow the first seeds of humanity in the heart of the young adolescent. This advantage is all the greater because this is the only time in his life when such efforts may be really successful.

I have always observed that young men, corrupted in early youth and addicted to women and debauchery, are inhuman and cruel; their passionate temperament makes them impatient, vindictive, and angry; their imagination fixed on one object only, refuses all others; mercy and pity are alike unknown to them; they would have sacrificed father, mother, the whole world, to the least of their pleasures. A young man, on the other hand, brought up in happy innocence, is drawn by the first stirrings of nature to the tender and affectionate passions; his warm heart is touched by the sufferings of his fellow-creatures; he trembles with delight when he meets his comrade, his arms can embrace tenderly, his eyes can shed tears of pity; he learns to be sorry for offending others through his shame at causing annoyance. If the eager warmth of his blood makes him quick, hasty, and passionate, a moment later you see all his natural kindness of heart in the eagerness of his repentance; he weeps, he groans over the wound he has given; he would atone for the blood he has shed with his own; his anger dies away, his pride abases itself before the consciousness of his wrong-doing. Is he the injured party, in the height of his fury an excuse, a word, disarms him; he forgives the wrongs of others as whole-heartedly as he repairs his own. Adolescence is not the age of hatred or vengeance; it is the age of pity, mercy, and generosity. Yes, I maintain, and I am not afraid of the testimony of experience, a youth of good birth, one who has preserved his innocence up to the age of twenty, is at that age the best, the most generous, the most loving, and the most lovable of men. You never heard such a thing; I can well believe that philosophers such as you, brought up among the corruption of the public schools, are unaware of it.

Man's weakness makes him sociable. Our common sufferings draw our hearts to our fellow-creatures; we should have no duties to mankind if we were not men. Every affection is a sign of insufficiency; if each of us had no need of others, we should hardly think of associating with them. So our frail happiness has its roots in our weakness. A really happy man is a hermit; God only enjoys absolute happiness; but which of us has any idea what that means? If any imperfect creature were self-sufficing, what would he have to enjoy? To our thinking he would be wretched and alone. I do not understand how one who has need of nothing could love anything, nor do I understand how he who loves nothing can be happy.

Hence it follows that we are drawn towards our fellow-creatures less by our feeling for their joys than for their sorrows; for in them we discern more plainly a nature like our own, and a pledge of their affection for us. If our common needs create a bond of interest our common sufferings create a bond of affection. The sight of a happy man arouses in others envy rather than love, we are ready to accuse him of usurping a right which is not his, of seeking happiness for himself alone, and our selfishness suffers an additional pang in the thought that this man has no need of us. But who does not pity the wretch when he beholds his sufferings? who would not deliver him from his woes if a wish could do it? Imagination puts us more readily in the place of the miserable man than of the happy man; we feel that the one condition touches us more nearly than the other. Pity is sweet, because, when we put ourselves in the place of one who suffers, we are aware, nevertheless, of the pleasure of not suffering like him. Envy is bitter, because the sight of a happy man, far from putting the envious in his place, inspires him with regret that he is not there. The one seems to exempt us from the pains he suffers, the other seems to deprive us of the good things he enjoys.

Do you desire to stimulate and nourish the first stirrings of awakening sensibility in the heart of a young man, do you desire to incline his disposition towards kindly deed and thought, do not cause the seeds of pride, vanity, and envy to spring up in him through the misleading picture of the happiness of mankind; do not show him to begin with the pomp of courts, the pride of palaces, the delights of pageants; do not take him into society and into brilliant assemblies; do not show him the outside of society till you have made him capable of estimating it at its true worth. To show him the world before he is acquainted with men, is not to train him, but to corrupt him; not to teach, but to mislead.

By nature men are neither kings, nobles, courtiers, nor millionaires. All men are born poor and naked, all are liable to the sorrows of life, its disappointments, its ills, its needs, its suffering of every kind; and all are condemned at length to die. This is what it really means to be a man, this is what no mortal can escape. Begin then with the study of the essentials of humanity, that which really constitutes mankind.

At sixteen the adolescent knows what it is to suffer, for he himself has suffered; but he scarcely realises that others suffer too; to see without feeling is not knowledge, and as I have said again and again the child who does not picture the feelings of others knows no ills but his own; but when his imagination is kindled by the first beginnings of growing sensibility, he begins to perceive himself in his fellow-creatures, to be touched by their cries, to suffer in their sufferings. It is at this time that the sorrowful picture of suffering humanity should stir his heart with the first touch of pity he has ever known.

If it is not easy to discover this opportunity in your scholars, whose fault is it? You taught them so soon to play at feeling, you taught them so early its language, that speaking continually in the same strain they turn your lessons against yourself, and give you no chance of discovering when they cease to lie, and begin to feel what they say. But look at Emile; I have led him up to this age, and he has neither felt nor pretended to feel. He has never said, "I love you dearly," till he knew what it was to love; he has never been taught what expression to assume when he enters the room of his father, his mother, or his sick tutor; he has not learnt the art of affecting a sorrow he does not feel. He has never pretended to weep for the death of any one, for he does not know what it is to die. There is the same insensibility in his heart as in his manners. Indifferent, like every child, to every one but himself, he takes no interest in any one; his only peculiarity is that he will not pretend to take such an interest; he is less deceitful than others.

Emile having thought little about creatures of feeling will be a long time before he knows what is meant by pain and death. Groans and cries will begin to stir his compassion, he will turn away his eyes at the sight of blood; the convulsions of a dying animal will cause him I know not what anguish before he knows the source of these impulses. If he were still stupid and barbarous he would not feel them; if he were more learned he would recognise their source; he has compared ideas too frequently already to be insensible, but not enough to know what he feels.

So pity is born, the first relative sentiment which touches the human heart according to the order of nature. To become sensitive and pitiful the child must know that he has fellow-creatures who suffer as he has suffered, who feel the pains he has felt, and others which he can form some idea of, being capable of feeling them himself. Indeed, how can we let ourselves be stirred by pity unless we go beyond ourselves, and identify ourselves with the suffering animal, by leaving, so to speak, our own nature and taking his. We only suffer so far as we suppose he suffers; the suffering is not ours but his. So no one becomes sensitive till his imagination is aroused and begins to carry him outside himself.

What should we do to stimulate and nourish this growing sensibility, to direct it, and to follow its natural bent? Should we not present to the young man objects on which the expansive force of his heart may take effect, objects which dilate it, which extend it to other creatures, which take him outside himself? should we not carefully remove everything that narrows, concentrates, and strengthens the power of the human self? that is to say, in other words, we should arouse in him kindness, goodness, pity, and beneficence, all the gentle and attractive passions which are naturally pleasing to man; those passions prevent the growth of envy, covetousness, hatred, all the repulsive and cruel passions which make our sensibility not merely a cipher but a minus quantity, passions which are the curse of those who feel them.

I think I can sum up the whole of the preceding reflections in two or three maxims, definite, straightforward, and easy to understand.

FIRST MAXIM.—It is not in human nature to put ourselves in the place of those who are happier than ourselves, but only in the place of those who can claim our pity.

If you find exceptions to this rule, they are more apparent than real. Thus we do not put ourselves in the place of the rich or great when we become fond of them; even when our affection is real, we only appropriate to ourselves a part of their welfare. Sometimes we love the rich man in the midst of misfortunes; but so long as he prospers he has no real friend, except the man who is not deceived by appearances, who pities rather than envies him in spite of his prosperity.

The happiness belonging to certain states of life appeals to us; take, for instance, the life of a shepherd in the country. The charm of seeing these good people so happy is not poisoned by envy; we are genuinely interested in them. Why is this? Because we feel we can descend into this state of peace and innocence and enjoy the same happiness; it is an alternative which only calls up pleasant thoughts, so long as the wish is as good as the deed. It is always pleasant to examine our stores, to contemplate our own wealth, even when we do not mean to spend it.

From this we see that to incline a young man to humanity you must not make him admire the brilliant lot of others; you must show him life in its sorrowful aspects and arouse his fears. Thus it becomes clear that he must force his own way to happiness, without interfering with the happiness of others.

SECOND MAXIM.—We never pity another's woes unless we know we may suffer in like manner ourselves.

"Non ignara mali, miseris succurrere disco."—Virgil.

I know nothing go fine, so full of meaning, so touching, so true as these words.

Why have kings no pity on their people? Because they never expect to be ordinary men. Why are the rich so hard on the poor? Because they have no fear of becoming poor. Why do the nobles look down upon the people? Because a nobleman will never be one of the lower classes. Why are the Turks generally kinder and more hospitable than ourselves? Because, under their wholly arbitrary system of government, the rank and wealth of individuals are always uncertain and precarious, so that they do not regard poverty and degradation as conditions with which they have no concern; to-morrow, any one may himself be in the same position as those on whom he bestows alms to-day. This thought, which occurs again and again in eastern romances, lends them a certain tenderness which is not to be found in our pretentious and harsh morality.

So do not train your pupil to look down from the height of his glory upon the sufferings of the unfortunate, the labours of the wretched, and do not hope to teach him to pity them while he considers them as far removed from himself. Make him thoroughly aware of the fact that the fate of these unhappy persons may one day be his own, that his feet are standing on the edge of the abyss, into which he may be plunged at any moment by a thousand unexpected irresistible misfortunes. Teach him to put no trust in birth, health, or riches; show him all the changes of fortune; find him examples — there are only too many of them — in which men of higher rank than himself have sunk below the condition of these wretched ones. Whether by their own fault or another's is for the present no concern of ours; does he indeed know the meaning of the word fault? Never interfere with the order in which he acquires knowledge, and teach him only through the means within his reach; it needs no great learning to perceive that all the prudence of mankind cannot make certain whether he will be alive or dead in an hour's time, whether before nightfall he will not be grinding his teeth in the pangs of nephritis, whether a month hence he will be rich or poor, whether in a year's time he may not be rowing an Algerian galley under the lash of the slave-driver. Above all do not teach him this, like his catechism, in cold blood; let him see and feel the calamities which overtake men; surprise and startle his imagination with the perils which lurk continually about a man's path; let him see the pitfalls all about him, and when he hears you speak of them, let him cling more closely to you for fear lest he should fall. "You will make him timid and cowardly," do you say? We shall see; let us make him kindly to begin with, that is what matters most.

THIRD MAXIM. — The pity we feel for others is proportionate, not to the amount of the evil, but to the feelings we attribute to the sufferers.

We only pity the wretched so far as we think they feel the need of pity. The bodily effect of our sufferings is less than one would suppose; it is memory that prolongs the pain, imagination which projects it into the future, and makes us really to be pitied. This is, I think, one of the reasons why we are more callous to the sufferings of animals than of men, although a fellow-feeling ought to make us identify ourselves equally with either. We scarcely pity the cart-horse in his shed, for we do not suppose that while he is eating his hay he is thinking of the blows he has received and the labours in store for him. Neither do we pity the sheep grazing in the field, though we know it is about to be slaughtered, for we believe it knows nothing of the fate in store for it. In this way we also become callous to the fate of our fellow-men, and the rich console themselves for the harm done by them to the poor, by the assumption that the poor are too stupid to feel. I usually judge of the value any one puts on the welfare of his fellow-creatures by what he seems to think of them. We naturally think lightly of the happiness of those we despise. It need not surprise you that politicians speak so scornfully of the people, and philosophers profess to think mankind so wicked.

The people are mankind; those who do not belong to the people are so few in number that they are not worth counting. Man is the same in every station of life; if that be so, those ranks to which most men belong deserve most honour. All distinctions of rank fade away before the eyes of a thoughtful person; he sees the same passions, the same feelings in the noble and the guttersnipe; there is merely a slight difference in speech, and more or less artificiality of tone; and if there is indeed any essential difference between them, the disadvantage is all on the side of those who are more sophisticated. The people show themselves as they are, and they are not attractive; but the fashionable world is compelled to adopt a disguise; we should be horrified if we saw it as it really is.

There is, so our wiseacres tell us, the same amount of happiness and sorrow in every station. This saying is as deadly in its effects as it is incapable of proof; if all are equally happy why should I trouble myself about any one? Let every one stay where he is; leave the slave to be ill-treated, the sick man to suffer, and the wretched to perish; they have nothing to gain by any change in their condition. You enumerate the sorrows of the rich, and show the vanity of his empty pleasures; what barefaced sophistry! The rich man's sufferings do not come from his position, but from himself alone when he abuses it. He is not to be pitied were he indeed more miserable than the poor, for his ills are of his own making, and he could be happy if he chose. But the sufferings of the poor man come from external things, from the hardships fate has imposed upon him. No amount of habit can accustom him to the bodily ills of fatigue, exhaustion, and hunger. Neither head nor heart can serve to free him from the sufferings of his condition. How is Epictetus the better for knowing beforehand that his master will break his leg for him; does he do it any the less? He has to endure not only the pain itself but the pains of anticipation. If the people were as wise as we assume them to be stupid, how could they be other than they are? Observe persons of this class; you will see that, with a different way of speaking, they have as much intelligence and more common-sense than yourself. Have respect then for your species; remember that it consists essentially of the people, that if all the kings and all the philosophers were removed they would scarcely be missed, and things would go on none the worse. In a word, teach your pupil to love all men, even those who fail to appreciate him; act in such way that he is not a member of any class, but takes his place in all alike: speak in his hearing of the human race with tenderness, and even with pity, but never with scorn. You are a man; do not dishonour mankind.

It is by these ways and others like them—how different from the beaten paths—that we must reach the heart of the young adolescent, and stimulate in him the first impulses of nature; we must develop that heart and open its doors to his fellow-creatures, and there must be as little self-interest as possible mixed up with these impulses; above all, no vanity, no emulation, no boasting, none of those sentiments which force us to compare ourselves with others; for such comparisons are never made without arousing some measure of hatred against those who dispute our claim to the first place, were it only in our own estimation. Then we must be either blind or angry, a bad man or a fool; let us try to avoid this dilemma. Sooner or later these dangerous passions will appear, so you tell me, in spite of us. I do not deny it. There is a time and place for everything; I am only saying that we should not help to arouse these passions.

This is the spirit of the method to be laid down. In this case examples and illustrations are useless, for here we find the beginning of the countless differences of character, and every example I gave would possibly apply to only one case in a hundred thousand. It is at this age that the clever teacher begins his real business, as a student and a philosopher who knows how to probe the heart and strives to guide it aright. While the young man has not learnt to pretend, while he does not even know the meaning of pretence, you see by his look, his manner, his gestures, the impression he has received from any object presented to him; you read in his countenance every impulse of his heart; by watching his expression you learn to protect his impulses and actually to control them.

It has been commonly observed that blood, wounds, cries and groans, the preparations for painful operations, and everything which directs the senses towards things connected with suffering, are usually the first to make an impression on all men. The idea of destruction, a more complex matter, does not have so great an effect; the thought of death affects us later and less forcibly, for no one knows from his own experience what it is to die; you must have seen corpses to feel the agonies of the dying. But when once this idea is established in the mind, there is no spectacle more dreadful in our eyes, whether because of the idea of complete destruction which it arouses through our senses, or because we know that this moment must come for each one of us and we feel ourselves all the more keenly affected by a situation from which we know there is no escape.

These various impressions differ in manner and in degree, according to the individual character of each one of us and his former habits, but they are universal and no one is altogether free from them. There are other impressions less universal and of a later growth, impressions most suited to sensitive souls, such impressions as we receive from moral suffering, inward grief, the sufferings of the mind, depression, and sadness. There are men who can be touched by nothing but groans and tears; the suppressed sobs of a heart labouring under sorrow would never win a sigh; the sight of a downcast visage, a pale and gloomy countenance, eyes which can weep no longer, would never draw a tear from them. The sufferings of the mind are as nothing to them; they weigh them, their own mind feels nothing; expect nothing from such persons but inflexible severity, harshness, cruelty. They may be just and up-right, but not merciful, generous, or pitiful. They may, I say, be just, if a man can indeed be just without being merciful.

But do not be in a hurry to judge young people by this standard, more es-pecially those who have been educated rightly, who have no idea of the moral sufferings they have never had to endure; for once again they can only pity the ills they know, and this apparent insensibility is soon transformed into pity when they begin to feel that there are in human life a thousand ills of which they know nothing. As for Emile, if in childhood he was distinguished by simplicity and good sense, in his youth he will show a warm and tender heart; for the reality of the feelings depends to a great extent on the accuracy of the ideas.

But why call him hither? More than one reader will reproach me no doubt for departing from my first intention and forgetting the lasting happiness I promised my pupil. The sorrowful, the dying, such sights of pain and woe, what happiness, what delight is this for a young heart on the threshold of life? His gloomy tutor, who proposed to give him such a pleasant education, only introduces him to life that he may suffer. This is what they will say, but what care I? I promised to make him happy, not to make him seem happy. Am I to blame if, deceived as usual by the outward appearances, you take them for the reality?

Let us take two young men at the close of their early education, and let them enter the world by opposite doors. The one mounts at once to Olympus, and moves in the smartest society; he is taken to court, he is presented in the houses of the great, of the rich, of the pretty women. I assume that he is eve-rywhere made much of, and I do not regard too closely the effect of this re-ception on his reason; I assume it can stand it. Pleasures fly before him, every day provides him with fresh amusements; he flings himself into everything with an eagerness which carries you away. You find him busy, eager, and curious; his first wonder makes a great impression on you; you think him happy; but behold the state of his heart; you think he is rejoicing, I think he suffers.

What does he see when first he opens his eyes? all sorts of so-called pleas-ures, hitherto unknown. Most of these pleasures are only for a moment within his reach, and seem to show themselves only to inspire regret for their loss. Does he wander through a palace; you see by his uneasy curiosity that he is asking why his father's house is not like it. Every question shows you that he is comparing himself all the time with the owner of this grand place. And all the mortification arising from this comparison at once revolts and stimulates his vanity. If he meets a young man better dressed than himself, I find him secretly complaining of his parents' meanness. If he is better dressed than another, he suffers because the latter is his superior in birth or in intellect, and all his gold lace is put to shame by a plain cloth coat. Does he shine unrivalled in some assembly, does he stand on tiptoe that they may see him better, who is there who does not secretly desire to humble the pride and vanity of the young fop? Everybody is in league against him; the disquieting glances of a solemn man, the biting phrases of some satirical person, do not fail to reach him, and if it were only one man who despised him, the scorn of that one would poison in a moment the applause of the rest.

Let us grant him everything, let us not grudge him charm and worth; let him be well-made, witty, and attractive; the women will run after him; but by pursuing him before he is in love with them, they will inspire rage rather than love; he will have successes, but neither rapture nor passion to enjoy them. As his desires are always anticipated; they never have time to spring up among his pleasures, so he only feels the tedium of restraint. Even before he knows it he is disgusted and satiated with the sex formed to be the delight of his own; if he continues its pursuit it is only through vanity, and even should he really be devoted to women, he will not be the only brilliant, the only attractive young man, nor will he always find his mistresses prodigies of fidelity.

I say nothing of the vexation, the deceit, the crimes, and the remorse of all kinds, inseparable from such a life. We know that experience of the world disgusts us with it; I am speaking only of the drawbacks belonging to youthful illusions.

Hitherto the young man has lived in the bosom of his family and his friends, and has been the sole object of their care; what a change to enter all at once into a region where he counts for so little; to find himself plunged into another sphere, he who has been so long the centre of his own. What insults, what humiliation, must he endure, before he loses among strangers the ideas of his own importance which have been formed and nourished among his own people! As a child everything gave way to him, everybody flocked to him; as a young man he must give place to every one, or if he preserves ever so little of his former airs, what harsh lessons will bring him to himself! Accustomed to get everything he wants without any difficulty, his wants are many, and he feels continual privations. He is tempted by everything that flatters him; what others have, he must have too; he covets everything, he envies every one, he would always be master. He is devoured by vanity, his young heart is enflamed by unbridled passions, jealousy and hatred among the rest; all these violent passions burst out at once; their sting rankles in him in the busy world, they return with him at night, he comes back dissatisfied with himself, with others; he falls asleep among a thousand foolish schemes disturbed by a thousand fancies, and his pride shows him even in his dreams those fancied pleasures; he is tormented by a desire which will never be satisfied. So much for your pupil; let us turn to mine.

If the first thing to make an impression on him is something sorrowful his first return to himself is a feeling of pleasure. When he sees how many ills he has escaped he thinks he is happier than he fancied. He shares the suffering of his fellow-creatures, but he shares it of his own free will and finds pleasure in it. He enjoys at once the pity he feels for their woes and the joy of being exempt from them; he feels in himself that state of vigour which projects us beyond ourselves, and bids us carry elsewhere the superfluous activity of our well-being. To pity another's woes we must indeed know them, but we need not feel them. When we have suffered, when we are in fear of suffering, we pity those who suffer; but when we suffer ourselves, we pity none but ourselves. But if all of us, being subject ourselves to the ills of life, only bestow upon others the sensibility we do not actually require for ourselves, it follows that pity must be a very pleasant feeling, since it speaks on our behalf; and, on the other hand, a hard-hearted man is always unhappy, since the state of his heart leaves him no superfluous sensibility to bestow on the sufferings of others.

We are too apt to judge of happiness by appearances; we suppose it is to be found in the most unlikely places, we seek for it where it cannot possibly be; mirth is a very doubtful indication of its presence. A merry man is often a wretch who is trying to deceive others and distract himself. The men who are jovial, friendly, and contented at their club are almost always gloomy grumblers at home, and their servants have to pay for the amusement they give among their friends. True contentment is neither merry nor noisy; we are jealous of so sweet a sentiment, when we enjoy it we think about it, we delight in it for fear it should escape us. A really happy man says little and laughs little; he hugs his happiness, so to speak, to his heart. Noisy games, violent delight, conceal the disappointment of satiety. But melancholy is the friend of pleasure; tears and pity attend our sweetest enjoyment, and great joys call for tears rather than laughter.

If at first the number and variety of our amusements seem to contribute to our happiness, if at first the even tenor of a quiet life seems tedious, when we look at it more closely we discover that the pleasantest habit of mind consists in a moderate enjoyment which leaves little scope for desire and aversion. The unrest of passion causes curiosity and fickleness; the emptiness of noisy pleasures causes weariness. We never weary of our state when we know none more delightful. Savages suffer less than other men from curiosity and from tedium; everything is the same to them—themselves, not their possessions— and they are never weary.

The man of the world almost always wears a mask. He is scarcely ever himself and is almost a stranger to himself; he is ill at ease when he is forced into his own company. Not what he is, but what he seems, is all he cares for.

I cannot help picturing in the countenance of the young man I have just spoken of an indefinable but unpleasant impertinence, smoothness, and affectation, which is repulsive to a plain man, and in the countenance of my own pupil a simple and interesting expression which indicates the real contentment and the calm of his mind; an expression which inspires respect and confidence, and seems only to await the establishment of friendly relations to bestow his own confidence in return. It is thought that the expression is merely the development of certain features designed by nature. For my own part I think that over and above this development a man's face is shaped, all unconsciously, by the frequent and habitual influence of certain affections of the heart. These affections are shown on the face, there is nothing more certain;

and when they become habitual, they must surely leave lasting traces. This is why I think the expression shows the character, and that we can sometimes read one another without seeking mysterious explanations in powers we do not possess.

A child has only two distinct feelings, joy and sorrow; he laughs or he cries; he knows no middle course, and he is constantly passing from one extreme to the other. On account of these perpetual changes there is no lasting impression on the face, and no expression; but when the child is older and more sensitive, his feelings are keener or more permanent, and these deeper impressions leave traces more difficult to erase; and the habitual state of the feelings has an effect on the features which in course of time becomes ineffaceable. Still it is not uncommon to meet with men whose expression varies with their age. I have met with several, and I have always found that those whom I could observe and follow had also changed their habitual temper. This one observation thoroughly confirmed would seem to me decisive, and it is not out of place in a treatise on education, where it is a matter of importance, that we should learn to judge the feelings of the heart by external signs.

I do not know whether my young man will be any the less amiable for not having learnt to copy conventional manners and to feign sentiments which are not his own; that does not concern me at present, I only know he will be more affectionate; and I find it difficult to believe that he, who cares for nobody but himself, can so far disguise his true feelings as to please as readily as he who finds fresh happiness for himself in his affection for others. But with regard to this feeling of happiness, I think I have said enough already for the guidance of any sensible reader, and to show that I have not contradicted myself.

I return to my system, and I say, when the critical age approaches, present to young people spectacles which restrain rather than excite them; put off their dawning imagination with objects which, far from inflaming their senses, put a check to their activity. Remove them from great cities, where the flaunting attire and the boldness of the women hasten and anticipate the teaching of nature, where everything presents to their view pleasures of which they should know nothing till they are of an age to choose for themselves. Bring them back to their early home, where rural simplicity allows the passions of their age to develop more slowly; or if their taste for the arts keeps them in town, guard them by means of this very taste from a dangerous idleness. Choose carefully their company, their occupations, and their pleasures; show them nothing but modest and pathetic pictures which are touching but not seductive, and nourish their sensibility without stimulating their senses. Remember also, that the danger of excess is not confined to any one place, and that immoderate passions always do irreparable damage. You need not make your pupil a sick-nurse or a Brother of Pity; you need not distress him by the perpetual sight of pain and suffering; you need not take him from one hospital to another, from the gallows to the prison. He must be softened, not hardened, by the sight of human misery. When we have seen a sight it ceases to impress us, use is second nature, what is always before our eyes no longer appeals to the imagination, and it is only through the imagination that we can feel the sorrows of others; this is why priests and doctors who are always beholding death and suffering become so hardened. Let your pupil therefore know something of the lot of man and the woes of his fellow-creatures, but let him not see them too often. A single thing, carefully selected and shown at the right time, will fill him with pity and set him thinking for a month. His opinion about anything depends not so much on what he sees, but on how it reacts on himself; and his lasting impression of any object depends less on the object itself than on the point of view from which he regards it. Thus by a sparing use of examples, lessons, and pictures, you may blunt the sting of sense and delay nature while following her own lead.

As he acquires knowledge, choose what ideas he shall attach to it; as his passions awake, select scenes calculated to repress them. A veteran, as distinguished for his character as for his courage, once told me that in early youth his father, a sensible man but extremely pious, observed that through his growing sensibility he was attracted by women, and spared no pains to restrain him; but at last when, in spite of all his care, his son was about to escape from his control, he decided to take him to a hospital, and, without telling him what to expect, he introduced him into a room where a number of wretched creatures were expiating, under a terrible treatment, the vices which had brought them into this plight. This hideous and revolting spectacle sickened the young man. "Miserable libertine," said his father vehemently, "begone; follow your vile tastes; you will soon be only too glad to be admitted to this ward, and a victim to the most shameful sufferings, you will compel your father to thank God when you are dead."

These few words, together with the striking spectacle he beheld, made an impression on the young man which could never be effaced. Compelled by his profession to pass his youth in garrison, he preferred to face all the jests of his comrades rather than to share their evil ways. "I have been a man," he said to me, "I have had my weaknesses, but even to the present day the sight of a harlot inspires me with horror." Say little to your pupil, but choose time, place, and people; then rely on concrete examples for your teaching, and be sure it will take effect.

The way childhood is spent is no great matter; the evil which may find its way is not irremediable, and the good which may spring up might come later. But it is not so in those early years when a youth really begins to live. This time is never long enough for what there is to be done, and its importance demands unceasing attention; this is why I lay so much stress on the art of prolonging it. One of the best rules of good farming is to keep things back as much as possible. Let your progress also be slow and sure; prevent the youth from becoming a man all at once. While the body is growing the spirits destined to give vigour to the blood and strength to the muscles are in process of formation and elaboration. If you turn them into another channel, and permit that strength which should have gone to the perfecting of one person to go to the making of another, both remain in a state of weakness and the work of nature is unfinished. The workings of the mind, in their turn, are affected by this change, and the mind, as sickly as the body, functions languidly and feebly. Length and strength of limb are not the same thing as courage or genius, and I grant that strength of mind does not always accompany strength of body, when the means of connection between the two are otherwise faulty. But however well planned they may be, they will always work feebly if for motive power they depend upon an exhausted, impoverished supply of blood, deprived of the substance which gives strength and elasticity to all the springs of the machinery. There is generally more vigour of mind to be found among men whose early years have been preserved from precocious vice, than among those whose evil living has begun at the earliest opportunity; and this is no doubt the reason why nations whose morals are pure are generally superior in sense and courage to those whose morals are bad. The latter shine only through I know not what small and trifling qualities, which they call wit, sagacity, cunning; but those great and noble features of goodness and reason, by which a man is distinguished and honoured through good deeds, virtues, really useful efforts, are scarcely to be found except among the nations whose morals are pure.

Teachers complain that the energy of this age makes their pupils unruly; I see that it is so, but are not they themselves to blame? When once they have let this energy flow through the channel of the senses, do they not know that they cannot change its course? Will the long and dreary sermons of the pedant efface from the mind of his scholar the thoughts of pleasure when once they have found an entrance; will they banish from his heart the desires by which it is tormented; will they chill the heat of a passion whose meaning the scholar realises? Will not the pupil be roused to anger by the obstacles opposed to the only kind of happiness of which he has any notion? And in the harsh law imposed upon him before he can understand it, what will he see but the caprice and hatred of a man who is trying to torment him? Is it strange that he rebels and hates you too?

I know very well that if one is easy-going one may be tolerated, and one may keep up a show of authority. But I fail to see the use of an authority over the pupil which is only maintained by fomenting the vices it ought to repress; it is like attempting to soothe a fiery steed by making it leap over a precipice.

Far from being a hindrance to education, this enthusiasm of adolescence is its crown and coping-stone; this it is that gives you a hold on the youth's heart when he is no longer weaker than you. His first affections are the reins by which you control his movements; he was free, and now I behold him in your power. So long as he loved nothing, he was independent of everything but himself and his own necessities; as soon as he loves, he is dependent on his affections. Thus the first ties which unite him to his species are already formed. When you direct his increasing sensibility in this direction, do not expect that it will at once include all men, and that the word "mankind" will have any meaning for him. Not so; this sensibility will at first confine itself to those like himself, and these will not be strangers to him, but those he knows, those whom habit has made dear to him or necessary to him, those who are evidently thinking and feeling as he does, those whom he perceives to be exposed to the pains he has endured, those who enjoy the pleasures he has enjoyed; in a word, those who are so like himself that he is the more disposed to self-love. It is only after long training, after much consideration as to his own feelings and the feelings he observes in others, that he will be able to generalise his individual notions under the abstract idea of humanity, and add to his individual affections those which may identify him with the race.

When he becomes capable of affection, he becomes aware of the affection of others, [Footnote: Affection may be unrequited; not so friendship. Friendship is a bargain, a contract like any other; though a bargain more sacred than the rest. The word "friend" has no other correlation. Any man who is not the friend of his friend is undoubtedly a rascal; for one can only obtain friendship by giving it, or pretending to give it.] and he is on the lookout for the signs of that affection. Do you not see how you will acquire a fresh hold on him? What bands have you bound about his heart while he was yet unaware of them! What will he feel, when he beholds himself and sees what you have done for him; when he can compare himself with other youths, and other tutors with you! I say, "When he sees it," but beware lest you tell him of it; if you tell him he will not perceive it. If you claim his obedience in return for the care bestowed upon him, he will think you have over-reached him; he will see that while you profess to have cared for him without reward, you meant to saddle him with a debt and to bind him to a bargain which he never made. In vain you will add that what you demand is for his own good; you demand it, and you demand it in virtue of what you have done without his consent. When a man down on his luck accepts the shilling which the sergeant professes to give him, and finds he has enlisted without knowing what he was about, you protest against the injustice; is it not still more unjust to demand from your pupil the price of care which he has not even accepted!

Ingratitude would be rarer if kindness were less often the investment of a usurer. We love those who have done us a kindness; what a natural feeling! Ingratitude is not to be found in the heart of man, but self-interest is there; those who are ungrateful for benefits received are fewer than those who do a kindness for their own ends. If you sell me your gifts, I will haggle over the price; but if you pretend to give, in order to sell later on at your own price, you are guilty of fraud; it is the free gift which is beyond price. The heart is a law to itself; if you try to bind it, you lose it; give it its liberty, and you make it your own.

When the fisherman baits his line, the fish come round him without suspicion; but when they are caught on the hook concealed in the bait, they feel the line tighten and they try to escape. Is the fisherman a benefactor? Is the fish ungrateful? Do we find a man forgotten by his benefactor, unmindful of that benefactor? On the contrary, he delights to speak of him, he cannot think of him without emotion; if he gets a chance of showing him, by some unexpected service, that he remembers what he did for him, how delighted he is to satisfy his gratitude; what a pleasure it is to earn the gratitude of his benefactor. How delightful to say, "It is my turn now." This is indeed the teaching of nature; a good deed never caused ingratitude.

If therefore gratitude is a natural feeling, and you do not destroy its effects by your blunders, be sure your pupil, as he begins to understand the value of your care for him, will be grateful for it, provided you have not put a price upon it; and this will give you an authority over his heart which nothing can overthrow. But beware of losing this advantage before it is really yours, beware of insisting on your own importance. Boast of your services and they become intolerable; forget them and they will not be forgotten. Until the time comes to treat him as a man let there be no question of his duty to you, but his duty to himself. Let him have his freedom if you would make him docile; hide yourself so that he may seek you; raise his heart to the noble sentiment of gratitude by only speaking of his own interest. Until he was able to understand I would not have him told that what was done was for his good; he would only have understood such words to mean that you were dependent on him and he would merely have made you his servant. But now that he is beginning to feel what love is, he also knows what a tender affection may bind a man to what he loves; and in the zeal which keeps you busy on his account, he now sees not the bonds of a slave, but the affection of a friend. Now there is nothing which carries so much weight with the human heart as the voice of friendship recognised as such, for we know that it never speaks but for our good. We may think our friend is mistaken, but we never believe he is deceiving us. We may reject his advice now and then, but we never scorn it.

We have reached the moral order at last; we have just taken the second step towards manhood. If this were the place for it, I would try to show how the first impulses of the heart give rise to the first stirrings of conscience, and how from the feelings of love and hatred spring the first notions of good and evil. I would show that justice and kindness are no mere abstract terms, no mere moral conceptions framed by the understanding, but true affections of the heart enlightened by reason, the natural outcome of our primitive affections; that by reason alone, unaided by conscience, we cannot establish any natural law, and that all natural right is a vain dream if it does not rest upon some instinctive need of the human heart. [Footnote: The precept "Do unto others as you would have them do unto you" has no true foundation but that of conscience and feeling; for what valid reason is there why I, being myself, should do what I would do if I were some one else, especially when I am morally certain I never shall find myself in exactly the same case; and who will answer for it that if I faithfully follow out this maxim, I shall get others to follow it with regard to me? The wicked takes advantage both of the uprightness of the just and of his own injustice; he will gladly have everybody just but himself. This bargain, whatever you may say, is not greatly to the advantage of the just. But if the enthusiasm of an overflowing heart identifies me with my fellow-creature, if I feel, so to speak, that I will not let him suffer lest I should suffer too, I care for him because I care for myself, and the reason of the precept is found in nature herself, which inspires me with the desire for my own welfare wherever I may be. From this I conclude that it is false to say that the precepts of natural law are based on reason only; they have a firmer and more solid foundation. The love of others springing from self-love, is the source of human justice. The whole of morality is summed up in the gospel in this summary of the law.] But I do not think it is my business at present to prepare treatises on metaphysics and morals, nor courses of study of any kind whatsoever; it is enough if I indicate the order and development of our feelings and our knowledge in relation to our growth. Others will perhaps work out what I have here merely indicated.

Hitherto my Emile has thought only of himself, so his first glance at his equals leads him to compare himself with them; and the first feeling excited by this comparison is the desire to be first. It is here that self-love is transformed into selfishness, and this is the starting point of all the passions which spring from selfishness. But to determine whether the passions by which his life will be governed shall be humane and gentle or harsh and cruel, whether they shall be the passions of benevolence and pity or those of envy and covetousness, we must know what he believes his place among men to be, and what sort of obstacles he expects to have to overcome in order to attain to the position he seeks.

To guide him in this inquiry, after we have shown him men by means of the accidents common to the species, we must now show him them by means of their differences. This is the time for estimating inequality natural and civil, and for the scheme of the whole social order.

Society must be studied in the individual and the individual in society; those who desire to treat politics and morals apart from one another will never understand either. By confining ourselves at first to the primitive relations, we see how men should be influenced by them and what passions should spring from them; we see that it is in proportion to the development of these passions that a man's relations with others expand or contract. It is not so much strength of arm as moderation of spirit which makes men free and independent. The man whose wants are few is dependent on but few people, but those who constantly confound our vain desires with our bodily needs, those who have made these needs the basis of human society, are continually mistaking effects for causes, and they have only confused themselves by their own reasoning.

Since it is impossible in the state of nature that the difference between man and man should be great enough to make one dependent on another, there is in fact in this state of nature an actual and indestructible equality. In the civil state there is a vain and chimerical equality of right; the means intended for its maintenance, themselves serve to destroy it; and the power of the community, added to the power of the strongest for the oppression of the weak, disturbs the sort of equilibrium which nature has established between them. [Footnote: The universal spirit of the laws of every country is always to take the part of the strong against the weak, and the part of him who has against him who has not; this defect is inevitable, and there is no exception to it.] From this first contradiction spring all the other contradictions between the real and the apparent, which are to be found in the civil order. The many will always be sacrificed to the few, the common weal to private interest; those specious words—justice and subordination—will always serve as the tools of violence and the weapons of injustice; hence it follows that the higher classes which claim to be useful to the rest are really only seeking their own welfare at the expense of others; from this we may judge how much consideration is due to them according to right and justice. It remains to be seen if the rank to which they have attained is more favourable to their own happiness to know what opinion each one of us should form with regard to his own lot. This is the study with which we are now concerned; but to do it thoroughly we must begin with a knowledge of the human heart.

If it were only a question of showing young people man in his mask, there would be no need to point him out, and he would always be before their eyes; but since the mask is not the man, and since they must not be led away by its specious appearance, when you paint men for your scholar, paint them as they are, not that he may hate them, but that he may pity them and have no wish to be like them. In my opinion that is the most reasonable view a man can hold with regard to his fellow-men.

With this object in view we must take the opposite way from that hitherto followed, and instruct the youth rather through the experience of others than through his own. If men deceive him he will hate them; but, if, while they treat him with respect, he sees them deceiving each other, he will pity them. "The spectacle of the world," said Pythagoras, "is like the Olympic games; some are buying and selling and think only of their gains; others take an active part and strive for glory; others, and these not the worst, are content to be lookers-on."

I would have you so choose the company of a youth that he should think well of those among whom he lives, and I would have you so teach him to know the world that he should think ill of all that takes place in it. Let him know that man is by nature good, let him feel it, let him judge his neighbour by himself; but let him see how men are depraved and perverted by society; let him find the source of all their vices in their preconceived opinions; let him be disposed to respect the individual, but to despise the multitude; let him see that all men wear almost the same mask, but let him also know that some faces are fairer than the mask that conceals them.

It must be admitted that this method has its drawbacks, and it is not easy to carry it out; for if he becomes too soon engrossed in watching other people, if you train him to mark too closely the actions of others, you will make him spiteful and satirical, quick and decided in his judgments of others; he will find a hateful pleasure in seeking bad motives, and will fail to see the good even in that which is really good. He will, at least, get used to the sight of vice, he will behold the wicked without horror, just as we get used to seeing the wretched without pity. Soon the perversity of mankind will be not so much a warning as an excuse; he will say, "Man is made so," and he will have no wish to be different from the rest.

But if you wish to teach him theoretically to make him acquainted, not only with the heart of man, but also with the application of the external causes which turn our inclinations into vices; when you thus transport him all at once from the objects of sense to the objects of reason, you employ a system of metaphysics which he is not in a position to understand; you fall back into the error, so carefully avoided hitherto, of giving him lessons which are like lessons, of substituting in his mind the experience and the authority of the master for his own experience and the development of his own reason.

To remove these two obstacles at once, and to bring the human heart within his reach without risk of spoiling his own, I would show him men from afar, in other times or in other places, so that he may behold the scene but cannot take part in it. This is the time for history; with its help he will read the hearts of men without any lessons in philosophy; with its help he will view them as a mere spectator, dispassionate and without prejudice; he will view them as their judge, not as their accomplice or their accuser.

To know men you must behold their actions. In society we hear them talk; they show their words and hide their deeds; but in history the veil is drawn aside, and they are judged by their deeds. Their sayings even help us to understand them; for comparing what they say and what they do, we see not only what they are but what they would appear; the more they disguise themselves the more thoroughly they stand revealed.

Unluckily this study has its dangers, its drawbacks of several kinds. It is difficult to adopt a point of view which will enable one to judge one's fellow-creatures fairly. It is one of the chief defects of history to paint men's evil deeds rather than their good ones; it is revolutions and catastrophes that make history interesting; so long as a nation grows and prospers quietly in the tranquillity of a peaceful government, history says nothing; she only begins to speak of nations when, no longer able to be self-sufficing, they interfere with their neighbours' business, or allow their neighbours to interfere with their own; history only makes them famous when they are on the downward path; all our histories begin where they ought to end. We have very accurate accounts of declining nations; what we lack is the history of those nations which are multiplying; they are so happy and so good that history has nothing to tell us of them; and we see indeed in our own times that the most successful governments are least talked of. We only hear what is bad; the good is scarcely mentioned. Only the wicked become famous, the good are forgotten or laughed to scorn, and thus history, like philosophy, is for ever slandering mankind.

Moreover, it is inevitable that the facts described in history should not give an exact picture of what really happened; they are transformed in the brain of the historian, they are moulded by his interests and coloured by his prejudices. Who can place the reader precisely in a position to see the event as it really happened? Ignorance or partiality disguises everything. What a different impression may be given merely by expanding or contracting the circumstances of the case without altering a single historical incident. The same object may be seen from several points of view, and it will hardly seem the same thing, yet there has been no change except in the eye that beholds it. Do you indeed do honour to truth when what you tell me is a genuine fact, but you make it appear something quite different? A tree more or less, a rock to the right or to the left, a cloud of dust raised by the wind, how often have these decided the result of a battle without any one knowing it? Does that prevent history from telling you the cause of defeat or victory with as much assurance as if she had been on the spot? But what are the facts to me, while I am ignorant of their causes, and what lessons can I draw from an event, whose true cause is unknown to me? The historian indeed gives me a reason, but he invents it; and criticism itself, of which we hear so much, is only the art of guessing, the art of choosing from among several lies, the lie that is most like truth.

Have you ever read Cleopatra or Cassandra or any books of the kind? The author selects some well-known event, he then adapts it to his purpose, adorns it with details of his own invention, with people who never existed, with imaginary portraits; thus he piles fiction on fiction to lend a charm to his story. I see little difference between such romances and your histories, unless it is that the novelist draws more on his own imagination, while the historian slavishly copies what another has imagined; I will also admit, if you please, that the novelist has some moral purpose good or bad, about which the historian scarcely concerns himself.

You will tell me that accuracy in history is of less interest than a true picture of men and manners; provided the human heart is truly portrayed, it matters little that events should be accurately recorded; for after all you say, what does it matter to us what happened two thousand years ago? You are right if the portraits are indeed truly given according to nature; but if the model is to be found for the most part in the historian's imagination, are you not falling into the very error you intended to avoid, and surrendering to the authority of the historian what you would not yield to the authority of the teacher? If my pupil is merely to see fancy pictures, I would rather draw them myself; they will, at least, be better suited to him.

The worst historians for a youth are those who give their opinions. Facts! Facts! and let him decide for himself; this is how he will learn to know mankind. If he is always directed by the opinion of the author, he is only seeing through the eyes of another person, and when those ayes are no longer at his disposal he can see nothing.

I leave modern history on one side, not only because it has no character and all our people are alike, but because our historians, wholly taken up with effect, think of nothing but highly coloured portraits, which often represent nothing. [Footnote: Take, for instance, Guicciardini, Streda, Solis, Machiavelli, and sometimes even De Thou himself. Vertot is almost the only one who knows how to describe without giving fancy portraits.] The old historians generally give fewer portraits and bring more intelligence and common-sense to their judgments; but even among them there is plenty of scope for choice, and you must not begin with the wisest but with the simplest. I would not put Polybius or Sallust into the hands of a youth; Tacitus is the author of the old, young men cannot understand him; you must learn to see in human actions the simplest features of the heart of man before you try to sound its depths. You must be able to read facts clearly before you begin to study maxims. Philosophy in the form of maxims is only fit for the experienced. Youth should never deal with the general, all its teaching should deal with individual instances.

To my mind Thucydides is the true model of historians. He relates facts without giving his opinion; but he omits no circumstance adapted to make us judge for ourselves. He puts everything that he relates before his reader; far from interposing between the facts and the readers, he conceals himself; we seem not to read but to see. Unfortunately he speaks of nothing but war, and in his stories we only see the least instructive part of the world, that is to say the battles. The virtues and defects of the Retreat of the Ten Thousand and the Commentaries of Caesar are almost the same. The kindly Herodotus, without portraits, without maxims, yet flowing, simple, full of details calculated to delight and interest in the highest degree, would be perhaps the best historian if these very details did not often degenerate into childish folly, better adapted to spoil the taste of youth than to form it; we need discretion before we can read him. I say nothing of Livy, his turn will come; but he is a statesman, a rhetorician, he is everything which is unsuitable for a youth.

History in general is lacking because it only takes note of striking and clearly marked facts which may be fixed by names, places, and dates; but the slow evolution of these facts, which cannot be definitely noted in this way, still remains unknown. We often find in some battle, lost or won, the ostensible cause of a revolution which was inevitable before this battle took place. War only makes manifest events already determined by moral causes, which few historians can perceive.

The philosophic spirit has turned the thoughts of many of the historians of our times in this direction; but I doubt whether truth has profited by their labours. The rage for systems has got possession of all alike, no one seeks to see things as they are, but only as they agree with his system.

Add to all these considerations the fact that history shows us actions rather than men, because she only seizes men at certain chosen times in full dress; she only portrays the statesman when he is prepared to be seen; she does not follow him to his home, to his study, among his family and his friends; she only shows him in state; it is his clothes rather than himself that she describes.

I would prefer to begin the study of the human heart with reading the lives of individuals; for then the man hides himself in vain, the historian follows him everywhere; he never gives him a moment's grace nor any corner where he can escape the piercing eye of the spectator; and when he thinks he is concealing himself, then it is that the writer shows him up most plainly.

"Those who write lives," says Montaigne, "in so far as they delight more in ideas than in events, more in that which comes from within than in that which comes from without, these are the writers I prefer; for this reason Plutarch is in every way the man for me."

It is true that the genius of men in groups or nations is very different from the character of the individual man, and that we have a very imperfect knowledge of the human heart if we do not also examine it in crowds; but it is none the less true that to judge of men we must study the individual man, and that he who had a perfect knowledge of the inclinations of each individual might foresee all their combined effects in the body of the nation.

We must go back again to the ancients, for the reasons already stated, and also because all the details common and familiar, but true and characteristic, are banished by modern stylists, so that men are as much tricked out by our modern authors in their private life as in public. Propriety, no less strict in literature than in life, no longer permits us to say anything in public which we might not do in public; and as we may only show the man dressed up for his part, we never see a man in our books any more than we do on the stage. The lives of kings may be written a hundred times, but to no purpose; we shall never have another Suetonius.

The excellence of Plutarch consists in these very details which we are no longer permitted to describe. With inimitable grace he paints the great man in little things; and he is so happy in the choice of his instances that a word, a smile, a gesture, will often suffice to indicate the nature of his hero. With a jest Hannibal cheers his frightened soldiers, and leads them laughing to the battle which will lay Italy at his feet; Agesilaus riding on a stick makes me love the conqueror of the great king; Caesar passing through a poor village and chatting with his friends unconsciously betrays the traitor who professed that he only wished to be Pompey's equal. Alexander swallows a draught without a word—it is the finest moment in his life; Aristides writes his own name on the shell and so justifies his title; Philopoemen, his mantle laid aside, chops firewood in the kitchen of his host. This is the true art of portraiture. Our disposition does not show itself in our features, nor our character in our great deeds; it is trifles that show what we really are. What is done in public is either too commonplace or too artificial, and our modern authors are almost too grand to tell us anything else.

M. de Turenne was undoubtedly one of the greatest men of the last century. They have had the courage to make his life interesting by the little details which make us know and love him; but how many details have they felt obliged to omit which might have made us know and love him better still? I will only quote one which I have on good authority, one which Plutarch would never have omitted, and one which Ramsai would never have inserted

193

had he been acquainted with it.

On a hot summer's day Viscount Turenne in a little white vest and night-cap was standing at the window of his antechamber; one of his men came up and, misled by the dress, took him for one of the kitchen lads whom he knew. He crept up behind him and smacked him with no light hand. The man he struck turned round hastily. The valet saw it was his master and trembled at the sight of his face. He fell on his knees in desperation. "Sir, I thought it was George." "Well, even if it was George," exclaimed Turenne rubbing the in-jured part, "you need not have struck so hard." You do not dare to say this, you miserable writers! Remain for ever without humanity and without feel-ing; steel your hard hearts in your vile propriety, make yourselves contempt-ible through your high-mightiness. But as for you, dear youth, when you read this anecdote, when you are touched by all the kindliness displayed even on the impulse of the moment, read also the littleness of this great man when it was a question of his name and birth. Remember it was this very Turenne who always professed to yield precedence to his nephew, so that all men might see that this child was the head of a royal house. Look on this picture and on that, love nature, despise popular prejudice, and know the man as he was.

There are few people able to realise what an effect such reading, carefully directed, will have upon the unspoilt mind of a youth. Weighed down by books from our earliest childhood, accustomed to read without thinking, what we read strikes us even less, because we already bear in ourselves the passions and prejudices with which history and the lives of men are filled; all that they do strikes us as only natural, for we ourselves are unnatural and we judge others by ourselves. But imagine my Emile, who has been carefully guarded for eighteen years with the sole object of preserving a right judgment and a healthy heart, imagine him when the curtain goes up casting his eyes for the first time upon the world's stage; or rather picture him behind the scenes watching the actors don their costumes, and counting the cords and pulleys which deceive with their feigned shows the eyes of the spectators. His first surprise will soon give place to feelings of shame and scorn of his fellow-man; he will be indignant at the sight of the whole human race deceiving it-self and stooping to this childish folly; he will grieve to see his brothers tear-ing each other limb from limb for a mere dream, and transforming themselves into wild beasts because they could not be content to be men.

Given the natural disposition of the pupil, there is no doubt that if the master exercises any sort of prudence or discretion in his choice of reading, however little he may put him in the way of reflecting on the subject-matter, this exercise will serve as a course in practical philosophy, a philosophy better understood and more thoroughly mastered than all the empty speculations with which the brains of lads are muddled in our schools. After following the romantic schemes of Pyrrhus, Cineas asks him what real good he would gain by the conquest of the world, which he can never enjoy without such great sufferings; this only arouses in us a passing interest as a smart saying; but

Emile will think it a very wise thought, one which had already occurred to himself, and one which he will never forget, because there is no hostile prejudice in his mind to prevent it sinking in. When he reads more of the life of this madman, he will find that all his great plans resulted in his death at the hands of a woman, and instead of admiring this pinchbeck heroism, what will he see in the exploits of this great captain and the schemes of this great statesman but so many steps towards that unlucky tile which was to bring life and schemes alike to a shameful death?

All conquerors have not been killed; all usurpers have not failed in their plans; to minds imbued with vulgar prejudices many of them will seem happy, but he who looks below the surface and reckons men's happiness by the condition of their hearts will perceive their wretchedness even in the midst of their successes; he will see them panting after advancement and never attaining their prize, he will find them like those inexperienced travellers among the Alps, who think that every height they see is the last, who reach its summit only to find to their disappointment there are loftier peaks beyond.

Augustus, when he had subdued his fellow-citizens and destroyed his rivals, reigned for forty years over the greatest empire that ever existed; but all this vast power could not hinder him from beating his head against the walls, and filling his palace with his groans as he cried to Varus to restore his slaughtered legions. If he had conquered all his foes what good would his empty triumphs have done him, when troubles of every kind beset his path, when his life was threatened by his dearest friends, and when he had to mourn the disgrace or death of all near and dear to him? The wretched man desired to rule the world and failed to rule his own household. What was the result of this neglect? He beheld his nephew, his adopted child, his son-in-law, perish in the flower of youth, his grandson reduced to eat the stuffing of his mattress to prolong his wretched existence for a few hours; his daughter and his granddaughter, after they had covered him with infamy, died, the one of hunger and want on a desert island, the other in prison by the hand of a common archer. He himself, the last survivor of his unhappy house, found himself compelled by his own wife to acknowledge a monster as his heir. Such was the fate of the master of the world, so famous for his glory and his good fortune. I cannot believe that any one of those who admire his glory and fortune would accept them at the same price.

I have taken ambition as my example, but the play of every human passion offers similar lessons to any one who will study history to make himself wise and good at the expense of those who went before. The time is drawing near when the teaching of the life of Anthony will appeal more forcibly to the youth than the life of Augustus. Emile will scarcely know where he is among the many strange sights in his new studies; but he will know beforehand how to avoid the illusion of passions before they arise, and seeing how in all ages they have blinded men's eyes, he will be forewarned of the way in which they may one day blind his own should he abandon himself to them. [Footnote: It is always prejudice which stirs up passion in our heart. He who only sees what really exists and only values what he knows, rarely becomes angry. The errors of our judgment produce the warmth of our desires.] These lessons, I know, are unsuited to him, perhaps at need they may prove scanty and ill-timed; but remember they are not the lessons I wished to draw from this study. To begin with, I had quite another end in view; and indeed, if this purpose is unfulfilled, the teacher will be to blame.

Remember that, as soon as selfishness has developed, the self in its relations to others is always with us, and the youth never observes others without coming back to himself and comparing himself with them. From the way young men are taught to study history I see that they are transformed, so to speak, into the people they behold, that you strive to make a Cicero, a Trajan, or an Alexander of them, to discourage them when they are themselves again, to make every one regret that he is merely himself. There are certain advantages in this plan which I do not deny; but, so far as Emile is concerned, should it happen at any time when he is making these comparisons that he wishes to be any one but himself—were it Socrates or Cato—I have failed entirely; he who begins to regard himself as a stranger will soon forget himself altogether.

It is not philosophers who know most about men; they only view them through the preconceived ideas of philosophy, and I know no one so prejudiced as philosophers. A savage would judge us more sanely. The philosopher is aware of his own vices, he is indignant at ours, and he says to himself, "We are all bad alike;" the savage beholds us unmoved and says, "You are mad." He is right, for no one does evil for evil's sake. My pupil is that savage, with this difference: Emile has thought more, he has compared ideas, seen our errors at close quarters, he is more on his guard against himself, and only judges of what he knows.

It is our own passions that excite us against the passions of others; it is our self-interest which makes us hate the wicked; if they did us no harm we should pity rather than hate them. We should readily forgive their vices if we could perceive how their own heart punishes those vices. We are aware of the offence, but we do not see the punishment; the advantages are plain, the penalty is hidden. The man who thinks he is enjoying the fruits of his vices is no less tormented by them than if they had not been successful; the object is different, the anxiety is the same; in vain he displays his good fortune and hides his heart; in spite of himself his conduct betrays him; but to discern this, our own heart must be utterly unlike his.

We are led astray by those passions which we share; we are disgusted by those that militate against our own interests; and with a want of logic due to these very passions, we blame in others what we fain would imitate. Aversion and self-deception are inevitable when we are forced to endure at another's hands what we ourselves would do in his place.

What then is required for the proper study of men? A great wish to know men, great impartiality of judgment, a heart sufficiently sensitive to understand every human passion, and calm enough to be free from passion. If there is any time in our life when this study is likely to be appreciated, it is this that I have chosen for Emile; before this time men would have been strangers to him; later on he would have been like them. Convention, the effects of which he already perceives, has not yet made him its slave, the passions, whose consequences he realises, have not yet stirred his heart. He is a man; he takes an interest in his brethren; he is a just man and he judges his peers. Now it is certain that if he judges them rightly he will not want to change places with any one of them, for the goal of all their anxious efforts is the result of prejudices which he does not share, and that goal seems to him a mere dream. For his own part, he has all he wants within his reach. How should he be dependent on any one when he is self-sufficing and free from prejudice? Strong arms, good health, [Footnote: I think I may fairly reckon health and strength among the advantages he has obtained by his education, or rather among the gifts of nature which his education has preserved for him.] moderation, few needs, together with the means to satisfy those needs, are his. He has been brought up in complete liberty and servitude is the greatest ill he understands. He pities these miserable kings, the slaves of all who obey them; he pities these false prophets fettered by their empty fame; he pities these rich fools, martyrs to their own pomp; he pities these ostentatious voluptuaries, who spend their life in deadly dullness that they may seem to enjoy its pleasures. He would pity the very foe who harmed him, for he would discern his wretchedness beneath his cloak of spite. He would say to himself, "This man has yielded to his desire to hurt me, and this need of his places him at my mercy."

One step more and our goal is attained. Selfishness is a dangerous tool though a useful one; it often wounds the hand that uses it, and it rarely does good unmixed with evil. When Emile considers his place among men, when he finds himself so fortunately situated, he will be tempted to give credit to his own reason for the work of yours, and to attribute to his own deserts what is really the result of his good fortune. He will say to himself, "I am wise and other men are fools." He will pity and despise them and will congratulate himself all the more heartily; and as he knows he is happier than they, he will think his deserts are greater. This is the fault we have most to fear, for it is the most difficult to eradicate. If he remained in this state of mind, he would have profited little by all our care; and if I had to choose, I hardly know whether I would not rather choose the illusions of prejudice than those of pride.

Great men are under no illusion with respect to their superiority; they see it and know it, but they are none the less modest. The more they have, the better they know what they lack. They are less vain of their superiority over us than ashamed by the consciousness of their weakness, and among the good things they really possess, they are too wise to pride themselves on a gift which is none of their getting. The good man may be proud of his virtue for it is his own, but what cause for pride has the man of intellect? What has Racine done that he is not Pradon, and Boileau that he is not Cotin?

The circumstances with which we are concerned are quite different. Let us keep to the common level. I assumed that my pupil had neither surpassing

197

genius nor a defective understanding. I chose him of an ordinary mind to show what education could do for man. Exceptions defy all rules. If, therefore, as a result of my care, Emile prefers his way of living, seeing, and feeling to that of others, he is right; but if he thinks because of this that he is nobler and better born than they, he is wrong; he is deceiving himself; he must be undeceived, or rather let us prevent the mistake, lest it be too late to correct it.

Provided a man is not mad, he can be cured of any folly but vanity; there is no cure for this but experience, if indeed there is any cure for it at all; when it first appears we can at least prevent its further growth. But do not on this account waste your breath on empty arguments to prove to the youth that he is like other men and subject to the same weaknesses. Make him feel it or he will never know it. This is another instance of an exception to my own rules; I must voluntarily expose my pupil to every accident which may convince him that he is no wiser than we. The adventure with the conjurer will be repeated again and again in different ways; I shall let flatterers take advantage of him; if rash comrades draw him into some perilous adventure, I will let him run the risk; if he falls into the hands of sharpers at the card-table, I will abandon him to them as their dupe.[Footnote: Moreover our pupil will be little tempted by this snare; he has so many amusements about him, he has never been bored in his life, and he scarcely knows the use of money. As children have been led by these two motives, self-interest and vanity, rogues and courtesans use the same means to get hold of them later. When you see their greediness encouraged by prizes and rewards, when you find their public performances at ten years old applauded at school or college, you see too how at twenty they will be induced to leave their purse in a gambling hell and their health in a worse place. You may safely wager that the sharpest boy in the class will become the greatest gambler and debauchee. Now the means which have not been employed in childhood have not the same effect in youth. But we must bear in mind my constant plan and take the thing at its worst. First I try to prevent the vice; then I assume its existence in order to correct it.] I will let them flatter him, pluck him, and rob him; and when having sucked him dry they turn and mock him, I will even thank them to his face for the lessons they have been good enough to give him. The only snares from which I will guard him with my utmost care are the wiles of wanton women. The only precaution I shall take will be to share all the dangers I let him run, and all the insults I let him receive. I will bear everything in silence, without a murmur or reproach, without a word to him, and be sure that if this wise conduct is faithfully adhered to, what he sees me endure on his account will make more impression on his heart than what he himself suffers.

I cannot refrain at this point from drawing attention to the sham dignity of tutors, who foolishly pretend to be wise, who discourage their pupils by always professing to treat them as children, and by emphasising the difference between themselves and their scholars in everything they do. Far from damping their youthful spirits in this fashion, spare no effort to stimulate their courage; that they may become your equals, treat them as such already, and if they cannot rise to your level, do not scruple to come down to theirs without being ashamed of it. Remember that your honour is no longer in your own keeping but in your pupil's. Share his faults that you may correct them, bear his disgrace that you may wipe it out; follow the example of that brave Roman who, unable to rally his fleeing soldiers, placed himself at their head, exclaiming, "They do not flee, they follow their captain!" Did this dishonour him? Not so; by sacrificing his glory he increased it. The power of duty, the beauty of virtue, compel our respect in spite of all our foolish prejudices. If I received a blow in the course of my duties to Emile, far from avenging it I would boast of it; and I doubt whether there is in the whole world a man so vile as to respect me any the less on this account.

I do not intend the pupil to suppose his master to be as ignorant, or as liable to be led astray, as he is himself. This idea is all very well for a child who can neither see nor compare things, who thinks everything is within his reach, and only bestows his confidence on those who know how to come down to his level. But a youth of Emile's age and sense is no longer so foolish as to make this mistake, and it would not be desirable that he should. The confidence he ought to have in his tutor is of another kind; it should rest on the authority of reason, and on superior knowledge, advantages which the young man is capable of appreciating while he perceives how useful they are to himself. Long experience has convinced him that his tutor loves him, that he is a wise and good man who desires his happiness and knows how to procure it. He ought to know that it is to his own advantage to listen to his advice. But if the master lets himself be taken in like the disciple, he will lose his right to expect deference from him, and to give him instruction. Still less should the pupil suppose that his master is purposely letting him fall into snares or preparing pitfalls for his inexperience. How can we avoid these two difficulties? Choose the best and most natural means; be frank and straightforward like himself; warn him of the dangers to which he is exposed, point them out plainly and sensibly, without exaggeration, without temper, without pedantic display, and above all without giving your opinions in the form of orders, until they have become such, and until this imperious tone is absolutely necessary. Should he still be obstinate as he often will be, leave him free to follow his own choice, follow him, copy his example, and that cheerfully and frankly; if possible fling yourself into things, amuse yourself as much as he does. If the consequences become too serious, you are at hand to prevent them; and yet when this young man has beheld your foresight and your kindliness, will he not be at once struck by the one and touched by the other? All his faults are but so many hands with which he himself provides you to restrain him at need. Now under these circumstances the great art of the master consists in controlling events and directing his exhortations so that he may know beforehand when the youth will give in, and when he will refuse to do so, so that all around him he may encompass him with the lessons of experience, and yet never let him run too great a risk.

Warn him of his faults before he commits them; do not blame him when once they are committed; you would only stir his self-love to mutiny. We learn nothing from a lesson we detest. I know nothing more foolish than the phrase, "I told you so." The best way to make him remember what you told him is to seem to have forgotten it. Go further than this, and when you find him ashamed of having refused to believe you, gently smooth away the shame with kindly words. He will indeed hold you dear when he sees how you forget yourself on his account, and how you console him instead of reproaching him. But if you increase his annoyance by your reproaches he will hate you, and will make it a rule never to heed you, as if to show you that he does not agree with you as to the value of your opinion.

The turn you give to your consolation may itself be a lesson to him, and all the more because he does not suspect it. When you tell him, for example, that many other people have made the same mistakes, this is not what he was expecting; you are administering correction under the guise of pity; for when one thinks oneself better than other people it is a very mortifying excuse to console oneself by their example; it means that we must realise that the most we can say is that they are no better than we.

The time of faults is the time for fables. When we blame the guilty under the cover of a story we instruct without offending him; and he then understands that the story is not untrue by means of the truth he finds in its application to himself. The child who has never been deceived by flattery understands nothing of the fable I recently examined; but the rash youth who has just become the dupe of a flatterer perceives only too readily that the crow was a fool. Thus he acquires a maxim from the fact, and the experience he would soon have forgotten is engraved on his mind by means of the fable. There is no knowledge of morals which cannot be acquired through our own experience or that of others. When there is danger, instead of letting him try the experiment himself, we have recourse to history. When the risk is comparatively slight, it is just as well that the youth should be exposed to it; then by means of the apologue the special cases with which the young man is now acquainted are transformed into maxims.

It is not, however, my intention that these maxims should be explained, nor even formulated. Nothing is so foolish and unwise as the moral at the end of most of the fables; as if the moral was not, or ought not to be so clear in the fable itself that the reader cannot fail to perceive it. Why then add the moral at the end, and go deprive him of the pleasure of discovering it for himself. The art of teaching consists in making the pupil wish to learn. But if the pupil is to wish to learn, his mind must not remain in such a passive state with regard to what you tell him that there is really nothing for him to do but listen to you. The master's vanity must always give way to the scholars; he must be able to say, I understand, I see it, I am getting at it, I am learning something. One of the things which makes the Pantaloon in the Italian comedies so wearisome is the pains taken by him to explain to the audience the platitudes they understand only too well already. We must always be intelligible, but we need not say all there is to be said. If you talk much you will say little, for at last no one will listen to you. What is the sense of the four lines at the end of La Fontaine's fable of the frog who puffed herself up. Is he afraid we should not understand it? Does this great painter need to write the names beneath the things he has painted? His morals, far from generalising, restrict the lesson to some extent to the examples given, and prevent our applying them to others. Before I put the fables of this inimitable author into the hands of a youth, I should like to cut out all the conclusions with which he strives to explain what he has just said so clearly and pleasantly. If your pupil does not understand the fable without the explanation, he will not understand it with it.

Moreover, the fables would require to be arranged in a more didactic order, one more in agreement with the feelings and knowledge of the young adolescent. Can you imagine anything so foolish as to follow the mere numerical order of the book without regard to our requirements or our opportunities. First the grasshopper, then the crow, then the frog, then the two mules, etc. I am sick of these two mules; I remember seeing a child who was being educated for finance; they never let him alone, but were always insisting on the profession he was to follow; they made him read this fable, learn it, say it, repeat it again and again without finding in it the slightest argument against his future calling. Not only have I never found children make any real use of the fables they learn, but I have never found anybody who took the trouble to see that they made such a use of them. The study claims to be instruction in morals; but the real aim of mother and child is nothing but to set a whole party watching the child while he recites his fables; when he is too old to recite them and old enough to make use of them, they are altogether forgotten. Only men, I repeat, can learn from fables, and Emile is now old enough to begin.

I do not mean to tell you everything, so I only indicate the paths which diverge from the right way, so that you may know how to avoid them. If you follow the road I have marked out for you, I think your pupil will buy his knowledge of mankind and his knowledge of himself in the cheapest market; you will enable him to behold the tricks of fortune without envying the lot of her favourites, and to be content with himself without thinking himself better than others. You have begun by making him an actor that he may learn to be one of the audience; you must continue your task, for from the theatre things are what they seem, from the stage they seem what they are. For the general effect we must get a distant view, for the details we must observe more closely. But how can a young man take part in the business of life? What right has he to be initiated into its dark secrets? His interests are confined within the limits of his own pleasures, he has no power over others, it is much the same as if he had no power at all. Man is the cheapest commodity on the market, and among all our important rights of property, the rights of the individual are always considered last of all.

When I see the studies of young men at the period of their greatest activity confined to purely speculative matters, while later on they are suddenly plunged, without any sort of experience, into the world of men and affairs, it strikes me as contrary alike to reason and to nature, and I cease to be surprised that so few men know what to do. How strange a choice to teach us so many useless things, while the art of doing is never touched upon! They profess to fit us for society, and we are taught as if each of us were to live a life of contemplation in a solitary cell, or to discuss theories with persons whom they did not concern. You think you are teaching your scholars how to live, and you teach them certain bodily contortions and certain forms of words without meaning. I, too, have taught Emile how to live; for I have taught him to enjoy his own society and, more than that, to earn his own bread. But this is not enough. To live in the world he must know how to get on with other people, he must know what forces move them, he must calculate the action and re-action of self-interest in civil society, he must estimate the results so accurately that he will rarely fail in his undertakings, or he will at least have tried in the best possible way. The law does not allow young people to manage their own affairs nor to dispose of their own property; but what would be the use of these precautions if they never gained any experience until they were of age. They would have gained nothing by the delay, and would have no more experience at five-and-twenty than at fifteen. No doubt we must take precautions, so that a youth, blinded by ignorance or misled by passion, may not hurt himself; but at any age there are opportunities when deeds of kindness and of care for the weak may be performed under the direction of a wise man, on behalf of the unfortunate who need help.

Mothers and nurses grow fond of children because of the care they lavish on them; the practice of social virtues touches the very heart with the love of humanity; by doing good we become good; and I know no surer way to this end. Keep your pupil busy with the good deeds that are within his power, let the cause of the poor be his own, let him help them not merely with his money, but with his service; let him work for them, protect them, let his person and his time be at their disposal; let him be their agent; he will never all his life long have a more honourable office. How many of the oppressed, who have never got a hearing, will obtain justice when he demands it for them with that courage and firmness which the practice of virtue inspires; when he makes his way into the presence of the rich and great, when he goes, if need be, to the footstool of the king himself, to plead the cause of the wretched, the cause of those who find all doors closed to them by their poverty, those who are so afraid of being punished for their misfortunes that they do not dare to complain?

But shall we make of Emile a knight-errant, a redresser of wrongs, a paladin? Shall he thrust himself into public life, play the sage and the defender of the laws before the great, before the magistrates, before the king? Shall he lay petitions before the judges and plead in the law courts? That I cannot say. The nature of things is not changed by terms of mockery and scorn. He will do all that he knows to be useful and good. He will do nothing more, and he knows that nothing is useful and good for him which is unbefitting his age. He knows that his first duty is to himself; that young men should distrust themselves; that they should act circumspectly; that they should show respect to those older than themselves, reticence and discretion in talking without cause, modesty in things indifferent, but courage in well doing, and boldness to speak the truth. Such were those illustrious Romans who, having been admitted into public life, spent their days in bringing criminals to justice and in protecting the innocent, without any motives beyond those of learning, and of the furtherance of justice and of the protection of right conduct.

Emile is not fond of noise or quarrelling, not only among men, but among animals. [Footnote: "But what will he do if any one seeks a quarrel with him?" My answer is that no one will ever quarrel with him, he will never lend himself to such a thing. But, indeed, you continue, who can be safe from a blow, or an insult from a bully, a drunkard, a bravo, who for the joy of killing his man begins by dishonouring him? That is another matter. The life and honour of the citizens should not be at the mercy of a bully, a drunkard, or a bravo, and one can no more insure oneself against such an accident than against a falling tile. A blow given, or a lie in the teeth, if he submit to them, have social consequences which no wisdom can prevent and no tribunal can avenge. The weakness of the laws, therefore, so far restores a man's independence; he is the sole magistrate and judge between the offender and himself, the sole interpreter and administrator of natural law. Justice is his due, and he alone can obtain it, and in such a case there is no government on earth so foolish as to punish him for so doing. I do not say he must fight; that is absurd; I say justice is his due, and he alone can dispense it. If I were king, I promise you that in my kingdom no one would ever strike a man or call him a liar, and yet I would do without all those useless laws against duels; the means are simple and require no law courts. However that may be, Emile knows what is due to himself in such a case, and the example due from him to the safety of men of honour. The strongest of men cannot prevent insult, but he can take good care that his adversary has no opportunity to boast of that insult.] He will never set two dogs to fight, he will never set a dog to chase a cat. This peaceful spirit is one of the results of his education, which has never stimulated self-love or a high opinion of himself, and so has not encouraged him to seek his pleasure in domination and in the sufferings of others. The sight of suffering makes him suffer too; this is a natural feeling. It is one of the after effects of vanity that hardens a young man and makes him take a delight in seeing the torments of a living and feeling creature; it makes him consider himself beyond the reach of similar sufferings through his superior wisdom or virtue. He who is beyond the reach of vanity cannot fall into the vice which results from vanity. So Emile loves peace. He is delighted at the sight of happiness, and if he can help to bring it about, this is an additional reason for sharing it. I do not assume that when he sees the unhappy he will merely feel for them that barren and cruel pity which is content to pity the ills it can heal. His kindness is active and teaches him much he would have learnt far more slowly, or he would never have learnt at all, if his heart had been harder. If he finds his comrades at strife, he tries to reconcile them; if he sees the afflicted, he inquires as to the cause of their sufferings; if he meets two men who hate each other, he wants to know the reason of their enmity; if he finds one who is down-trodden groaning under the oppression of the rich and powerful, he tries to discover by what means he can counteract this oppression, and in the interest he takes with regard to all these unhappy persons, the means of removing their sufferings are never out of his sight. What use shall we make of this disposition so that it may re-act in a way suited to his age? Let us direct his efforts and his knowledge, and use his zeal to increase them.

I am never weary of repeating: let all the lessons of young people take the form of doing rather than talking; let them learn nothing from books which they can learn from experience. How absurd to attempt to give them practice in speaking when they have nothing to say, to expect to make them feel, at their school desks, the vigour of the language of passion and all the force of the arts of persuasion when they have nothing and nobody to persuade! All the rules of rhetoric are mere waste of words to those who do not know how to use them for their own purposes. How does it concern a schoolboy to know how Hannibal encouraged his soldiers to cross the Alps? If instead of these grand speeches you showed him how to induce his prefect to give him a holiday, you may be sure he would pay more attention to your rules.

If I wanted to teach rhetoric to a youth whose passions were as yet undeveloped, I would draw his attention continually to things that would stir his passions, and I would discuss with him how he should talk to people so as to get them to regard his wishes favourably. But Emile is not in a condition so favourable to the art of oratory. Concerned mainly with his physical well-being, he has less need of others than they of him; and having nothing to ask of others on his own account, what he wants to persuade them to do does not affect him sufficiently to awake any very strong feeling. From this it follows that his language will be on the whole simple and literal. He usually speaks to the point and only to make himself understood. He is not sententious, for he has not learnt to generalise; he does not speak in figures, for he is rarely impassioned.

Yet this is not because he is altogether cold and phlegmatic, neither his age, his character, nor his tastes permit of this. In the fire of adolescence the life-giving spirits, retained in the blood and distilled again and again, inspire his young heart with a warmth which glows in his eye, a warmth which is felt in his words and perceived in his actions. The lofty feeling with which he is inspired gives him strength and nobility; imbued with tender love for mankind his words betray the thoughts of his heart; I know not how it is, but there is more charm in his open-hearted generosity than in the artificial eloquence of others; or rather this eloquence of his is the only true eloquence, for he has only to show what he feels to make others share his feelings.

The more I think of it the more convinced I am that by thus translating our kindly impulses into action, by drawing from our good or ill success conclusions as to their cause, we shall find that there is little useful knowledge that cannot be imparted to a youth; and that together with such true learning as may be got at college he will learn a science of more importance than all the rest together, the application of what he has learned to the purposes of life. Taking such an interest in his fellow-creatures, it is impossible that he should fail to learn very quickly how to note and weigh their actions, their tastes, their pleasures, and to estimate generally at their true value what may increase or diminish the happiness of men; he should do this better than those who care for nobody and never do anything for any one. The feelings of those who are always occupied with their own concerns are too keenly affected for them to judge wisely of things. They consider everything as it affects themselves, they form their ideas of good and ill solely on their own experience, their minds are filled with all sorts of absurd prejudices, and anything which affects their own advantage ever so little, seems an upheaval of the universe.

Extend self-love to others and it is transformed into virtue, a virtue which has its root in the heart of every one of us. The less the object of our care is directly dependent on ourselves, the less we have to fear from the illusion of self-interest; the more general this interest becomes, the juster it is; and the love of the human race is nothing but the love of justice within us. If therefore we desire Emile to be a lover of truth, if we desire that he should indeed perceive it, let us keep him far from self-interest in all his business. The more care he bestows upon the happiness of others the wiser and better he is, and the fewer mistakes he will make between good and evil; but never allow him any blind preference founded merely on personal predilection or unfair prejudice. Why should he harm one person to serve another? What does it matter to him who has the greater share of happiness, providing he promotes the happiness of all? Apart from self-interest this care for the general well-being is the first concern of the wise man, for each of us forms part of the human race and not part of any individual member of that race.

To prevent pity degenerating into weakness we must generalise it and extend it to mankind. Then we only yield to it when it is in accordance with justice, since justice is of all the virtues that which contributes most to the common good. Reason and self-love compel us to love mankind even more than our neighbour, and to pity the wicked is to be very cruel to other men.

Moreover, you must bear in mind that all these means employed to project my pupil beyond himself have also a distinct relation to himself; since they not only cause him inward delight, but I am also endeavouring to instruct him, while I am making him kindly disposed towards others.

First I showed the means employed, now I will show the result. What wide prospects do I perceive unfolding themselves before his mind! What noble feelings stifle the lesser passions in his heart! What clearness of judgment, what accuracy in reasoning, do I see developing from the inclinations we have cultivated, from the experience which concentrates the desires of a great heart within the narrow bounds of possibility, so that a man superior to others can come down to their level if he cannot raise them to his own! True principles of justice, true types of beauty, all moral relations between man and man, all ideas of order, these are engraved on his understanding; he sees the right place for everything and the causes which drive it from that place; he sees what may do good, and what hinders it. Without having felt the passions of mankind, he knows the illusions they produce and their mode of action.

I proceed along the path which the force of circumstances compels me to tread, but I do not insist that my readers shall follow me. Long ago they have made up their minds that I am wandering in the land of chimeras, while for my part I think they are dwelling in the country of prejudice. When I wander so far from popular beliefs I do not cease to bear them in mind; I examine them, I consider them, not that I may follow them or shun them, but that I may weigh them in the balance of reason. Whenever reason compels me to abandon these popular beliefs, I know by experience that my readers will not follow my example; I know that they will persist in refusing to go beyond what they can see, and that they will take the youth I am describing for the creation of my fanciful imagination, merely because he is unlike the youths with whom they compare him; they forget that he must needs be different, because he has been brought up in a totally different fashion; he has been influenced by wholly different feelings, instructed in a wholly different manner, so that it would be far stranger if he were like your pupils than if he were what I have supposed. He is a man of nature's making, not man's. No wonder men find him strange.

When I began this work I took for granted nothing but what could be observed as readily by others as by myself; for our starting-point, the birth of man, is the same for all; but the further we go, while I am seeking to cultivate nature and you are seeking to deprave it, the further apart we find ourselves. At six years old my pupil was not so very unlike yours, whom you had not yet had time to disfigure; now there is nothing in common between them; and when they reach the age of manhood, which is now approaching, they will show themselves utterly different from each other, unless all my pains have been thrown away. There may not be so very great a difference in the amount of knowledge they possess, but there is all the difference in the world in the kind of knowledge. You are amazed to find that the one has noble sentiments of which the others have not the smallest germ, but remember that the latter are already philosophers and theologians while Emile does not even know what is meant by a philosopher and has scarcely heard the name of God.

But if you come and tell me, "There are no such young men, young people are not made that way; they have this passion or that, they do this or that," it is as if you denied that a pear tree could ever be a tall tree because the pear trees in our gardens are all dwarfs.

I beg these critics who are so ready with their blame to consider that I am as well acquainted as they are with everything they say, that I have probably given more thought to it, and that, as I have no private end to serve in getting them to agree with me, I have a right to demand that they should at least take time to find out where I am mistaken. Let them thoroughly examine the nature of man, let them follow the earliest growth of the heart in any given circumstances, so as to see what a difference education may make in the individual; then let them compare my method of education with the results I ascribe to it; and let them tell me where my reasoning is unsound, and I shall have no answer to give them.

It is this that makes me speak so strongly, and as I think with good excuse: I have not pledged myself to any system, I depend as little as possible on arguments, and I trust to what I myself have observed. I do not base my ideas on what I have imagined, but on what I have seen. It is true that I have not confined my observations within the walls of any one town, nor to a single class of people; but having compared men of every class and every nation which I have been able to observe in the course of a life spent in this pursuit, I have discarded as artificial what belonged to one nation and not to another, to one rank and not to another; and I have regarded as proper to mankind what was common to all, at any age, in any station, and in any nation whatsoever.

Now if in accordance with this method you follow from infancy the course of a youth who has not been shaped to any special mould, one who depends as little as possible on authority and the opinions of others, which will he most resemble, my pupil or yours? It seems to me that this is the question you must answer if you would know if I am mistaken.

It is not easy for a man to begin to think; but when once he has begun he will never leave off. Once a thinker, always a thinker, and the understanding once practised in reflection will never rest. You may therefore think that I do too much or too little; that the human mind is not by nature so quick to unfold; and that after having given it opportunities it has not got, I keep it too long confined within a circle of ideas which it ought to have outgrown.

But remember, in the first place, that when I want to train a natural man, I do not want to make him a savage and to send him back to the woods, but that living in the whirl of social life it is enough that he should not let himself be carried away by the passions and prejudices of men; let him see with his eyes and feel with his heart, let him own no sway but that of reason. Under these conditions it is plain that many things will strike him; the oft-recurring feelings which affect him, the different ways of satisfying his real needs, must give him many ideas he would not otherwise have acquired or would only have acquired much later. The natural progress of the mind is quickened but not reversed. The same man who would remain stupid in the forests should become wise and reasonable in towns, if he were merely a spectator in them. Nothing is better fitted to make one wise than the sight of follies we do not share, and even if we share them, we still learn, provided we are not the dupe of our follies and provided we do not bring to them the same mistakes as the others.

Consider also that while our faculties are confined to the things of sense, we offer scarcely any hold to the abstractions of philosophy or to purely intellectual ideas. To attain to these we require either to free ourselves from the body to which we are so strongly bound, or to proceed step by step in a slow and gradual course, or else to leap across the intervening space with a gigantic bound of which no child is capable, one for which grown men even require many steps hewn on purpose for them; but I find it very difficult to see how you propose to construct such steps.

The Incomprehensible embraces all, he gives its motion to the earth, and shapes the system of all creatures, but our eyes cannot see him nor can our hands search him out, he evades the efforts of our senses; we behold the work, but the workman is hidden from our eyes. It is no small matter to know that he exists, and when we have got so far, and when we ask. What is he? Where is he? our mind is overwhelmed, we lose ourselves, we know not what to think.

Locke would have us begin with the study of spirits and go on to that of bodies. This is the method of superstition, prejudice, and error; it is not the method of nature, nor even that of well-ordered reason; it is to learn to see by shutting our eyes. We must have studied bodies long enough before we can form any true idea of spirits, or even suspect that there are such beings. The contrary practice merely puts materialism on a firmer footing.

Since our senses are the first instruments to our learning, corporeal and sensible bodies are the only bodies we directly apprehend. The word "spirit" has no meaning for any one who has not philosophised. To the unlearned and to the child a spirit is merely a body. Do they not fancy that spirits groan, speak, fight, and make noises? Now you must own that spirits with arms and voices are very like bodies. This is why every nation on the face of the earth, not even excepting the Jews, have made to themselves idols. We, ourselves, with our words, Spirit, Trinity, Persons, are for the most part quite anthropomorphic. I admit that we are taught that God is everywhere; but we also believe that there is air everywhere, at least in our atmosphere; and the word Spirit meant originally nothing more than breath and wind. Once you teach people to say what they do not understand, it is easy enough to get them to say anything you like.

The perception of our action upon other bodies must have first induced us to suppose that their action upon us was effected in like manner. Thus man began by thinking that all things whose action affected him were alive. He did not recognise the limits of their powers, and he therefore supposed that they were boundless; as soon as he had supplied them with bodies they became his gods. In the earliest times men went in terror of everything and everything in nature seemed alive. The idea of matter was developed as slowly as that of spirit, for the former is itself an abstraction.

Thus the universe was peopled with gods like themselves. The stars, the winds and the mountains, rivers, trees, and towns, their very dwellings, each had its soul, its god, its life. The teraphim of Laban, the manitos of savages, the fetishes of the negroes, every work of nature and of man, were the first gods of mortals; polytheism was their first religion and idolatry their earliest form of worship. The idea of one God was beyond their grasp, till little by little they formed general ideas, and they rose to the idea of a first cause and gave meaning to the word "substance," which is at bottom the greatest of abstractions. So every child who believes in God is of necessity an idolater or at least he regards the Deity as a man, and when once the imagination has perceived God, it is very seldom that the understanding conceives him. Locke's order leads us into this same mistake.

Having arrived, I know not how, at the idea of substance, it is clear that to allow of a single substance it must be assumed that this substance is endowed with incompatible and mutually exclusive properties, such as thought and size, one of which is by its nature divisible and the other wholly incapable of division. Moreover it is assumed that thought or, if you prefer it, feeling is a primitive quality inseparable from the substance to which it belongs, that its relation to the substance is like the relation between substance and size. Hence it is inferred that beings who lose one of these attributes lose the substance to which it belongs, and that death is, therefore, but a separation of substances, and that those beings in whom the two attributes are found are composed of the two substances to which those two qualities belong.

But consider what a gulf there still is between the idea of two substances and that of the divine nature, between the incomprehensible idea of the influence of our soul upon our body and the idea of the influence of God upon every living creature. The ideas of creation, destruction, ubiquity, eternity, almighty power, those of the divine attributes—these are all ideas so confused and obscure that few men succeed in grasping them; yet there is nothing obscure about them to the common people, because they do not understand them in the least; how then should they present themselves in full force, that is to say in all their obscurity, to the young mind which is still occupied with the first working of the senses, and fails to realise anything but what it handles? In vain do the abysses of the Infinite open around us, a child does not know the meaning of fear; his weak eyes cannot gauge their depths. To children everything is infinite, they cannot assign limits to anything; not that their measure is so large, but because their understanding is so small. I have even noticed that they place the infinite rather below than above the dimensions known to them. They judge a distance to be immense rather by their feet than by their eyes; infinity is bounded for them, not so much by what they can see, but how far they can go. If you talk to them of the power of God, they will think he is nearly as strong as their father. As their own knowledge is in everything the standard by which they judge of what is possible, they always picture what is described to them as rather smaller than what they know. Such are the natural reasonings of an ignorant and feeble mind. Ajax was afraid to measure his strength against Achilles, yet he challenged Jupiter to combat, for he knew Achilles and did not know Jupiter. A Swiss peasant thought himself the richest man alive; when they tried to explain to him what a king was, he asked with pride, "Has the king got a hundred cows on the high pastures?"

I am aware that many of my readers will be surprised to find me tracing the course of my scholar through his early years without speaking to him of religion. At fifteen he will not even know that he has a soul, at eighteen even he may not be ready to learn about it. For if he learns about it too soon, there is the risk of his never really knowing anything about it.

If I had to depict the most heart-breaking stupidity, I would paint a pedant teaching children the catechism; if I wanted to drive a child crazy I would set him to explain what he learned in his catechism. You will reply that as most of the Christian doctrines are mysteries, you must wait, not merely till the child is a man, but till the man is dead, before the human mind will understand those doctrines. To that I reply, that there are mysteries which the heart of man can neither conceive nor believe, and I see no use in teaching them to children, unless you want to make liars of them. Moreover, I assert that to admit that there are mysteries, you must at least realise that they are incomprehensible, and children are not even capable of this conception! At an age when everything is mysterious, there are no mysteries properly so-called.

"We must believe in God if we would be saved." This doctrine wrongly understood is the root of bloodthirsty intolerance and the cause of all the futile teaching which strikes a deadly blow at human reason by training it to cheat itself with mere words. No doubt there is not a moment to be lost if we would deserve eternal salvation; but if the repetition of certain words suffices to obtain it, I do not see why we should not people heaven with starlings and magpies as well as with children.

The obligation of faith assumes the possibility of belief. The philosopher who does not believe is wrong, for he misuses the reason he has cultivated, and he is able to understand the truths he rejects. But the child who professes the Christian faith—what does he believe? Just what he understands; and he understands so little of what he is made to repeat that if you tell him to say just the opposite he will be quite ready to do it. The faith of children and the faith of many men is a matter of geography. Will they be rewarded for having been born in Rome rather than in Mecca? One is told that Mahomet is the prophet of God and he says, "Mahomet is the prophet of God." The other is told that Mahomet is a rogue and he says, "Mahomet is a rogue." Either of them would have said just the opposite had he stood in the other's shoes. When they are so much alike to begin with, can the one be consigned to Paradise and the other to Hell? When a child says he believes in God, it is not God he believes in, but Peter or James who told him that there is something called God, and he believes it after the fashion of Euripides—

"O Jupiter, of whom I know nothing but thy name."

[Footnote: Plutarch. It is thus that the tragedy of Menalippus originally began, but the clamour of the Athenians compelled Euripides to change these opening lines.]

We hold that no child who dies before the age of reason will be deprived of everlasting happiness; the Catholics believe the same of all children who have been baptised, even though they have never heard of God. There are, therefore, circumstances in which one can be saved without belief in God, and these circumstances occur in the case of children or madmen when the human mind is incapable of the operations necessary to perceive the Godhead. The only difference I see between you and me is that you profess that children of seven years old are able to do this and I do not think them ready for it at fifteen. Whether I am right or wrong depends, not on an article of the creed, but on a simple observation in natural history.

From the same principle it is plain that any man having reached old age without faith in God will not, therefore, be deprived of God's presence in another life if his blindness was not wilful; and I maintain that it is not always wilful. You admit that it is so in the case of lunatics deprived by disease of their spiritual faculties, but not of their manhood, and therefore still entitled to the goodness of their Creator. Why then should we not admit it in the case of those brought up from infancy in seclusion, those who have led the life of a savage and are without the knowledge that comes from intercourse with other men. [Footnote: For the natural condition of the human mind and its slow development, cf. the first part of the Discours sur Inegalite.] For it is clearly impossible that such a savage could ever raise his thoughts to the knowledge of the true God. Reason tells that man should only be punished for his wilful faults, and that invincible ignorance can never be imputed to him as a crime. Hence it follows that in the sight of the Eternal Justice every man who would believe if he had the necessary knowledge is counted a believer, and that there will be no unbelievers to be punished except those who have closed their hearts against the truth.

Let us beware of proclaiming the truth to those who cannot as yet comprehend it, for to do so is to try to inculcate error. It would be better to have no idea at all of the Divinity than to have mean, grotesque, harmful, and unworthy ideas; to fail to perceive the Divine is a lesser evil than to insult it. The worthy Plutarch says, "I would rather men said, 'There is no such person as Plutarch,' than that they should say, 'Plutarch is unjust, envious, jealous, and such a tyrant that he demands more than can be performed.'"

The chief harm which results from the monstrous ideas of God which are instilled into the minds of children is that they last all their life long, and as men they understand no more of God than they did as children. In Switzerland I once saw a good and pious mother who was so convinced of the truth of this maxim that she refused to teach her son religion when he was a little child for fear lest he should be satisfied with this crude teaching and neglect a better teaching when he reached the age of reason. This child never heard the name of God pronounced except with reverence and devotion, and as soon as he attempted to say the word he was told to hold his tongue, as if the subject were too sublime and great for him. This reticence aroused his curiosity and his self-love; he looked forward to the time when he would know this mystery so carefully hidden from him. The less they spoke of God to him, the less he was himself permitted to speak of God, the more he thought about Him; this child beheld God everywhere. What I should most dread as the result of this unwise affectation of mystery is this: by over-stimulating the youth's imagination you may turn his head, and make him at the best a fanatic rather than a believer.

But we need fear nothing of the sort for Emile, who always declines to pay attention to what is beyond his reach, and listens with profound indifference to things he does not understand. There are so many things of which he is accustomed to say, "That is no concern of mine," that one more or less makes little difference to him; and when he does begin to perplex himself with these great matters, it is because the natural growth of his knowledge is turning his thoughts that way.

We have seen the road by which the cultivated human mind approaches these mysteries, and I am ready to admit that it would not attain to them naturally, even in the bosom of society, till a much later age. But as there are in this same society inevitable causes which hasten the development of the passions, if we did not also hasten the development of the knowledge which controls these passions we should indeed depart from the path of nature and disturb her equilibrium. When we can no longer restrain a precocious development in one direction we must promote a corresponding development in another direction, so that the order of nature may not be inverted, and so that things should progress together, not separately, so that the man, complete at every moment of his life, may never find himself at one stage in one of his faculties and at another stage in another faculty.

What a difficulty do I see before me! A difficulty all the greater because it depends less on actual facts than on the cowardice of those who dare not look the difficulty in the face. Let us at least venture to state our problem. A child should always be brought up in his father's religion; he is always given plain proofs that this religion, whatever it may be, is the only true religion, that all others are ridiculous and absurd. The force of the argument depends entirely on the country in which it is put forward. Let a Turk, who thinks Christianity so absurd at Constantinople, come to Paris and see what they think of Mahomet. It is in matters of religion more than in anything else that prejudice is triumphant. But when we who profess to shake off its yoke entirely, we who refuse to yield any homage to authority, decline to teach Emile anything which he could not learn for himself in any country, what religion shall we give him, to what sect shall this child of nature belong? The answer strikes me as quite easy. We will not attach him to any sect, but we will give him the means to choose for himself according to the right use of his own reason.

Incedo per ignes
Supposito cineri doloso. – Horace, lib. ii. ode I.

No matter! Thus far zeal and prudence have taken the place of caution. I hope that these guardians will not fail me now. Reader, do not fear lest I should take precautions unworthy of a lover of truth; I shall never forget my motto, but I distrust my own judgment all too easily. Instead of telling you what I think myself, I will tell you the thoughts of one whose opinions carry more weight than mine. I guarantee the truth of the facts I am about to relate; they actually happened to the author whose writings I am about to transcribe; it is for you to judge whether we can draw from them any considerations bearing on the matter in hand. I do not offer you my own idea or another's as your rule; I merely present them for your examination.

Thirty years ago there was a young man in an Italian town; he was an exile from his native land and found himself reduced to the depths of poverty. He had been born a Calvinist, but the consequences of his own folly had made him a fugitive in a strange land; he had no money and he changed his religion for a morsel of bread. There was a hostel for proselytes in that town to which he gained admission. The study of controversy inspired doubts he had never felt before, and he made acquaintance with evil hitherto unsuspected by him; he heard strange doctrines and he met with morals still stranger to him; he beheld this evil conduct and nearly fell a victim to it. He longed to escape, but he was locked up; he complained, but his complaints were unheeded; at the mercy of his tyrants, he found himself treated as a criminal because he would not share their crimes. The anger kindled in a young and untried heart by the first experience of violence and injustice may be realised by those who have themselves experienced it. Tears of anger flowed from his eyes, he was wild with rage; he prayed to heaven and to man, and his prayers were unheard; he spoke to every one and no one listened to him. He saw no one but the vilest servants under the control of the wretch who insulted him, or accomplices in the same crime who laughed at his resistance and encouraged him to follow their example. He would have been ruined had not a worthy priest visited the hostel on some matter of business. He found an opportunity of consulting him secretly. The priest was poor and in need of help himself, but the victim had more need of his assistance, and he did not hesitate to help him to escape at the risk of making a dangerous enemy.

Having escaped from vice to return to poverty, the young man struggled vainly against fate: for a moment he thought he had gained the victory. At the first gleam of good fortune his woes and his protector were alike forgotten. He was soon punished for this ingratitude; all his hopes vanished; youth indeed was on his side, but his romantic ideas spoiled everything. He had neither talent nor skill to make his way easily, he could neither be commonplace nor wicked, he expected so much that he got nothing. When he had sunk to his former poverty, when he was without food or shelter and ready to die of hunger, he remembered his benefactor.

He went back to him, found him, and was kindly welcomed; the sight of him reminded the priest of a good deed he had done; such a memory always rejoices the heart. This man was by nature humane and pitiful; he felt the sufferings of others through his own, and his heart had not been hardened by prosperity; in a word, the lessons of wisdom and an enlightened virtue had reinforced his natural kindness of heart. He welcomed the young man, found him a lodging, and recommended him; he shared with him his living which was barely enough for two. He did more, he instructed him, consoled him, and taught him the difficult art of bearing adversity in patience. You prejudiced people, would you have expected to find all this in a priest and in Italy?

This worthy priest was a poor Savoyard clergyman who had offended his bishop by some youthful fault; he had crossed the Alps to find a position which he could not obtain in his own country. He lacked neither wit nor learning, and with his interesting countenance he had met with patrons who found him a place in the household of one of the ministers, as tutor to his son. He preferred poverty to dependence, and he did not know how to get on with the great. He did not stay long with this minister, and when he departed he took with him his good opinion; and as he lived a good life and gained the hearts of everybody, he was glad to be forgiven by his bishop and to obtain from him a small parish among the mountains, where he might pass the rest of his life. This was the limit of his ambition.

He was attracted by the young fugitive and he questioned him closely. He saw that ill-fortune had already seared his heart, that scorn and disgrace had overthrown his courage, and that his pride, transformed into bitterness and spite, led him to see nothing in the harshness and injustice of men but their evil disposition and the vanity of all virtue. He had seen that religion was but a mask for selfishness, and its holy services but a screen for hypocrisy; he had found in the subtleties of empty disputations heaven and hell awarded as prizes for mere words; he had seen the sublime and primitive idea of Divinity disfigured by the vain fancies of men; and when, as he thought, faith in God required him to renounce the reason God himself had given him, he held in equal scorn our foolish imaginings and the object with which they are concerned. With no knowledge of things as they are, without any idea of their origins, he was immersed in his stubborn ignorance and utterly despised those who thought they knew more than himself.

The neglect of all religion soon leads to the neglect of a man's duties. The heart of this young libertine was already far on this road. Yet his was not a bad nature, though incredulity and misery were gradually stifling his natural disposition and dragging him down to ruin; they were leading him into the conduct of a rascal and the morals of an atheist.

The almost inevitable evil was not actually consummated. The young man was not ignorant, his education had not been neglected. He was at that happy age when the pulse beats strongly and the heart is warm, but is not yet enslaved by the madness of the senses. His heart had not lost its elasticity. A native modesty, a timid disposition restrained him, and prolonged for him that period during which you watch your pupil so carefully. The hateful example of brutal depravity, of vice without any charm, had not merely failed to quicken his imagination, it had deadened it. For a long time disgust rather than virtue preserved his innocence, which would only succumb to more seductive charms.

The priest saw the danger and the way of escape. He was not discouraged by difficulties, he took a pleasure in his task; he determined to complete it and to restore to virtue the victim he had snatched from vice. He set about it cautiously; the beauty of the motive gave him courage and inspired him with means worthy of his zeal. Whatever might be the result, his pains would not be wasted. We are always successful when our sole aim is to do good.

He began to win the confidence of the proselyte by not asking any price for his kindness, by not intruding himself upon him, by not preaching at him, by always coming down to his level, and treating him as an equal. It was, so I think, a touching sight to see a serious person becoming the comrade of a young scamp, and virtue putting up with the speech of licence in order to triumph over it more completely. When the young fool came to him with his silly confidences and opened his heart to him, the priest listened and set him at his ease; without giving his approval to what was bad, he took an interest in everything; no tactless reproof checked his chatter or closed his heart; the pleasure which he thought was given by his conversation increased his pleasure in telling everything; thus he made his general confession without knowing he was confessing anything.

After he had made a thorough study of his feelings and disposition, the priest saw plainly that, although he was not ignorant for his age, he had forgotten everything that he most needed to know, and that the disgrace which fortune had brought upon him had stifled in him all real sense of good and evil. There is a stage of degradation which robs the soul of its life; and the inner voice cannot be heard by one whose whole mind is bent on getting food. To protect the unlucky youth from the moral death which threatened him, he began to revive his self-love and his good opinion of himself. He showed him a happier future in the right use of his talents; he revived the generous warmth of his heart by stories of the noble deeds of others; by rousing his admiration for the doers of these deeds he revived his desire to do like deeds himself. To draw him gradually from his idle and wandering life, he made him copy out extracts from well-chosen books; he pretended to want these extracts, and so nourished in him the noble feeling of gratitude. He taught him indirectly through these books, and thus he made him sufficiently regain his good opinion of himself so that he would no longer think himself good for nothing, and would not make himself despicable in his own eyes.

A trifling incident will show how this kindly man tried, unknown to him, to raise the heart of his disciple out of its degradation, without seeming to think of teaching. The priest was so well known for his uprightness and his discretion, that many people preferred to entrust their alms to him, rather than to the wealthy clergy of the town. One day some one had given him some money to distribute among the poor, and the young man was mean enough to ask for some of it on the score of poverty. "No," said he, "we are brothers, you belong to me and I must not touch the money entrusted to me." Then he gave him the sum he had asked for out of his own pocket. Lessons of this sort seldom fail to make an impression on the heart of young people who are not wholly corrupt.

I am weary of speaking in the third person, and the precaution is unnecessary; for you are well aware, my dear friend, that I myself was this unhappy fugitive; I think I am so far removed from the disorders of my youth that I may venture to confess them, and the hand which rescued me well deserves that I should at least do honour to its goodness at the cost of some slight shame.

What struck me most was to see in the private life of my worthy master, virtue without hypocrisy, humanity without weakness, speech always plain and straightforward, and conduct in accordance with this speech. I never saw him trouble himself whether those whom he assisted went to vespers or confession, whether they fasted at the appointed seasons and went without meat; nor did he impose upon them any other like conditions, without which you might die of hunger before you could hope for any help from the devout.

Far from displaying before him the zeal of a new convert, I was encouraged by these observations and I made no secret of my way of thinking, nor did he seem to be shocked by it. Sometimes I would say to myself, he overlooks my indifference to the religion I have adopted because he sees I am equally indifferent to the religion in which I was brought up; he knows that my scorn for religion is not confined to one sect. But what could I think when I sometimes heard him give his approval to doctrines contrary to those of the Roman Catholic Church, and apparently having but a poor opinion of its ceremonies. I should have thought him a Protestant in disguise if I had not beheld him so faithful to those very customs which he seemed to value so lightly; but I knew he fulfilled his priestly duties as carefully in private as in public, and I knew not what to think of these apparent contradictions. Except for the fault which had formerly brought about his disgrace, a fault which he had only partially overcome, his life was exemplary, his conduct beyond reproach, his conversation honest and discreet. While I lived on very friendly terms with him, I learnt day by day to respect him more; and when he had completely won my heart by such great kindness, I awaited with eager curiosity the time when I should learn what was the principle on which the uniformity of this strange life was based.

This opportunity was a long time coming. Before taking his disciple into his confidence, he tried to get the seeds of reason and kindness which he had sown in my heart to germinate. The most difficult fault to overcome in me was a certain haughty misanthropy, a certain bitterness against the rich and successful, as if their wealth and happiness had been gained at my own expense, and as if their supposed happiness had been unjustly taken from my own. The foolish vanity of youth, which kicks against the pricks of humiliation, made me only too much inclined to this angry temper; and the self-respect, which my mentor strove to revive, led to pride, which made men still more vile in my eyes, and only added scorn to my hatred.

Without directly attacking this pride, he prevented it from developing into hardness of heart; and without depriving me of my self-esteem, he made me less scornful of my neighbours. By continually drawing my attention from the empty show, and directing it to the genuine sufferings concealed by it, he taught me to deplore the faults of my fellows and feel for their sufferings, to pity rather than envy them. Touched with compassion towards human weaknesses through the profound conviction of his own failings, he viewed all men as the victims of their own vices and those of others; he beheld the poor groaning under the tyranny of the rich, and the rich under the tyranny of their own prejudices. "Believe me," said he, "our illusions, far from concealing our woes, only increase them by giving value to what is in itself valueless, in making us aware of all sorts of fancied privations which we should not otherwise feel. Peace of heart consists in despising everything that might disturb that peace; the man who clings most closely to life is the man who can least enjoy it; and the man who most eagerly desires happiness is always most miserable."

"What gloomy ideas!" I exclaimed bitterly. "If we must deny ourselves everything, we might as well never have been born; and if we must despise even happiness itself who can be happy?" "I am," replied the priest one day, in a tone which made a great impression on me. "You happy! So little favoured by fortune, so poor, an exile and persecuted, you are happy! How have you contrived to be happy?" "My child," he answered, "I will gladly tell you."

Thereupon he explained that, having heard my confessions, he would confess to me. "I will open my whole heart to yours," he said, embracing me. "You will see me, if not as I am, at least as I seem to myself. When you have heard my whole confession of faith, when you really know the condition of my heart, you will know why I think myself happy, and if you think as I do, you will know how to be happy too. But these explanations are not the affair of a moment, it will take time to show you all my ideas about the lot of man and the true value of life; let us choose a fitting time and a place where we may continue this conversation without interruption."

I showed him how eager I was to hear him. The meeting was fixed for the very next morning. It was summer time; we rose at daybreak. He took me out of the town on to a high hill above the river Po, whose course we beheld as it flowed between its fertile banks; in the distance the landscape was crowned by the vast chain of the Alps; the beams of the rising sun already touched the plains and cast across the fields long shadows of trees, hillocks, and houses, and enriched with a thousand gleams of light the fairest picture which the human eye can see. You would have thought that nature was displaying all her splendour before our eyes to furnish a text for our conversation. After contemplating this scene for a space in silence, the man of peace spoke to me.

☐☐ ☐☐☐☐☐ O☐☐ ☐☐☐O☐☐☐☐ ☐☐I☐☐☐

My child, do not look to me for learned speeches or profound arguments. I am no great philosopher, nor do I desire to be one. I have, however, a certain amount of common-sense and a constant devotion to truth. I have no wish to argue with you nor even to convince you; it is enough for me to show you, in all simplicity of heart, what I really think. Consult your own heart while I speak; that is all I ask. If I am mistaken, I am honestly mistaken, and therefore my error will not be counted to me as a crime; if you, too, are honestly mistaken, there is no great harm done. If I am right, we are both endowed with reason, we have both the same motive for listening to the voice of reason. Why should not you think as I do?

By birth I was a peasant and poor; to till the ground was my portion; but my parents thought it a finer thing that I should learn to get my living as a priest and they found means to send me to college. I am quite sure that neither my parents nor I had any idea of seeking after what was good, useful, or true; we only sought what was wanted to get me ordained. I learned what was taught me, I said what I was told to say, I promised all that was required, and I became a priest. But I soon discovered that when I promised not to be a man, I had promised more than I could perform.

Conscience, they tell us, is the creature of prejudice, but I know from experience that conscience persists in following the order of nature in spite of all the laws of man. In vain is this or that forbidden; remorse makes her voice heard but feebly when what we do is permitted by well-ordered nature, and still more when we are doing her bidding. My good youth, nature has not yet appealed to your senses; may you long remain in this happy state when her voice is the voice of innocence. Remember that to anticipate her teaching is to offend more deeply against her than to resist her teaching; you must first learn to resist, that you may know when to yield without wrong-doing.

From my youth up I had reverenced the married state as the first and most sacred institution of nature. Having renounced the right to marry, I was resolved not to profane the sanctity of marriage; for in spite of my education and reading I had always led a simple and regular life, and my mind had preserved the innocence of its natural instincts; these instincts had not been obscured by worldly wisdom, while my poverty kept me remote from the temptations dictated by the sophistry of vice.

This very resolution proved my ruin. My respect for marriage led to the discovery of my misconduct. The scandal must be expiated; I was arrested, suspended, and dismissed; I was the victim of my scruples rather than of my incontinence, and I had reason to believe, from the reproaches which accompanied my disgrace, that one can often escape punishment by being guilty of a worse fault.

A thoughtful mind soon learns from such experiences. I found my former ideas of justice, honesty, and every duty of man overturned by these painful events, and day by day I was losing my hold on one or another of the opinions I had accepted. What was left was not enough to form a body of ideas which could stand alone, and I felt that the evidence on which my principles rested was being weakened; at last I knew not what to think, and I came to the same conclusion as yourself, but with this difference: My lack of faith was the slow growth of manhood, attained with great difficulty, and all the harder to uproot.

I was in that state of doubt and uncertainty which Descartes considers essential to the search for truth. It is a state which cannot continue, it is disquieting and painful; only vicious tendencies and an idle heart can keep us in that state. My heart was not so corrupt as to delight in it, and there is nothing which so maintains the habit of thinking as being better pleased with oneself than with one's lot.

I pondered, therefore, on the sad fate of mortals, adrift upon this sea of human opinions, without compass or rudder, and abandoned to their stormy passions with no guide but an inexperienced pilot who does not know whence he comes or whither he is going. I said to myself, "I love truth, I seek her, and cannot find her. Show me truth and I will hold her fast; why does she hide her face from the eager heart that would fain worship her?"

Although I have often experienced worse sufferings, I have never led a life so uniformly distressing as this period of unrest and anxiety, when I wandered incessantly from one doubt to another, gaining nothing from my prolonged meditations but uncertainty, darkness, and contradiction with regard to the source of my being and the rule of my duties.

I cannot understand how any one can be a sceptic sincerely and on principle. Either such philosophers do not exist or they are the most miserable of men. Doubt with regard to what we ought to know is a condition too violent for the human mind; it cannot long be endured; in spite of itself the mind decides one way or another, and it prefers to be deceived rather than to believe nothing.

My perplexity was increased by the fact that I had been brought up in a church which decides everything and permits no doubts, so that having rejected one article of faith I was forced to reject the rest; as I could not accept absurd decisions, I was deprived of those which were not absurd. When I was told to believe everything, I could believe nothing, and I knew not where to stop.

I consulted the philosophers, I searched their books and examined their various theories; I found them all alike proud, assertive, dogmatic, professing, even in their so-called scepticism, to know everything, proving nothing, scoffing at each other. This last trait, which was common to all of them, struck me as the only point in which they were right. Braggarts in attack, they are weaklings in defence. Weigh their arguments, they are all destructive; count their voices, every one speaks for himself; they are only agreed in arguing with each other. I could find no way out of my uncertainty by listening to them.

I suppose this prodigious diversity of opinion is caused, in the first place, by the weakness of the human intellect; and, in the second, by pride. We have no means of measuring this vast machine, we are unable to calculate its workings; we know neither its guiding principles nor its final purpose; we do not know ourselves, we know neither our nature nor the spirit that moves us; we scarcely know whether man is one or many; we are surrounded by impenetrable mysteries. These mysteries are beyond the region of sense, we think we can penetrate them by the light of reason, but we fall back on our imagination. Through this imagined world each forces a way for himself which he holds to be right; none can tell whether his path will lead him to the goal. Yet we long to know and understand it all. The one thing we do not know is the limit of the knowable. We prefer to trust to chance and to believe what is not true, rather than to own that not one of us can see what really is. A fragment of some vast whole whose bounds are beyond our gaze, a fragment abandoned by its Creator to our foolish quarrels, we are vain enough to want to determine the nature of that whole and our own relations with regard to it.

If the philosophers were in a position to declare the truth, which of them would care to do so? Every one of them knows that his own system rests on no surer foundations than the rest, but he maintains it because it is his own. There is not one of them who, if he chanced to discover the difference between truth and falsehood, would not prefer his own lie to the truth which another had discovered. Where is the philosopher who would not deceive the whole world for his own glory? If he can rise above the crowd, if he can excel his rivals, what more does he want? Among believers he is an atheist; among atheists he would be a believer.

The first thing I learned from these considerations was to restrict my inquiries to what directly concerned myself, to rest in profound ignorance of everything else, and not even to trouble myself to doubt anything beyond what I required to know.

I also realised that the philosophers, far from ridding me of my vain doubts, only multiplied the doubts that tormented me and failed to remove any one of them. So I chose another guide and said, "Let me follow the Inner Light; it will not lead me so far astray as others have done, or if it does it will be my own fault, and I shall not go so far wrong if I follow my own illusions as if I trusted to their deceits."

I then went over in my mind the various opinions which I had held in the course of my life, and I saw that although no one of them was plain enough to gain immediate belief, some were more probable than others, and my inward consent was given or withheld in proportion to this improbability. Having discovered this, I made an unprejudiced comparison of all these different ideas, and I perceived that the first and most general of them was also the simplest and the most reasonable, and that it would have been accepted by every one if only it had been last instead of first. Imagine all your philosophers, ancient and modern, having exhausted their strange systems of force, chance, fate, necessity, atoms, a living world, animated matter, and every variety of materialism. Then comes the illustrious Clarke who gives light to the world and proclaims the Being of beings and the Giver of things. What universal admiration, what unanimous applause would have greeted this new system—a system so great, so illuminating, and so simple. Other systems are full of absurdities; this system seems to me to contain fewer things which are beyond the understanding of the human mind. I said to myself, "Every system has its insoluble problems, for the finite mind of man is too small to deal with them; these difficulties are therefore no final arguments, against any system. But what a difference there is between the direct evidence on which these systems are based! Should we not prefer that theory which alone explains all the facts, when it is no more difficult than the rest?"

Bearing thus within my heart the love of truth as my only philosophy, and as my only method a clear and simple rule which dispensed with the need for vain and subtle arguments, I returned with the help of this rule to the examination of such knowledge as concerned myself; I was resolved to admit as self-evident all that I could not honestly refuse to believe, and to admit as true all that seemed to follow directly from this; all the rest I determined to leave undecided, neither accepting nor rejecting it, nor yet troubling myself to clear up difficulties which did not lead to any practical ends.

But who am I? What right have I to decide? What is it that determines my judgments? If they are inevitable, if they are the results of the impressions I receive, I am wasting my strength in such inquiries; they would be made or not without any interference of mine. I must therefore first turn my eyes upon myself to acquaint myself with the instrument I desire to use, and to discover how far it is reliable.

I exist, and I have senses through which I receive impressions. This is the first truth that strikes me and I am forced to accept it. Have I any independent knowledge of my existence, or am I only aware of it through my sensations? This is my first difficulty, and so far I cannot solve it. For I continually experience sensations, either directly or indirectly through memory, so how can I know if the feeling of self is something beyond these sensations or if it can exist independently of them?

My sensations take place in myself, for they make me aware of my own existence; but their cause is outside me, for they affect me whether I have any reason for them or not, and they are produced or destroyed independently of me. So I clearly perceive that my sensation, which is within me, and its cause or its object, which is outside me, are different things.

Thus, not only do I exist, but other entities exist also, that is to say, the objects of my sensations; and even if these objects are merely ideas, still these ideas are not me.

But everything outside myself, everything which acts upon my senses, I call matter, and all the particles of matter which I suppose to be united into separate entities I call bodies. Thus all the disputes of the idealists and the realists have no meaning for me; their distinctions between the appearance and the reality of bodies are wholly fanciful.

I am now as convinced of the existence of the universe as of my own. I next consider the objects of my sensations, and I find that I have the power of comparing them, so I perceive that I am endowed with an active force of which I was not previously aware.

To perceive is to feel; to compare is to judge; to judge and to feel are not the same. Through sensation objects present themselves to me separately and singly as they are in nature; by comparing them I rearrange them, I shift them so to speak, I place one upon another to decide whether they are alike or different, or more generally to find out their relations. To my mind, the distinctive faculty of an active or intelligent being is the power of understanding this word "is." I seek in vain in the merely sensitive entity that intelligent force which compares and judges; I can find no trace of it in its nature. This passive entity will be aware of each object separately, it will even be aware of the whole formed by the two together, but having no power to place them side by side it can never compare them, it can never form a judgment with regard to them.

To see two things at once is not to see their relations nor to judge of their differences; to perceive several objects, one beyond the other, is not to relate them. I may have at the same moment an idea of a big stick and a little stick without comparing them, without judging that one is less than the other, just as I can see my whole hand without counting my fingers. [Footnote: M. de le Cordamines' narratives tell of a people who only know how to count up to three. Yet the men of this nation, having hands, have often seen their fingers without learning to count up to five.] These comparative ideas, 'greater', 'smaller', together with number ideas of 'one', 'two', etc. are certainly not sensations, although my mind only produces them when my sensations occur.

We are told that a sensitive being distinguishes sensations from each other by the inherent differences in the sensations; this requires explanation. When the sensations are different, the sensitive being distinguishes them by their differences; when they are alike, he distinguishes them because he is aware of them one beyond the other. Otherwise, how could he distinguish between two equal objects simultaneously experienced? He would necessarily confound the two objects and take them for one object, especially under a system which professed that the representative sensations of space have no extension.

When we become aware of the two sensations to be compared, their impression is made, each object is perceived, both are perceived, but for all that their relation is not perceived. If the judgment of this relation were merely a sensation, and came to me solely from the object itself, my judgments would never be mistaken, for it is never untrue that I feel what I feel.

Why then am I mistaken as to the relation between these two sticks, especially when they are not parallel? Why, for example, do I say the small stick is a third of the large, when it is only a quarter? Why is the picture, which is the sensation, unlike its model which is the object? It is because I am active when I judge, because the operation of comparison is at fault; because my understanding, which judges of relations, mingles its errors with the truth of sensations, which only reveal to me things.

Add to this a consideration which will, I feel sure, appeal to you when you have thought about it: it is this—If we were purely passive in the use of our senses, there would be no communication between them; it would be impossible to know that the body we are touching and the thing we are looking at is the same. Either we should never perceive anything outside ourselves, or there would be for us five substances perceptible by the senses, whose identity we should have no means of perceiving.

This power of my mind which brings my sensations together and compares them may be called by any name; let it be called attention, meditation, reflection, or what you will; it is still true that it is in me and not in things, that it is I alone who produce it, though I only produce it when I receive an impression from things. Though I am compelled to feel or not to feel, I am free to examine more or less what I feel.

Being now, so to speak, sure of myself, I begin to look at things outside myself, and I behold myself with a sort of shudder flung at random into this vast universe, plunged as it were into the vast number of entities, knowing nothing of what they are in themselves or in relation to me. I study them, I observe them; and the first object which suggests itself for comparison with them is myself.

All that I perceive through the senses is matter, and I deduce all the essential properties of matter from the sensible qualities which make me perceive it, qualities which are inseparable from it. I see it sometimes in motion, sometimes at rest, [Footnote: This repose is, if you prefer it, merely relative; but as we perceive more or less of motion, we may plainly conceive one of two extremes, which is rest; and we conceive it so clearly that we are even disposed to take for absolute rest what is only relative. But it is not true that motion is of the essence of matter, if matter may be conceived of as at rest.] hence I infer that neither motion nor rest is essential to it, but motion, being an action, is the result of a cause of which rest is only the absence. When, therefore, there is nothing acting upon matter it does not move, and for the very reason that rest and motion are indifferent to it, its natural state is a state of rest.

I perceive two sorts of motions of bodies, acquired motion and spontaneous or voluntary motion. In the first the cause is external to the body moved, in the second it is within. I shall not conclude from that that the motion, say of a watch, is spontaneous, for if no external cause operated upon the spring it would run down and the watch would cease to go. For the same reason I should not admit that the movements of fluids are spontaneous, neither should I attribute spontaneous motion to fire which causes their fluidity. [Footnote: Chemists regard phlogiston or the element of fire as diffused, motionless, and stagnant in the compounds of which it forms part, until external forces set it free, collect it and set it in motion, and change it into fire.]

You ask me if the movements of animals are spontaneous; my answer is, "I cannot tell," but analogy points that way. You ask me again, how do I know that there are spontaneous movements? I tell you, "I know it because I feel them." I want to move my arm and I move it without any other immediate cause of the movement but my own will. In vain would any one try to argue me out of this feeling, it is stronger than any proofs; you might as well try to convince me that I do not exist.

If there were no spontaneity in men's actions, nor in anything that happens on this earth, it would be all the more difficult to imagine a first cause for all motion. For my own part, I feel myself so thoroughly convinced that the natural state of matter is a state of rest, and that it has no power of action in itself, that when I see a body in motion I at once assume that it is either a living body or that this motion has been imparted to it. My mind declines to accept in any way the idea of inorganic matter moving of its own accord, or giving rise to any action.

Yet this visible universe consists of matter, matter diffused and dead, [Footnote: I have tried hard to grasp the idea of a living molecule, but in vain. The idea of matter feeling without any senses seems to me unintelligible and self-contradictory. To accept or reject this idea one must first understand it, and I confess that so far I have not succeeded.] matter which has none of the cohesion, the organisation, the common feeling of the parts of a living body, for it is certain that we who are parts have no consciousness of the whole. This same universe is in motion, and in its movements, ordered, uniform, and subject to fixed laws, it has none of that freedom which appears in the spontaneous movements of men and animals. So the world is not some huge animal which moves of its own accord; its movements are therefore due to some external cause, a cause which I cannot perceive, but the inner voice makes this cause so apparent to me that I cannot watch the course of the sun without imagining a force which drives it, and when the earth revolves I think I see the hand that sets it in motion.

If I must accept general laws whose essential relation to matter is unperceived by me, how much further have I got? These laws, not being real things, not being substances, have therefore some other basis unknown to me. Experiment and observation have acquainted us with the laws of motion; these laws determine the results without showing their causes; they are quite inadequate to explain the system of the world and the course of the universe. With the help of dice Descartes made heaven and earth; but he could not set his dice in motion, nor start the action of his centrifugal force without the help of rotation. Newton discovered the law of gravitation; but gravitation alone would soon reduce the universe to a motionless mass; he was compelled to add a projectile force to account for the elliptical course of the celestial bodies; let Newton show us the hand that launched the planets in the tangent of their orbits.

The first causes of motion are not to be found in matter; matter receives and transmits motion, but does not produce it. The more I observe the action and reaction of the forces of nature playing on one another, the more I see that we must always go back from one effect to another, till we arrive at a first cause in some will; for to assume an infinite succession of causes is to assume that there is no first cause. In a word, no motion which is not caused by another motion can take place, except by a spontaneous, voluntary action; inanimate bodies have no action but motion, and there is no real action without will. This is my first principle. I believe, therefore, that there is a will which sets the universe in motion and gives life to nature. This is my first dogma, or the first article of my creed.

How does a will produce a physical and corporeal action? I cannot tell, but I perceive that it does so in myself; I will to do something and I do it; I will to move my body and it moves, but if an inanimate body, when at rest, should begin to move itself, the thing is incomprehensible and without precedent. The will is known to me in its action, not in its nature. I know this will as a cause of motion, but to conceive of matter as producing motion is clearly to conceive of an effect without a cause, which is not to conceive at all.

It is no more possible for me to conceive how my will moves my body than to conceive how my sensations affect my mind. I do not even know why one of these mysteries has seemed less inexplicable than the other. For my own part, whether I am active or passive, the means of union of the two substances seem to me absolutely incomprehensible. It is very strange that people make this very incomprehensibility a step towards the compounding of the two substances, as if operations so different in kind were more easily explained in one case than in two.

The doctrine I have just laid down is indeed obscure; but at least it suggests a meaning and there is nothing in it repugnant to reason or experience; can we say as much of materialism? Is it not plain that if motion is essential to matter it would be inseparable from it, it would always be present in it in the same degree, always present in every particle of matter, always the same in each particle of matter, it would not be capable of transmission, it could neither increase nor diminish, nor could we ever conceive of matter at rest. When you tell me that motion is not essential to matter but necessary to it, you try to cheat me with words which would be easier to refute if there was a little more sense in them. For either the motion of matter arises from the matter itself and is therefore essential to it; or it arises from an external cause and is not necessary to the matter, because the motive cause acts upon it; we have got back to our original difficulty.

The chief source of human error is to be found in general and abstract ideas; the jargon of metaphysics has never led to the discovery of any single truth, and it has filled philosophy with absurdities of which we are ashamed as soon as we strip them of their long words. Tell me, my friend, when they talk to you of a blind force diffused throughout nature, do they present any real idea to your mind? They think they are saying something by these vague expressions—universal force, essential motion—but they are saying nothing at all. The idea of motion is nothing more than the idea of transference from place to place; there is no motion without direction; for no individual can move all ways at once. In what direction then does matter move of necessity? Has the whole body of matter a uniform motion, or has each atom its own motion? According to the first idea the whole universe must form a solid and indivisible mass; according to the second it can only form a diffused and incoherent fluid, which would make the union of any two atoms impossible. What direction shall be taken by this motion common to all matter? Shall it be in a straight line, in a circle, or from above downwards, to the right or to the left? If each molecule has its own direction, what are the causes of all these directions and all these differences? If every molecule or atom only revolved on its own axis, nothing would ever leave its place and there would be no

225

transmitted motion, and even then this circular movement would require to follow some direction. To set matter in motion by an abstraction is to utter words without meaning, and to attribute to matter a given direction is to assume a determining cause. The more examples I take, the more causes I have to explain, without ever finding a common agent which controls them. Far from being able to picture to myself an entire absence of order in the fortuitous concurrence of elements, I cannot even imagine such a strife, and the chaos of the universe is less conceivable to me than its harmony. I can understand that the mechanism of the universe may not be intelligible to the human mind, but when a man sets to work to explain it, he must say what men can understand.

If matter in motion points me to a will, matter in motion according to fixed laws points me to an intelligence; that is the second article of my creed. To act, to compare, to choose, are the operations of an active, thinking being; so this being exists. Where do you find him existing, you will say? Not merely in the revolving heavens, nor in the sun which gives us light, not in myself alone, but in the sheep that grazes, the bird that flies, the stone that falls, and the leaf blown by the wind.

I judge of the order of the world, although I know nothing of its purpose, for to judge of this order it is enough for me to compare the parts one with another, to study their co-operation, their relations, and to observe their united action. I know not why the universe exists, but I see continually how it is changed; I never fail to perceive the close connection by which the entities of which it consists lend their aid one to another. I am like a man who sees the works of a watch for the first time; he is never weary of admiring the mechanism, though he does not know the use of the instrument and has never seen its face. I do not know what this is for, says he, but I see that each part of it is fitted to the rest, I admire the workman in the details of his work, and I am quite certain that all these wheels only work together in this fashion for some common end which I cannot perceive.

Let us compare the special ends, the means, the ordered relations of every kind, then let us listen to the inner voice of feeling; what healthy mind can reject its evidence? Unless the eyes are blinded by prejudices, can they fail to see that the visible order of the universe proclaims a supreme intelligence? What sophisms must be brought together before we fail to understand the harmony of existence and the wonderful co-operation of every part for the maintenance of the rest? Say what you will of combinations and probabilities; what do you gain by reducing me to silence if you cannot gain my consent? And how can you rob me of the spontaneous feeling which, in spite of myself, continually gives you the lie? If organised bodies had come together fortuitously in all sorts of ways before assuming settled forms, if stomachs are made without mouths, feet without heads, hands without arms, imperfect organs of every kind which died because they could not preserve their life, why do none of these imperfect attempts now meet our eyes; why has nature at length prescribed laws to herself which she did not at first recognise? I must not be surprised if that which is possible should happen, and if the improbability of the event is compensated for by the number of the attempts. I grant this; yet if any one told me that printed characters scattered broadcast had produced the Aeneid all complete, I would not condescend to take a single step to verify this falsehood. You will tell me I am forgetting the multitude of attempts. But how many such attempts must I assume to bring the combination within the bounds of probability? For my own part the only possible assumption is that the chances are infinity to one that the product is not the work of chance. In addition to this, chance combinations yield nothing but products of the same nature as the elements combined, so that life and organisation will not be produced by a flow of atoms, and a chemist when making his compounds will never give them thought and feeling in his crucible. [Footnote: Could one believe, if one had not seen it, that human absurdity could go so far? Amatus Lusitanus asserts that he saw a little man an inch long enclosed in a glass, which Julius Camillus, like a second Prometheus, had made by alchemy. Paracelsis (De natura rerum) teaches the method of making these tiny men, and he maintains that the pygmies, fauns, satyrs, and nymphs have been made by chemistry. Indeed I cannot see that there is anything more to be done, to establish the possibility of these facts, unless it is to assert that organic matter resists the heat of fire and that its molecules can preserve their life in the hottest furnace.]

I was surprised and almost shocked when I read Neuwentit. How could this man desire to make a book out of the wonders of nature, wonders which show the wisdom of the author of nature? His book would have been as large as the world itself before he had exhausted his subject, and as soon as we attempt to give details, that greatest wonder of all, the concord and harmony of the whole, escapes us. The mere generation of living organic bodies is the despair of the human mind; the insurmountable barrier raised by nature between the various species, so that they should not mix with one another, is the clearest proof of her intention. She is not content to have established order, she has taken adequate measures to prevent the disturbance of that order.

There is not a being in the universe which may not be regarded as in some respects the common centre of all, around which they are grouped, so that they are all reciprocally end and means in relation to each other. The mind is confused and lost amid these innumerable relations, not one of which is itself confused or lost in the crowd. What absurd assumptions are required to deduce all this harmony from the blind mechanism of matter set in motion by chance! In vain do those who deny the unity of intention manifested in the relations of all the parts of this great whole, in vain do they conceal their nonsense under abstractions, co-ordinations, general principles, symbolic expressions; whatever they do I find it impossible to conceive of a system of entities so firmly ordered unless I believe in an intelligence that orders them. It is not in my power to believe that passive and dead matter can have brought forth living and feeling beings, that blind chance has brought forth intelligent beings, that that which does not think has brought forth thinking beings.

I believe, therefore, that the world is governed by a wise and powerful will; I see it or rather I feel it, and it is a great thing to know this. But has this same world always existed, or has it been created? Is there one source of all things? Are there two or many? What is their nature? I know not; and what concern is it of mine? When these things become of importance to me I will try to learn them; till then I abjure these idle speculations, which may trouble my peace, but cannot affect my conduct nor be comprehended by my reason.

Recollect that I am not preaching my own opinion but explaining it. Whether matter is eternal or created, whether its origin is passive or not, it is still certain that the whole is one, and that it proclaims a single intelligence; for I see nothing that is not part of the same ordered system, nothing which does not co-operate to the same end, namely, the conservation of all within the established order. This being who wills and can perform his will, this being active through his own power, this being, whoever he may be, who moves the universe and orders all things, is what I call God. To this name I add the ideas of intelligence, power, will, which I have brought together, and that of kindness which is their necessary consequence; but for all this I know no more of the being to which I ascribe them. He hides himself alike from my senses and my understanding; the more I think of him, the more perplexed I am; I know full well that he exists, and that he exists of himself alone; I know that my existence depends on his, and that everything I know depends upon him also. I see God everywhere in his works; I feel him within myself; I behold him all around me; but if I try to ponder him himself, if I try to find out where he is, what he is, what is his substance, he escapes me and my troubled spirit finds nothing.

Convinced of my unfitness, I shall never argue about the nature of God unless I am driven to it by the feeling of his relations with myself. Such reasonings are always rash; a wise man should venture on them with trembling, he should be certain that he can never sound their abysses; for the most insolent attitude towards God is not to abstain from thinking of him, but to think evil of him.

After the discovery of such of his attributes as enable me to conceive of his existence, I return to myself, and I try to discover what is my place in the order of things which he governs, and I can myself examine. At once, and beyond possibility of doubt, I discover my species; for by my own will and the instruments I can control to carry out my will, I have more power to act upon all bodies about me, either to make use of or to avoid their action at my pleasure, than any of them has power to act upon me against my will by mere physical impulsion; and through my intelligence I am the only one who can examine all the rest. What being here below, except man, can observe others, measure, calculate, forecast their motions, their effects, and unite, so to speak, the feeling of a common existence with that of his individual existence? What is there so absurd in the thought that all things are made for me, when I alone can relate all things to myself?

It is true, therefore, that man is lord of the earth on which he dwells; for not only does he tame all the beasts, not only does he control its elements through his industry; but he alone knows how to control it; by contemplation he takes possession of the stars which he cannot approach. Show me any other creature on earth who can make a fire and who can behold with admiration the sun. What! can I observe and know all creatures and their relations; can I feel what is meant by order, beauty, and virtue; can I consider the universe and raise myself towards the hand that guides it; can I love good and perform it; and should I then liken myself to the beasts? Wretched soul, it is your gloomy philosophy which makes you like the beasts; or rather in vain do you seek to degrade yourself; your genius belies your principles, your kindly heart belies your doctrines, and even the abuse of your powers proves their excellence in your own despite.

For myself, I am not pledged to the support of any system. I am a plain and honest man, one who is not carried away by party spirit, one who has no ambition to be head of a sect; I am content with the place where God has set me; I see nothing, next to God himself, which is better than my species; and if I had to choose my place in the order of creation, what more could I choose than to be a man!

I am not puffed up by this thought, I am deeply moved by it; for this state was no choice of mine, it was not due to the deserts of a creature who as yet did not exist. Can I behold myself thus distinguished without congratulating myself on this post of honour, without blessing the hand which bestowed it? The first return to self has given birth to a feeling of gratitude and thankfulness to the author of my species, and this feeling calls forth my first homage to the beneficent Godhead. I worship his Almighty power and my heart acknowledges his mercies. Is it not a natural consequence of our self-love to honour our protector and to love our benefactor?

But when, in my desire to discover my own place within my species, I consider its different ranks and the men who fill them, where am I now? What a sight meets my eyes! Where is now the order I perceived? Nature showed me a scene of harmony and proportion; the human race shows me nothing but confusion and disorder. The elements agree together; men are in a state of chaos. The beasts are happy; their king alone is wretched. O Wisdom, where are thy laws? O Providence, is this thy rule over the world? Merciful God, where is thy Power? I behold the earth, and there is evil upon it.

Would you believe it, dear friend, from these gloomy thoughts and apparent contradictions, there was shaped in my mind the sublime idea of the soul, which all my seeking had hitherto failed to discover? While I meditated upon man's nature, I seemed to discover two distinct principles in it; one of them raised him to the study of the eternal truths, to the love of justice, and of true morality, to the regions of the world of thought, which the wise delight to contemplate; the other led him downwards to himself, made him the slave of his senses, of the passions which are their instruments, and thus opposed everything suggested to him by the former principle. When I felt myself carried away, distracted by these conflicting motives, I said, No; man is not one; I will and I will not; I feel myself at once a slave and a free man; I perceive what is right, I love it, and I do what is wrong; I am active when I listen to the voice of reason; I am passive when I am carried away by my passions; and when I yield, my worst suffering is the knowledge that I might have resisted.

Young man, hear me with confidence. I will always be honest with you. If conscience is the creature of prejudice, I am certainly wrong, and there is no such thing as a proof of morality; but if to put oneself first is an inclination natural to man, and if the first sentiment of justice is moreover inborn in the human heart, let those who say man is a simple creature remove these contradictions and I will grant that there is but one substance.

You will note that by this term 'substance' I understand generally the being endowed with some primitive quality, apart from all special and secondary modifications. If then all the primitive qualities which are known to us can be united in one and the same being, we should only acknowledge one substance; but if there are qualities which are mutually exclusive, there are as many different substances as there are such exclusions. You will think this over; for my own part, whatever Locke may say, it is enough for me to recognise matter as having merely extension and divisibility to convince myself that it cannot think, and if a philosopher tells me that trees feel and rocks think [Footnote: It seems to me that modern philosophy, far from saying that rocks think, has discovered that men do not think. It perceives nothing more in nature than sensitive beings; and the only difference it finds between a man and a stone is that a man is a sensitive being which experiences sensations, and a stone is a sensitive being which does not experience sensations. But if it is true that all matter feels, where shall I find the sensitive unit, the individual ego? Shall it be in each molecule of matter or in bodies as aggregates of molecules? Shall I place this unity in fluids and solids alike, in compounds and in elements? You tell me nature consists of individuals. But what are these individuals? Is that stone an individual or an aggregate of individuals? Is it a single sensitive being, or are there as many beings in it as there are grains of sand? If every elementary atom is a sensitive being, how shall I conceive of that intimate communication by which one feels within the other, so that their two egos are blended in one? Attraction may be a law of nature whose mystery is unknown to us; but at least we conceive that there is nothing in attraction acting in proportion to mass which is contrary to extension and divisibility. Can you conceive of sensation in the same way? The sensitive parts have extension, but the sensitive being is one and indivisible; he cannot be cut in two, he is a whole or he is nothing; therefore the sensitive being is not a material body. I know not how our materialists understand it, but it seems to me that the same difficulties which have led them to reject thought, should have made them also reject feeling; and I see no reason why, when the first step has been taken, they should not take the second too; what more would it cost them? Since they are certain they do not think, why do they dare to affirm that they feel?] in vain will he perplex me with his cunning arguments; I merely regard him as a dishonest sophist, who prefers to say that stones have feeling rather than that men have souls.

Suppose a deaf man denies the existence of sounds because he has never heard them. I put before his eyes a stringed instrument and cause it to sound in unison by means of another instrument concealed from him; the deaf man sees the chord vibrate. I tell him, "The sound makes it do that." "Not at all," says he, "the string itself is the cause of the vibration; to vibrate in that way is a quality common to all bodies." "Then show me this vibration in other bodies," I answer, "or at least show me its cause in this string." "I cannot," replies the deaf man; "but because I do not understand how that string vibrates why should I try to explain it by means of your sounds, of which I have not the least idea? It is explaining one obscure fact by means of a cause still more obscure. Make me perceive your sounds; or I say there are no such things."

The more I consider thought and the nature of the human mind, the more likeness I find between the arguments of the materialists and those of the deaf man. Indeed, they are deaf to the inner voice which cries aloud to them, in a tone which can hardly be mistaken. A machine does not think, there is neither movement nor form which can produce reflection; something within thee tries to break the bands which confine it; space is not thy measure, the whole universe does not suffice to contain thee; thy sentiments, thy desires, thy anxiety, thy pride itself, have another origin than this small body in which thou art imprisoned.

No material creature is in itself active, and I am active. In vain do you argue this point with me; I feel it, and it is this feeling which speaks to me more forcibly than the reason which disputes it. I have a body which is acted upon by other bodies, and it acts in turn upon them; there is no doubt about this reciprocal action; but my will is independent of my senses; I consent or I resist; I yield or I win the victory, and I know very well in myself when I have done what I wanted and when I have merely given way to my passions. I have always the power to will, but not always the strength to do what I will. When I yield to temptation I surrender myself to the action of external objects. When I blame myself for this weakness, I listen to my own will alone; I am a slave in my vices, a free man in my remorse; the feeling of freedom is never effaced in me but when I myself do wrong, and when I at length prevent the voice of the soul from protesting against the authority of the body.

I am only aware of will through the consciousness of my own will, and intelligence is no better known to me. When you ask me what is the cause which determines my will, it is my turn to ask what cause determines my judgment; for it is plain that these two causes are but one; and if you understand clearly that man is active in his judgments, that his intelligence is only the power to compare and judge, you will see that his freedom is only a similar power or one derived from this; he chooses between good and evil as he judges between truth and falsehood; if his judgment is at fault, he chooses amiss. What then is the cause that determines his will? It is his judgment. And what is the cause that determines his judgment? It is his intelligence, his power of judging; the determining cause is in himself. Beyond that, I understand nothing.

No doubt I am not free not to desire my own welfare, I am not free to desire my own hurt; but my freedom consists in this very thing, that I can will what is for my own good, or what I esteem as such, without any external compulsion. Does it follow that I am not my own master because I cannot be other than myself?

The motive power of all action is in the will of a free creature; we can go no farther. It is not the word freedom that is meaningless, but the word necessity. To suppose some action which is not the effect of an active motive power is indeed to suppose effects without cause, to reason in a vicious circle. Either there is no original impulse, or every original impulse has no antecedent cause, and there is no will properly so-called without freedom. Man is therefore free to act, and as such he is animated by an immaterial substance; that is the third article of my creed. From these three you will easily deduce the rest, so that I need not enumerate them.

If man is at once active and free, he acts of his own accord; what he does freely is no part of the system marked out by Providence and it cannot be imputed to Providence. Providence does not will the evil that man does when he misuses the freedom given to him; neither does Providence prevent him doing it, either because the wrong done by so feeble a creature is as nothing in its eyes, or because it could not prevent it without doing a greater wrong and degrading his nature. Providence has made him free that he may choose the good and refuse the evil. It has made him capable of this choice if he uses rightly the faculties bestowed upon him, but it has so strictly limited his powers that the misuse of his freedom cannot disturb the general order. The evil that man does reacts upon himself without affecting the system of the world, without preventing the preservation of the human species in spite of itself. To complain that God does not prevent us from doing wrong is to complain because he has made man of so excellent a nature, that he has endowed his actions with that morality by which they are ennobled, that he has made virtue man's birthright. Supreme happiness consists in self-content; that we may gain this self-content we are placed upon this earth and endowed with freedom, we are tempted by our passions and restrained by conscience. What more could divine power itself have done on our behalf? Could it have made our nature a contradiction, and have given the prize of well-doing to one who was incapable of evil? To prevent a man from wickedness, should Providence have restricted him to instinct and made him a fool? Not so, O God of my soul, I will never reproach thee that thou hast created me in thine own image, that I may be free and good and happy like my Maker!

It is the abuse of our powers that makes us unhappy and wicked. Our cares, our sorrows, our sufferings are of our own making. Moral ills are undoubtedly the work of man, and physical ills would be nothing but for our vices which have made us liable to them. Has not nature made us feel our needs as a means to our preservation! Is not bodily suffering a sign that the machine is out of order and needs attention? Death.... Do not the wicked poison their own life and ours? Who would wish to live for ever? Death is the cure for the evils you bring upon yourself; nature would not have you suffer perpetually. How few sufferings are felt by man living in a state of primitive simplicity! His life is almost entirely free from suffering and from passion; he neither fears nor feels death; if he feels it, his sufferings make him desire it; henceforth it is no evil in his eyes. If we were but content to be ourselves we should have no cause to complain of our lot; but in the search for an imaginary good we find a thousand real ills. He who cannot bear a little pain must expect to suffer greatly. If a man injures his constitution by dissipation, you try to cure him with medicine; the ill he fears is added to the ill he feels; the thought of death makes it horrible and hastens its approach; the more we seek to escape from it, the more we are aware of it; and we go through life in the fear of death, blaming nature for the evils we have inflicted on ourselves by our neglect of her laws.

O Man! seek no further for the author of evil; thou art he. There is no evil but the evil you do or the evil you suffer, and both come from yourself. Evil in general can only spring from disorder, and in the order of the world I find a never failing system. Evil in particular cases exists only in the mind of those who experience it; and this feeling is not the gift of nature, but the work of man himself. Pain has little power over those who, having thought little, look neither before nor after. Take away our fatal progress, take away our faults and our vices, take away man's handiwork, and all is well.

Where all is well, there is no such thing as injustice. Justice and goodness are inseparable; now goodness is the necessary result of boundless power and of that self-love which is innate in all sentient beings. The omnipotent projects himself, so to speak, into the being of his creatures. Creation and preservation are the everlasting work of power; it does not act on that which has no existence; God is not the God of the dead; he could not harm and destroy without injury to himself. The omnipotent can only will what is good. [Footnote: The ancients were right when they called the supreme God Optimus Maximus, but it would have been better to say Maximus Optimus, for his goodness springs from his power, he is good because he is great.] Therefore he who is supremely good, because he is supremely powerful, must also be supremely just, otherwise he would contradict himself; for that love of order which creates order we call goodness and that love of order which preserves order we call justice.

Men say God owes nothing to his creatures. I think he owes them all he promised when he gave them their being. Now to give them the idea of something good and to make them feel the need of it, is to promise it to them. The more closely I study myself, the more carefully I consider, the more plainly do I read these words, "Be just and you will be happy." It is not so, however, in the present condition of things, the wicked prospers and the oppression of the righteous continues. Observe how angry we are when this expectation is disappointed. Conscience revolts and murmurs against her Creator; she exclaims with cries and groans, "Thou hast deceived me."

"I have deceived thee, rash soul! Who told thee this? Is thy soul destroyed? Hast thou ceased to exist? O Brutus! O my son! let there be no stain upon the close of thy noble life; do not abandon thy hope and thy glory with thy corpse upon the plains of Philippi. Why dost thou say, 'Virtue is naught,' when thou art about to enjoy the reward of virtue? Thou art about to die! Nay, thou shalt live, and thus my promise is fulfilled."

One might judge from the complaints of impatient men that God owes them the reward before they have deserved it, that he is bound to pay for virtue in advance. Oh! let us first be good and then we shall be happy. Let us not claim the prize before we have won it, nor demand our wages before we have finished our work. "It is not in the lists that we crown the victors in the sacred games," says Plutarch, "it is when they have finished their course."

If the soul is immaterial, it may survive the body; and if it so survives, Providence is justified. Had I no other proof of the immaterial nature of the soul, the triumph of the wicked and the oppression of the righteous in this world would be enough to convince me. I should seek to resolve so appalling a discord in the universal harmony. I should say to myself, "All is not over with life, everything finds its place at death." I should still have to answer the question, "What becomes of man when all we know of him through our senses has vanished?" This question no longer presents any difficulty to me when I admit the two substances. It is easy to understand that what is imperceptible to those senses escapes me, during my bodily life, when I perceive through my senses only. When the union of soul and body is destroyed, I think one may be dissolved and the other may be preserved. Why should the destruction of the one imply the destruction of the other? On the contrary, so unlike in their nature, they were during their union in a highly unstable condition, and when this union comes to an end they both return to their natural state; the active vital substance regains all the force which it expended to set in motion the passive dead substance. Alas! my vices make me only too well aware that man is but half alive during this life; the life of the soul only begins with the death of the body.

But what is that life? Is the soul of man in its nature immortal? I know not. My finite understanding cannot hold the infinite; what is called eternity eludes my grasp. What can I assert or deny, how can I reason with regard to what I cannot conceive? I believe that the soul survives the body for the maintenance of order; who knows if this is enough to make it eternal? However, I know that the body is worn out and destroyed by the division of its parts, but I cannot conceive a similar destruction of the conscious nature, and as I cannot imagine how it can die, I presume that it does not die. As this assumption is consoling and in itself not unreasonable, why should I fear to accept it?

I am aware of my soul; it is known to me in feeling and in thought; I know what it is without knowing its essence; I cannot reason about ideas which are unknown to me. What I do know is this, that my personal identity depends upon memory, and that to be indeed the same self I must remember that I have existed. Now after death I could not recall what I was when alive unless I also remembered what I felt and therefore what I did; and I have no doubt that this remembrance will one day form the happiness of the good and the torment of the bad. In this world our inner consciousness is absorbed by the crowd of eager passions which cheat remorse. The humiliation and disgrace involved in the practice of virtue do not permit us to realise its charm. But when, freed from the illusions of the bodily senses, we behold with joy the supreme Being and the eternal truths which flow from him; when all the powers of our soul are alive to the beauty of order and we are wholly occupied in comparing what we have done with what we ought to have done, then it is that the voice of conscience will regain its strength and sway; then it is that the pure delight which springs from self-content, and the sharp regret for our own degradation of that self, will decide by means of overpowering feeling what shall be the fate which each has prepared for himself. My good friend, do not ask me whether there are other sources of happiness or suffering; I cannot tell; that which my fancy pictures is enough to console me in this life and to bid me look for a life to come. I do not say the good will be rewarded, for what greater good can a truly good being expect than to exist in accordance with his nature? But I do assert that the good will be happy, because their maker, the author of all justice, who has made them capable of feeling, has not made them that they may suffer; moreover, they have not abused their freedom upon earth and they have not changed their fate through any fault of their own; yet they have suffered in this life and it will be made up to them in the life to come. This feeling relies not so much on man's deserts as on the idea of good which seems to me inseparable from the divine essence. I only assume that the laws of order are constant and that God is true to himself.

Do not ask me whether the torments of the wicked will endure for ever, whether the goodness of their creator can condemn them to the eternal suffering; again, I cannot tell, and I have no empty curiosity for the investigation of useless problems. How does the fate of the wicked concern me? I take little interest in it. All the same I find it hard to believe that they will be condemned to everlasting torments. If the supreme justice calls for vengeance, it claims it in this life. The nations of the world with their errors are its ministers. Justice uses self-inflicted ills to punish the crimes which have deserved them. It is in your own insatiable souls, devoured by envy, greed, and ambition, it is in the midst of your false prosperity, that the avenging passions find the due reward of your crimes. What need to seek a hell in the future life? It is here in the breast of the wicked.

When our fleeting needs are over, and our mad desires are at rest, there should also be an end of our passions and our crimes. Can pure spirits be capable of any perversity? Having need of nothing, why should they be wicked? If they are free from our gross senses, if their happiness consists in the contemplation of other beings, they can only desire what is good; and he who ceases to be bad can never be miserable. This is what I am inclined to think though I have not been at the pains to come to any decision. O God, merciful and good, whatever thy decrees may be I adore them; if thou shouldst commit the wicked to everlasting punishment, I abandon my feeble reason to thy justice; but if the remorse of these wretched beings should in the course of time be extinguished, if their sufferings should come to an end, and if the same peace shall one day be the lot of all mankind, I give thanks to thee for this. Is not the wicked my brother? How often have I been tempted to be like him? Let him be delivered from his misery and freed from the spirit of hatred that accompanied it; let him be as happy as I myself; his happiness, far from arousing my jealousy, will only increase my own.

Thus it is that, in the contemplation of God in his works, and in the study of such of his attributes as it concerned me to know, I have slowly grasped and developed the idea, at first partial and imperfect, which I have formed of this Infinite Being. But if this idea has become nobler and greater it is also more suited to the human reason. As I approach in spirit the eternal light, I am confused and dazzled by its glory, and compelled to abandon all the earthly notions which helped me to picture it to myself. God is no longer corporeal and sensible; the supreme mind which rules the world is no longer the world itself; in vain do I strive to grasp his inconceivable essence. When I think that it is he that gives life and movement to the living and moving substance which controls all living bodies; when I hear it said that my soul is spiritual and that God is a spirit, I revolt against this abasement of the divine essence; as if God and my soul were of one and the same nature! As if God were not the one and only absolute being, the only really active, feeling, thinking, willing being, from whom we derive our thought, feeling, motion, will, our freedom and our very existence! We are free because he wills our freedom, and his inexplicable substance is to our souls what our souls are to our bodies. I know not whether he has created matter, body, soul, the world itself. The idea of creation confounds me and eludes my grasp; so far as I can conceive of it I believe it; but I know that he has formed the universe and all that is, that he has made and ordered all things. No doubt God is eternal; but can my mind grasp the idea of eternity? Why should I cheat myself with meaningless words? This is what I do understand; before things were—God was; he will be when they are no more, and if all things come to an end he will still endure. That a being beyond my comprehension should give life to other beings, this is merely difficult and beyond my understanding; but that Being and Nothing should be convertible terms, this is indeed a palpable contradiction, an evident absurdity.

God is intelligent, but how? Man is intelligent when he reasons, but the Supreme Intelligence does not need to reason; there is neither premise nor conclusion for him, there is not even a proposition. The Supreme Intelligence is wholly intuitive, it sees what is and what shall be; all truths are one for it, as all places are but one point and all time but one moment. Man's power makes use of means, the divine power is self-active. God can because he wills; his will is his power. God is good; this is certain; but man finds his happiness in the welfare of his kind. God's happiness consists in the love of order; for it is through order that he maintains what is, and unites each part in the whole. God is just; of this I am sure, it is a consequence of his goodness; man's injustice is not God's work, but his own; that moral justice which seems to the philosophers a presumption against Providence, is to me a proof of its existence. But man's justice consists in giving to each his due; God's justice consists in demanding from each of us an account of that which he has given us.

If I have succeeded in discerning these attributes of which I have no absolute idea, it is in the form of unavoidable deductions, and by the right use of my reason; but I affirm them without understanding them, and at bottom that is no affirmation at all. In vain do I say, God is thus, I feel it, I experience it, none the more do I understand how God can be thus.

In a word: the more I strive to envisage his infinite essence the less do I comprehend it; but it is, and that is enough for me; the less I understand, the more I adore. I abase myself, saying, "Being of beings, I am because thou art; to fix my thoughts on thee is to ascend to the source of my being. The best use I can make of my reason is to resign it before thee; my mind delights, my weakness rejoices, to feel myself overwhelmed by thy greatness."

Having thus deduced from the perception of objects of sense and from my inner consciousness, which leads me to judge of causes by my native reason, the principal truths which I require to know, I must now seek such principles of conduct as I can draw from them, and such rules as I must lay down for my guidance in the fulfilment of my destiny in this world, according to the purpose of my Maker. Still following the same method, I do not derive these rules from the principles of the higher philosophy, I find them in the depths of my heart, traced by nature in characters which nothing can efface. I need only consult myself with regard to what I wish to do; what I feel to be right is right, what I feel to be wrong is wrong; conscience is the best casuist; and it is only when we haggle with conscience that we have recourse to the subtleties of argument. Our first duty is towards ourself; yet how often does the voice of others tell us that in seeking our good at the expense of others we are doing ill? We think we are following the guidance of nature, and we are resisting it; we listen to what she says to our senses, and we neglect what she says to our heart; the active being obeys, the passive commands. Conscience is the voice of the soul, the passions are the voice of the body. It is strange that these voices often contradict each other? And then to which should we give heed? Too often does reason deceive us; we have only too good a right to doubt her; but conscience never deceives us; she is the true guide of man; it is to the soul what instinct is to the body, [Footnote: Modern philosophy, which only admits what it can understand, is careful not to admit this obscure power called instinct which seems to guide the animals to some end without any acquired experience. Instinct, according to some of our wise philosophers, is only a secret habit of reflection, acquired by reflection; and from the way in which they explain this development one ought to suppose that children reflect more than grown-up people: a paradox strange enough to be worth examining. Without entering upon this discussion I must ask what name I shall give to the eagerness with which my dog makes war on the moles he does not eat, or to the patience with which he sometimes watches them for hours and the skill with which he seizes them, throws them to a distance from their earth as soon as they emerge, and then kills them and leaves them. Yet no one has trained him to this sport, nor even told him there were such things as moles. Again, I ask, and this is a more important question, why, when I threatened this same dog for the first time, why did he throw himself on the ground with his paws folded, in such a suppliant attitude .....calculated to touch me, a position which he would have maintained if, without being touched by it, I had continued to beat him in that position? What! Had my dog, little more than a puppy, acquired moral ideas? Did he know the meaning of mercy and generosity? By what acquired knowledge did he seek to appease my wrath by yielding to my discretion? Every dog in the world does almost the same thing in similar circumstances, and I am asserting nothing but what any one can verify for himself. Will the philosophers, who so scornfully reject instinct, kindly explain this fact by the mere play of sensations and experience which they assume we have acquired? Let them give an account of it which will satisfy any sensible man; in that case I have nothing further to urge, and I will say no more of instinct.] he who obeys his conscience is following nature and he need not fear that he will go astray. This is a matter of great importance, continued my benefactor, seeing that I was about to interrupt him; let me stop awhile to explain it more fully.

The morality of our actions consists entirely in the judgments we ourselves form with regard to them. If good is good, it must be good in the depth of our heart as well as in our actions; and the first reward of justice is the consciousness that we are acting justly. If moral goodness is in accordance with our nature, man can only be healthy in mind and body when he is good. If it is not so, and if man is by nature evil, he cannot cease to be evil without corrupting his nature, and goodness in him is a crime against nature. If he is made to do harm to his fellow-creatures, as the wolf is made to devour his prey, a humane man would be as depraved a creature as a pitiful wolf; and virtue alone would cause remorse.

My young friend, let us look within, let us set aside all personal prejudices and see whither our inclinations lead us. Do we take more pleasure in the sight of the sufferings of others or their joys? Is it pleasanter to do a kind action or an unkind action, and which leaves the more delightful memory behind it? Why do you enjoy the theatre? Do you delight in the crimes you behold? Do you weep over the punishment which overtakes the criminal? They say we are indifferent to everything but self-interest; yet we find our consolation in our sufferings in the charms of friendship and humanity, and even in our pleasures we should be too lonely and miserable if we had no one to share them with us. If there is no such thing as morality in man's heart, what is the source of his rapturous admiration of noble deeds, his passionate devotion to great men? What connection is there between self-interest and this enthusiasm for virtue? Why should I choose to be Cato dying by his own hand, rather than Caesar in his triumphs? Take from our hearts this love of what is noble and you rob us of the joy of life. The mean-spirited man in whom these delicious feelings have been stifled among vile passions, who by thinking of no one but himself comes at last to love no one but himself, this man feels no raptures, his cold heart no longer throbs with joy, and his eyes no longer fill with the sweet tears of sympathy, he delights in nothing; the wretch has neither life nor feeling, he is already dead.

There are many bad men in this world, but there are few of these dead souls, alive only to self-interest, and insensible to all that is right and good. We only delight in injustice so long as it is to our own advantage; in every other case we wish the innocent to be protected. If we see some act of violence or injustice in town or country, our hearts are at once stirred to their depths by an instinctive anger and wrath, which bids us go to the help of the oppressed; but we are restrained by a stronger duty, and the law deprives us of our right to protect the innocent. On the other hand, if some deed of mercy or generosity meets our eye, what reverence and love does it inspire! Do we not say to ourselves, "I should like to have done that myself"? What does it matter to us that two thousand years ago a man was just or unjust? and yet we take the same interest in ancient history as if it happened yesterday. What are the crimes of Cataline to me? I shall not be his victim. Why then have I the same horror of his crimes as if he were living now? We do not hate the wicked merely because of the harm they do to ourselves, but because they are wicked. Not only do we wish to be happy ourselves, we wish others to be happy too, and if this happiness does not interfere with our own happiness, it increases it. In conclusion, whether we will or not, we pity the unfortunate; when we see their suffering we suffer too. Even the most depraved are not wholly without this instinct, and it often leads them to self-contradiction. The highwayman who robs the traveller, clothes the nakedness of the poor; the fiercest murderer supports a fainting man.

Men speak of the voice of remorse, the secret punishment of hidden crimes, by which such are often brought to light. Alas! who does not know its unwelcome voice? We speak from experience, and we would gladly stifle this imperious feeling which causes us such agony. Let us obey the call of nature; we shall see that her yoke is easy and that when we give heed to her voice we find a joy in the answer of a good conscience. The wicked fears and flees from her; he delights to escape from himself; his anxious eyes look around him for some object of diversion; without bitter satire and rude mockery he would always be sorrowful; the scornful laugh is his one pleasure. Not so the just man, who finds his peace within himself; there is joy not malice in his laughter, a joy which springs from his own heart; he is as cheerful alone as in company, his satisfaction does not depend on those who approach him; it includes them.

Cast your eyes over every nation of the world; peruse every volume of its history; in the midst of all these strange and cruel forms of worship, among this amazing variety of manners and customs, you will everywhere find the same ideas of right and justice; everywhere the same principles of morality, the same ideas of good and evil. The old paganism gave birth to abominable gods who would have been punished as scoundrels here below, gods who merely offered, as a picture of supreme happiness, crimes to be committed and lust to be gratified. But in vain did vice descend from the abode of the gods armed with their sacred authority; the moral instinct refused to admit it into the heart of man. While the debaucheries of Jupiter were celebrated, the continence of Xenocrates was revered; the chaste Lucrece adored the shameless Venus; the bold Roman offered sacrifices to Fear; he invoked the god who mutilated his father, and he died without a murmur at the hand of his own father. The most unworthy gods were worshipped by the noblest men. The sacred voice of nature was stronger than the voice of the gods, and won reverence upon earth; it seemed to relegate guilt and the guilty alike to heaven.

There is therefore at the bottom of our hearts an innate principle of justice and virtue, by which, in spite of our maxims, we judge our own actions or those of others to be good or evil; and it is this principle that I call conscience.

But at this word I hear the murmurs of all the wise men so-called. Childish errors, prejudices of our upbringing, they exclaim in concert! There is nothing in the human mind but what it has gained by experience; and we judge everything solely by means of the ideas we have acquired. They go further; they even venture to reject the clear and universal agreement of all peoples, and to set against this striking unanimity in the judgment of mankind, they seek out some obscure exception known to themselves alone; as if the whole trend of nature were rendered null by the depravity of a single nation, and as if the existence of monstrosities made an end of species. But to what purpose does the sceptic Montaigne strive himself to unearth in some obscure corner of the world a custom which is contrary to the ideas of justice? To what purpose does he credit the most untrustworthy travellers, while he refuses to believe the greatest writers? A few strange and doubtful customs, based on local causes, unknown to us; shall these destroy a general inference based on the agreement of all the nations of the earth, differing from each other in all else, but agreed in this? O Montaigne, you pride yourself on your truth and honesty; be sincere and truthful, if a philosopher can be so, and tell me if there is any country upon earth where it is a crime to keep one's plighted word, to be merciful, helpful, and generous, where the good man is scorned, and the traitor is held in honour.

Self-interest, so they say, induces each of us to agree for the common good. But how is it that the good man consents to this to his own hurt? Does a man go to death from self-interest? No doubt each man acts for his own good, but if there is no such thing as moral good to be taken into consideration, self-interest will only enable you to account for the deeds of the wicked; possibly you will not attempt to do more. A philosophy which could find no place for good deeds would be too detestable; you would find yourself compelled either to find some mean purpose, some wicked motive, or to abuse Socrates and slander Regulus. If such doctrines ever took root among us, the voice of nature, together with the voice of reason, would constantly protest against them, till no adherent of such teaching could plead an honest excuse for his partisanship.

It is no part of my scheme to enter at present into metaphysical discussions which neither you nor I can understand, discussions which really lead nowhere. I have told you already that I do not wish to philosophise with you, but to help you to consult your own heart. If all the philosophers in the world should prove that I am wrong, and you feel that I am right, that is all I ask.

For this purpose it is enough to lead you to distinguish between our acquired ideas and our natural feelings; for feeling precedes knowledge; and since we do not learn to seek what is good for us and avoid what is bad for us, but get this desire from nature, in the same way the love of good and the hatred of evil are as natural to us as our self-love. The decrees of conscience are not judgments but feelings. Although all our ideas come from without, the feelings by which they are weighed are within us, and it is by these feelings alone that we perceive fitness or unfitness of things in relation to ourselves, which leads us to seek or shun these things.

To exist is to feel; our feeling is undoubtedly earlier than our intelligence, and we had feelings before we had ideas.[Footnote: In some respects ideas are feelings and feelings are ideas. Both terms are appropriate to any perception with which we are concerned, appropriate both to the object of that perception and to ourselves who are affected by it; it is merely the order in which we are affected which decides the appropriate term. When we are chiefly concerned with the object and only think of ourselves as it were by reflection, that is an idea; when, on the other hand, the impression received excites our chief attention and we only think in the second place of the object which caused it, it is a feeling.] Whatever may be the cause of our being, it has provided for our preservation by giving us feelings suited to our nature; and no one can deny that these at least are innate. These feelings, so far as the individual is concerned, are self-love, fear, pain, the dread of death, the desire for comfort. Again, if, as it is impossible to doubt, man is by nature sociable, or at least fitted to become sociable, he can only be so by means of other innate feelings, relative to his kind; for if only physical well-being were considered, men would certainly be scattered rather than brought together. But the motive power of conscience is derived from the moral system formed through this twofold relation to himself and to his fellow-men. To know good is not to love it; this knowledge is not innate in man; but as soon as his reason leads him to perceive it, his conscience impels him to love it; it is this feeling which is innate.

So I do not think, my young friend, that it is impossible to explain the immediate force of conscience as a result of our own nature, independent of reason itself. And even should it be impossible, it is unnecessary; for those who deny this principle, admitted and received by everybody else in the world, do not prove that there is no such thing; they are content to affirm, and when we affirm its existence we have quite as good grounds as they, while we have moreover the witness within us, the voice of conscience, which speaks on its own behalf. If the first beams of judgment dazzle us and confuse the objects we behold, let us wait till our feeble sight grows clear and strong, and in the light of reason we shall soon behold these very objects as nature has already showed them to us. Or rather let us be simpler and less pretentious; let us be content with the first feelings we experience in ourselves, since science always brings us back to these, unless it has led us astray.

Conscience! Conscience! Divine instinct, immortal voice from heaven; sure guide for a creature ignorant and finite indeed, yet intelligent and free; infallible judge of good and evil, making man like to God! In thee consists the excellence of man's nature and the morality of his actions; apart from thee, I find nothing in myself to raise me above the beasts—nothing but the sad privilege of wandering from one error to another, by the help of an unbridled understanding and a reason which knows no principle.

Thank heaven we have now got rid of all that alarming show of philosophy; we may be men without being scholars; now that we need not spend our life in the study of morality, we have found a less costly and surer guide through this vast labyrinth of human thought. But it is not enough to be aware that there is such a guide; we must know her and follow her. If she speaks to all hearts, how is it that so few give heed to her voice? She speaks to us in the language of nature, and everything leads us to forget that tongue. Conscience is timid, she loves peace and retirement; she is startled by noise and numbers; the prejudices from which she is said to arise are her worst enemies. She flees before them or she is silent; their noisy voices drown her words, so that she cannot get a hearing; fanaticism dares to counterfeit her voice and to inspire crimes in her name. She is discouraged by ill-treatment; she no longer speaks to us, no longer answers to our call; when she has been scorned so long, it is as hard to recall her as it was to banish her.

How often in the course of my inquiries have I grown weary of my own coldness of heart! How often have grief and weariness poured their poison into my first meditations and made them hateful to me! My barren heart yielded nothing but a feeble zeal and a lukewarm love of truth. I said to myself: Why should I strive to find what does not exist? Moral good is a dream, the pleasures of sense are the only real good. When once we have lost the taste for the pleasures of the soul, how hard it is to recover it! How much more difficult to acquire it if we have never possessed it! If there were any man so wretched as never to have done anything all his life long which he could remember with pleasure, and which would make him glad to have lived, that man would be incapable of self-knowledge, and for want of knowledge of goodness, of which his nature is capable, he would be constrained to remain in his wickedness and would be for ever miserable. But do you think there is any one man upon earth so depraved that he has never yielded to the temptation of well-doing? This temptation is so natural, so pleasant, that it is impossible always to resist it; and the thought of the pleasure it has once afforded is enough to recall it constantly to our memory. Unluckily it is hard at first to find satisfaction for it; we have any number of reasons for refusing to follow the inclinations of our heart; prudence, so called, restricts the heart within the limits of the self; a thousand efforts are needed to break these bonds. The joy of well-doing is the prize of having done well, and we must deserve the prize before we win it. There is nothing sweeter than virtue; but we do not know this till we have tried it. Like Proteus in the fable, she first assumes a thousand terrible shapes when we would embrace her, and only shows her true self to those who refuse to let her go.

Ever at strife between my natural feelings, which spoke of the common weal, and my reason, which spoke of self, I should have drifted through life in perpetual uncertainty, hating evil, loving good, and always at war with myself, if my heart had not received further light, if that truth which determined my opinions had not also settled my conduct, and set me at peace with myself. Reason alone is not a sufficient foundation for virtue; what solid ground can be found? Virtue we are told is love of order. But can this love prevail over my love for my own well-being, and ought it so to prevail? Let them give me clear and sufficient reason for this preference. Their so-called principle is in truth a mere playing with words; for I also say that vice is love of order, differently understood. Wherever there is feeling and intelligence, there is some sort of moral order. The difference is this: the good man orders his life with regard to all men; the wicked orders it for self alone. The latter centres all things round himself; the other measures his radius and remains on the circumference. Thus his place depends on the common centre, which is God, and on all the concentric circles which are His creatures. If there is no God, the wicked is right and the good man is nothing but a fool.

My child! May you one day feel what a burden is removed when, having fathomed the vanity of human thoughts and tasted the bitterness of passion, you find at length near at hand the path of wisdom, the prize of this life's labours, the source of that happiness which you despaired of. Every duty of natural law, which man's injustice had almost effaced from my heart, is engraven there, for the second time in the name of that eternal justice which lays these duties upon me and beholds my fulfilment of them. I feel myself merely the instrument of the Omnipotent, who wills what is good, who performs it, who will bring about my own good through the co-operation of my will with his own, and by the right use of my liberty. I acquiesce in the order he establishes, certain that one day I shall enjoy that order and find my happiness in it; for what sweeter joy is there than this, to feel oneself a part of a system where all is good? A prey to pain, I bear it in patience, remembering that it will soon be over, and that it results from a body which is not mine. If I do a good deed in secret, I know that it is seen, and my conduct in this life is a pledge of the life to come. When I suffer injustice, I say to myself, the Almighty who does all things well will reward me: my bodily needs, my poverty, make the idea of death less intolerable. There will be all the fewer bonds to be broken when my hour comes.

Why is my soul subjected to my senses, and imprisoned in this body by which it is enslaved and thwarted? I know not; have I entered into the counsels of the Almighty? But I may, without rashness, venture on a modest conjecture. I say to myself: If man's soul had remained in a state of freedom and innocence, what merit would there have been in loving and obeying the order he found established, an order which it would not have been to his advantage to disturb? He would be happy, no doubt, but his happiness would not attain to the highest point, the pride of virtue, and the witness of a good conscience within him; he would be but as the angels are, and no doubt the good man will be more than they. Bound to a mortal body, by bonds as strange as they are powerful, his care for the preservation of this body tempts the soul to think only of self, and gives it an interest opposed to the general order of things, which it is still capable of knowing and loving; then it is that the right use of his freedom becomes at once the merit and the reward; then it is that it prepares for itself unending happiness, by resisting its earthly passions and following its original direction.

If even in the lowly position in which we are placed during our present life our first impulses are always good, if all our vices are of our own making, why should we complain that they are our masters? Why should we blame the Creator for the ills we have ourselves created, and the enemies we ourselves have armed against us? Oh, let us leave man unspoilt; he will always find it easy to be good and he will always be happy without remorse. The guilty, who assert that they are driven to crime, are liars as well as evil-doers; how is it that they fail to perceive that the weakness they bewail is of their own making; that their earliest depravity was the result of their own will; that by dint of wishing to yield to temptations, they at length yield to them whether they will or no and make them irresistible? No doubt they can no longer avoid being weak and wicked, but they need not have become weak and wicked. Oh, how easy would it be to preserve control of ourselves and of our passions, even in this life, if with habits still unformed, with a mind beginning to expand, we were able to keep to such things as we ought to know, in order to value rightly what is unknown; if we really wished to learn, not that we might shine before the eyes of others, but that we might be wise and good in accordance with our nature, that we might be happy in the performance of our duty. This study seems tedious and painful to us, for we do not attempt it till we are already corrupted by vice and enslaved by our passions. Our judgments and our standards of worth are determined before we have the knowledge of good and evil; and then we measure all things by this false standard, and give nothing its true worth.

There is an age when the heart is still free, but eager, unquiet, greedy of a happiness which is still unknown, a happiness which it seeks in curiosity and doubt; deceived by the senses it settles at length upon the empty show of happiness and thinks it has found it where it is not. In my own case these illusions endured for a long time. Alas! too late did I become aware of them, and I have not succeeded in overcoming them altogether; they will last as long as this mortal body from which they arise. If they lead me astray, I am at least no longer deceived by them; I know them for what they are, and even when I give way to them, I despise myself; far from regarding them as the goal of my happiness, I behold in them an obstacle to it. I long for the time when, freed from the fetters of the body, I shall be myself, at one with myself, no longer torn in two, when I myself shall suffice for my own happiness. Meanwhile I am happy even in this life, for I make small account of all its evils, in which I regard myself as having little or no part, while all the real good that I can get out of this life depends on myself alone.

To raise myself so far as may be even now to this state of happiness, strength, and freedom, I exercise myself in lofty contemplation. I consider the order of the universe, not to explain it by any futile system, but to revere it without ceasing, to adore the wise Author who reveals himself in it. I hold intercourse with him; I immerse all my powers in his divine essence; I am overwhelmed by his kindness, I bless him and his gifts, but I do not pray to him. What should I ask of him — to change the order of nature, to work miracles on my behalf? Should I, who am bound to love above all things the order which he has established in his wisdom and maintained by his providence, should I desire the disturbance of that order on my own account? No, that rash prayer would deserve to be punished rather than to be granted. Neither do I ask of him the power to do right; why should I ask what he has given me already? Has he not given me conscience that I may love the right, reason that I may perceive it, and freedom that I may choose it? If I do evil, I have no excuse; I do it of my own free will; to ask him to change my will is to ask him to do what he asks of me; it is to want him to do the work while I get the wages; to be dissatisfied with my lot is to wish to be no longer a man, to wish to be other than what I am, to wish for disorder and evil. Thou source of justice and truth, merciful and gracious God, in thee do I trust, and the desire of my heart is — Thy will be done. When I unite my will with thine, I do what thou doest; I have a share in thy goodness; I believe that I enjoy beforehand the supreme happiness which is the reward of goodness.

In my well-founded self-distrust the only thing that I ask of God, or rather expect from his justice, is to correct my error if I go astray, if that error is dangerous to me. To be honest I need not think myself infallible; my opinions, which seem to me true, may be so many lies; for what man is there who does not cling to his own beliefs; and how many men are agreed in everything? The illusion which deceives me may indeed have its source in myself, but it is God alone who can remove it. I have done all I can to attain to truth; but its source is beyond my reach; is it my fault if my strength fails me and I can go no further; it is for Truth to draw near to me.

The good priest had spoken with passion; he and I were overcome with emotion. It seemed to me as if I were listening to the divine Orpheus when he sang the earliest hymns and taught men the worship of the gods. I saw any number of objections which might be raised; yet I raised none, for I perceived that they were more perplexing than serious, and that my inclination took his part. When he spoke to me according to his conscience, my own seemed to confirm what he said.

"The novelty of the sentiments you have made known to me," said I, "strikes me all the more because of what you confess you do not know, than because of what you say you believe. They seem to be very like that theism or natural religion, which Christians profess to confound with atheism or irreligion which is their exact opposite. But in the present state of my faith I should have to ascend rather than descend to accept your views, and I find it difficult to remain just where you are unless I were as wise as you. That I may be at least as honest, I want time to take counsel with myself. By your own showing, the inner voice must be my guide, and you have yourself told me that when it has long been silenced it cannot be recalled in a moment. I take what you have said to heart, and I must consider it. If after I have thought things out, I am as convinced as you are, you will be my final teacher, and I will be your disciple till death. Continue your teaching however; you have only told me half what I must know. Speak to me of revelation, of the Scriptures, of those difficult doctrines among which I have strayed ever since I was a child, incapable either of understanding or believing them, unable to adopt or reject them."

"Yes, my child," said he, embracing me, "I will tell you all I think; I will not open my heart to you by halves; but the desire you express was necessary before I could cast aside all reserve. So far I have told you nothing but what I thought would be of service to you, nothing but what I was quite convinced of. The inquiry which remains to be made is very difficult. It seems to me full of perplexity, mystery, and darkness; I bring to it only doubt and distrust. I make up my mind with trembling, and I tell you my doubts rather than my convictions. If your own opinions were more settled I should hesitate to show you mine; but in your present condition, to think like me would be gain. [Footnote: I think the worthy clergyman might say this at the present time to the general public.] Moreover, give to my words only the authority of reason; I know not whether I am mistaken. It is difficult in discussion to avoid assuming sometimes a dogmatic tone; but remember in this respect that all my assertions are but reasons to doubt me. Seek truth for yourself, for my own part I only promise you sincerity.

"In my exposition you find nothing but natural religion; strange that we should need more! How shall I become aware of this need? What guilt can be mine so long as I serve God according to the knowledge he has given to my mind, and the feelings he has put into my heart? What purity of morals, what dogma useful to man and worthy of its author, can I derive from a positive doctrine which cannot be derived without the aid of this doctrine by the right use of my faculties? Show me what you can add to the duties of the natural law, for the glory of God, for the good of mankind, and for my own welfare; and what virtue you will get from the new form of religion which does not result from mine. The grandest ideas of the Divine nature come to us from reason only. Behold the spectacle of nature; listen to the inner voice. Has not

246

God spoken it all to our eyes, to our conscience, to our reason? What more can man tell us? Their revelations do but degrade God, by investing him with passions like our own. Far from throwing light upon the ideas of the Supreme Being, special doctrines seem to me to confuse these ideas; far from ennobling them, they degrade them; to the inconceivable mysteries which surround the Almighty, they add absurd contradictions, they make man proud, intolerant, and cruel; instead of bringing peace upon earth, they bring fire and sword. I ask myself what is the use of it all, and I find no answer. I see nothing but the crimes of men and the misery of mankind.

"They tell me a revelation was required to teach men how God would be served; as a proof of this they point to the many strange rites which men have instituted, and they do not perceive that this very diversity springs from the fanciful nature of the revelations. As soon as the nations took to making God speak, every one made him speak in his own fashion, and made him say what he himself wanted. Had they listened only to what God says in the heart of man, there would have been but one religion upon earth.

"One form of worship was required; just so, but was this a matter of such importance as to require all the power of the Godhead to establish it? Do not let us confuse the outward forms of religion with religion itself. The service God requires is of the heart; and when the heart is sincere that is ever the same. It is a strange sort of conceit which fancies that God takes such an interest in the shape of the priest's vestments, the form of words he utters, the gestures he makes before the altar and all his genuflections. Oh, my friend, stand upright, you will still be too near the earth. God desires to be worshipped in spirit and in truth; this duty belongs to every religion, every country, every individual. As to the form of worship, if order demands uniformity, that is only a matter of discipline and needs no revelation.

"These thoughts did not come to me to begin with. Carried away by the prejudices of my education, and by that dangerous vanity which always strives to lift man out of his proper sphere, when I could not raise my feeble thoughts up to the great Being, I tried to bring him down to my own level. I tried to reduce the distance he has placed between his nature and mine. I desired more immediate relations, more individual instruction; not content to make God in the image of man that I might be favoured above my fellows, I desired supernatural knowledge; I required a special form of worship; I wanted God to tell me what he had not told others, or what others had not understood like myself.

"Considering the point I had now reached as the common centre from which all believers set out on the quest for a more enlightened form of religion, I merely found in natural religion the elements of all religion. I beheld the multitude of diverse sects which hold sway upon earth, each of which accuses the other of falsehood and error; which of these, I asked, is the right? Every one replied, 'My own;' every one said, 'I alone and those who agree with me think rightly, all the others are mistaken.' And how do you know that your sect is in the right? Because God said so. And how do you know

God said so? [Footnote: "All men," said a wise and good priest, "maintain that they hold and believe their religion (and all use the same jargon), not of man, nor of any creature, but of God. But to speak truly, without pretence or flattery, none of them do so; whatever they may say, religions are taught by human hands and means; take, for example, the way in which religions have been received by the world, the way in which they are still received every day by individuals; the nation, the country, the locality gives the religion; we belong to the religion of the place where we are born and brought up; we are baptised or circumcised, we are Christians, Jews, Mohametans before we know that we are men; we do not pick and choose our religion for see how ill the life and conduct agree with the religion, see for what slight and human causes men go against the teaching of their religion." —Charron, De la Sagesse. —It seems clear that the honest creed of the holy theologian of Condom would not have differed greatly from that of the Savoyard priest.] And who told you that God said it? My pastor, who knows all about it. My pastor tells me what to believe and I believe it; he assures me that any one who says anything else is mistaken, and I give not heed to them.

"What! thought I, is not truth one; can that which is true for me be false for you? If those who follow the right path and those who go astray have the same method, what merit or what blame can be assigned to one more than to the other? Their choice is the result of chance; it is unjust to hold them responsible for it, to reward or punish them for being born in one country or another. To dare to say that God judges us in this manner is an outrage on his justice.

"Either all religions are good and pleasing to God, or if there is one which he prescribes for men, if they will be punished for despising it, he will have distinguished it by plain and certain signs by which it can be known as the only true religion; these signs are alike in every time and place, equally plain to all men, great or small, learned or unlearned, Europeans, Indians, Africans, savages. If there were but one religion upon earth, and if all beyond its pale were condemned to eternal punishment, and if there were in any corner of the world one single honest man who was not convinced by this evidence, the God of that religion would be the most unjust and cruel of tyrants.

"Let us therefore seek honestly after truth; let us yield nothing to the claims of birth, to the authority of parents and pastors, but let us summon to the bar of conscience and of reason all that they have taught us from our childhood. In vain do they exclaim, 'Submit your reason;' a deceiver might say as much; I must have reasons for submitting my reason.

"All the theology I can get for myself by observation of the universe and by the use of my faculties is contained in what I have already told you. To know more one must have recourse to strange means. These means cannot be the authority of men, for every man is of the same species as myself, and all that a man knows by nature I am capable of knowing, and another may be deceived as much as I; when I believe what he says, it is not because he says it but because he proves its truth. The witness of man is therefore nothing more than the witness of my own reason, and it adds nothing to the natural means which God has given me for the knowledge of truth.

"Apostle of truth, what have you to tell me of which I am not the sole judge? God himself has spoken; give heed to his revelation. That is another matter. God has spoken, these are indeed words which demand attention. To whom has he spoken? He has spoken to men. Why then have I heard nothing? He has instructed others to make known his words to you. I understand; it is men who come and tell me what God has said. I would rather have heard the words of God himself; it would have been as easy for him and I should have been secure from fraud. He protects you from fraud by showing that his envoys come from him. How does he show this? By miracles. Where are these miracles? In the books. And who wrote the books? Men. And who saw the miracles? The men who bear witness to them. What! Nothing but human testimony! Nothing but men who tell me what others told them! How many men between God and me! Let us see, however, let us examine, compare, and verify. Oh! if God had but deigned to free me from all this labour, I would have served him with all my heart.

"Consider, my friend, the terrible controversy in which I am now engaged; what vast learning is required to go back to the remotest antiquity, to examine, weigh, confront prophecies, revelations, facts, all the monuments of faith set forth throughout the world, to assign their date, place, authorship, and occasion. What exactness of critical judgment is needed to distinguish genuine documents from forgeries, to compare objections with their answers, translations with their originals; to decide as to the impartiality of witnesses, their common-sense, their knowledge; to make sure that nothing has been omitted, nothing added, nothing transposed, altered, or falsified; to point out any remaining contradictions, to determine what weight should be given to the silence of our adversaries with regard to the charges brought against them; how far were they aware of those charges; did they think them sufficiently serious to require an answer; were books sufficiently well known for our books to reach them; have we been honest enough to allow their books to circulate among ourselves and to leave their strongest objections unaltered?

"When the authenticity of all these documents is accepted, we must now pass to the evidence of their authors' mission; we must know the laws of chance, and probability, to decide which prophecy cannot be fulfilled without a miracle; we must know the spirit of the original languages, to distinguish between prophecy and figures of speech; we must know what facts are in accordance with nature and what facts are not, so that we may say how far a clever man may deceive the eyes of the simple and may even astonish the learned; we must discover what are the characteristics of a prodigy and how its authenticity may be established, not only so far as to gain credence, but so that doubt may be deserving of punishment; we must compare the evidence for true and false miracles, and find sure tests to distinguish between them; lastly we must say why God chose as a witness to his words means which themselves require so much evidence on their behalf, as if he were playing with human credulity, and avoiding of set purpose the true means of persuasion.

"Assuming that the divine majesty condescends so far as to make a man the channel of his sacred will, is it reasonable, is it fair, to demand that the whole of mankind should obey the voice of this minister without making him known as such? Is it just to give him as his sole credentials certain private signs, performed in the presence of a few obscure persons, signs which everybody else can only know by hearsay? If one were to believe all the miracles that the uneducated and credulous profess to have seen in every country upon earth, every sect would be in the right; there would be more miracles than ordinary events; and it would be the greatest miracle if there were no miracles wherever there were persecuted fanatics. The unchangeable order of nature is the chief witness to the wise hand that guides it; if there were many exceptions, I should hardly know what to think; for my own part I have too great a faith in God to believe in so many miracles which are so little worthy of him.

"Let a man come and say to us: Mortals, I proclaim to you the will of the Most Highest; accept my words as those of him who has sent me; I bid the sun to change his course, the stars to range themselves in a fresh order, the high places to become smooth, the floods to rise up, the earth to change her face. By these miracles who will not recognise the master of nature? She does not obey impostors, their miracles are wrought in holes and corners, in deserts, within closed doors, where they find easy dupes among a small company of spectators already disposed to believe them. Who will venture to tell me how many eye-witnesses are required to make a miracle credible! What use are your miracles, performed if proof of your doctrine, if they themselves require so much proof! You might as well have let them alone.

"There still remains the most important inquiry of all with regard to the doctrine proclaimed; for since those who tell us God works miracles in this world, profess that the devil sometimes imitates them, when we have found the best attested miracles we have got very little further; and since the magicians of Pharaoh dared in the presence of Moses to counterfeit the very signs he wrought at God's command, why should they not, behind his back, claim a like authority? So when we have proved our doctrine by means of miracles, we must prove our miracles by means of doctrine, [Footnote: This is expressly stated in many passages of Scripture, among others in Deuteronomy xiii., where it is said that when a prophet preaching strange gods confirms his words by means of miracles and what he foretells comes to pass, far from giving heed to him, this prophet must be put to death. If then the heathen put the apostles to death when they preached a strange god and confirmed their words by miracles which came to pass I cannot see what grounds we have for complaint which they could not at once turn against us. Now, what should be done in such a case? There is only one course; to return to argument and let the miracles alone. It would have been better not to have had recourse to them at all. That is plain common-sense which can only be obscured by great subtlety of distinction. Subtleties in Christianity! So Jesus Christ was mistaken when he promised the kingdom of heaven to the simple, he was mistaken when he began his finest discourse with the praise of the poor in spirit, if so much wit is needed to understand his teaching and to get others to believe in him. When you have convinced me that submission is my duty, all will be well; but to convince me of this, come down to my level; adapt your arguments to a lowly mind, or I shall not recognise you as a true disciple of your master, and it is not his doctrine that you are teaching me.] for fear lest we should take the devil's doings for the handiwork of God. What think you of this dilemma?

"This doctrine, if it comes from God, should bear the sacred stamp of the godhead; not only should it illumine the troubled thoughts which reason imprints on our minds, but it should also offer us a form of worship, a morality, and rules of conduct in accordance with the attributes by means of which we alone conceive of God's essence. If then it teaches us what is absurd and unreasonable, if it inspires us with feelings of aversion for our fellows and terror for ourselves, if it paints us a God, angry, jealous, revengeful, partial, hating men, a God of war and battles, ever ready to strike and to destroy, ever speaking of punishment and torment, boasting even of the punishment of the innocent, my heart would not be drawn towards this terrible God, I would take good care not to quit the realm of natural religion to embrace such a religion as that; for you see plainly I must choose between them. Your God is not ours. He who begins by selecting a chosen people, and proscribing the rest of mankind, is not our common father; he who consigns to eternal punishment the greater part of his creatures, is not the merciful and gracious God revealed to me by my reason.

"Reason tells me that dogmas should be plain, clear, and striking in their simplicity. If there is something lacking in natural religion, it is with respect to the obscurity in which it leaves the great truths it teaches; revelation should teach us these truths in a way which the mind of man can understand; it should bring them within his reach, make him comprehend them, so that he may believe them. Faith is confirmed and strengthened by understanding; the best religion is of necessity the simplest. He who hides beneath mysteries and contradictions the religion that he preaches to me, teaches me at the same time to distrust that religion. The God whom I adore is not the God of darkness, he has not given me understanding in order to forbid me to use it; to tell me to submit my reason is to insult the giver of reason. The minister of truth does not tyrannise over my reason, he enlightens it.

"We have set aside all human authority, and without it I do not see how any man can convince another by preaching a doctrine contrary to reason. Let them fight it out, and let us see what they have to say with that harshness of speech which is common to both.

"INSPIRATION: Reason tells you that the whole is greater than the part; but I tell you, in God's name, that the part is greater than the whole.

"REASON: And who are you to dare to tell me that God contradicts himself? And which shall I choose to believe. God who teaches me, through my reason, the eternal truth, or you who, in his name, proclaim an absurdity?

"INSPIRATION: Believe me, for my teaching is more positive; and I will prove to you beyond all manner of doubt that he has sent me.

"REASON: What! you will convince me that God has sent you to bear witness against himself? What sort of proofs will you adduce to convince me that God speaks more surely by your mouth than through the understanding he has given me?

"INSPIRATION: The understanding he has given you! Petty, conceited creature! As if you were the first impious person who had been led astray through his reason corrupted by sin.

"REASON: Man of God, you would not be the first scoundrel who asserts his arrogance as a proof of his mission.

"INSPIRATION: What! do even philosophers call names?

"REASON: Sometimes, when the saints set them the example.

"INSPIRATION: Oh, but I have a right to do it, for I am speaking on God's behalf.

"REASON: You would do well to show your credentials before you make use of your privileges.

"INSPIRATION: My credentials are authentic, earth and heaven will bear witness on my behalf. Follow my arguments carefully, if you please.

"REASON: Your arguments! You forget what you are saying. When you teach me that my reason misleads me, do you not refute what it might have said on your behalf? He who denies the right of reason, must convince me without recourse to her aid. For suppose you have convinced me by reason, how am I to know that it is not my reason, corrupted by sin, which makes me accept what you say? besides, what proof, what demonstration, can you advance, more self-evident than the axiom it is to destroy? It is more credible that a good syllogism is a lie, than that the part is greater than the whole.

"INSPIRATION: What a difference! There is no answer to my evidence; it is of a supernatural kind.

"REASON: Supernatural! What do you mean by the word? I do not understand it.

"INSPIRATION: I mean changes in the order of nature, prophecies, signs, and wonders of every kind.

"REASON: Signs and wonders! I have never seen anything of the kind.

"INSPIRATION: Others have seen them for you. Clouds of witnesses—the witness of whole nations....

"REASON: Is the witness of nations supernatural?

"INSPIRATION: No; but when it is unanimous, it is incontestable.

"REASON: There is nothing so incontestable as the principles of reason, and one cannot accept an absurdity on human evidence. Once more, let us see your supernatural evidence, for the consent of mankind is not supernatural.

"INSPIRATION: Oh, hardened heart, grace does not speak to you.

"REASON: That is not my fault; for by your own showing, one must have already received grace before one is able to ask for it. Begin by speaking to me in its stead.

"INSPIRATION: But that is just what I am doing, and you will not listen. But what do you say to prophecy?

"REASON: In the first place, I say I have no more heard a prophet than I have seen a miracle. In the next, I say that no prophet could claim authority over me.

"INSPIRATION: Follower of the devil! Why should not the words of the prophets have authority over you?

"REASON: Because three things are required, three things which will never happen: firstly, I must have heard the prophecy; secondly, I must have seen its fulfilment; and thirdly, it must be clearly proved that the fulfilment of the prophecy could not by any possibility have been a mere coincidence; for even if it was as precise, as plain, and clear as an axiom of geometry, since the clearness of a chance prediction does not make its fulfilment impossible, this fulfilment when it does take place does not, strictly speaking, prove what was foretold.

"See what your so-called supernatural proofs, your miracles, your prophecies come to: believe all this upon the word of another. Submit to the authority of men the authority of God which speaks to my reason. If the eternal truths which my mind conceives of could suffer any shock, there would be no sort of certainty for me; and far from being sure that you speak to me on God's behalf, I should not even be sure that there is a God.

"My child, here are difficulties enough, but these are not all. Among so many religions, mutually excluding and proscribing each other, one only is true, if indeed any one of them is true. To recognise the true religion we must inquire into, not one, but all; and in any question whatsoever we have no right to condemn unheard. [Footnote: On the other hand, Plutarch relates that the Stoics maintained, among other strange paradoxes, that it was no use hearing both sides; for, said they, the first either proves his point or he does not prove it; if he has proved it, there is an end of it, and the other should be condemned: if he has not proved it, he himself is in the wrong and judgment should be given against him. I consider the method of those who accept an exclusive revelation very much like that of these Stoics. When each of them claims to be the sole guardian of truth, we must hear them all before we can choose between them without injustice.] The objections must be compared with the evidence; we must know what accusation each brings against the other, and what answers they receive. The plainer any feeling appears to us, the more we must try to discover why so many other people refuse to accept it. We should be simple, indeed, if we thought it enough to hear the doctors on our own side, in order to acquaint ourselves with the arguments of the other. Where can you find theologians who pride themselves on their honesty? Where are those who, to refute the arguments of their opponents, do not begin by making out that they are of little importance? A man may make a good show among his own friends, and be very proud of his arguments, who would cut a very poor figure with those same arguments among those who are on the other side. Would you find out for yourself from books? What learning you will need! What languages you must learn; what libraries you must ransack; what an amount of reading must be got through! Who will guide me in such a choice? It will be hard to find the best books on the opposite side in any one country, and all the harder to find those on all sides; when found they would be easily answered. The absent are always in the wrong, and bad arguments boldly asserted easily efface good arguments put forward with scorn. Besides books are often very misleading, and scarcely express the opinions of their authors. If you think you can judge the Catholic faith from the writings of Bossuet, you will find yourself greatly mistaken when you have lived among us. You will see that the doctrines with which Protestants are answered are quite different from those of the pulpit. To judge a religion rightly, you must not study it in the books of its partisans, you must learn it in their lives; this is quite another matter. Each religion has its own traditions, meaning, customs, prejudices, which form the spirit of its creed, and must be taken in connection with it.

"How many great nations neither print books of their own nor read ours! How shall they judge of our opinions, or we of theirs? We laugh at them, they despise us; and if our travellers turn them into ridicule, they need only travel among us to pay us back in our own coin. Are there not, in every country, men of common-sense, honesty, and good faith, lovers of truth, who only seek to know what truth is that they may profess it? Yet every one finds truth in his own religion, and thinks the religion of other nations absurd; so all these foreign religions are not so absurd as they seem to us, or else the reason we find for our own proves nothing.

"We have three principal forms of religion in Europe. One accepts one revelation, another two, and another three. Each hates the others, showers curses on them, accuses them of blindness, obstinacy, hardness of heart, and falsehood. What fair-minded man will dare to decide between them without first carefully weighing their evidence, without listening attentively to their arguments? That which accepts only one revelation is the oldest and seems the best established; that which accepts three is the newest and seems the most consistent; that which accepts two revelations and rejects the third may perhaps be the best, but prejudice is certainly against it; its inconsistency is glaring.

"In all three revelations the sacred books are written in languages unknown to the people who believe in them. The Jews no longer understand Hebrew, the Christians understand neither Hebrew nor Greek; the Turks and Persians do not understand Arabic, and the Arabs of our time do not speak the language of Mahomet. Is not it a very foolish way of teaching, to teach people in an unknown tongue? These books are translated, you say. What an answer! How am I to know that the translations are correct, or how am I to make sure that such a thing as a correct translation is possible? If God has gone so far as to speak to men, why should he require an interpreter?

"I can never believe that every man is obliged to know what is contained